'Those who came before me,' said Baudin, 'called it *Terre Australe*, the southern land.'

'I am your southern lands?' she said. 'That will not do. A name of any consequence must be in Latin.'

He was half asleep. He touched her shoulder. She understood, and turned with her back towards him, and he covered them both with the bedclothes and curled himself around her, with his face in the nape of her neck.

Then, into her hair, he murmured, 'I will say *Australia*. Is that Latin enough for you? I shall call you Australia.' She moved her head in assent, took his arm and placed it round her, and they slept.

# SOUTHERN CROSS

Terry Coleman

ARROW BOOKS

Arrow Books Limited
17–21 Conway Street, London W1P 6JD

An imprint of the Hutchinson Publishing Group

London Melbourne Sydney Auckland
Johannesburg and agencies
throughout the world

First published by Hutchinson 1979
Arrow edition 1980
Reprinted 1981 and 1982
© Terry Coleman 1979

Made and printed in Great Britain
by The Anchor Press Ltd
Tiptree, Essex

ISBN 0 09 921690 6

# Contents

# PART ONE

# I

# In Which Susannah Receives Her Lover

On an evening in October, which in those southern parts of the world is early summer, Susannah stood alone on the lawns before Government House, gazing across the Domain and then out across the noblest harbour on earth as a sheer-lined ship, under topsails, moved slowly into Sydney Cove. The ship flew at her stern the tricolor of Revolutionary France and at her mainyard, as a courtesy to the monarch whose port she was entering, the union flag of George III of Great Britain. She dropped anchor, and the port-officer's cutter put out to her. In half an hour it would be sunset. On the Domain lawns the air was warm and full of the scent of frangipanni, Great Moreton Bay figs, and sabina cedars. The corvette whose approach the woman had observed was known to her. She had walked the decks, taken tea in the captain's cabin with him and his officers, and gravely attended as he unfolded charts to entertain her, showing her those coasts of the great southern land he had already explored. One day, on board, she had said, 'There is something here, I do not know what, but there is the feeling – I could be in the gardens of my father's Domain?' And he replied, 'My ship, you see, has to be fast. She is as fast a ship as there is. She is made from Bermuda cedar, which is a fast wood for a ship. That is what you sense. The timbers might be from the young cedars of your Domain, when they are a little grown.'

In the evening, in front of the house, the woman still waited, rarely taking her eyes from the ship, though she knew it would be an hour before salutations were exchanged between the ship's captain and the port-officer, and glasses of Madeira

accepted, and that only then would the vessel slip to her mainland mooring, directly beneath the Residency, where the lawns
sloped right down to the cove. As the sun sank below the
horizon, the riding lights of the corvette showed up at first
faintly against the flaring orange of the western sky and then
more clearly against the pink glow which succeeded. Now was
the time of day when the Domain was at its most beautiful, a
time of infinite greens – the subdued grey-and-blue tints of the
native eucalypts, the more vivid green of the cedars and oaks
the English had planted, and the greens of the many grasses.
Near the house the lawns were of velvet bent, as lustrous and
soft as those of an English country house, but not easily tended
in the climate of that southern latitude. Nearer the cove, the
lawns were of couch or buffalo, coarser and hardier, but lighter
in tone. As the light went, the woman walked a few yards
towards a frangipanni, a small tree whose white flowers, with
yellow hearts, like five-petalled *fleurs-de-lis*, give the lightest of
scents. The head gardener had told her that morning that he
had never seen a frangipanni flower that early, and said it was
for her. Twenty minutes after sunset, when the trees were still
of discernibly different shades of green, and the lights of the
ship cast a soft sheen over the waters of the cove, the woman
returned to the spot before the house where she had first waited.

Still she stood there. The trees became silhouettes, no longer
green. The light was between what a landsman calls twilight,
when a person may see to walk easily over uneven ground, and
that darker state which a sailor calls nautical twilight, when
shapes are only dimly visible at a hundred yards. Then at last
the corvette moved to her mooring and the captain strode up
the grassed slope towards Government House.

When she began to wait the woman had stood in golden light,
and the house, with its verandahs and shading trees, in cool
shadow. But when the man at last approached she stood in a
dusk that was almost night, with the house no longer obscure
but lit inside with the soft light of mirrored candelabras and
sending that light faintly on to the lawns behind her. Against
the night sky, her long hair was darkness made visible by the
faint haze of the harbour lights before her, and by the stars
above. Through her slight muslin gown the house lights shone,
penetrating, tracing, and transluminating the petals, ferns, and

quatrefoils of the embroidery, so that she seemed herself the source of light. The man took the woman's outstretched hands in his, drew her to him and clasped her, raising her a little so that she came half up on her toes. They held each other. Then she withdrew enough to be able to take his head in her hands and regard his features. Post-captain Nicolas Baudin was commander of the French corvette, and Susannah's lover. He was not returning from a long absence – the separation had been for only ten days while he prospected the neighbouring inlets for the specimens of mahogany and blackbutt tree that would be required of him on his return to Europe – but he had sailed with his memories of her, and her name, every hour in his mind. He loved her; and she saw this. The moment of that perception is one that reveals a woman's soul. He knew that she would cherish him. The winking points of the Southern Cross looked down on the broad bay, on the cove with its ships riding easily, on the town, on the Domain, on the lawn, on the two figures on that lawn, on the translucencies of the woman's dress, and on the man's transfigured face, which he lowered and buried in her hair.

'My love?' she said.

He raised his head a little.

'How clear a night it is,' she said. 'Your stars are clear.'

He was so intent on her that he hardly glanced up. But he was a navigator and had explained the southern heavens to her, showing her stars seen in no northern sky. The Southern Cross, which he had especially shown her, lies on the edge of a gap in the Milky Way, on the edge of a black void which sets off the brilliance of its five points. The southern skies are less crowded than the northern, just as the southern oceans run for many thousands of miles unbroken by land. But those south seas enclose one entire island continent, then called New Holland, and on one fragment of that continent Susannah and Baudin stood embraced.

This was in the year 1802. Susannah was the daughter of Philip Gidley King, Captain General and Governor-in-Chief of His Majesty's colony of New South Wales. Baudin commanded two French men o'war of thirty guns, which both now lay in the

cove. Britain and France had been at war and would be again –
those long wars that began with the French Revolution and
ended with Waterloo. It did happen, on that evening, that the
two powers had been for a few months briefly at peace, in the
interval, as it were, between two acts of a drama. But that news
had not reached the ends of the earth, and it was on the ends
of the earth that Susannah and Baudin found themselves. There
was nothing farther. There is nothing farther. How they came
there must be told. All around them was the spirit of this last,
loneliest place, its apartness and its grandeur. But neither the
genius of the place nor any sense of her own insignificance
under so vast a heaven, awed Susannah. She was a woman of
will and of wilfulness, and with that will she could give herself
with a full heart.

She took Baudin by the hand and led him towards the house
and towards the light. She was eighteen and he was her first
love: he was twice her age, and she was to be his last. It was a
night she never forgot, and it determined the whole course of
her long life.

# 2

# Transported beyond the Seas

Susannah and Baudin were observed as they entered the house by John Easty, the Governor's head gardener, who lived in a cottage within the Domain. Easty was a man whose memory went back as far as there was any colony to be remembered. In 1787, as a private soldier, he sailed with the First Fleet of convict ships from England to Botany Bay. The convicts were the first settlers. Before them, only Captain Cook and his crew had seen that bay, when they discovered it in 1770. Easty remembered some of the officers of that first convict fleet. One of them was Lieutenant King, who had stayed to become the colony's third governor. Easty remembered, the day they sailed, how the lieutenant's little daughter was held up at the dockside to wave goodbye. That was Susannah, who was three at the time. She came out much later. He could remember some of the felons. He well remembered George Bryant, who in 1802 was still in the colony. He had become quite friends with Bryant, as far as a soldier and a felon could be friends. He remembered Bryant and other convicts telling him about their trials.

Trials in 1786 were apt to be brief. One summer's day at the Old Bailey, in the City of London, Mr Justice Hotham got through six. All the offences were capital. First, Mary Abeil, alias Tilley, of Islington, was put up.

'Why alias Tilley?' asked the judge, looking up from his nosegay of sweet flowers, whose fragrance was supposed to refresh the judicial mind and repel the miasma which floated up from the prisoners in the dock. The prisoners did stink. Mary

Abell stank. She would, after four months in Newgate jail,
waiting for her trial.

'Because, my lord,' said Mr Rhodes, counsel for the
Crown, 'she has committed other crimes under that name,
which . . .'

'Mr Rhodes,' said the Judge, 'you really must not tell me
that. She is charged upon indictment with one count, although
that, God knows, is enough.' It was. Mary Abell was a whore,
which did not matter and was no concern of the law. She was
a procuress, which could hardly help appearing in the evidence,
but that did not much matter. What mattered was that, failing
to procure enough girls for her uses, though the wretchedly poor
were easily enough procured, she cruelly kidnapped Ann Shore,
aged twelve years and four months, and deprived the said Ann
Shore of her freedom, and brought about the death of Ann
Shore. The indictment did not say all that, because the girl,
having already escaped from the house of Mary Abell, had
drowned herself. Such a death could not be charged to Mary
Abell. It was no murder. But it was an evil kidnapping. The
prisoner wept, and not a man in court believed her tears. The
jury did not retire. The foreman said, 'Guilty,' and the Judge,
turning to the woman, said to her, 'Do you think there will be
mercy for your soul?' She was hustled away.

Put up George Abrams. He did not know his age, but thought
twenty-seven, and was indicted for the very thorough highway
robbery of Fleetwood Bury, Esquire, whom he had deprived of
one pair men's leather breeches, value ten shillings; one linen
ruffled shirt, five shillings; one man's peruke, two shillings; one
pair leather boot garters, twelve pence; one gold repeater
watch, ten guineas; and One Proper Coin of the Realm called
half a guinea, value half a guinea.

'In that order?' said the Judge. 'Breeches first?'

There was a little, permitted, laughter in court before the
verdict of guilty was pronounced.

And so on. Robert Spencer, for forging cheques in the name
of the Earl of Harington: Guilty. Jane Bowing, for stealing a
tub with 100 oysters in it at Billingsgate, it being strongly
urged against her that she had been defended from arrest by
a gang of girls, one of whom had a knife: Guilty. William
Pearce, for that, having been employed at His Majesty's Mint

in the cleaning of sovereigns, he did feloniously steal forty-seven of the objects of his work: Guilty.

Then came George Bryant, aged sixteen, for having taken and carried away with intent at the time of such taking to deprive the owner permanently thereof, one blue broadcloth cloak, with fur collar, lined with blue silk, and buckled with a silver buckle, the property of the Right Reverend Father in God James, Lord Bishop of Peterborough, from his London residence: Guilty. Bryant was exceptional. Not only had he stolen a bishop's cloak, no less, but he was the only prisoner in court that day to have chattels with him. The other prisoners were penniless. Bryant's chattel was the cloak, which had been too good to sell, as no receiver of stolen goods would touch so distinctive a thing, and some even had religious scruples, or said they had. It was of course the Bishop's, but the Bishop would not reclaim it for fear that it might have attracted to it the taint of prison fever, which might communicate itself in turn to the Bishop. Now prisoners could indeed have chattels, and, if they did, this was written down in the court record. A prisoner might have forty guineas, evidently stolen, but if they were not the subject of the indictment brought against him they were his to take with him to prison, or to Botany Bay: that is, if the jailors had not already, in the broader interests of justice, in their turn robbed the prisoner. Bryant's chattel had survived his jailors because it had to be produced in court. Since it was unclaimed it was his. Since it was his it had to be written down: 'George Bryant. Chattel, One bishop's cloak,' and while the clerk was doing this, the Judge looked at the prisoner for the first time.

'Where do you come from?'

'Dorchester, sir.'

The Judge remembered Dorchester, a county town 150 miles from London, a western provincial capital in its own way, a town laid out by the Romans, with broad, straight roads. He had been on assize there. He knew Weymouth too, a watering place on the coast, six miles away. It was a place much loved by the King, and the Judge had been there as the King's guest at a place called Gloucester House. He remembered the name. But what he most remembered was that, one morning some years before, he had bought at a Weymouth linen draper's five pairs of women's gloves, for a woman who lay deep in his affection. The recollection of this touched the mind of the Judge, and he looked again at the boy and at the cloak. The court had completed its business. Counsel were waiting, the clerks sat still, the ushers' hands were on the doors. All were awaiting His Lordship's pleasure, but all wanted to get away.

'Put it on,' said the Judge.

The boy looked helplessly around, until a clerk motioned to him what to do, and Bryant took the cloak and draped it over his shoulders, and looked up. He did not know whether he was being mocked. He was not. The assembled counsel, clerks, and ushers had already seen that the Judge was not playing with the prisoner, and they kept silence.

'Very well,' said Mr Justice Hotham. 'George Bryant, I wish you better for the future. And' – this to the clerk – 'let it be recorded that I wish that he *shall* have the cloak, and that whoever robs him of it may count on my displeasure. You know who should be told. See they know.'

The Judge's chance recollection of a chance happiness saved that cloak for George Bryant. It was small affair, of course; or so everyone thought.

The Judge said again to the boy, 'I wish you well,' and then the court rose.

In those days each prisoner was not sentenced at the end of his own trial, but at the end of the session all were brought back to be sentenced together. That was the end of the assize. There were no more prisoners to try, and so next morning they were all brought back. All were cast for death. Mary Abell, alias Tilley, wept throughout. Pearce, the thief of the sovereigns, and Henry Abrams, the thorough highwayman, both joked with their friends in court. They joked to keep up their courage, because they were in real fear of their lives. Most sentences of death were known to be only formal. That was why the Judge could wish the boy Bryant well the evening before, and in the morning tell him he was to be taken to a place of execution and there hanged by the neck until he was dead. In that year, no fewer than 222 crimes were capital. You could hardly hang one-eighth of the population of London, which would have been the result of a literal interpretation of the law. And so almost all sentences were commuted to transportation, but a

flagrant highwayman or a thief in the Mint itself could not
count on that mercy. Mary Abell, had she been a man, would
have died, but the law was kinder to women. In the end, only
Pearce, the thief of the sovereigns, was told to resign himself to
death. Early one morning he was suspended outside Newgate
in the sight of God and in the face of a large press of men and
women assembled for the entertainment. The other five, with
Abrams the thorough highwayman marvelling at his luck,
were condemned to be transported to Africa, beyond the seas.
The commission to the keeper of Newgate did say Africa,
because at that time it was simply not known where to ship
them, and Africa sounded far enough beyond the seas. The
American colonies, no longer being colonies, could no longer
receive them. His Majesty's Secretary of State considered
Jamaica, but that caused an uproar among the slaving interests
there and in London. It eventually became necessary for the
Prime Minister, Pitt, to give the matter twenty minutes of his
time, which he did one afternoon, when Bryant and his fellow
convicts had already been waiting in Newgate for three months
after their sentences.

William Pitt had greater things than convicts to worry about.
He had just been obliged to appoint commissioners to look into
ways of reducing the national debt, which was politically
awkward since most Englishmen had no idea that there was a
national debt, and would have been unable to understand how
England came to owe anybody anything. Warren Hastings, the
Governor General of India, appeared to have been guilty of
various kinds of cruelty and peculation, to have profited indiscreetly from the opium trade, and to have hanged an Indian
prince who accused him of corruption, before the prince could
speak against him. Some members of Parliament wanted to
impeach Hastings, and this was worrying. India mattered. The
national debt mattered. It did not weigh heavily on Pitt's mind
that thousands of condemned felons were lying either in His
Majesty's jails or, if they were unlucky, in His Majesty's hulks
in the Thames, waiting to know to which corner of the earth
they would be transported, most of them for the rest of their
lives. But there they were, and Lord Sydney, Secretary of State
for the Home Department, appeared incapable of signing some
piece of paper and disposing of them somewhere, quickly. So

Pitt himself, one afternoon, gave the matter twenty minutes of his time, meeting and listening to a dozen or so interested gentlemen.

He barely looked around the table to acknowledge their presence. He had the reputation of a cold man. He read aloud the heading from a sheaf of papers placed before him by the Under Secretary who sat by his side throughout.

' "A Receptacle for Felons," ' he said. Then he pushed away the papers, taking from the pile only one sheet. ' "Stealing Linen from Bleaching Grounds," ' he read, again aloud, and then explained. "Now this, gentlemen, is a list of crimes for which a man may be punished by deprivation of life or by transportation. It is not our business to reform the laws of the kingdom. We have not the time for that this afternoon. But I suppose the nature of the crimes committed by those we are ourselves about to commit somewhere beyond the seas, may determine, in our minds, the savagery or the softness of the place to which we decide to send them. So, I will read. I am of course selecting. There are Murder, Forcible Violation of Chastity, Forcible Hindering of Captains of Ships at Sea from Fighting – these I take it are heinous enough. We would agree on that. And it would not matter where we sent such people. Pulling Down Houses or Churches. I have seen no church or house recently pulled down. Sending Threatening Letters: I am constantly in receipt of threatening letters, perhaps any minister is, but I take that as a normal part of the business of government, and would not wish to send all the writers to some of the swamps that have been recommended to me. Destroying Velvet in the Loom. Grave, if you are a proprietor of velvet looms. Attempting to Kill Privy Councillors. I see that only two of us are Privy Councillors. Stealing an Heiress. I have known good men stolen *by* heiresses, but there seems to be no punishment prescribed for that. Stealing a Shroud out of a Grave: uncommon, I believe, except in Scotland, where the resurrection men really want the body, not the shroud. Marrying More Wives or Husbands Than One, Clandestinely Solemnizing Marriage, and, I see, Carrying Too Many Passengers in the Thames if Any Drown.'

He slid the paper carefully aside.

'But most will be common thieves, and we must now find

a receptacle for them. I have heard Africa mentioned. Mr Smeatham?'

Mr Smeatham had lived four years on the west coast of Africa. He said: 'Put two hundred convicts on an island in the Gambia river, and not one in a hundred will survive the first six months.'

'Mr Boon? Would you say that was a fact?'

Mr Boon, who had been a surgeon in Africa, would give no opinion as to that, but he would say that from the middle of July to the end of November there was putrid fever, that from December to the end of March there was the flux, and that, on each of his own three visits, two-thirds of the King's forces had perished each year.

'Sir James?'

Sir James Old, a merchant, was anxious that no felons should be sent to Gambia or Senegal because, if they were, it would put an end to all trade there, as none of the traders who at present went up the rivers in their long boats would dare to continue doing so, for fear of being plundered.

'And, Sir George,' – it was Edmund Burke interrupting from the end of the table – 'will you give us your opinion as to the practicability of Europeans subsisting, by field labour, in the Tropics?'

'Death,' said Sir George, 'would be the consequence of their continuing an hour exposed to the sun.'

Burke pronounced. 'The capital seat of plague,' he said. 'For there all life dies and all death lives.'

'And with that phrase,' said Pitt, 'I take it we have disposed of Africa?'

From Africa they went to the idyllic enthusiasm of Robert West, a medical man who had abjured Christianity and the hope of an after-life and created a fashionable following in London as the chief apostle of the perfectibility of life on earth. He gave lectures illustrated with diagrams of the human physiognomy as it displayed itself in the various races of the world, and with paintings of the women of the South Seas, particularly of Tahiti, as recently discovered. He wanted to send out male convicts and mate them with such women. 'From the union of these Europeans – who, though fallen, are specimens of a race of advanced intellect and civilization – from their union with the most beautifully formed women that the sun beholds, a colony might be peopled with beings, their offspring, that would be an ornament to human nature.'

The Prime Minister enquired, 'You have been to the South Seas, Mr West?' He had not.

'Mr Banks?' said Pitt. This was Joseph Banks, naturalist and President of the Royal Society, who had been at Botany Bay with Captain Cook, and it was Botany Bay in New Holland that he put forward as the site for the new colony of felons. There were kangaroos the size of middling sheep, but very swift and hard to catch. There were no beasts of prey, and it was Banks's opinion that sheep, if taken there, would thrive. The grass was long and luxuriant. There was a lot of wild spinach. There were plenty of skate, all very large. One they caught had weighed 366 pounds. If 800 people were sent out, with a year's supply of food and drink, and with tools, they would thrive. It was not to be doubted that a tract of land such as New Holland, which was larger than the whole of Europe, could support a colony.

'The climate?' said Pitt.

'Mild and moderate. I apprehend it is similar to that of the South of France.'

'Mr Dalrymple?' said Pitt.

Alexander Dalrymple had been visibly anxious to speak, and now out it came. 'We often see men grow giddy and lose their senses. This happens not less frequently in the political than in the natural world.'

'Continue,' said Pitt.

It was Mr Dalrymple's opinion that to send felons to New Holland would be to encourage rather than deter crime. To make them their own masters, in a temperate climate, where they would have every object of comfort before them! That would *incite* men to become convicts. If England had nothing to lose in the South Seas, it might be a curiously interesting experiment to see what sort of government a set of lawless ruffians would set up amongst themselves, but we had much to lose in the South Seas.

'Ah,' said Pitt, 'I think I begin to follow your reasoning now.'

Dalrymple did not have the sense to take warning from this, and went on to say it would be madness, folly, and a hazard,

to allow felons to subvert a sacred charter, that of the East
India Company. Pitt heard him out. He was arguing in effect
that the charter of that company gave it entire control over all
commerce in about half of the southern hemisphere, and that
this power would be infringed by the establishment of a new
colony which might trade not with the company but directly
with England or, worse still, with foreign countries. He finished
his harangue.

'You are disinterested in your opinion?' asked Pitt.

'I tell the plain truth as I see it.'

'But you are at present in the employment of the East India
Company?' Mr Dalrymple admitted that he was. Mr Pitt
indicated that he had given enough of his time to the matter,
and the meeting was ended. He told the Under Secretary to
weigh the evidence and make the decision himself.

The Under Secretary had observed the Prime Minister
closely, read his mind correctly, and seen that the objections of
the East India Company to New Holland had convincingly
demonstrated the superiority of that site over all others suggested for the new colony. So Botany Bay was chosen, and the
destination on the jailor's commission to transport the prisoners
was altered from Africa to New Holland. The Under Secretary
also bore in mind the representations of the Admiralty that
such a colony could grow hemp superior to Baltic hemp, and
that South Sea island pines could make better and taller masts
for men o'war, but the decision had been taken at that twenty
minutes' meeting of a Prime Minister, who had better things to
worry about, with a dozen men only one of whom had ever
seen New Holland. That man was Joseph Banks, and he had
been there once, sixteen years before, for ten days. The decision
was announced at the Opening of Parliament in one sentence
in the King's Speech. There was no debate. And so George
Bryant and his four remaining companions were shipped in
chains down the Thames and into the English Channel, where
at Portsmouth they met the other 582 men and 190 women who
were to be the convicts of the First Fleet.

As they waited to sail, an impresario with an eye for the idea
of the moment presented at the Royal Circus Theatre in
London an opera entitled *Botany Bay*, in which the hero has this
aria, this snatch of song:

> I'll kill them tyrants one by one
> And shoot the flogger down;
> I'll give the law a little shock,
> Remember what I say.
> They'll yet regret they sent Jim Jones
> In chains to Botany Bay.

The Governor of that First Fleet, Arthur Phillip, the man to whose office King was eventually to succeed, was a mild Christian gentleman. He was born the son of a German immigrant and teacher of foreign languages, and had raised himself to be a captain in the Royal Navy. But for the twelve years before 1787 he had been retired on half pay, farming down in the New Forest in Hampshire, hardly expecting to sail again, certainly expecting no high command. Not that Botany Bay was so high a command. Nobody wanted it until this gentleman farmer was made the most casual offer of it by the Secretary to the Navy, who was by chance a neighbour. Whereupon George III, by the Grace of God, caused a commission to be drawn up in which he called the gentleman farmer his trusty and well-beloved servant, recited that he had especial confidence in his prudence, courage, and loyalty, and gave him despotic powers over a continent.

'I would not,' said the Governor to the Secretary of the Navy, over a glass of punch three days before they sailed, 'I would not wish convicts to lay the foundation of an empire.'

'Convicts is what you have got.'

'I think convicts should ever remain separated from the garrison soldiers, and other settlers that may come in from Europe.'

'None will come.' And the Secretary was right. In the first two decades, fewer than 100 did.

'Then we shall be a fragile colony. I should wish to show clemency.' So he did wish. He wished indeed to retain only two offences as capital – murder, and unnatural crime, by which he meant sodomy.

'You must hold out a little more terror than that,' said the Secretary. But then, the Governor did have in mind the holding out of some terror. Though he would desire only two crimes to be capital, yet those guilty of such crimes he proposed not to hang but to deliver up to the native blacks, to be eaten.

'Cannibals?' said the Secretary.

The Governor assented.

'Cannibals. Who might, then, acquire a taste for white meat greater than your tribute to them of the occasional assassin would satisfy?'

But by then the Home Office in London had already received just such a modest proposal from the Governor-designate and had, for reasons unstated, declined it. Excessive clemency was to be avoided, but no one was to be eaten.

So, on a fine Sunday morning, they sailed. One day out, in light breezes, John Easty, a soldier on the convict transport *Scarborough*, gazed astern at the Lizard, the last of England. One month out the rum measures were suspected, complained of by the sailors, and found to be one-third short. Two months out, a large shoal of flying fish flew on board. Three months out, they lay in sight of Rio de Janeiro. From Rio they sailed eastwards across the South Atlantic to the Cape of Good Hope, which was then Dutch.

Easty and Bryant had become friends. Bryant had kept the Bishop's cloak. The Judge's writ ran as far as Portsmouth. No one had dared to take it before then. But at Portsmouth, when the prisoners were taken on board the convict ships, they were stripped, sluiced down with buckets of salt water, compelled to dress in slop-clothes of yellow and brown, and their own clothes, even if still good, were thrown overboard. Easty had saved Bryant's cloak, mostly out of the kindness of his heart, and would return it to him at the end of the voyage, minus the silver buckle. It was understood Easty would keep that.

From Cape Town they made eastwards again, in the roaring forties, through the heaviest seas they had ever seen, under the sharpest lightning, and towards the reddest skies, until, eight months and one week out from England, they came to New Holland. Joseph Banks had said the climate was that of the south of France, and the gentlemen of the Admiralty, and the Prime Minister, relied upon his judgement. The men of the First Fleet found a very complete harbour in which a thousand ships of the line, all the navies of the world, could safely shelter, and then they discovered the cove which, on 26 January 1788, they named Sydney after the British Home Secretary of the day. But they had not found the south of France, only a magnificent desert.

# 3

# The Hundred Hungry Days

The marine sentries shuffled backwards and forwards on the dirt path in front of what would one day, if they ever completed it, be Government House, but was still, a year after the colony was established, only a wooden shanty, a bit larger than the others of the town. There were four sentries, Luke Hines, Richard Aske, James Baker, and Joseph Hunt, and only the last had boots. The others wore the ruined remains of boots, cracked uppers from which the leather soles had long ago fallen away and been replaced by wooden slats. The leather uppers and wooden soles were bound together with canvas strips wound round and round. Only Joseph Hunt had boots, and the others knew why and said nothing. The uniforms of all four were no longer recognizable as uniforms. The red cloth was faded and torn and no longer even patchable. Only Joseph Hunt had eaten meat in the last week, and that had been salt pork – meat from pigs brought from England, animals from which they should have bred, but almost all the colony's livestock had been slaughtered for food. The flour in the government stores was low. The crops planted had shrivelled in the ground. Only a few orange trees, planted in the Domain, were flourishing. Of the four sentries, only Joseph Hunt was not hungry.

Richard Aske gazed at the barren lawns of struggling grass, and over the barren government farm where no crops grew, and then at the distant, barren hills.

'We'll starve,' he said, 'unless we're lucky.'

'We'll be lucky then,' said Luke Hines. 'A black cat crossed our path the other day, James Baker and me, when we were down by the stores.'

'Black cat's lucky,' said Richard Aske.

'Lucky for us,' said Luke Hines. 'Poor beast went almost mewing down our throats.'

'Like rabbit pie,' said Baker. 'As good as. Only, that was two weeks ago, and that, I b'lieve, was the extermination of the breed in the colony.'

'There was a woman,' said Hines, 'ate grass on Greenhill, and died; and when the surgeon opened her, there was only grass.'

Aske said, 'It will be a hundred hungry days for us.'

Only Joseph Hunt was sanguine. The stock was slaughtered and the crops shrivelled, but he was sure the supply ships would come. Since the colony was established, no single ship had come. The First Fleet had been the only fleet so far. But Hunt was sanguine. The other three said nothing, and then the little group separated and drew themselves to some sort of attention as the first of the Governor's guests began to arrive, walking up the slope from the settlement. They were the officers of the colony and its magistrates. The more provident or dishonest still had good shoes.

The Governor still had clothes because he had come out with three uniforms. There were servants. The Governor's table had silver and fine china, but little food. The Governor had put his own supplies into the common store. He had tried to govern his colony with mercy, and often pardoned the larcenies of half-starved men. His own table had silver and fine china, but for food only a broth, a thick soup with very little meat in it made to go a long way. The Governor said Grace himself, and then each guest produced from his pocket a hunk of bread, which he placed on the polished walnut table beside the solid silver spoon. In Sydney, even at Government House, the unwritten rule was, 'Bring your own Bread'.

'The Irishmen, sir,' said Lieutenant Johnston of the New South Wales Corps, among general laughter, 'have set off for China.' The lieutenant's colleagues had known what he was going to say and were delighted to observe the Governor as he received the news. The lieutenant had a reputation as a wit. The Corps was getting to be a law unto itself in the colony, even this early. The Governor was a captain in the Royal Navy, and he had practically the powers of a viceroy over every man in the colony – except for the officers of the Corps. They were certainly, in the end, under his command, and had come out to guard the convicts. But they were not from his own service. They were soldiers, who wore red coats, and in the day-to-day running of their own affairs they pleased themselves. If the Governor cared to give a direct order to their commanding officer, that would be that. It would be obeyed. But in practice he was unlikely to do so, because, at the other end of the earth, he was dependent on the Corps to keep order.

Governor Phillip waited for the laughter to die down. 'Poor men,' he said. 'I tried to save them.' The Governor and Lieutenant King had gone to the Irish when they heard of this belief that a colony of white people flourished three to four hundred miles south-west of Sydney, white people in a country that the Irish nevertheless believed was China.

'Only a tolerable walk, sir,' said Johnston. 'So the Paddies are reported to have gone to China, fourteen of them, with bits of boiled beef over their shoulders, gone rotten from being saved so long from their rations, and bags of biscuits at their belts, and each man with a screw of paper full of sugar stored in the crown of his hat. The sugar to put in the infusion of tea they propose to brew with the leaves they pull off the bushes as they cross the Chinese border.'

'It was a wild and cruel fancy of theirs,' said King, 'and they would not be reasoned out of it.' The soldiers were indignant that the Governor and one of his officers should have descended to talk to Irish convicts at all, because to do so was to lower not only their own dignity but also that of the military. The Corps officers would have flogged the Irishmen out of their fancy, and one of them said as much. The Governor looked bleakly round his table. Only King and another naval lieutenant, his own men, appeared in sympathy with him. The navy was an unfashionable service, because in it a man might rise by his own exertions and luck, whereas in the army a commission was bought. In his former service he had met lieutenant-colonels fourteen years old, who had attained that rank by purchase. But he was continually amazed at the resource and humanity of his own officers when he compared them with their counterparts in the military. He had once requested the Corps

officers in the colony, when they saw the convicts diligent, to
say a few words of encouragement to them, and, when they
met them idle, or straggling in the woods, to threaten them
with punishment. To this their commanding officer replied that
this was not in his written orders, and that he considered it no
business of his officers to associate in any way, however slightly,
with criminals. Except, the Governor supposed, to order them
flogged. He was sick of the incessant dignity of the military
officers. He was dismayed by their insensibility. He thought the
Irish had cruelly deluded themselves, but even though he put
this down largely to their Papism, he would not flog a man for
his delusions. For what else kept a man alive in New South
Wales? The Irish pined most for home, and their Celtic
imagination was the most easily stirred. Many Irishmen had no
idea how far they had come, no idea of the shape of the world,
and no idea where Australia lay in relation to Ireland. Sailors
told them that if you sailed south from Sydney it got colder.
The Irishmen knew Ireland was colder than New South Wales.
Therefore they reasoned that if you sailed south you would
come again to Ireland. Some put out in open boats, bound for
Antarctica, and were never seen again. Now these Irishmen,
fourteen of them, had conceived the idea of China. It was a
delusion, spread by a half-mad old woman, which had been
nourished by hope until it was a conviction. And New Holland
itself nourished delusion. It was a continent like no other, with
plants like no other, and animals nowhere else found. Away
from the coast there were few trees, and most of those were
eucalypts. Eucalypt could be scrub, or it could grow to trees
two hundred feet high. When the hot wind blew, bark hanging
from the trunks in strips rustled and chafed and almost moaned.
The outback moaned. It was a fragment of another planet, and
on it men took on other minds. Few could stand the loneliness.
Perhaps the sailors did better because they were used to years
of solitude at sea. But all of them, for more than a year, had
heard nothing and seen nothing that they had not brought with
them, or that was not already on the land. Delusion was their
only hope, and the Governor, surveying his dwindling stores,
sometimes thought hope itself was a delusion.

'What of the gold?' he asked.

'The mine is being searched for,' said King.

A week before, a convict had come in to the commissariat and tried to buy food with ore of some sort, which he said was gold. He was refused the food, but the Governor did send a detachment of soldiers to seek out the mine. The man was leading them to it. The soldiers were searching without much hope, since large fresh-water rivers, quarries of limestone and even marble, and mines of various rare ores, were proclaimed by the convicts every day. No claim had once proved true. But the chance of gold was worth a search. The officers were also asking among the convicts for a goldsmith who could assay the stuff brought in, which was certainly yellow and heavy. But gold in New South Wales? The man said it was, and insisted that he had found another Peru. It might be so, or it might be as insubstantial as the Irishmen's China. The Governor and his officers ate their broth.

Outside, Joseph Hunt took his three colleagues into his confidence and promised to make them rich in a way which could gain them boots like his and fill their stomachs. They hesitated.

Next morning, in the convict barracks, John Orton, a common felon, earnestly told his mates and his guards that John Orton was no more than an alias, and that he was by rights Count Grigori Orlov, favourite for many years of the Tsarina Catherine II, who had of course been his mistress. This was a tale thought unnecessarily flamboyant. Count Orlov already had a greater fame. He had been a prince of pickpockets. He had once dipped a jewelled snuff-box valued at £4000 from a royal duke, and he had enjoyed a remarkably long run. In the London of the 1780s a felon was judged like a play – the longer the run the more estimable the criminal, and Orlov had run for ever. For fourteen years, in fact, before he made the mistake of passing himself off as a Member of Parliament, entering the Commons chamber, and rising to speak. The Speaker, not quite recalling his constituency, said, 'The Member for . . .?', to which Orlov replied, 'For St Petersburg.'

That morning too, in front of the barracks, a funeral cortège was drawn up – a dray to carry the coffin of Captain DuCann, late of the New South Wales Corps, whose principal achievement in life was to devise an iron man-collar with long spikes

each side of the neck, so that gangs of convicts wearing it looked,
as they approached, like herds of horned cattle. As his representative at the funeral the Governor sent King, whose
precedence in the dusty march to the burying ground was being
disputed by Lieutenant Johnston of the Corps. There was no
doubt that King's naval rank was senior to the military, and no
doubt that as Governor's representative he had to take precedence. King did not care to brawl by a coffin, in public,
watched by private soldiers and convicts, but the midshipman
with him was zealous for the honour of the service, and was
quietly reasoning with the military officer, who was shouting
about his honour. It was hot. King approached to end the
matter, saying he would be perfectly happy to bring up the
rear, at which Johnston was determined he should not have that
privilege either, and howled at him, 'Damn your soul and
uniform, King, go first. Go first. I shall be delighted to see any
navy man go before me to the grave.'

Two weeks later the broken-off wards of a key were found
by the night patrol in the lock of the government storehouse.
The shaft of the key was discovered after a search at daybreak
next morning under the bed of Joseph Hunt, and in his quarters
were found two pair of new boots and twelve ounces of government tobacco. In the house of the bootmaker, quantities of
flour, meat, spirits, and tobacco were found, which he admitted
he had received from Hunt. Hunt, being in danger of his life,
informed on six of his fellow soldiers and turned King's evidence
at their trial. The six included his three colleagues of the guard
at Government House – Luke Hines, Richard Aske, James Baker,
and three others, Brown, Dykes, and Jones. Hunt betrayed men
he had himself seduced into the robberies. At half past two
they were pronounced guilty by a court of their own officers
and sentenced to death. The six stood to attention under the
high sun beside the storehouse while the warrant for their
execution was taken for the Governor's signature. He was a long
half-hour before he brought himself to sign it, and then the
paper was taken to the execution place and read aloud to
the men. They had already been degraded of all the badges and
numbers of their regiment, and now the brass buttons of their
tunics were cut away. All wore new boots, from which the laces
had been removed. The convicts assembled for the spectacle

kept silence. A woman offered the six men rum, which all took, except James Baker, who asked for water. The hangman trussed their arms and placed the rope around their throats. Dykes wept, and Aske said a word to comfort him. Luke Hines squared his shoulders in the bright red coat made by the tailor only three days before for a leg of bacon. The Governor did not attend. He refused the invitation of the Corps captain in charge, saying that with the signing of the warrant he already felt executioner enough. There was no drop. The hanging was strangulation by slow struggle. Though the Governor did not go, he could not avoid seeing, from his window, the new and vivid red coat of Luke Hines as at first it jerked, and then as it twisted in a half-circle slowly left and then right.

The hanging was by the store the men had robbed.

Easty said: 'The gallows was erected before the sentence was cast upon them, and before they had any trial.'

Lieutenant King glanced at him, and said, 'They were the flower of the regiment.'

'Sir,' said Easty, 'Joseph Hunt was the occasion of all their deaths as he was the first that began the robbery, but he received a free pardon.'

The convicts maintained their silence. The soldiers looked down at the red dust. The six dying in front of them were six men known to them all, and, in so small a colony, six out of so very few. There was hardly a soldier present but shed tears, officers and men.

'What did poor Aske say to Dykes,' asked King, 'before they were turned off? Did you catch it?'

Easty answered him. 'Sir, I think he might have said, "Such is life." '

And such was life in the colony in March of 1789, a month before George Washington was inaugurated as first president of the United States, and less than three months before the Paris mob stormed the Bastille. Then the second and third fleets limped into Sydney Cove, trebling the population and bringing food and supplies. The hungry days were over. The *Lady Vane* transport put into the cove carrying London newspapers and the Twelve Apostles, young women sent out by a religious society in London and so named by the sailors. Most were found pregnant by the reverend inspector who visited the vessel in order to certify the young women's high state of moral improvement. The newspapers, arriving eight months late from England, carried an item which amused the Governor for days. Washington DC, it appeared, had at last been laid out, three years later, as he never tired of remarking, than his own city of Sydney. But Washington DC was still on paper, and it was also, as he was uncharitable enough to perceive from the newspaper account, situated on a swamp. The projected great avenues, he said, if they were ever built, would for fifty years lead only to other swamps; for more than fifty years he was right. Not that New South Wales was a flourishing settlement. There were no swamps because there was so little water. Avenues from Sydney would have led to arid deserts. The searchers for the gold mine had long ago returned, having found nothing, and in their absence the fraudulent ore had been assayed and found to contain a mixture of sand, redstone, and powdered red brass. The discoverer confessed the brass came from two doorknobs. 'Gold!' said the Governor. 'Doorknobs is all the gold there ever will be in New Holland.' Everyone agreed.

Two of the fourteen Irishmen returned half demented from China, the other twelve having fallen victim to starvation or aborigines. The two survivors were apprehended at the outskirts of the town and had the misfortune to be brought before Lieutenant Johnston. 'Arrah there, Colonel,' said the first Irishman, 'and long life to ye.' This counted as insolence, and the lieutenant set about having them flogged, selecting as scourgers two convicts of bodily height and power, who inflicted alternate strokes with the cat o'nine tails. Each Irishman received fifty strokes, after which one man died.

Fifty was a commonplace punishment, as Lieutenant Johnston said when he was summoned by the Governor to give an account of himself. The Governor had wished to rule by clemency, and now saw the colony reduced to a state of near-savagery, a savagery he felt as much in himself as in the felons. The execution of the six marines, which he had countenanced with such great reluctance, signing the warrants after half an hour of agonizing over those men and the power he had over their lives, but also having to consider the example he must make of those who looted the stores of a half-starving settlement, had been on his mind ever since. And now a man had been

flogged to death for believing an old woman who told him
China was within walking distance, and for a few words of
greeting to Johnston. The Governor could not arrest Johnston.
It was within the power of any officer summarily to order a
flogging of fifty lashes. More required a magistrate. But the
Governor was angry, and brought Johnston before him as
nearly under appearance of arrest as he could, having him
conducted into the room by an escort of two naval lieutenants.

'You may order a punishment of fifty lashes, Mr Johnston,
but did it not occur to your mind that these were men exhausted
by months of privation, and probably starved?'

'We gave water to the one who asked, sir.' Mr Johnston at
this point said, as further evidence of his concern for the state
of the two men, that he had ordered a surgeon to be present.

'Bring him,' said the Governor, and the surgeon was brought,
and read from his notes.

'The first man,' he said, 'uttered a piercing scream at the first
lash, and continued to bellow at every succeeding lash. The
skin was lacerated at the fifth lash, the blood came at the sixth,
and ran at the eighth. He asked for water at the tenth lash,
which was given. I am of opinion that he was sufficiently
punished at the twenty-fifth lash. He fainted at the thirtieth.
More blood appeared than I had previously discerned on any
other criminal.'

'He fainted, but was still flogged?'

'Yes, sir.'

'And the second man?'

'The skin lacerated at the ninth, and there was a slight
effusion of blood. The prisoner subdued his sense of pain by
biting his lips. The skin of this man was thick to an exceptional
degree. Both his mind and his body must have been hardened
by former punishments. He did not cry out, but at the eighteenth he began to writhe. Still he did not cry out. He was a
criminal known to be "flash" or "game". After the punishment
was completed he stood and shook himself like a bear, and said,
"Domino." '

'The first man fainted and was continued to be flogged?'

'Yes.'

'Did it occur to you that after the thirtieth stroke Lieutenant
Johnston might have been flogging a dead man?'

'It was not the first who died, sir, but the second.'

'The harder man died?'

'An hour afterwards. He did not speak after the punishment, but sat and looked to sea.'

'And this word "Domino" that he said, when he was cut down, what was that?'

Lieutenant Johnston explained that it was a word spoken by the winner at the game of dominoes.

'At the end of the game he says, "Domino"?' asked the Governor.

The surgeon said, 'It is an ejaculation of completion.'

'Yes,' said the Governor. There was nothing he could do except take the extreme step of court-martialling Johnston but there was no charge that would warrant that.

'Go back to your duty,' he said. 'Get out.'

Then, as the lieutenant and the surgeon left, he called back the surgeon.

'There is blood on your coat? Is that blood?' It was only a tiny spattering, but it did appear to be blood.

'I could not remove it, sir. As the scourgers flourished their cats, to clean them after each stroke, a little blood and flesh flew from the instruments.'

'How far away were you standing?'

The surgeon reflected. 'About thirty feet, sir.'

For the next two days the Governor rode round his city, taking stock of what he saw, and then wrote a despatch to the Secretary of State in London.

'The crops are now fair, but there is not a barn, granary, or storehouse in which to preserve them, nor are these even thought of yet. There are too few mechanics in the colony to erect them. Our boats have gone to ruin and decay. Nor is there any place of public worship. There is a tendency to evil not so much among the felons as among those appointed to guard them, which the greatest diligence on my part has been unable wholly to check. Officers grow overweening in brutality. Men become beasts. Even the Sacred Character of the Redeemer, were He to appear in the colony in its present dark state, might well find gentlemen readier to prepare for His head a second crown of thorns than to welcome Him as their Saviour.'

The Under Secretary in London, when he read this, did not

pass it to the Secretary of State but put it aside. There were other matters to think of. War with the French was imminent. The Under Secretary glanced again at the letter he had put aside. 'Deluded,' he said to himself.

# 4

# Felons' Gala and the Night of the Wives

Bennelong, an aborigine, sat at a side table in the Governor's dining room eating lamb chops daintily with his fingers and a knife. When he had finished he reached instinctively to wipe his hands on the fabric at the back of the brocaded chair on which he was sitting but Easty, who had been charged with his training from the moment of his capture, looked hard at him and Bennelong grinned, dipped his fingers in the finger bowl, and dabbed them on the napkin.

'Might think he'd dined in good company all his life,' said Governor Phillip.

It had not always been so. The first time he was brought to the Governor's table he bowed to the company, as he had been taught, ate his food cleanly, as he had been taught, and then sat back and threw his plate and knife out of the open window. The Governor said they had expected too much too soon, and must persevere. They had persevered, until Bennelong was now perfect in all the usages of civilization, not excepting the finger bowl. The time of the Hundred Hungry Days was well behind the colony. There was now abundant food, though when Bennelong first appeared there had not been, and the servants murmured at the amount he was fed. He was sturdy for an aborigine, five feet eight inches tall, and in the famine time a week's ration kept him content for barely a day. Since it was the Governor's policy to keep him content, he was fed as much as he could eat. Bennelong's introduction to good society had given the Governor pleasure. His commission as Governor enjoined him to conciliate the affections of the natives, to encourage the convicts to live in amity and kindness with them, and to punish those who wantonly hindered their pursuits or destroyed their persons. He had always assured his superiors in London that he did everything possible to prevent their being offered insults, that he would teach them the advantages of civilization and how to sow corn so that they might not die of starvation in the season when the fish were short, and that when he had time he would himself go among them. 'And mix with them myself,' he wrote to the Secretary. The Governor well remembered the day, a year after his arrival, when he and a party of twelve white men went to the north shore of Botany Bay, twenty miles from Sydney, and were surrounded by 212 aborigines who, when he offered friendship, laid down their spears and stone hatchets, sat beside their weapons, and afterwards brought some of their women to receive gifts of beads, kettles, and little bells. He was inclined to forget that he and his party of twelve had first set out to find the murderers of two convicts who were speared while they were cutting rushes. But he knew that the aborigines were treacherous. They could invite a man to eat with them, and then, after a convivial meal, kill him. There were few escapes by convicts into the interior because a man unarmed or alone was invariably murdered, as most of the Irishmen had been. He chose not to believe tales that an aborigine woman who had given birth to a half-caste child, fathered by a convict, had tried to darken its skin by holding it over a fire. It died, but the aborigines would have killed it in any case, as they always did any white man's child, and the white men, with so few white women, had many children by aboriginal women. The white man had also, as the Governor well knew, taken the aborigines' land. The Governor's honest mind, when it contemplated aborigines, led him to act humanely because he was a Christian who believed in the equality of all men in the eyes of God, and because he had not been untouched by Rousseau's concept of the Noble Savage. He believed that in his natural state, from which he departed only to decay, Man was good and happy. So he was delighted when Bennelong was captured, submitted to instruction, wore European clothes, declined all spirituous liquor and drank only water, and showed pleasure at a portrait of the Duchess of Cumberland. The Duchess was sister-in-law of George III.

Easty did not tell the Governor that Bennelong, when first
shown the portrait, said of it, as he had been instructed by the
servants to say of any female convict who took his fancy, 'Now
there's a flash covess. I like to dab it up with her.' *Covess* was the
feminine of *cove*, and meant a likely-looking woman: and the
rest speaks for itself. Bennelong's command of English was
rapidly increasing, which pleased the Governor. He overlooked
Bennelong's habit of absconding for the night to pursue women
of his own kind, only finding it strange that on such occasions
the man should leave his European clothes, of which he was so
proud, in a thrown-off heap on the floor of this or that drawing
room. One day Easty found Bennelong with his ear half bitten
through by a man whose woman he was dragging off, and had
it secretly sewn up for him by a surgeon. After a year Bennelong
was no longer guarded but was allowed to live in a brick hut
on the eastern point of the cove, appearing at the Governor's
for dinner. The part of the cove where he lived was named
Bennelong Point.

When the first Governor returned home to London after
seven years he took Bennelong with him, to demonstrate that
aborigines existed, to show that they could master both etiquette
and English, and to be presented to the monarch. Black men
were not then unknown in London. Negroes were fashionable
as ladies' servants. But Bennelong was not a Negro. It was much
noted that he was much closer in his features to an Indian than
to any African Negro. He was fitted out like a gentleman in a
red tail suit and doeskin breeches, and was altogether one of the
attractions of the season, behaving, except at a concert of music
by Handel, in a most genteel fashion, chatting to all and
learning to make an excellent bow, a most excellent leg.

Lieutenant King had returned to England on leave at the same
time, and was employed in conducting Bennelong from town
house to town house. To the Handel concert King brought his
daughter Susannah, then aged ten. She did not see him at his
best. He made his leg when presented to her, which was elegant
enough, but when the music began he was so affected by the
clavichord and by the singing of an admittedly indifferent
soprano that he covered his ears and gave a great howl.

He was instructed not to howl at his presentation a few days
later to George III. His Majesty chose to receive Bennelong,

along with Lieutenant King, in his library. The King was expecting a savage. When he saw Bennelong in the dress of an English gentleman, he could think only to address him as a gentleman, and asked with which books written on the topography of New Holland he was familiar. Bennelong was mute, merely making repeated legs until he was escorted from the room. His Majesty asked the lieutenant to remain.

'Now, sir,' he said, 'tell me. I have read despatches from Botany Bay, which speak of hardship. But is not a fine colony to be made there?'

'It is, sir,' the officer said, 'so fine a harbour as I never before saw. But inland a mile, sir, and it is beyond all description a wretched country.'

Few men spoke with candour to George III. He liked this young officer. 'Wretched?' he said. 'Wretched, you say?'

'Sir,' said the lieutenant, 'every man almost laments himself of being there.'

'Ah,' said His Majesty, 'ah – but they said as much of Virginia, when that was first settled. We have lost Virginia. I will be very frank with you. I was the last to consent to the separation.'

The lieutenant had the good fortune to have served in that lost American colony, and so monarch and naval officer talked for half an hour. Conversation pleased George III, and the young man – though he had said Sydney was a wretched place, and though the King had strangely American hopes of his new southern colony – also pleased him.

'And when,' asked the King, 'do you return?'

The lieutenant did not at that moment intend to return at all. He rather looked for promotion in the navy, and some command. Again he said what he thought, and told the King he believed he had already done his part in New South Wales.

'I should have thought so too,' said George III, 'if you had not done it so well.' Now this was either great courtesy on the part of a monarch, or an empty compliment (but he was not given to such things), or more likely an expression of hope, because he wished the young man *would* do well. Whatever it was, the fact is that he had no knowledge at all, at that moment, of whether the lieutenant had done well, or done badly, or done anything. But it was decisive. When in 1800 another new governor was required for this new Virginia, George III remembered Philip Gidley King. And that is how he returned to Sydney as Governor, and how Susannah, his daughter, came there too.

Six months out from London, on a warm summer evening, the convoy of King's ships and four convict vessels entered the great harbour. It was already sunset, so the fleet anchored for the night in open waters. They would wait until daylight to enter the cove. On board, as his flagship rode at anchor, King entertained the ship's officers to dinner in the great stern cabin. Toasts were drunk to the monarch, to the colony in whose waters they lay, and then, as was the custom, the last toast was proposed by the youngest lieutenant of the ship's company.

'To His Excellency the Governor, and to Miss King, the Governor's lady.'

Susannah had never been toasted in that way before. Nor had she ever been referred to in that way. She was at first surprised, but then she inclined her head in acknowledgement to the officers who drank her health, and to the young man who had proposed it.

When his officers left, and Susannah stood to leave with them, to go to her cabin, King called her back.

'Susannah. Wait.'

The officers said their goodnights. King resumed his place at the head of the long table, and motioned his daughter to take her place again, at the side.

King was a widower. Susannah's mother had died when she was three years old. She was his only daughter. Little more than six months before, she had still been at her finishing school at Bath.

King poured himself a glass of port, leaned back in his chair, and regarded his daughter. She was sitting with her back very straight, and her head high. She waited.

'That young man who proposed your health is seventeen,' he said. 'It will be years before he has any command.'

'He is very young,' she said.

'Dear Susannah, you are younger still.'

She was sixteen.

'And from tomorrow,' said King, 'you will be the first lady of this colony. You will receive my guests. Government House is not a palace, but it will be yours to run. It will be your house.'

She looked down at her lap, at the folds of her dress. He rose and walked round the table to her, and kissed her head. She sat still, and then suddenly reached up and encircled him with her arms.

'I shall do it,' she said.

King nodded. He knew very well she would.

'Now go to bed,' he said, and then, as she rose to go, he said, 'Susannah. It is a very young colony. Younger than you.'

But even in so young a colony there were already two traditions. The first was that a play should be given, of course by the convicts, in a theatre newly built by them, to celebrate any great event. The coming of a new governor was such an event. The second was that, the day after the arrival of a convict fleet bringing women convicts, the ticket-of-leave men, convicts who had completed four years of a seven-year sentence, should be permitted to visit the new women's quarters, in a strictly orderly and supervised manner, to select wives. The play was given on the night of the Governor's arrival. The wiving was to be the next day.

The play had a fetching prologue, written by an author who had at home gained by his works great praise and little cash, and had in the end been driven so to desperation by the dilatory payment of a celebrated publisher that he accosted the man in Fleet Street, was once again refused, and in uncontrolled fury dragged the man to the banks of the Thames and threw him in. Alas, he had mischosen his man. The publisher had the ear of those in high places, the warrant for the poor hack's arrest was issued at Downing Street itself, and the penal colony of New South Wales acquired a writer of spirit. This was his prologue:

> From distant climes, o'er wide-spread seas we come,
> Though not with much *éclat* or beat of drum:
> True patriots all, for, be it understood,
> We left our country for our country's good.

Much laughter in the boxes. Susannah was delighted.

> But, you inquire, what could our breasts inflame
> With this new passion for theatric fame?
> Your patience, sirs; some observations made,
> You'll grant us equal to the scenic trade.
> Too oft, alas, we've wept th'unwilling tear,
> And petrified our hearts with real fear.
> Macbeth a harvest of applause will reap,
> For some of us, I fear, have murdered sleep.

This was greeted with silence by all. Many had murdered sleep. Many never knew a lasting peace of mind. The prologue continued:

> His lady, too, with grace will sleep and talk,
> Our females have been used at night to walk.

Back to laughter.

> Sometimes, indeed, so various is our art,
> An actor may improve and mend his part.
> 'Give me a horse,' bawls Richard, like a drone;
> *We'll* find a man will help himself to one.
> Grant us your favour, put us to the test,
> To gain your smiles we'll do our very best;
> And, without fear of turnkey lockits,
> Thus, in an honest way, still pick your pockets.

The officers were amused, the Governor diverted, and Susannah delighted. She applauded, clapping her white-gloved hands. Next day the seamstresses and dressmakers of Sydney received visit after visit from ladies wanting gloves made up – cotton gloves, silk gloves, but always white gloves. Within a week, white gloves became a fashion in Sydney. It was this more than anything else that told Susannah that she was indeed first lady. She was amused.

After the play, the audience all went home in high spirits, where the officers found that their quarters had been looted in their absence of all eatables, drinkables, shoes – of which there was still scarcely a pair to be had in all Sydney, for want of both shoemakers and leather – and of anything transportable and saleable. All feather mattresses had disappeared. The play had been called *The Revenge*.

A few men were apprehended the next day, and each endured fifty lashes. Susannah, walking near the hospital, caught a brief sight of a scourged man being carried there from the prison. He was writhing, and calling out. King wished she had not seen this so soon, but knew he could not keep it from her. It was a thing of everyday occurrence. He did, however, keep her from the wiving, which was less difficult to do since the women's prison, called the factory, was fifteen miles out, at Parramatta. The newly arrived women had been taken to the factory the previous day. There was generally a substantial difference in the criminality of a transported man and a transported woman. The male convicts were not saints. Those from the cities, and most were from London or Liverpool or such places, were a pack of lying, thieving rogues. Some were violent, but few were murderous, few evil. But the women were worse. There were some who had simply been unlucky, but on the whole a woman, to be transported, had to be a more persistent, hard, pitiless criminal, a whore who would strip her drunken client of all he wore and leave him naked in the frozen streets, or a kidnapper of children. The women were not only worse, but were also under less restraint than the men. On board convict ships carrying females – for once a woman became a convict she was no longer, By Authority, to be called a woman, but a female – there were no soldiers to mount guard. The females were not chained as men often were. It was much lamented that the means of disciplining females were few. Females could scarcely be flogged, though a few were. The master of the *Orion*, in the First Fleet, tied Mary Abell to the rigging and ordered twenty-five lashes, which the boatswain laid on with a will because she had bitten half through the tongue of one of his shipmates. That was the Mary Abell convicted of abducting a twelve-year-old girl. But such a flogging was unusual. Furthermore, the seduction of the ship's crew, on a voyage of many months, was taken for granted. The females were certainly wanton. Very few, however innocently convicted, retained after the voyage an innocence of any sort.

When they arrived in the colony they were most welcome. In 1800 there were five men to each woman in New South Wales, so the 200 who sailed with Susannah were eagerly awaited. The colony was conducted on Christian principles.

The officers had a wholesome horror of unnatural offences,
offences to which females, though depraved, were known to be
a preventive. Therefore the lawful union of male and female
was held to conduce to the best interests of the colony. So a
ticket-of-leave man might also have a ticket of admission to the
factory, under strict supervision, and on the explicit understanding that his visit was made with the purpose of selecting
a wife. The union envisaged was that of holy matrimony,
but it was not enquired too rigorously, and sometimes
not at all, whether either partner was previously married in
England.

So, the day after the arrival, tickets were given in batches to
the males. Each was allowed an hour – to view, converse, invite,
and strike the bargain. It was remarked as a sad fact by the
magistrate conducting the factory, who was also a clergyman,
that the females did most of the viewing and made most of the
terms. The magistrate was assisted in keeping order by his
subordinates, corporals in the New South Wales Regiment.
Things could not proceed too far while the reverend magistrate
was present, but on the day after the Governor's arrival, while
the viewing was proceeding, he departed at dusk for the
Governor's banquet, whereupon the corporals were cozened,
coneyed, traduced by promises and stupefied by liquor, and
males and females became men and women again. Then
followed a reckless lasciviousness which, though he could not for
a moment have countenanced it, would not much have surprised the Governor. The ground was strewn with copulating
forms, the more delicate seeking the privacy of kitchens, lofts,
or stables. Women rolled from one man to another, and bar-
gained themselves for liquor, for food, for any possession a man
might have upon him.

Two hundred women had newly arrived, all declaring themselves single. Three hundred men presented themselves with
tickets. It should have been the night of the two hundred wives.
That is the name the convicts gave it. The next day, fifty-eight
couples did present themselves as candidates for Christian
marriage, and were, after the proper time prescribed by the
church for the publishing of banns – banns 13,000 miles from
any ears that might need to hear them – joined in the sacred
bonds of matrimony.

But, before that, dark word of what happened that night came to the ears of the Rev. Peregrine Judd, and he, in black habit, came to the Governor.

'The females comported themselves, Your Excellency, like . . . like wanton colts.'

'Fillies, Mr Judd, I take it; fillies. You do see? And fillies are pretty chaste, you know. Ever tried to take a stallion to a filly? Ever *seen* a stallion with a filly, come to that? I suppose you must have done; and been forcibly impressed with the, what would you say, Mr Judd?'

'By the animality, sir.'

'Men and women, if we bring them here, and if *you* give them tickets, are likely to be animals, and a great deal more ingenious and various than animals. Marry the fifty-eight fillies and save their souls.'

But it was a strange thing that, among these deplored animals, there were both men and women who, finding in each other a personal attachment they had not known before – for which they had had no opportunity, coming as they did from teeming lodgings and filthy alleys – stood by each other faithfully. Two such were George Bryant, the boy of the cloak, now about thirty, and Jane Broad. They married, not with the fifty-eight couples, as not wishing to be precipitate, but two months later.

# 5

# The Summons to the Tuileries

It was so long since he had worn full-dress uniform that, when he received his astonishing summons to the Tuileries, Nicolas Baudin had to borrow the sword, his own having long ago been sold. His had been the sort of service that rarely called for full dress, and, for that matter, he had not for two years worn even the sea-going uniform of a lieutenant of the French navy. These two years he spent in his Paris lodgings, writing the memoirs of past voyages. He was poor. He was the son of a small provincial merchant and had entered the French marine when Louis XVI was still alive and King of France. For fifteen years he had held the rank of lieutenant, unpromoted. He had no connections. He had made one bad error, which haunted him. But it was forgotten by almost everyone except himself, and it had not been an error of seamanship. He was, and he knew it, a much more than good sailor. But by the month of March of 1802 he had not for two years been at sea.

'Who,' Napoléon Bonaparte had demanded three days before of an aged admiral whose loyalty and judgement he trusted, 'is the best navigator we have? I am thinking of the south seas.'

The old man said straightaway, 'Baudin.'

'Why?'

'He was under my command twelve years ago. I know him. Bougainville will know him.' Bougainville was a great man, old and full of honours, the navigator who gave his name to the crimson bougainvillaea, a man as renowned as Captain Cook.

'And *where* is this Baudin?' said Napoléon, thinking he would probably be cruising off Martinique or somewhere equally remote, not likely to put into a French port for months or years and therefore useless to his present purpose. 'What is his command?'

'To my knowledge, he has none.'

'And that man, you say, and Bougainville would say, is the best navigator in France; and he has no command?'

The admiral explained.


Baudin was found rapidly, and in due time presented himself at the Tuileries, the royal palace of the guillotined king. Napoléon had moved his quarters there only a month before. He was not yet Emperor; that would take another four years. But he was First Consul. He was the man who was making an empire out of a revolution, which was thought by some to be treason to the revolution, and by others a miracle.

Baudin entered the great room knowing nothing. Napoléon did not greet him, but regarded him for ten seconds, which is a long time. He knew Baudin to be older than himself, and now he saw, as he had often seen in his officers of the marine, that a life spent largely at sea is a hard one. Baudin was also not of a sailor's build. He was not tall, well short of six feet, but neither was he broad. His hair was dark, his eyes hazel, or a shade darker than hazel. His life was in his eyes. He could keep the other features of his face impassive, but never his eyes, which revealed his mind. Bonaparte took this in, and then motioned him to a window, where there was a globe, a chased and gilded globe. His finger traced the ports of Canton and Macao, and the island of Timor.

'For three centuries Europeans have formed settlements here.'

Baudin assented.

'And for three centuries this,' said Bonaparte, indicating the sketchy contour of New Holland, 'has been forgotten?'

Baudin let his silence assent again, though for three centuries that land had been not forgotten but unknown. It was only thirty years since the east coast had been mapped at all. In the lifetimes of both men in that room it had been thought possible that a vast, new, unknown continent lay somewhere in the Pacific, much further north than New Holland. There was room for one. It was only in their time that Captain Cook had disproved that thesis, and mapped a fragment of the eastern coast of New South Wales.

'Well' – and Napoléon sat – 'we shall come to know the coastline of that great south land.' Baudin was thinking that he had himself come close to that coast twelve years before, and never touched it, having to retreat before a tempest. He was thinking of the mocking story put about by the English that other French navigators had also come as close, and had been deterred by the croaking of the monstrous New Holland frogs.

'Baudin,' said the First Consul, 'I am told you are as good a navigator as I have. I have also been informed that you have spent most of the last few years cruising the Indian and Pacific Oceans collecting botanical specimens for the Emperor of Austria, or for his nephew of Hungary, and that you appear to have stocked the more exotic gardens and glasshouses of Vienna and Budapest.'

'I am an officer of the French marine, sir, and I carried out those expeditions with the leave of my superiors. It was a leave I did not want. I would have served on any French ship, but none was offered.'

'Two are offered now. You will take two corvettes, and do for me along the coasts of New Holland what you did for Vienna and Budapest. And, as well, you will chart, survey, and bring back specimens of these.' Baudin found himself taking tinted engravings of emus and kangaroos held out to him. He had never seen such creatures. He had never heard of the First Consul's sudden interest in zoology.

'Sir, to do that we shall have to put in at Sydney to victual, and Sydney . . .'

'You are perhaps reminding me that we are at war with England? Captain Cook sailed in time of war, a British ship with passports from the former government of France and the present government of the United States of America. You seem to have been about the business of the Emperor of Austria, with, you say, the approval of my admirals, and we are, you will recall, at war with him too. We already have passports from the English, who have sent them along with a learned quotation to the effect that even in times of war men in search of the truth need fear no enemy. Voltaire, they say.'

'Sir, Cook was sailing what I understand to have been a sort of collier brig. I am to have two corvettes? Two men o'war, each of thirty guns?'

'Baudin, you have been a lieutenant for some fifteen years, and I begin to see why. In part I see why. You will take command of these ships with the rank of post-captain, you will select your own officers, you will rename your ships, let us say, *Géographe* and *Naturaliste*, you will make France's name honoured in all the countries you touch on, you will make us beloved of those uncivilized people to whom you will be taking nothing but benefits, and you will show, oh, the great and liberal designs of the Consulate for the pacification of Europe.'

Baudin hardly heard these last words. He had never been an ambitious man, but now he had just received the greatest preferment of his life. He had been given *carte blanche* to explore the only utterly unknown continent of the world, and knew that should he remotely succeed he would leave at least a name to posterity. He said, with some passion, that with God's help he would do it.

'You must not,' said Napoléon, 'confuse even the First Consul with God.'

Then he said, 'I shall not dwell further, Citizen Baudin, on what solely concerns your inner conduct, so to speak.' Baudin bowed. That matter of the past again.

So there they were. Corvettes, passports, surveys, emus. And of course more than that. Baudin could never remember the First Consul's exact words, and nor were those words later embodied in any formal orders, but he was told indirectly, though plainly enough, that the great southern route to China and the east was the concern of France as well as of Britain, and that Sydney commanded that route. He understood. Ten years later Napoléon would order the taking of Sydney, though by then he would lack the ships to do it.

As Baudin left his presence, Bonaparte called after him, 'Outward bound, take on wine at Tenerife.' Five weeks later, Baudin sailed for New South Wales.

# 6

# The Sighting of the French Sail

By 1802 Sydney had a town clock. The loss of eight sheep
and a hog killed by lightning was no longer a public calamity.
As early as 1790 shops opened in the town. Houses were numbered by 1796. There was progress. The colony was a flourishing
jail. It could also be said by its presence to be guarding the
southern trade routes. The other things hoped of it had failed.
South Sea pines proved too brittle or downright rotten to
provide masts for His Majesty's ships. The southern flax of
which so much was hoped, since it had a longer fibre than the
Baltic flax on which for years Britain had perilously depended
for the ropes and rigging of its ships, would not make even a
decent cat o'nine tails. The knotted cords tended to fray soon
after the fiftieth lash. By 1802 six convicts had suffered as many
as a thousand lashes each but, as one despairing officer remarked, they were so little reclaimed by the lash as if so many
drops of water had been poured upon their backs. He might
also have remarked that four of them, if not reformed, were at
least so crippled that they could never again work, only steal.

Bennelong had returned from England civilized, and continued to wear the clothes of an English gentleman. He went
so far as to bring back laced petticoats which he made his
wives wear for decency's sake. They obeyed until they were
ridiculed by their own people. Bennelong's noble savagery had
been so thoroughly civilized out of him that he took to drink.
He was no longer asked to eat at Government House. Easty
tried to look after him, but found the man intractable. Captain
Johnston of the Corps, a few days after his promotion from
lieutenant, found that his elevation had given him a new sense

of concern for the safety of the convicts and went round an-
nouncing he would shoot the Bennelong fellow the next time
he saw him drunk. He was only prevented from doing this by a
direct order from the Governor. Bennelong was not given new
western clothes, and his old ones soon wore to rags. In the end
he went bush, living alone in the outback, and was not seen for
months at a time.

Governor King continued to be irritated by the atrociousness
of the military officers who were the colony's magistrates. Two
women, Bridget Rose and Margaret Murphy, on no more than
suspicion of stealing a gown and selling it for liquor, were
ordered to be chained together and to remain chained until
the gown was restored. King released them when he heard of it.
Then there was the affair of John Macarthur, formerly a
London corset-maker who had risen to be a lieutenant in the
Corps. Macarthur, with farsightedness, had devoted himself to
sheep-farming for profit, but overstepped himself when he
picked a quarrel with the Lieutenant-Governor and wounded
him in a duel. King took the opportunity to be rid of the man
and sent him to England for court-martial, together with a
report intended to put a final stop to his military career. He
wrote that Macarthur's chief employment during his years in
the colony had been that of making a large fortune for himself,
helping his brother officers to make small ones, mostly at the
public expense, and generally sowing discord and strife. He
had also wounded the Lieutenant-Governor. That, thought
King, sealing the despatch, should be enough.

What with all this, the Governor could not help reflecting
that few of his magistrates and even fewer of his officers were
gentlemen. He often consoled himself by conversing with those
few of the newly arrived convicts who, back in England, had
been, if not gentlemen, at least more like gentlemen than his
colleagues in the administration of the colony. These conver-
sations were known as his 'At Homes'.

'Well, Mr Burgoyne,' he would say to a man brought before
him, 'and what were you sent here for?'

Mr Burgoyne would explain that he had suffered the misfortune to be acquainted with a person of bad character, and
that . . .

'But, Mr Burgoyne, come to the point. I don't want you to

go round here and then back again and round the other way.'
Here the Governor traced circles on the table with his finger
as he spoke, and fixed the man with an amiable stare. 'Really,
sir, you are not at the bar of the Old Bailey now. Come to the
point.'

The point was that Mr Burgoyne, having the misfortune to
introduce himself to a royal levée at St James's Palace attended
by the Lord Chancellor and some of the greatest quality in the
land, had cut off and made away with the insignia of the Order
of the Bath, encrusted with brilliants of the first water, worn by
the Duke of Buccleuch.

'So you are of the better class of pickpocket, Mr Burgoyne?'

'Though your Excellency may doubt my assertion, I solemnly
assure you I was innocent of the charge.'

'Oh I dare say, Mr Burgoyne, very innocent, no doubt.
Quite innocent, I dare say.'

'I am happy you should think so, sir.'

'Yes. And what trade were you brought up to, Mr Burgoyne?'

To this the man replied that he had no trade at all, since he
was, though now regrettably declined, a gentleman by birth.
The Governor nodded and nodded and gave the man a
scribbled note to be a clerk at the commissary stores where, he
said, there were no brilliants of any water. This kept the man
off the road gangs and out of fetters.

It was one afternoon in late June when Sir Harry Browne
Hayes, knight, made his appearance and he, though not only a
transported felon but also an Irishman, was as near a gentleman
as could be got.

He was shown in while the Governor was putting the finishing
touches to a water colour of a black man, whom he had portrayed standing on a rock of flat sandstone at the east side of the
cove. The pencilled outline was complete, and the Governor
was tinting in the colours.

'A moment, if you please,' he said over his shoulder. Sir
Harry did wait a moment but then, when he caught sight of the
painting, he stepped over to regard it.

'A fine thing, sir,' he said. 'A very fine thing. To the life. It is
a gift you have, sir, to get so near the life.'

The Governor put down his brush and turned round.

'Indeed?' he said.

Sir Harry apologized. 'I beg your pardon, sir, to have come
between you and your work. But at home, in Cork, the walls of
my house were covered with fine paintings, though I could never
myself as much as draw a mouse, or not so that even a cat
would recognize it. I beg you pardon, sir.'

'Not at all, not at all,' said the Governor. 'But now I fear I
must ask you what came between you and your house in Cork,
with its fine paintings. Pray, Sir Harry, why were you sent here?'

'I am an Irishman, sir.'

'I am sorry for that; but, Sir Harry . . .?'

'Sir, I was a freeman of Cork and High Sheriff of that city.'

'But even for that, Sir Harry?' And the Governor, making his
circles on the table, was saying don't go round here and back
again, when Sir Harry volunteered that he had been condemned
for abducting an heiress.

'Ah,' said the Governor, waving him to a chair. 'You were
of course innocent? Quite innocent?'

'Oh, no, sir, quite guilty, very guilty. Though she was a
Quaker.'

'Ah,' repeated the Governor, and, dismissing his escort and
calling for a decanter, he was soon settling down to chat with
Sir Harry as if with a member of his own club in London. A
gentleman was rare.

'Not at all for the money, Sir Harry, I take it, though she was
an heiress?'

'There was a matter of twenty thousand pounds that she had,
sir, and a man could not say, knowing of such a sum, that his
conduct might not be swayed, but it was mostly for Mary Pike
herself, for she was as fine a woman as a man could wake to see
as his first sight of a new day. But she was never of one mind.
First she would, and then she would not, and seeing the poor
woman's hesitation . . .'

'There was nothing you could do but make up her mind for
her?'

'It was so. But there was no violence offered to Miss Pike,
except the forcing of her from her father's house, and she
assented to that, sir, as you might say, afterwards. Three
months we lived together, as man and woman, and going openly
to assemblies and other public companies, where the natural
gaiety of her was a great thing to see; and a great thing for me

in company to have it said behind my back that such a fine girl
was mine. There are some things a man likes to hear said behind
his back, and him not intended to hear. There *was* the sin of
pride in it.'

'And the, ah, forcible marriage was taken exception to by
the father?'

'A marriage there never was, though I offered it, and me
having her already too. We lived as man and woman, and such
a woman, who could hold out her wild arms to me at dinner
with the Lord Mayor himself, and take me away, in the eyes
of the company, between the soup and the roast, to her bed.
She was a dear wanton. But she was half-hearted in the deeper
things. We lived as man and woman, not man and wife. She
would not be my wife. Sir, the indictment said, 'Carrying off
with intent to marry,' and I would not demur at that indictment
as all my friends cried out to me that I should. I would not
deny the intent. It was always my dearest intent. If I had
wanted *her*, not marriage, it would never have come to the
assizes. So there's the outcome of an honourable intent.'

Sir Harry laughed, and the Governor leaned forward to refill
his glass.

'But you were thinking,' said Sir Harry, 'that the money went
with the marriage? No marriage, no fortune? I do not blame
the natural course of your thoughts, sir. It is very likely, but it
is not the truth. Banker's daughter though she was, she ran
through half her fortune unasked. I never asked a penny of it,
but she gave it. But she was a Quaker, and thought it a sin to
marry having been abducted, as if the good God could read
between the lines of a marriage register but not see between the
sheets of her bed. And I could not carry away her mind, much
as I tried. I said the abduction was on my soul, not hers. Still
she asserted that we were living in sin, a state from which we
could not marry, even to cure that sin. It was a Quaker logic
that escaped me. The Irish Church, being older, is more con-
versant with man's frailties. So I told her. And as for living in
sin, sir, I denied that premise, given my intent to marry. "Living
in the sin of abduction, then, Sir Harry?" she would say, "living
in abduction," and she was not to be moved.'

'But what brought you here, Sir Harry? Who laid the
information?'

'Zealots, her brothers. Broadsheets all over Cork, five hundred pounds' reward for my discovery, and I walking at liberty past the whole town every day and all the world knowing me and smiling with me. Then some poor man in need, God rest his soul, took the five hundred, and I was taken. Do you know, sir, when the day came in court, Mary Pike spoke as clearly against me as if I were a man she had observed, but did not know. But I swear she did it without malice, for she would have thought that a sin. I knew the jury, all of them, and they said, as I saw, that she was unembarrassed on the occasion. When I was brought in guilty, I asked the Judge to hang me that day, but he would not, and then, while I waited three months in jail expecting my death, I had the Dead March in *Saul* played every day on a barrel-organ as I dined. A man should prepare his soul.'

'But you are prepared for Heaven, not New South Wales, Sir Harry. And what became of Mary Pike?'

'I never heard. Gay at other assemblies, and in other company? She was a dear wanton.'

The Governor was asking what he could do to make his guest's stay in the colony less arduous, and Sir Harry was requesting the loan of books from his library, when a ship was signalled in the bay. King begged Sir Harry not to disturb himself, and by all means to finish the decanter, but to excuse him while he attended to his duties. He went to see the ship.

She was a French corvette, in tatters, only twelve of her crew fit out of 180, and unable to work herself into the cove. King sent sailors to bring her in. The men were received at the hospital with care, and the officers by the Governor and his daughter Susannah with all sweet help and gentle visitation.

# 7

# The Sandalwood Bed, and the Conception of Australia

Baudin was fit in two weeks, and he owed much of his recovery to Susannah. She was a woman of vivid spirit and, besides, having been brought up in decent English society in the last decade of the eighteenth century, the century of the Enlightenment, she spoke better French than he did English, and was almost as competent a botanist. So she was with him a great deal. He insisted, as soon as he could insist on anything, that they should speak English. It was all very well, he said, for a man in a fever to be nursed in his own language, but now he was well he should speak hers. She laughed at his pride, and he laughed at it himself. She undertook his further instruction in English, in his turn he instructed her in astronomy, and they were altogether happy. He was tender with her. She touched his heart, and, when she saw this, there was no defence left to her, or to him. A wound which had afflicted his heart for twelve years – for he was a man who remembered and remembered, and tormented himself with remembrance – was at last solaced. He truly loved Susannah, and within a month they were grateful lovers. He could remember days as intense, but never happier. He could even bear a ten days' absence from her to prospect the near-by coast for specimens of timber-wood, and to trap the required kangaroos. It was from this brief expedition that Susannah watched him return, at the beginning of our story. She waited for him in the dark, and then took him to the house. Her father was away for the night at Parramatta.

Susannah was a beautiful woman. She stood quite still, by the great bed in her room, while Baudin looked from her windows into the cove. There were the lights of his own ship, the *Géographe*, and of his second vessel, the *Naturaliste*, which had reached Sydney some weeks after him, and the lights of an American trader, a beautiful ship, he thought, as trim a merchantman as he had ever seen. She was the *Caroline*, out of New York. Yankee captains were learning that sugar, tobacco, muslins, silks, and above all rum, commanded a price in Sydney. Susannah was dressed in Chinese silks and Irish linens that had come in the cargoes of American ships. The bed too was of American pine, pine that had been the gift of an American skipper who desired the Governor to enlarge his licence to import West Indies sugar. The wood had been worked by a convict as a labour of love, because he had been a cabinet-maker before a thief, and longed to make fine things. It was a fine bed. At its head he had set an inlay of red sandalwood, from Djakarta. He said it was the kind of sandalwood which had lined King Solomon's temple. The bed was always known as the sandalwood bed, and had always been Susannah's.

Baudin closed the shutters and turned to her. The whole length of the room was between them. She was lit by the three candles in the gilt triple candlestick she still carried.

'Put it down,' he said.

She placed it on the rosewood chest, and then stood as before, and smiled directly at him. Baudin always told her that her hair was black, but it was brown, though so dark a brown as to be black in any light but open day. Her dark eyes and all her features were, he had often told her, those of Raphael's portrait of St Cecilia, which he had often seen before the Revolution in the cathedral at Bayeux. Susannah was no saint. Her time as a girl in London and Bath, as a daughter of a lieutenant in the colonies, had not been easy. There she was not the Governor's daughter. There she was poor, and lonely, and it had made her wary. This wariness she hid under an assumed assurance that was almost coquettish. She had not acquired naturally, but had been taught at her finishing school, the assurance of a lady. She had been *taught* how to walk through a doorway, and how to hold her head high. This she did with such style that it might

have been to the manner born, but she knew it had been taught.
And she could at times seem to flirt with her father's aides,
though she did not know she did this, or with the man who held
her horse, or with a ferryman. She did smile directly at any
man, in the most trivial of transactions. She could be proud,
and hurt, and so preserved this wariness. She was always, as it
were, remembering to walk through doorways with her head
held high. Baudin loved her, but that did not stop him seeing
this touch of the coquette in her. He saw it all the more clearly.
He was older than her, and wiser than he had been a few years
before. He loved her most when she was grave. In repose she
was grave, and her gravity moved him to tenderness and sometimes near to tears of gratitude for the great gift she was to him;
a gift he had never expected again. But he was now wise enough
to see her coquettishness for what it was, for an uncertainty, a
tentativeness. He had the sense to know she was whole-hearted.
He was a fortunate man to know this, because it was true. She
stood by the bed with a smile that a jealous man, or a man less
happy – a man made less happy by the smallest doubt – might
have thought a mocking smile.

He walked across to her and loosened her long hair. He
unfastened the many buttons of her silk dress, and she moved
her shoulders, held her arms straight at her sides, and let the
slight garment slip down her arms and over her hips on to
the floor. He loosened the waistband of her linen slip, and
let that fall. He knelt and removed her shoes. He rose and
kissed her eyes, and took her hands in his for a moment,
and only then did she move on to the bed and lie waiting for
him.

When he came to lie beside her, half arched above her, she
held out both arms to welcome him, and spoke his name. As
he entered her, he spoke her name again and again, making of
the words a litany of hope and faith. He was not a man of any
formal religious belief. These were the only moments of his life
in which he felt the gift of Grace, and she was as beyond herself
as he was.

They slept for a while, perhaps for half an hour, until he
awoke and woke her. She laid her hand on his head, a touch
almost of ceremony, and then moved towards him and held
him. They talked drowsily. She lay with her eyes closed, her

hair over her face, and her arms thrown wide on the pillows. He raised himself, lightly kissed the parting of her legs, and then her forehead, and then with the edge of his right hand traced a course from her throat, down across her belly, towards the slightly raised knees.

'*Terre Napoléon?*' she said.

He smiled. When they had first met, at any rate as soon as he was sufficiently recovered to walk with her in the gardens of the Domain, he had told her, most indiscreetly – so indiscreetly that they both knew then that a great intimacy had already grown up between them – that he would on his charts mark New Holland as *Terre Napoléon.*

'Napoleon's land?' she had said. 'So much for your passports then? So much for your botany? So much for your kangaroos? And of what will my father then be governor?'

Of the corner of a continent no one had ever mapped, he could have said, and that continent as large as North America and much less known. In that continent, which might be a waste or as rich as Europe, her father had a commission as Captain General and Governor-in-Chief of a tract of unknown land stretching westwards to the 135th meridian of longitude, more than a thousand miles to the west of Sydney. The frontier was a notional line over which, he would have guessed, no man would ever walk for another twenty years, and that would have been a good guess. But he did not say anything like that, partly because he did not wish to be discourteous to a British governor whose kindness to him had been so great, and partly because he already loved that governor's daughter. But '*Terre Napoléon*' he certainly intended to mark on the charts he would present, on his return, to the First Consul. That had been the conversation in the garden.

In bed, Susannah now said, 'Nicolas, you have circumnavigated the world?' She knew he had, and when he returned to France would have done it a second time. When he returned to France – they had rarely talked of that. Her mind ran from the thought. Her mind fled from it. But the return would have to be soon.

Susannah had the gift of abandon, of a carnality that was right with a true lover, and this is a gift beyond words. She took his hand, guided it gently to her maidenhair and between,

below, and said, 'You have circumnavigated me. You discovered me. So name me.'

'Not for Napoléon,' he said, and then went on. 'The Frenchmen who came to New Holland before me . . .'

But she interrupted him, took his hand and kissed it, and said,
completing his sentence, '. . . and who ran away because of the
frogs?'

'Those who came before me,' said Baudin, 'called it *Terre
Australe*, the southern land.'

'I am your southern lands?' she said. 'That will not do. A
name of any consequence must be in Latin.'

He was half asleep. He touched her shoulder. She understood,
and turned with her back towards him, and he covered them
both with the bedclothes, and curled himself around her, with
his face in the nape of her neck.

Then, into her hair, he murmured, 'I will say, *Australia*. Is
that Latin enough for you? I shall call you Australia.' She
moved her head in assent, took his arm and placed it round her,
and they slept.

Next day at dinner, when her father had returned, Captain
General of *Terre Napoléon*, Susannah glanced round the table at
his guests – at Baudin, at two lieutenants from the French ships
who were also there, and at Sir Harry Browne Hayes, who
could not possibly be invited to the Governor's table, but was.
She caught Baudin's eye, and then, addressing the company at
large, expressed the view that Australia would do very well as
a name for the whole continent. Didn't they think so? Better
than New Holland, she said, seeing there had been no Dutch-
men for years. Much better than New South Wales, because
who could name a continent after Wales? Australia would do
very well: did not Captain Baudin think so? Whereupon the
gentlemen all agreed, and, what was more important, Sir
Harry Browne Hayes said he would willingly abduct a continent
of that name, and so told his convict friends, and they began to
use the name in what was known as the 'flash language'. It
became current. It was settled in a year.

At the dinner table Baudin returned her smile, and spread
both his hands open towards her in a gesture which was entirely
comprehended by the Governor, and very well understood by
Baudin's fellow officers, and by Sir Harry Browne Hayes. All

this was fifteen years before a future governor of the colony, in a despatch to Westminster, was to suggest that Australia, which did appear to be the given name, the name generally used, might be a good name to adopt, did they think, for the whole continent?

# 8

# Them that Sells, and Them that Drinks

On a barren plot a mile from Sydney, twenty feet from his shack which was in turn only twenty feet from the road to Parramatta, George Abrams sat in the heat of the day drinking one glass of rum, and then refilling the glass and with a muttering of words tipping the contents slowly on to the ground beside him where a rough cross of wood was planted in the earth. All this was plainly visible from the road, and the Governor, returning from Parramatta, ordered his carriage to stop. He watched as the man went through the same ritual for a second time, but could not hear the words he uttered.

He got down from the carriage.

'Take care, Y'r Excellency,' said the sergeant of his guard. 'The man is mad drunk.'

'No, the man is despairing drunk.'

He walked across the red dust to the man, who was pouring another libation over what the Governor could now see was a fresh grave.

'I loved you in this life, Retty, though I showed it little enough. I had little to share, and I didn't share that much. But I'll share this now, if you'll take a drink from me.'

He looked up and saw the Governor and sergeant, and pointed to the earth. 'She does take it down, you see.' He watched, and the Governor and the sergeant watched, as the rum soaked into the sodden patch at the foot of the cross.

'She does, you see.'

'What are you?' asked the Governor.

'I'm George Abrams. And that's Retty. But no more of that. It's too late for reason now.'

'I know him, Y'r Excellency,' said the sergeant. 'Abrams, a highwayman that was. Came out First Fleet and pardoned two year ago, but never prospered.' Then to Abrams the sergeant said, 'She was your wife that drowned?'

Abrams refilled the glass with care, and offered it first to the sergeant and then to the Governor, who shook their heads. 'We put out in a boat,' he said. 'But that was afterwards. First there was Ellen Breen, and we revelled the day in the town. I don't know that I liked Ellen, but we were all day in the town. And at four we came back to the water, where there was a boat. Ellen got in the boat, and that was when Retty came round.'

'Came round?' said King.

'Came round. Came round the cove to find me, and saw Ellen in the boat. She did use language then, and all but pushed me in the cove, and Ellen hit Retty with an oar, but she missed. And all the time Retty cursed me, by the child that was in her, that I'd be damned for Ellen, and I dare say I am.'

He drank. 'First Fleet we both was, and then ticket-of-leave, and then the King's pardon, and then my own land.' He gazed at the arid patch around him. 'But it would never yet grow.'

'Were you First Fleet, sir?' This he asked of the sergeant who seemed to him, as wearing a uniform, of greater authority than the other man who was standing watching.

The sergeant said, 'What happened with the boat?'

'Capsized. We all know that. Capsized near Breakfast Point. We made peace, and after Retty cursed me again she came into the boat too. I think Ellen was asleep. But, you see, we lost an oar. Ellen hit Retty with an oar, which was the one that was lost, because it floated away.'

He poured another glass for himself, and another for the grave. 'I sculled out to Breakfast Point, with one oar, and then Retty saw the second, where it had drifted, and she reached for it and fell, and took the boat with her, and us all in the cove drowning. I never saw Retty again, and Ellen drowned asleep. I was the fullest of us all but I did swim. I was the fullest of the three of us, and I never knew rum did float.'

He looked up at the sergeant's red coat. 'Were you in the First Fleet? There was an officer there spoke wise words to me.

Wise words. He was always saying the same, mind, but he did
say – this was when we was in the chain gangs, and in the heat
of day, like now – he did say, "Abrams, you have a precious
gift, denied to many. You have peace of mind. For," he would
say, "the remembrance of your past vices is for the moment
absorbed in the greatness of your present punishment." Wise
words. Damn fool that he was, saying always the same. Damn
fool.'

The man poured more rum straight from the bottle into the
earth, watching until the last drop soaked in.

'Rum,' said the Governor. 'Blasted rum.'

'Oh, rum,' repeated the man on the ground, looking at the
Governor as if aware for the first time who he might be, and
then waving his hand out over the water to where a cutter
loaded with kegs was moving away from a supply shop. 'But
this colony is made up half of them who sells rum, as you sees,'
gesturing towards the cutter and the ship, 'and half,' taking the
bottle and with infinite care tipping the last few drops into the
grave, 'and half of them that drinks it.'

The Governor did not need to look twice to know that the
cutter was Johnston's, recently promoted major and now commander of the New South Wales Corps. He knew Johnston of
old. He knew well that the major and his officers made far and
away the greater part of their income from a monopoly in rum,
a monopoly they enforced with the rifle butts of their troops,
who simply stove in any casks found in the colony to have been
acquired from other sources. King was disposed not to see many
things that he did see. He relied on the good sense of Johnston
not to allow his greed to carry things too far. Johnston, in his
turn, ought to have known, and knew, that a letter from the
Governor to London could have him recalled – though that
would take perhaps a year. The Governor, looking out into the
cove at the cutter and the supply ship, and then at a brig lying
off the mouth of the cove, waiting as he knew to enter the next
day with another cargo of rum, resolved to say a few quiet
words. Johnston was asked that night to dinner.

'Major Johnston,' said the Governor, having taken him aside
beforehand, 'what was the asking price, per gallon, of the master
of the *Solent*?' That was the ship already in the cove, discharging
rum. The Governor had never before asked such a question.

The major assured him that a dozen kegs would, naturally, be delivered to Government House the next day if the Governor wished. He never had before, but the major considered himself a reasonable man and the Governor's hint, as he took it to be, a reasonable one.

'No, Johnston, I was just wondering about the asking price.'

'Twenty shillings,' said the major.

The Governor had made careful enquiries and found the figure to be eight shillings. He said nothing of that.

'Ah, and what will it fetch, would you say? A fair figure?'

'Thirty,' said the major, 'but some of it is poor stuff and will not make that.'

The Governor had heard eighty shillings was already being extorted from the publicans of Sydney, and guessed that the price would rise before it fell. He also had information that the quality was excellent.

'A plentiful supply?' he enquired.

The major attempted a light answer. 'The colony does have a thirst.'

'I have seen the results of that thirst. But shall we say we have enough for the moment? It would be better if the ship that works in tomorrow were to discharge no rum here, and I shall be obliged if you will see that she does not.'

Johnston had already begun to negotiate with the master of the second ship. 'I shall require that order in writing, sir,' he said.

'No,' said the Governor, 'I do not think that you will, on reflection, find that necessary at all. Now, let us go in.'

At dinner the conversation was not about rum but wine. Baudin's third lieutenant, Pelegrin, who was only a boy of twenty, was saying he had met two wine-growers from Bordeaux. The Governor knew them: they had come out on a Dutch merchantman the year before and had by all been thought slightly mad in their enthusiasm at the colony's future as a producer of wine. Now they had met the French lieutenant and communicated their enthusiasm to him.

'They told me,' said the officer, 'that no other part of the world they knew, not one of the great wine regions of France, could grow a vine with such force as New South Wales.'

'Nowhere else so fast?' said the Governor.

'So they said.'

'So they told me too. But the trouble is, the first north-westerly off that desert that none of us has yet explored, and the whole lot shrivels up. So, as I remember it, they moved away somewhere up country.' The Governor recalled giving them his formal permission to go where they liked, only not to get made into stew by the aborigines, and off they went carrying their cherished cuttings with them, which they had brought out in the Dutch ship.

'Well,' said the lieutenant, 'they found the slopes of a valley where everything has flourished. North of the city. Fifteen miles north. I tasted their new wine and thought it more than fair. Not quite this' – the Governor's guests were drinking a Burgundy from the same Dutchman that had brought the French wine-growers – 'by no means this, but fair wine, much fairer than I have drunk in some French inns, and some French ships.'

Major Johnston, whose thoughts were on a cargo of West Indies rum waiting in the cove, a cargo he could not now touch, drank a great deal of the Governor's good Burgundy and kept a stubborn silence.

The Governor wished the wine-growers success. England was, he supposed, the only maritime power in the world in whose empire no wine of any consequence was made. France, Spain, Portugal, Holland, all had their vineyards either at home or somewhere in their overseas possessions, and England, he thought – though his tone of voice hardly showed any great concern for it – must spend a fair part of her wealth on Madeiras and Burgundies and Sherries.

The French and English officers were now very easy with one another, easy enough for Pelegrin to remark that if England had her own vineyards she wouldn't have needed to try, twice each, to take the Canary Islands and the Cape; and for the Governor to reply that, as for the Canaries, they were probably worth the taking, but, as far as the wine went, he would not risk a sloop for the Cape.

Johnston, summoning the footman to refill his glass, growled at this, and Susannah, whose misfortune it was to have the man next to her, turned to address Baudin across the table. Had he met these French wine-growers?

'No. Just a forger.'

'Plenty of those,' said the Governor. 'Good climate for those.'

'From Paris,' said Baudin.

'French? Didn't know we had any French convicts. Must try and do something for the fellow. Could he teach a smattering of French to the daughters of the garrison? What's his name?'

'Morand,' said Baudin. 'And he's persuasive enough. He did put it rather well, saying all he'd ever done was wish to associate himself with the Bank of England. . . .'

'Laudable enough wish,' said the Governor.

'But without, as he put it, having first gone through the formality of opening an account there.'

The evening was well enough advanced for them to laugh at this, and to be highly entertained by what followed.

'Notes of hand for five pounds,' said Baudin. 'Notes on the Bank of England, only he got slightly confused in his etching of the plates, and Britannia came out sitting the wrong way round.'

A voice from next to Susannah interrupted the laughter.

'Subvert the whole economy,' said Johnston.

'What?' asked the Governor.

'Undermine the whole economy. Damned rogue intended to print a million of the things, useless paper, honoured for gold, and the whole economy of England crashing round our ears.'

Susannah laughed helplessly, Baudin had to look away for fear he might do much the same. Pelegrin buried his face in his napkin, and the Governor gave a great roar of laughter. This was all a pity. For once, Major Johnston was on the fringes of the truth. Morand had intended to print a million notes, with the precise, mad purpose Johnston had expressed.

'I'll give him a ticket of leave tomorrow,' said the Governor. 'He can teach the ladies how to sketch too.' But Johnston was on his feet in half-drunken anger. First his rum lost to him, and now this mockery. It was too much humiliation, and he turned furiously to Baudin, who was the only man at the table who had managed to keep his face, and then to the Governor. 'Your Excellency will know,' he said, trembling, 'that the brig standing out in the cove, the brig whose rum is not to be introduced into the colony, has already contracted eight hundred gallons to Captain Baudin, who will be enabled to sell it at a vast profit?' And with that he threw his napkin in Baudin's face.

Out of the silence which followed, the Governor said, 'Major Johnston, it is with my knowledge and permission that Captain Baudin has revictualled his ships for their return passage, and with that knowledge and permission that he has contracted for rum from that brig. Now, sir?'

Johnston realized the enormity of what he had said and done, bowed to the Governor, and apologized to Baudin, saying, with the weird echo of some form of words he had got from a manual of etiquette, 'I am in your hands.' Phrases such as 'the demanding of satisfaction', and the 'putting himself at Baudin's disposal', slurred across his mind.

Baudin, anxious that Johnston should be humiliated no further, replied, 'I beg you to think no more of it.'

Johnston left. Baudin, by his gentle conduct, had made an enemy, because such generosity is rarely forgiven. By intending not to humiliate Johnston he had placed him greatly in his debt and had therefore greatly humiliated him. The Governor by his laughter had made a scourge for himself and his successor; and Susannah, by hers, had engendered an enmity that would last longer than she could have dreamed.

# 9

# And Remember Silkylinings

Government House was built in the Italian style, with colon-
nades, but to it there was attached, in the English style by an
English builder, an orangery. The builder was a man who,
some years before, while in the employment of the Crown estates
in London, had stolen many tons of ready-cut Portland stone
from the Crown's yards. He did this openly, getting his wagoners
to call at the government depot with their drays and teams of
horses, and to present an order signed by himself. His signature
was known and trusted. For many years he had been patching
up Kensington Palace and other royal residences, and collecting
many tons of cut stone to carry out the work. But he began to
use more and more of the stone to build handsome houses on
his own account, which he sold at a handsome profit, until one
day he was found out, and transported. In New South Wales
he was put to the making of Government House, and, since he
had often worked at Kensington Palace and admired the
orangery there, he built another at Sydney. It was elegant but it
was not needed. In Sydney, orange trees need no shelter to
grow. The orangery was not used, it fell into disuse, and was
over-grown outside by vines. No one went there. But there it
remained, an arched summer house, aside from the residence,
and the vines gave shade. What was intended as a shelter for
orange trees, to warm and encourage them, became a summer
house for Nicolas and Susannah, to shade them. At the one end
of the orangery the builder had placed a marble table, six feet
long. He wished, after all, to make something not of Portland
stone. The curiously olive marble, almost like onyx, came from

the hold of a Spanish ship, and the builder gave it to his masons
to fashion after a design he sketched in pencil on the white wall
of the orangery. The masons did well. The table top was smooth.
Its four legs were shaped like those of a lion, with lions' paws.

It was the orangery and this table which Nicolas and
Susannah discovered. On an afternoon a few days after the
naming of Australia, she sat on the table, and leaned back,
supporting herself with her hands on the table behind her. Her
head was thrown back so that her hair spread out, also behind
her. Nicolas stood by an archway. Outside it was full afternoon.
Inside it was cool. The table was cool through Susannah's dress.

'I must tell your father,' said Nicolas.

'My love, he knows,' she said, to the ceiling.

'He knows, but I must tell him.'

She stayed as she was, then first turned her head to look
across at him, and then, without moving, closed her eyes. There
was already a language between them that takes years to grow
between others, or never grows. With most it never grows. It
could be direct, and then it was mostly she who was direct,
either speaking to him in words that were most open, or else
holding out her arms to him, again openly. Or it could be
indirect, as in a feigned withdrawal, a silence, or a closing of
the eyes. It was the most subtle of semiotics, a language of
silences and signs shared by them. She closed her eyes, and he
crossed to her, and waited, and then let his hand fall on the line
of her hair as it fell from her brow, and from the back of her
head, and behind her shoulders. She never showed she felt this,
unless with the faintest of smiles.

This is a moment at which the manner of her dress matters
least, but whatever she wore became part of Susannah, so this
is how she was dressed. She could have been Greek. She was
certainly what passed for Greek in the imagination of the time.
It was a time when a woman probably wore as little as women
ever have worn. The farthingales and frills and wigs of ten years
before were all gone, and so was almost everything gone. Ten
years before it would have been unthinkable not to be nipped
in at the waist by tight lacing: in 1802 it was as unthinkable to
be constricted in this way. Ten years before everything would
have been elaborate: now everything was simplicity. By those
in England who did not fight, the French Revolution and the

wars that followed were felt mostly in the changing out of
women's clothes. The Revolution took away the old, and put
the new in its place. The new felt the need to be pure, and
purity was classical Greek. Susannah's hair, at all times of the
day and on all occasions, was her own. She had no wigs. On
her face she wore no colouring. The Directory was mostly
known not as a French political institution but as the name of
all that was new in fashion. Her dress was in the style of the
Directory. It was muslin, so high-waisted that the fabric was
shaped over her breasts and then fell sheer. She wore no petticoats, only a linen slip. She wore no stockings, and her silk shoes
were without heels. She wore no decoration, not even a bow of
flowers between the breasts. That year, a woman's dress of silk or
muslin might be a little embroidered, as Susannah's was. It was
a fashion often too cold for London, but it might have been
designed for the climate of Sydney. It was a line cruel to a
woman of no figure, but fortunate for Susannah. She was a
woman in white muslin and a little linen, leaning back on a table
of olive marble, and throwing back her head so that her black
hair fell straight.

When she smiled, Baudin caressed her lips with his fingers,
parting them a little, so that he touched, no more than touched,
her teeth and the tip of her tongue. He leaned to brush his
cheek against her hair, and parted her lips with his lips, and
then he raised his head a little and began to talk to her. Sometimes they were silent. At other times he talked to her, and now
he talked.

'I shall come into you,' he said.

She said nothing, not a word, but opened her eyes to look
into his for a moment, and then let her head fall back again.

He caressed her hair, and she smiled.

'But if I stay here, your hair will keep me,' Nicolas murmured
to her. 'Or' – not kissing her but letting his lips rest on hers for
an instant – 'this will keep me.'

She made again the almost imperceptible movement of her
head which meant yes, she agreed that he must not be kept
there.

'Or here,' he said, touching the line of her throat: and again
she agreed, showing this by the smallest arching of the neck.

'Or I should be kept here.' With his right hand he caressed

not her breasts, but her side, and at that she moved, in agreement, yes, but by now involuntarily.

'And so,' he said, and let his hand fall in one caress from her side, to her waist and then her hips, then down to her knees and to her ankles, and then he was kneeling on the floor of the orangery before her. It was a soft floor to kneel on, because it was carpeted with the petals and leaves of the flowers and plants a gardener had grown there many years before, which were now dried and powdered and half an inch thick on the floor. Baudin slipped off her shoes, which were so insubstantial they could scarcely be called shoes, rather slippers, and kissed her toes and the insteps of her feet, and then held both her ankles in his hands. Raising himself slowly, he caressed the line of her calves with his lips, and then his head was between her knees and she held it there with the lightest sideways pressing of her parted legs. The muslin dress of the Directory was light but long, and full in the skirt, so that Nicolas, when he rose from Susannah's ankles, buried his head under the dress, and the muslin was a canopy over his head. His hands were at her waist, and he held her there as his lips travelled up from her knees, and he stroked the inside of her legs with the hair of his head.

She said one word, his name, and he took his hands from her waist, embraced her hips, and kissed her gently between the legs, kissing her softly and then exploring with his lips and entering with his tongue. His senses were surrounded by the airiness of muslin, the scented musk of Susannah, and the silkiness of her.

'Nicolas, Nicolas, Nicolas,' she said.

He rose, and she slid herself towards him on the marble table, and, no longer supporting herself on her arms, lay back on the table with her hands behind her head, and then, standing, he entered her. She no longer closed her eyes, but looked into his, and at his hands where they held her, and at his body as it moved and moved into hers, and then held out a hand to take his.

He said, 'Lie still a moment then,' and, taking her hand, entwined his fingers in hers. For a moment they were motionless. In the summer house, what was happening? To say merely the conjunction of two bodies would have been the most bitter of misapprehensions. It was their minds and spirits that were one. He was a Frenchman and an officer of the Republic, but he was also, and could never wish to be free from it, a Roman Catholic. He was a man of the Age of Reason and yet, in spite of all that reason, his whole instinct told him that he had a soul. With his dear love Susannah, how could he not at least hope that he might have a soul, and that she might have? No man enters a woman he truly loves without that hope. And what was she? She, but that was the last consideration in the world, was the Governor's daughter, and that was nothing to her. At that moment it was not on the fringes of her consciousness. She was a girl, she was a woman, and as changed since she met Baudin as a human being can be changed, realizing worlds she had not guessed at, but she was also an Englishwoman and a Protestant. She would have been hard put to say what a Protestant was. But whereas Baudin would go to his priest, and expect the priest to intercede between himself and his God, Susannah took it for granted that she could, if she wished, pray to her God alone, without intercession of saints or priests. Priests of the Established Church in eighteenth-century England were men of pleasant education who could be asked to dinner. She would never have thought of a priest of the English church as a man in whom she could confide her greatest longings, sins, and hopes. She would not have thrust so great a burden on a man whom one could ask to dinner. If she prayed, it would have been directly to her God. She never did pray, though later she would, but she too believed in an immortal soul. Of Baudin's soul, of the soul of the man she adored and loved, she had no doubt. She would not have used the word *soul*, but that was the idea that was in her mind and body, and her mind and body were at that moment one. So they held hands, and lay still.

He began to move inside her again, she put up her arms at first to hold his waist, and then his shoulders, and then his head, bringing him closer to her, and then she averted her head, a gesture he knew so well, and moments (or how long?) afterwards, she tossed her head, exclaiming, 'Oh my dear love,' and came with that exaltation on her lips and in his ears: and at this he too was moved beyond himself and splashed helplessly into her.

Perhaps five minutes later, Susannah and Nicolas – lovers disentwined – stood in the arched doorway of the summer house,

and she turned in his arms to rise on her toes and kiss him o
the brow. They had been half an hour in the orangery. What
ever an observer might have thought, though there was n
observer, it was not done wantonly or recklessly, or, if ther
were colours of recklessness or wantonness, they were nothin
to set against the knowledge of both that all was done, at hear
discreetly, soberly, fittingly. Nicolas said, for the first time, 'W
shall marry.' And she said, '*Oh yes*,' and they walked in sunligh
hand in hand over the lawns of the Domain towards her father
not disguising where they came from, and he, for his part
showed no surprise, because he had none. When they reache
him he embraced his daughter and then offered his hand t
Baudin. Yet neither had spoken one word to him.

Baudin looked at King, drawing himself up as if to for
words to speak, and then both men smiled.

'Sir,' said Baudin, and then stopped, because he was in shir
and breeches, and Susannah, as he saw at a glance, a glanc
he had not thought to make before, was, as plainly as could be
a woman who has just made love, which showed not only in he
dishevelled hair but in her eyes. Then he began again. He
father had noticed all that before Baudin, in his great happiness
had given any thought to appearance.

'Sir,' he said. 'I do fear this may be unexpected. . . .'

'Nicolas,' said King, 'My dear Nicolas. I do assure you i
is not.'

Both Baudin and King could have laughed for joy, but they
postponed that until necessary words could be spoken.

Baudin said, 'I am asking for your daughter.'

The Governor glanced at Susannah, knowing he did not nee
to. He said, 'There is nothing that could give me more happiness. Nothing.' The two men laughed, and the Governor -
officer, gentleman, and Englishman that he was – put a hand
on Baudin's shoulder, and then both hands on both shoulders
and nearly embraced him. He did again embrace his daughter

'Nicolas,' he said, 'there are a few things. Before dinner
would you care to take a glass with me in my room?'

There were a few things, and more than they could have
expected. It was now known that France and England were a
peace. Both Baudin and King, as naval officers, knew that this
might be an uneasy peace, but even if they supposed that wa

might break out again, what was a war between nations that could not be settled between gentlemen? If these two gentlemen ever met at sea they might be obliged to slaughter each other, but that really was to take matters to absurdity. This they agreed. Such an event was unlikely. Apart from that, even in war the civilities were observed. During the late hostilities, even trade of a sort had continued between Britain and France, though some of that trade had the tinge of smuggling about it. French brandy was still procurable in England. And safe conducts would of course be granted. Susannah would have no difficulty in obtaining a passage to France, and once there she would marry Baudin. She could not sail with the *Géographe*. That would be too precipitate, and, besides, it would be stretching the proprieties for the daughter of an English governor to sail aboard a French man o'war. But the Governor expected to be recalled the next year, and Susannah would return with him to Europe. Probably all would still be peace. If there was war, that would scarcely last long, and even if it did Susannah could of course join Baudin in Paris. If there was war he might be called to sea again, but a woman who married a sailor knew that. And of course there was this, that she was an Anglican and he a Roman Catholic, but she knew that too. Their children would be Catholic, but the Governor was tolerant in religion and expected his daughter would be too. And if there was a peace, either Baudin would flourish in the French marine or if he chose he might come to live with King in London or in the country. There *were* things to be talked of, but they would all resolve themselves – so these two gentlemen told themselves over their Madeira. They could not know that the war had already broken out again. They could not foresee that it would last another thirteen years. They could not foresee that French naval power would be broken at Trafalgar in only three years' time. They could not foresee, that day at the end of the earth, the early death of the Governor so soon after his return to England. They could not foresee so many things, but all was agreed as if they could.

Meanwhile, in the time left to them in Sydney, Susannah and Nicolas haunted the house and the Domain, illuminating it with their love and with the instinct of their attraction to each other. This was so strong an attraction, having so much a life of its own, that they did not at all need to be close before it was felt by them, and evident to all around. It was there if they walked in the garden twenty yards apart, she stepping on to the lawns from the east wing and he from the west, and, knowing each other to be there but not approaching more closely, walking parallel paths. He was as aware of her, and she of him, as if they held each other. It happened the first time by chance that they left the house this way, at the same time but apart: and then it happened not by chance.

At breakfast she said, 'Shall we be two paths?'

So they strolled their parallel walks, over the lawns, by the cedars, downwards to the cove, until she turned to face him, and then ran towards him with her gown flying behind her, and did not so much fall into his arms as give herself softly into them, even at a run, and then say, with her head on his breast, when she was breathing again quietly, 'You are a magnet.'

'*We* are magnets,' he said. 'We are fortunate. We have been happy. But magnets have two poles, north and south. And if you take two magnets, as you are one and I am another, the northern pole of one will seize and clasp the southern pole of the other. That is us. But put north to north and the two poles do not attract. They chase each other away. They fight.' She did not understand, so, on the chart table in his cabin on the *Géographe*, in the cove, where he had often before shown her charts of the seas and plans of the stars, he demonstrated for her, taking two tiny bar magnets, showing first how one moved to bring the other to it and hold it firm, so that it took the strength of her fingers to pull them apart. But then he reversed the bars, and one fled from the other until, by his manoeuvring, the first bar turned the other, and held it again.

'So they can fight,' she exclaimed.

It was in his cabin that Baudin and Susannah fought, when he told her he must sail on a certain day, in two weeks. Two weeks to that day. She asked for longer, confidently expecting that he would delay, but he could not. She did not comprehend.

'You won't?'

He shook his head. 'I cannot.'

'You refuse?' She took her hands from his.

'I do not refuse. I must. There is no choice. If I stay here another week after that day, I may lose three months on the

passage home.' He explained the prevailing winds, the mon-
soons, the precarious seasonal tempests of the southern seas, and
the peril of the passage to the Cape of Good Hope which he
must make, but she swept the charts from the table. She was a
girl again, with all her unsureness, a girl with her father away
God knew where, her mother dead, a little girl bewildered by
their absences which seemed to her the withdrawal of love. In
her mind, at the moment, she was losing Nicolas as she had so
often lost her father as he said goodbye at the outset of so many
voyages.

'Go,' she said. 'Go away. I shall never see you again. You
will forget. I shall be forgotten.'

He tried to be gentle. He was gentle. 'That *is* nonsense,' he
said, taking her by the shoulders, doing all in his power to
reassure a frightened girl he loved. Alas, her father, too many
times saying goodbye, had often touched her shoulders in just
such a way, and she whirled on Baudin and struck him, twice,
full in the face. This was a side of Susannah he had never seen.
He was astonished, and put up his arms to defend himself, and
when she struck at him again he caught her wrists. She pulled
him down, taking him off balance. He fell, and, as he did,
Susannah, curling her body into a half circle to break her own
fall, struck him in the chest with her knees. She meant it. He
caught his breath with the shock, released her, and stumbled to
his feet in amazement.

'Susannah?'

She lay on the floor as she had fallen. He stooped, but rose
when he saw her eyes full of bitter anger. He turned and
walked from the cabin on to the quarterdeck. It had not been
a silent scuffle. There is little privacy even for the captain on
board a corvette. As he stepped from his cabin the midshipman
of the watch, divided between duty and sense, looked enquir-
ingly at him from the flush deck, twenty feet away. Baudin
shook his head and the boy walked for'ard. Baudin closed the
door to his quarters and leaned over the rail. For the first time
he noticed the pain in his right side. When he re-entered the
cabin ten minutes later Susannah still lay where she had lain
before, no longer in fury but asleep. He sat and watched her as
she slept for half an hour. Then she stirred, realized where she
was, saw her lover sitting with his face away from her, as if

looking through one of the cabin lights, but seeing nothing. She came and knelt before him, laying her head in his lap, saying not a word. He caressed her hair, took the shape of her head in his hands, and his heart went out to her at that moment as never before. She never uttered the hint of an apology. She only said, 'I did not know it would be that soon.'

Two days later the ship's surgeon, told by Baudin some cock and bull story about a fall against a capstan on the quay, examined his captain and announced that he had come by three cracked ribs. 'Nothing much, sir, for a capstan. I should say you will feel it for a week or so, and then it will go. You may catch your breath every now and again. Nothing to that, though. Shouldn't lie on my right side for a bit if I were you.'

Baudin dined every evening now at the Governor's table. King laughed at the story of the capstan, not disbelieving it but amused that a British capstan, if not the government of New South Wales, knew a Frenchman when it saw one coming, and couldn't read passports signed by some Secretary of State in London enjoining all who owed allegiance to the British Crown to accord safe conduct to French botanists even though they might come in corvettes. Baudin would have said nothing whatever, except that as he reached for the salt he had been unable to hide a sharp twinge. Susannah had not realized either. There had been no bruise. Afterwards she said to him, 'I did not know.' The whole strange violence of that moment in the cabin brought them closer than ever, and she accepted that he did have to leave.


Two days before Baudin sailed, the Governor gave a masked ball in his honour.

'No one,' said the Governor, as they discussed the arrangements, 'is going to assassinate me, I take it?' It was only ten years before that the Swedish King Gustav III had been stabbed at a masked ball at the Stockholm opera. Baudin knew Stockholm, and so did the Governor. Both had put into that brilliant port, that harbour of the wooded islands, in high midsummer, sailing through Baltic seas where at that time of year the sun hardly sets, where light becomes twilight for the space of only three or four hours, and sunset and dawn are hardly separated. Both Baudin and the Governor, in their previous service, had paid courtesy visits to the Swedish king. He had entertained both. He had taken both to the opera, and, as both remembered, to Drottningholm, his summer palace a few miles from Stockholm, and there shown them his own opera house, not the city opera where he was to be assassinated but the elegant, narrow theatre built for the court.

'Turned into a granary or something, after his death?' asked the Governor. 'Wasn't it?'

Baudin only knew that the present King of Sweden had no taste for music.

'Drottningholm,' said the Governor, 'Queen's Island. Strange we should both have been there. So far off.' It was far: not from Europe, but from Sydney it could hardly have been farther. But it was not strange. Sweden was still the remains of a great power, and it was to be expected that both French and English men o'war would pay courtesy visits. What was strange was what the Governor said next, when the ladies had left the table and the port had been round twice.

'Those,' he said, 'were summer nights. The summer nights of my youth.'

Baudin refilled his glass.

'I cannot think that I have ever told Susannah,' said the Governor, 'or why I haven't. Her mother may have. I don't know, but I doubt it because she was little when her mother died. It was my first command, and there I was with a new ship, frigate, a thirty-four, and a new wife. And so I took her to Stockholm. It was there Susannah was conceived. We were always sure of that.'

Baudin smiled.

'Summer nights,' said the Governor.

Baudin proposed a toast to summer nights and to Susannah, and the masked ball was settled. It would be a farewell to him, and a commemoration of that summer night, whenever it was, long ago.

'No one,' said the Governor, 'will assassinate me. They're all scared to death of my deputies who would succeed me. So am I.'

Susannah's maid dressed her for the evening. The masked ball had been obliged to admit a small compromise. The gentlemen would be allowed to wear uniform, with the token disguise of a mask. There were still hardly enough men's clothes in the colony to permit more than that. The women were luckier, or more ingenious. Wigs could hardly be counterfeited, and were not, but the hair could be powdered, and picture hats, in the style much painted by Gainsborough, could be devised. Above all, the simple, clinging dresses of the Directory were abandoned for that night, and the old full skirts of what was after all only the fashion before that, were adapted. Most of the women who had come in the first years of the colony still possessed such gowns. The servants still wore them. Few convict women had anything else. So full skirts were to be had, and there are few extravagancies to which a full skirt will not lend its shape.

Susannah stepped naked into a creation of pleated frills, into a skirt layered and bunched and puffed and festooned with ribbon, and, which was her own touch, lined at the hem with paper so that as her maid drew the skirt round her waist, and as Susannah moved to view herself in the long pier-glass of her dressing room, the skirt rustled against itself and against her. The paper was from the five quires of tissue paper carried by the *Géographe*, to make tracings of charts, the ribbon from the twenty-five ells of silver fringe and gold fringe carried, along with snuff-boxes, drums, and tambourines, to trade with the natives. Then Susannah put on high-heeled shoes. For years she had not worn either a skirt that fastened at her real waist, or shoes that raised her heels. She swirled round and, what with the unaccustomed weight and momentum of the skirt and the unaccustomed height of the heels, all but fell over. She recovered herself and laughed, and regarded her long reflection in the looking-glass – the skirt, and above the skirt her undressed body, bare breasts, bare arms, and neck as yet unadorned. She extended her arms so far as she could by her sides, raised them above her head, and said aloud, 'This is how I am for Nicolas. This is how I look to Nicolas. This is how I shall be for Nicolas. This is how I shall be for Nicolas tonight.' She spun round again, and caught glimpses of her shoulders, admiring herself, knowing Nicolas would admire her, and that Nicolas loved her.

Her maid, being the daughter of a convict and therefore more proper, reproached her animal pride and exhilaration.

'Shame, ma'am.'

Susannah stopped spinning so suddenly that her skirt continued to move and rustle round her of its own volition, and looked at the girl. She knew Mary had men of her own. 'Mary,' she said, 'why not? Now, dress me. No, the hat first. No, first the powder.' The girl was unwilling, and there she showed sense.

'To muck up such hair as yours, black and just brushed shining, and cake it with this tack, is nothing but wicked.' It was true. The tack the girl spoke of was only bad flour, adulterated as usual in the colony with a little chalk.

'Leave it off,' said Susannah. 'The hat then.'

The hat was pinned in place.

'Now my necklace.'

A silver necklace was placed to encircle her throat, and fastened at the nape of the neck, and from it a pendant hung so that its single diamond fell between her breasts.

'Now the bracelets.'

Three bracelets were slipped over her extended fingers. The bracelet nearest the wrist was the gift of Baudin.

'And now cover me.'

It was warm. The maid placed a thin basque, with sleeves, over Susannah's arms and shoulders, and tied it at the back. That was all. Susannah viewed herself again, tossed her hair from her face, heard the music begin from below, and descended to welcome her father's guests. All evening, wherever she moved, the paper rustled in her skirts and the candles shone in reflection in her hair.

At the ball, all the softness was provided by the women, most of whom showed their shoulders. All the colour was provided by the men, who showed their uniforms. The female shoulders of New South Wales in 1802 were white. It was 16 November, a month to midsummer, and the Sydney sun was nearly tropical in intensity, but no lady would display herself to the sun. No lady would, if she could prevent it, allow the sun to see her face. At the ball nearly all the women adopted as fancy dress the extraordinary hoops, farthingales, and bunched petticoats of forty years before. One or two braver women had gone back another hundred years to Nell Gwynne and become for the night orange-sellers (a trade they would have despised, whatever its prospects) and kings' mistresses (an honourable estate to which many would have aspired, had there been monarchs in Sydney). So their skirts were all of unfamiliar fullness, and their shoulders were all alike bare because that was fancy dress, and white because they were ladies. The gentlemen were more glorious. The British naval officers, the aristocracy of the colony, wore full dress, the blue cutaway coat, single breasted, with white breeches, white stockings, and black shoes with gilt buckles. The blues were many in shade. Only those officers recently arrived from England wore unfaded coats. The Governor's was probably the most faded of all, but he was rather proud of that. All coats had high, turned-back cuffs, but, just as there were few blues that were dark blues, there were few whites that were doeskin white. The breeches were as likely to be of canvas as doeskin. The Governor did have doeskin, but it was, to say the best of it, a creamy white, or, to tell the truth, off-white with age. What predominated was the blue and the gold, the blue of the naval uniforms, and the gilt in the trimmings of the coats, on the braided pockets, at the sleeves, and in the epaulettes. The officers of the New South Wales Corps wore red. Susannah, receiving them at her father's side, greeted them as cordially as she did any naval officer. She was one of the few who did not consider all the Corps officers to be rogues. The French officers began to arrive. They were hardly as welcome to the generality of the guests as to the Governor. Most people, after showing great kindness at first, thought the Frenchmen had been too long in the colony, and had been too well entertained by the Governor. Besides, there was felt to be something between Susannah and the French captain. This was generally known, although what was known was little. The Governor's servants and his aides had been loyally discreet. The generality also did not approve the elaborate dress of the Frenchmen. It was noticed with some acerbity that the uniform dress of an officer of a Republican and presumably austere France was, if any-thing, more gilded than that of a British officer, and that was true. The silk breeches, the wigs, the buckles not merely of gilt but of gold, and the lace cravats of Louis XVI had all gone, but there was still a higher collar than any worn by His Britannic

Majesty's officers, and a red waistcoat under the blue coat, and, with full dress, even plumes in the tricorne hat. Baudin, when he arrived, by protocol the last of his officers, wore also round his waist a tricolor sash. Susannah had never seen him like this. In the eyes of the entire room she acknowledged his bow, and he kissed her hand.

They dined. Speeches of friendship were made, and toasts to amity proposed and responded to. Then they danced. A minuet is the most formal of dances, a convocation of patterns. As a dance, it is a French garden, with an intricacy of paths, but an intricacy of order. There was distance. Nor did a couple dance together and alone. The minuet is a dance of a gathered society of men and women. In the dance all meet. It is a dance of steps and glides to the left and right, forward and backwards in quarter turns, approaching and retreating, seeking and evading, a dance of courtship. From one end of the ball room to another, Susannah caught her lover's glance, and the first time they came together briefly and he made his bow to her, she said, 'We are two paths again.' And at the second round, curtsying to him, she contrived that though she could not enfold him, her rustling skirts should, and her eyes shone. The tips of his fingers touched hers, but that was in the dance.

'Two paths,' he replied, as she moved away.

It was during that minuet that the messenger came. Pelegrin, the lieutenant of the watch from the *Géographe*. He and his colleagues in the wardroom had all wished to accept the Governor's invitation to the ball, and Baudin had told them to draw lots to see which should stay behind, as one officer must. Now he was in the hallway, with an escort of two French marines, and at the end of the dance Baudin was taken aside and told this.

In an ante-room, Baudin said to his officer. 'Well?'

'Sir, at eleven o'clock a woman came on board. She said her name was Mary Bickaith. She is English.'

'A convict?'

'She says not, sir. She wishes to return to Europe with us.'

'So you brought her here?' Baudin was wishing the boy had simply landed her and left it at that.

'She is still on board.'

Baudin looked up. 'Why?'

'Sir, she says she is Susannah's . . . she says she is the maid of mademoiselle the daughter of the Governor, and that she is no convict, and that both you and the Governor would not refuse to hear her.'

At that moment Susannah came looking for Baudin. She half withdrew when she saw he was with one of his officers, but he called to her to come in.

'Susannah, is Mary Bickaith the Mary who is your maid?'

A nod.

'She's on my ship saying she is no convict, that she wants to sail with us, and that your father wouldn't refuse to listen to her, or words to that effect. Now, I can get her off quickly, and that will be that. Or I can, I suppose, talk to your father. If she's your maid, what do you want me to do?'

Susannah said, 'It's true she isn't a convict.'

'How then?'

'She came here with her mother, who was. Her mother stole some cloth. That was four years ago, or so Mary says. Mary came here with her mother. It was either that or go into a convent, and Mary is no nun.'

'And her mother?'

'Dead last year.'

'And you didn't know of this? That she would come to me?'

'I did not.' Susannah's temper nearly took fire, until she saw that Baudin had only meant to ask whether she would approve of the girl's going, and not whether she had connived at it. She made that motion of looking down and quickly up again which, he well knew, signified, 'I didn't mean that,' words she was never able to bring herself to say plainly. She said, 'Mary does want to go home, and I know how badly she wants it. She is always talking about Suffolk. If you want to go and ask my father, I wish her well.'

'All right.' Baudin turned to his lieutenant, who had been conspicuously hearing nothing, and said, 'Take off that sword you are carrying, go and find yourself a glass of claret, and then wait for me in the hallway.' The boy went off. Susannah exchanged the briefest of glances with Baudin. 'My father?' she said.

'Please. Better if you go. I don't want to send that boy to your father's aide and have half Sydney wondering what's happening. Will you ask if I could come and have a few words?'

The words were few and blunt, but easy.

'This place is a damn great jail, Nicolas, for anyone who happens to have got here and happens to be British. The girl's no convict, never was, Susannah won't mind, though she likes her. You say you'll take her, though one girl among a ship's company . . .? Still, that's your business.'

'Republicans and gentlemen to a man,' said Baudin.

'Well. As Governor I can throw her out. I could certainly throw her out for trying to escape, even though she's supposed to be free. I can't lawfully give her safe conduct to England. God knows what things are coming to. I'm damned if I'll deport her, but what I can't do is simply give her a letter telling whomsoever it concerns that I've just given her permission to go. What I can do is know nothing about it. So I suggest that you have told me nothing. What my daughter tells me oughtn't to be evidence, or if it is I never heard what she said either. Anyway, if it were to happen that two days out you found a stowaway . . .?'

So Mary Bickaith remained on board. Baudin told his lieutenant to return to the ship and do nothing either way, and say nothing. Then he and Susannah first returned to the minuet and then slipped outside into the Domain.

A Sydney summer midnight can be warm as the Caribbean, and the darkness as deep. When they were not quite away from the house lights an unseen sentry presented arms with a crash and Baudin cursed the man under his breath as he acknowledged the salute. Then he and Susannah sought the absolute darkness of the farther Domain, and the smooth bark of a blue eucalypt for her to rest against. Lovers in Sydney did not lie at night on lawns for fear of snakes. For that matter there were poisonous spiders in trees, but they were less thought of. He led her by the hand until they found the tree familiar to them. It was a massive tree, there for a hundred years. Of all the trees in the world the trunk of the blue eucalypt is smoothest to the touch. The bark falls naturally away, leaving a trunk of polished white with only an occasional patch of grey-blue, which gives the tree its name. She leaned back against it and they began the minuet of love-making, a dance as formal as before, with figures and paths, but now for a society of one

man and one woman, and in the paths of her body and his. He
stood before her. She kissed his lips and his mouth and his eyes.
He loosened the tapes which fastened her basque at the back,
and rested his face in her warm breasts. She held his head in
her hands, and then with her right hand discovered his face.
He held her by the hips, and then slid his hands under her skirts
to lift them.

'They will think it is surf,' she said, and he knew, because she
was looking in the direction of the cove at the riding lights of
the ships, what she meant. Her skirts lifted with a rustle of paper
that must, it seemed to their ears, have carried to the vessels
there and been heard by the watch.

She leaned backwards. He always thought the bones of her
hips, those two bones which are most prominent as a woman
stands, the most elegant of her body. He cupped them in his
hands, she pressed back against his palms, and he stroked the
concavity of her belly between the hip-bones. Then he parted
her legs with his hand, and brushed that hand lightly against
her. She was always the most fluid of women. He called it silky.
She stood, half-lying, against the tree as he went so easily into
her, penetrating the silkiest of women, entering the silkiest of girls.

This time she talked to him, as for a while they remained
standing still, he inside her, she enclosing him. 'After a week,'
she said, 'my love, a week after the first night you ever came
to my room, you sent me that signal, SUSANNAH REMEMBER
SILKYLININGS, from the ship, and my father's aide, when he
brought it to me, said he couldn't be sure he had rightly made
out the flags: perhaps it was just some way a French ship
dressed all over. And he was sorry, too, that he had taken it to
my father first, not being certain it was for me although it did
start with my name. He said my father read it and smiled and
said it was most undoubtedly for me, and to bring it to me, and
so he did.'

In the Domain, by the tree, Nicolas and Susannah were as
much together as man and woman could be. As they parted at
last, and her skirts fell again into place with their great rustle,
Nicolas was for the most fleeting of moments taken in his mind
out of his exhilaration and he saw himself, sadly and as if in
a dream, holding in his hands not Susannah but an instrument
of navigation called an astrolabe. That was a moment and no

more, and then his consciousness returned to the Domain, the dark, the warmth, the present, and Susannah whom he greatly loved. In the house, the strings still played a minuet.

'We must make an appearance,' she said.

'I know.'

And so they did, she not even caring to go first to her room even to brush her hair. When they came again within the lights of the mansion she said, 'Just look and see,' and turned round before him, and he smiled and nodded, to tell her she was assembled. They entered the ball room together, last toasts were proposed to Baudin, to his ship, to his officers, and to peace. Baudin replied, 'I bequeath to the French nation the duty of offering to you the deepest thanks for all, for everything, that you have done, but' – and at this he addressed himself directly to King – 'it is for me to thank you with my heart for your friendship and love.' Then the Governor himself, with a boldness neither he nor Baudin nor Susannah gave a jot for, called for a toast to Baudin and Susannah together. That was drunk in the last of the champagne.

It was three in the morning before Nicolas and Susannah lay together in the sandalwood bed. She said, 'I did not know about Mary. But she did say, as she dressed me, that she would not undress me tonight.' They slept. Of their parting, the next day, nothing shall be said. That was for them to endure alone, and so, after all these years, it shall remain. Captain Philip Gidley King, Royal Navy, Captain General and Governor-in-Chief of New South Wales, watched the corvettes sail out of the cove, and in his daily log, immediately after a note on the American brig *Fanny*, which had sailed that morning, bound for Batavia and then New England, with a cargo of speculative goods, he wrote:

Ships: *Géographe* and *Naturaliste*, French. Arrived, June 18. Departed, October 17. Whence, Discovery. Whither, Discovery, and, God Willing, France.

Nicolas Baudin, Post-Captain in the marine of Republican France, sailed away from Susannah, with whom he would, God Willing, be in a few months reunited, and away from the continent he and she had named.

# 10

# On 7 July 1803, a Boy, Robert

Susannah stood in the sunlight, delighted as a child, while two men, and the wife of one of them, told her the old story of the bishop's cloak, almost making a play of it for her, enacting it on the patch of grass in front of a cottage in the Domain. The two men were George Bryant, who stole the cloak in his youth, and John Easty, who was now pensioned from the army and had become the Governor's head gardener. Bryant worked as a gardener under him

'Now Mr Easty there,' said Bryant, 'he will be the Judge.'

Susannah inclined her head to Easty. 'My lord,' she said.

'No, ma'am,' he said, embarrassed at her addressing him in this way even in play.

'Easty,' she said, 'if you are a judge you are my lordship and you must stand up straight and look lord-like.'

Jane Bryant watched. She was the wife of George Bryant. They were the couple who had married not on the night of the wiving but discreetly, two months later, as not wishing to be precipitate.

'Well, ma'am,' said Bryant, 'as you see, Mr Easty is the Judge. And at my trial, while the clerk was writing me down in the court book, a great thing of leather, why, it was the Judge's pleasure that the cloak should be placed upon me, as I do place it now on you.' And with that, Bryant took the cloak, and draped it with ceremony over Susannah's shoulders. She stood still, stroked the fur collar, turned back the skirt of the cloak to see the blue silk lining, and then smiled at Jane.

'And then,' said Bryant, 'the whole court of people broke

from their reverend silence to applause, and the Judge and me
talked for ever so long about Dorchester, the which being, as I
have said, the city of my birth, and there were such "Hear
hears" as I never heard. And that is how the cloak came all this
way across the world.'

The tale had been often told over the years, and gained in
the telling.

'And then,' said Susannah, 'Easty took the silver buckle from
it on the boat?'

Bryant said, 'As was no more than Mr Easty's due, seeing it
was agreed.'

Susannah smiled, took the cloak from her shoulders and gave
it back to Bryant, and said, 'Very well then Jane, we too have
agreed, on another matter.'

Jane curtsied.

It was two weeks after Baudin's departure. The loss had been
very great to her, and that afternoon was the first time since
then that Susannah had been gay. She needed a maid, Mary
Bickaith having sailed with the *Géographe*, and her father said
she could do worse than look at Jane Bryant, a steady woman he
thought. Because Bryant was a gardener he lived in the cottage
in the Domain and, if this were agreeable to Susannah, Jane
could perfectly well return to her husband at nights, and come
to dress her in the mornings. Easty, whose judgement the
Governor trusted, had spoken for Bryant and his wife. The crime
for which Jane had been transported was trivial, the theft of two
lengths of silk, which showed, the Governor thought, a superior
taste. Most women stole muslin. So Easty had called at Government House that afternoon to take Susannah to the Bryants'
cottage. He thought it more proper that Jane should come to
Susannah, but Susannah was less interested in ceremony than in
seeing how a woman who might become her maid lived herself.
She had found Jane a sturdy, soft-spoken Dorset girl, with
steady hazel eyes. The cottage was whitewashed inside and out,
and smelled sweet, and Jane, after the first confused curtsys and
bobbings, looked Susannah in the eye, and that settled it. The
wage was not expressed in money. Jane was given to understand,
through Easty, that there would be enough cloth from the
government stores to clothe her, that legs of ham and the like
from the kitchens of Government House would find their way

to the cottage, and that after two years she might expect a pardon.

The Bryants were delighted.

'Dress the Governor's daughter in silk as penance for lifting your two lengths of felon's silk, Jane,' said her husband, after Susannah left.

Jane said, 'I have seen her often, and with the captain from the French ship, and I like the lady.'

'She is much liked,' said her husband. 'But she knows what she wants.'

'I see that.'

And Jane settled down to read to her husband from an old English newspaper. He had never learned to read himself.

'Fine goings on at Weymouth,' she said. 'Listen to this then.' She read the Court Circular:

'*Weymouth. August 14.*
Yesterday morning the King, Princess Augusta, and the Duke of Gloucester bathed. His Majesty, after breakfast, rode out on horseback.'

'I have been there,' said Bryant, 'when he did. And walked from Dorchester to see it.'

Jane continued.

'This morning at ten o'clock the Royal Family, with their usual party of nobility, went on board the *Charlotte* yacht.'

'And I have seen that party of nobility,' said Bryant. 'Fine gentlemen and their ladies, and the whole town turned out to wish them well. Often I remember it as a boy.'

Jane read and her husband listened, both convicts, both transported beyond the seas, both eager for news of the doings of the King in whose name they had been transported from a country they loved and could hardly hope ever to see again.


A month later it seemed likely to Susannah, and for two weeks before that had seemed a certainty to Jane, who had lived the last three of her twenty years in prisons, hulks, transport ships, and the female factory and had seen a great deal of life, that Susannah was carrying Baudin's child. At the first signs

Susannah sent word to Jane not to attend her that morning, and then not to come the next, and then not the next. Jane ignored the last message and found Susannah pale and white, already dressed but lying on the sandalwood bed with her face in the pillows.

She said, 'I have never been ill before.'

'You are not ill now, ma'am. And there is no matter for sadness either, if I see it straight. Nor tears. You will be going home to the captain soon. I beg your pardon, ma'am, but I saw you together, and he is a man who would rejoice.'

Susannah sat upright and looked at her maid, seeing in Jane's eyes the steadiness and sense she had recognized on the afternoon of their first interview in the cottage.

'I know he would, Jane. And I do too. Only, I am so wretched in the mornings. For the rest, I do rejoice.'

She told her father later that day, and he came round from behind his desk and kissed her head and rocked her in his arms. The instinct for happiness in a man is so great that for long moments he did not think at all, but surrendered himself to a welling-up of his love for his daughter and to a sense of pleasure that, with this coming grandchild, his own posterity was in a small way assured. Then he did think, and came and sat by her on a sofa, and told her what he was afraid she would not have considered, but had to be told.

'My dear,' he said, 'if this is so, I am a happy man. But, if this is so, then it does mean that you cannot sail as soon as you had hoped. You could have gone with the transport next month, but the passage, at best, is uncertain in length. There are perhaps, seven more months to your confinement, and seven months might find you still at sea, and you know that is unthinkable.'

She had *not* considered that, but she knew her father was right. She suddenly faced the certainty that she would be separated from Nicolas for more than another year, and would have to bear his child in the colony, alone. She was brave with her father, and brave all that day. It was only late at night, with Jane, that she wept bitterly, and the woman wept with her. That night, sleepless and alone, she prayed for the first time since she was a child, for Nicolas, for their unborn child, and for courage.

By the transport on which she should have sailed to Europe, she sent a letter to Baudin, which should reach France three months after his expected arrival.

'My dearest Nicolas,' she wrote, 'I cannot be certain, but I *know*, which is more than certainty, that our child was conceived the evening you came back to me, and walked up to the cove, and from my room saw the lights of the ships in the cove, and then took me to bed. It was the night we named Australia.'


Susannah was examined by the best surgeon her father could find. His name was Redmond, a ruined naval surgeon who, in order to pay gambling debts, had sold forceps, calipers, scalpels, saws and other instruments of his profession which were unfortunately the property of their lordships of the Admiralty. He had been transported, but then, since surgeons were rare in the colony, and since he had never gambled again, had rapidly been pardoned. He was twenty-five. He was not a bad surgeon, but in his naval career he had sawn off more legs than he had delivered children. In truth he had delivered no child at all, though he had watched two delivered at the naval hospital at Portsmouth. It was merciful that Jane, in her career of hulks and prisons, had seen many women delivered, and had delivered two with her own hands. Redmond did have academic advantages. As a surgeon's apprentice he had read the learned treatises of Le Motte, Simpson, Chapman, Gifford, and Gregoire. He also had access in the colony to the article on Midwifery in the *Encyclopaedia Britannica*, a work published in 1771 by a Society of Gentlemen in Scotland, in which the different Sciences and Arts were digested into distinct Treatises. This was in fact not so derisory a resource as would be thought nowadays. The treatise on midwifery was long, copiously illustrated, and intended to help and inform those who might need to act on the information.

Redmond had red hair. He was a big man. He attended Susannah in her sitting room, with Jane as chaperon. He had read the article on midwifery that morning.

'Midwifery, ma'am,' he assured her, 'is the art of assisting nature in bringing forth a perfect child from the womb of the mother.'

'Good,' she said. 'How big is it now?'

'Big?'

'How big is the perfect child within my womb?' It was unfair on Redmond, and put him at a distinct disadvantage, that Susannah too had read the article on midwifery in the same work that same morning in her father's library, and recognized his definition of midwifery as the first sentence of the article. It was also disconcerting for Redmond that she was prepared to ask bold questions that were not supposed to occur to the delicate minds of ladies of that time.

He hesitated to ask her the date of possible conception, but she conveyed to him that in her opinion the child might be three months old. Then, he replied, after considering gravely, the ovum would at that moment be the size of, let us say, a goose egg. She had read that too.

But she said to herself that she would not mock him any more. He was trying his best to put her mind at ease, and to explain. There was really nothing else he could do. At three months there was no point in examining her. Those were days when a doctor, at five months, could not be *certain* that a woman he was attending was pregnant or suffering from a disease producing superficially the same signs. He could be reasonably sure, but not certain. Jane, who knew Susannah more intimately than ever Redmond could have done after a dozen examinations, was more sure than any surgeon. She stood by the sofa on which Susannah reclined, watched Redmond, and never said a word. Redmond continued his business of putting Susannah at ease.

'A little later on, ma'am,' he said, 'the child, as it lies in the womb, and is grown . . .'

'More like a child?'

'When it is grown more like a child, it will recline in nearly a circular, or rather oval, figure, which is calculated to take up as little space as possible.'

Susannah waited.

'The chin,' said the surgeon, 'rests on the breasts, the thighs are pressed along the belly, the face being placed between the knees, while the arms cross each other round the legs. Do I explain myself? Do you see?'

Susannah did see, but what she saw was not the entwining of a child in her womb, but that of herself and Nicolas.

At that moment Baudin was sailing a course due north, one thousand miles from Sydney. He had sailed up the eastern coasts of Australia but well away from land. No mariner of his day would take the route which on a modern map looks obvious, that between the northern tip of Australia and the south of New Guinea. That was a narrow and then uncharted strait. Instead he would sail far north into the Pacific, thread his way through the Solomon Islands, cross the Equator northwards, then loop down east of Borneo, cross the Equator again, this time southwards, and only then sail west, south of Batavia and the city of Djakarta and across the Indian Ocean to round the Cape of Good Hope. It was the longest possible way round, but the only one known to be safe. Baudin, with a replenished ship, a rested crew, and the recollection and prospect of Susannah every hour in his mind, was a happy man. His cabin was now possessed by Susannah. He saw her figure as she walked towards him across the quarterdeck, and across the Persian carpets which covered the cabin deck in port but had been stowed once he put to sea. He heard the rustle of her dresses. His voyage of discovery was a success. He had charted the coast of southern New Holland, and part of the east coast. He had on board specimens of emus and kangaroos and countless plants. His charts of *Terre Napoléon*, which he saw himself presenting to the First Consul, were covered by names which made them sound like a French roll of honour. There was *Baie Tallyrand*, named after Napoléon's foreign minister. There was a *Golfe Bonaparte* and a *Golfe Josephine*. Desert capes and desert places were named for Montaigne, Lafayette, Voltaire, Molière, and even for Rabelais and Jeanne d'Arc. Baudin was going home with hope in his heart and mind. He was too good a navigator not to realize the risks on the passage still before him, but he knew also that, God willing, he would overcome them. He had accomplished what he had been sent to do. He had entirely reasonable hopes and expectations of preferment. Promotion to flag rank on his return was likely, and, though he was not ambitious, what good sailor does not wish to be an admiral? He had made his name, and, though he had named nothing *Cap Baudin*, he allowed himself the natural and not immodest hope that Napoléon, seizing a

pen, would dash down that name on the map and wave away
Baudin's protests. Above all, and it *was* above all, he carried in
his heart a confident hope of life to be lived with Susannah. His
officers, if they thought of their captain's hopes, would have
considered that the easiest to be achieved. Susannah had been
so wholeheartedly his, whereas flag rank was, they knew, a
lottery of preferment determined by a hundred imponderable
chances. But to Baudin, because Susannah was the greatest
thing he hoped for, it was her – through some mischance and in
spite of her glorious wholeness of heart – that he feared he
might lose. As he walked his quarterdeck he noticed, as he
never had done before Susannah came on board, the scent of
the cedar timbers of his ship. One day he summoned the
carpenter, asked if he had any item of sandalwood on board,
and received the man's astonished answer of, 'No, sir. It would
be no use.' Baudin thought of the sandalwood bed.


When Susannah was six months with child, Redmond said to
her, as if offering essential information, 'The woman is sometimes subject to longings besides.'

'Are you offering me strange fruit, Mr Redmond?' But the
man did not laugh. He never laughed. She half expected him
to send out for a basket of paw-paw immediately. Susannah had
her longings, but she did not think them strange. They were to
her the most natural thing. She longed for her lover, and tried
to re-create him in her senses by wandering in the Domain,
walking the path she had taken across the lawn when he had
walked the parallel path, and going again and again to the tree
against which they had leaned the night of the masked ball,
caressing with her fingers the texture of its smooth bark. She
was still not noticeably pregnant, especially not in the dresses
of the Directory, and she did not need to close her eyes, even in
daylight, to re-create the sounds and scents and movements,
longings and fruitions, of that night. She did not need to close
her eyes. With her eyes open but not seeing what was at present
before them, with her senses shut to what was there at present
but rather recalling the darkness, and the lights in the cove, and
the watchmen on the ships who must have heard the rustling of
the paper in her gown, like surf, she could take herself back in

mind – and her mind very nearly took the sensations of the body
with it – to the events of that night. At other times she loved to
walk among the cedars of the Domain, and recall the scent of
the corvette's timbers. She wondered occasionally about Mary
Bickaith, who had dressed her that night.


Mary Bickaith was a blessing to the wardroom of the *Géographe*,
whose officers had adopted her, and a blessing to the sailors.
What she did for the spirit of those men was very great. By being
a woman, and by being there and talking with them, and asking
them, in the few words of French she had learned, about Paris,
she kept them from the numbness and from some of the fear of
a long passage. The storms of the Indian Ocean can be terrible,
and a corvette is not built for them. A corvette is a messenger-
ship of a fleet, or a fast raider, too fine in her lines to be a good
sea boat in a gale. Mary was strong and a good sailor, mercifully
never seasick. The crew of the *Géographe* had crawled exhausted
into Sydney, and a rest of five months had only apparently
restored them. On the passage home, after four months at sea,
they were nearly worn out again. Once, for five days on end,
the ship was awash, every man was soaked, and there was no
way of keeping dry, and no hot food. No fire could be lit. A
fire was a danger in a pitching, rolling, yawing corvette. Even
if it had been prudent to light one, it would have been doused
in a moment by the sluicing seas running clean across the decks.
For days they all but drifted in shrouds, keeping only enough
sail to gain steerway. They had long ago lost touch with the
*Naturaliste*. The men shivered in tropical heat. The ship's biscuit
was powdered almost to dust by weevils, and then moistened by
the humid air into a wet paste. The salt beef stank so that the
men could not stomach it. On their hands sores grew the colour
of wine lees. Their lips shrivelled. Their joints stiffened. When
they emerged from those five days of hell into calm seas,
Baudin's first concern was for his men and his second for the
animals. The emus and kangaroos had suffered too. His
scientists were so incapacitated that Baudin fed the animals
himself, and Mary went with him to help. The third lieutenant,
Pelegrin, died. Baudin entered the death in his log, and sat with
his head in his hands.

Two hours later his servant entered the cabin and approached him.

'Sir, she is laying him out.'

Baudin raised his head.

The dead on men o'war were not usually laid out, but hustled into weighted hammocks and committed to the deep. Baudin went to see what she had done. He looked at the face of the young man he had known so well, and at the grave face of the English girl. He put a hand on her shoulder and thanked her. They sat in the 'tween decks with a swaying lantern between them shedding its light on their figures and that of the dead man.

'It is so many,' he said, 'so many.'

The captain of a man o'war feels the full weight of loneliness. At sea he must be separate and aloof. He may talk to his officers, but then only in the line of duty. He may talk to his servant. A perceptive servant, from the carrying-in of the captain's breakfast, may very well learn more of him than his first lieutenant. Under the lantern Baudin talked to Mary, and what came to his mind was the list of those who had left Havre with him and would never return.

'Stanislas died at sea. He was a botanist. That was two years ago. And Anselm, chief gardener, and Sautier, and Louis, and now Pelegrin, who was a boy. He came to me that night of the ball, to say you were on board.'

'That is what I remembered,' she said.

'And so many others, left ill at Timor, left ill God knows where. I knew them.'

'We shall come through, sir,' she said. Baudin smiled at this innocent assurance. He had sailed the seas of the world, he had been in far worse straits than this before, but he was grateful for this girl's reassurance and for her cheerfulness.

'We shall come to Paris sir. The men have told me about Paris.' Then she dared to come a little closer to his mind, and told him what she knew he wanted to know. Anywhere else, it would not have been her place to tell him, or to say a word, but they were in the vastness of the Indian Ocean, and what was her place there?

'Miss Susannah is a constant, loving woman; and I know her well, sir.'

'Thank you,' he said, and rose and went on deck.

As the watches changed, the first lieutenant brought him a pannikin of water from a cask just broached, and showed it to him, saying nothing. It was the colour of tea.

Baudin nodded. 'We shall hold our course to round the Cape,' he said. The lieutenant was thinking of Île de France, an island off the south-east coast of Africa where they could revictual and obtain good water. But that would take them too far north and lose them weeks. Baudin's orders remained what they had been, to hold course round the Cape.


Back in Sydney, Susannah was asking Redmond a great number of questions. Within a week she would be confined. How many births were difficult?

'In a town of three thousand women . . . ,' he said.

'Yes, Mr Redmond?'

'In a town of three thousand, one thousand women may be delivered in a year.'

She thought that excessive, but it was a fact that the women of Sydney had been fecund.

'And of those one thousand, in nine hundred and twenty cases the child will be born without any other than common assistance.'

'And the other eighty?'

'Require, ah, other assistance.'

Of course Susannah was afraid. That was why she showed such bright courage. It was just as well for her that she did not know Mr Redmond had never delivered a single child, with ordinary or extraordinary assistance. She did guess at his inexperience, but did not ask.


That day, in the middle of the stifling ocean, Baudin was shown the filthy contents of the third bad water cask to be broached in a week. So many of the crew were ill that both watches had to be turned out to execute the simplest manoeuvre. That day it was a fair sea and a fair wind, but he kept reefs in the courses and in all topsails. He did not want to fill the mainsail because it would have been impossible to furl it in the dark, if the squalls of the previous weeks came on them again. He saw the colour

of the drinking water held out for him to examine. He saw the
eyes of his officers. He saw the eyes of his men on the flush deck.
He looked up at the sun. 'Lay a course' he said, 'for Île de
France.' The joy was spontaneous. The men of the watch,
knowing this to be their deliverance, cheered in exaltation, and
the watch below, either hearing these cheers, or sensing the
vessel shift in her course, ran on deck if they could run, or
climbed slowly up if they could not run, but every man came
on deck and gazed at the new horizon beyond which lay Île de
France. Baudin's servant brought him a glass of a claret he had
not intended to open until they first sighted the coast of metropolitan France, having concealed it from his master. Baudin
told him to take a glass himself.

Susannah's was a natural and easy labour. Jane was to all
intents the midwife. Hers were the hands that helped Susannah
when she needed help. Jane also had the prison midwife waiting
in the next room, a woman who, though perhaps not belonging
at Government House, had delivered a thousand babies. If
there was any difficulty Jane had determined to call her in
whether Mr Redmond agreed or not. She rather thought he
would have agreed, but in the event it was not necessary. Jane
delivered the child, and Redmond supervised. All was proper.
Susannah lay on her left side on the sandalwood bed, wearing a
linen half shift, an open linen skirt, and a bed gown. Over the
undersheet were three layers of sheep skins, tied with tapes to
each side of the bed. She lay with her knees contracted to the
belly, and a pillow between her knees to keep them apart. It
was a remarkably easy labour. When she was delivered she was
bathed with a soft, warm towel, and then bound around with a
broad linen cloth, and the warmed sheets were folded upwards
from the foot of the bed and placed over her. In the delirium of
her pain before the birth she fiercely held Jane's hands as if they
were those of Nicolas, and called out his name.
'You have a son,' Jane told her. After the birth Susannah
slept. Jane took the child and washed it, wrapped it in linen,
and rubbed the head, temples, and breast with spirits. When
Susannah awoke the child was placed in her arms, and she
named him Robert. It was 7 July 1803.

The prison midwife was given a guinea and sent away. Redmond busied himself forbidding Susannah all nourishment except warm barley water, or chicken water boiled up with cinnamon, to which might be added a third or a fourth part of light wine. Susannah drank with appetite. 'Or *less* than a fourth part of wine,' said Redmond, 'if the patient drinks plentifully.' He said firmly that she was to have no solid food for five or six days. After one day, when Redmond was away, Jane gave Susannah boiled breast of chicken.

The Governor embraced his daughter with tears of gratitude in his eyes, and took his grandson from her arms with such exaggerated gentleness that she laughed at him. It was a fine boy.

'I am happy man,' said the Governor.

'And I am a happy woman,' said Susannah. 'Nicolas will be happy.'

All noise had been banished for the confinement. The wooden floors were laid with drugget and the stairs with cloths, the door hinges oiled, the knockers tied, the bells silenced, and the carriageway strewn with reeds.

'Do away with all that nonsense,' said Susannah. 'I want to hear the sounds of the house again.' On the fourth day – and this was unthinkable in the year 1803 – Susannah demanded to move for an hour to a chair in the window so that she could see the trees of the Domain and the sails in the cove, and she stayed there all afternoon.

The child was three months old when James Cobb, master of the *Columbia*, a full-rigged ship out of Boston with a cargo of flour, good salt pork, wine from the Cape, iron tools, and paper, paced up the slope from the cove over the Domain to Government House. It was almost a year since Baudin had ascended that same slope, awaited by Susannah. The *Columbia* was the first American vessel to enter Sydney that year. By that autumn, only thirteen vessels of any nation had entered the port. Susannah eagerly sent down to them all for news of the *Géographe*, though her father told her it was much too early to know anything. She missed the entrance of the *Columbia* because she and Jane and the child had been away the previous two days

at Parramatta, the Governor's second residence. The leisurely
ride there and back in the Governor's carriage eased her restlessness. As Captain Cobb walked up the hill she was just
returning. He saw her as she got down from the carriage
carrying the child, a hundred yards ahead of him. He heard
Susannah murmuring to the child, but could not hear what she
said. He saw the woman's white form go indoors, waited for a
minute, gazing round at the eucalypts he had never seen before,
and then continued his walk up to the house.

A servant ushered him into an ante-room, and returned
immediately to take him to the Governor.

'Captain Cobb, my compliments. But you have walked. I
sent a carriage for you to the quay.'

'I did not think of that,' said the American. 'The pilot pointed
out the house from the cove and I could see it was a walk. I
came as soon as I put ashore.'

The *Columbia* had entered the cove only two hours before and
was immediately noticed by King, who knew a well-run ship
when he saw one. He knew she was from Boston and then the
Cape, but her rigging seemed intact and even her paint fresh.
As she made in to her moorings as neatly as any man o'war –
neater, he could not help thinking, than some – he watched the
agility of the men at work in her shrouds, and the assured
easiness of those on deck who, having for the moment nothing
to do, lounged at the rails and scanned the new coastline. These
men had an ease which might have been mistaken for indolence,
but it was nothing of the sort. The Governor had rapidly learned
this from the men of previous American ships. It was not an
indolence, more a complete independence. King was a sailor
who did not need to watch a ship handled for more than a few
moments to know something about her officers and crew. He had
learned that American officers were often very good, and the
seamen, taken at large, far and away the best who ever entered
the port. After terrible voyages they were healthy. They could
read and write. American seamen were good enough to be
mates in the vessels of most other nations, and some of them
made this transition. Having landed at Sydney, they commonly
played hell in the waterfront inns, but he let that go. He had
fought Yankee ships in the War of Independence. He would
have preferred such seamen as allies.

'That is a very fine vessel, captain,' he said. 'I watched her put in.'

He had also read her signals before they had been relayed to him by his aide. Her captain had asked an immediate interview with the Governor.

'We spoke to a French corvette in the Indian Ocean.'

King had known this was coming.

'She was well off course for Île de France. I went on board. We helped provision her. Her water was foul.'

King looked sharply at the American, who went on. 'It was taken on here, at Sydney. I saw the casks. They were bad casks. I gave her what I could. She will have made Île de France.'

King was in a fury of mind. He wanted to know more, and yet his mind was full of those casks. On account of their blasted rum monopoly, almost all the sound casks in the colony passed through the hands of the New South Wales Corps. Most of the casks with which the *Géographe* was provisioned came from that source. King had seen himself that the water given to the French was sweet. He had watched the casks hoisted, and the casks had been whole, and not rotten. But now he realized that there was a question he had not asked himself. What had those apparently sound casks previously contained? If it was rum then, strangely enough, that was all right. Rum dregs do not much hurt sweet water. But if it was wine, and if the casks had not first been thoroughly charred, then he knew what would happen to that water. Major Johnston knew what would happen to that water. Johnston's men would have supplied those casks, and their monopoly was extending itself into wine.

'Wine casks?' he asked.

'As I guess.'

The American placed on the table a package wrapped in oilskin. 'Mr Governor,' he said, 'I was asked to bring these to you, and I am sorry it is bad news.'

'Baudin?'

'The captain's name was Baudin. When I went on board I was told he had not eaten for two days, nor spoken for hours. Their surgeon was dead. An English girl begged me to send for mine. I did, and he found the captain still warm, but dead. The French lieutenant gave me this package.' It was a bundle of papers addressed to Susannah. 'And he gave me this letter for you. I stayed for the burial of the French captain.'

The first lieutenant's letter to King was brief. Post-Captain Nicolas Baudin had died of fever. The lieutenant thought that the last pages of his personal log were intended for Susannah, and enclosed them in a separate package, which he was entrusting to Captain Cobb. Captain Baudin had never ceased to express his gratitude to His Excellency the Governor of New South Wales. As for the Governor's daughter, the lieutenant believed the journal would speak for itself. He offered the Governor and Susannah his deepest sympathy, and for his part could express only sorrow at the death of such a man as Baudin, and commiserate in others a grief he knew they would feel even more keenly than himself.

Captain Cobb looked away as the Governor read this, and then turned to see a man quite broken and not attempting to hide the silent tears on his face.

'Mr Governor,' said Cobb, 'I am sorry to bring you this news. I will go.'

King looked at him. 'Oh, no, you must forgive me. But you will need this.' He took a sheet of paper and scribbled instructions to his quartermaster general to supply the *Columbia*'s master with whatever he required, with no exception, and to the provost marshal of the New South Wales Corps that the master, officers, and men of the *Columbia* were to be allowed free access at all times to the quays and town of Sydney.

The Yankee captain left. In the hallway he passed a dark-haired girl in a white dress, holding a tiny child. She looked up and smiled straight at him. He recognized her as the woman he had seen get down from the carriage. He wondered whose the child was. Susannah thought the visitor very grave and went into her father to ask why. Cobb declined the carriage, which by this time had found him and was waiting outside, and walked down again over the lawns to his cutter waiting at the jetty.

Late that night Susannah read again, as she had been reading over and over all day, the papers her father had given her when she went in so gaily to ask about the American captain in the hallway. There was a painstaking note from Mary Bickaith, which said:

The American surgeon found these papers with Captain Baudin, which the lieutenant says he was writing at his last moment, and they are for you and will send them by the American ship to you. I was with him a lot, with the animals, and it was a fever. I thought the burial was French, but the lieutenant said it was Latin. The American captain lent me a book in English, and I read the words about the day the dead shall arise from the Sea; and I said the Our Father for his soul, and prayed for you. It was all properly done.

The package also contained Baudin's personal log. On its last page was a letter written to Susannah in his final hours. It was half a farewell to her and half a fevered account of the ship's working. It said:

Heavy seas all night, pitching, labouring, spraying all over. The emus and kangaroos are seasick. The sea gives them no peace. Morning and the sea is fair. Susannah, you were the greatest gift that was ever made to me. I never hoped for so much. I do not think I shall be able to write any more. May you be loved. May you be cherished in your heart, and in your mind, and in your bed. We made the emus eat by opening their beaks and gave them wine and sugar, and the seasick kangaroos too, though we were very short of these things for ourselves. I had to come to bed but do not find much relief here. I believe we are at latitude 7 degrees 30 minutes S. and longitude 95 degrees 41 minutes E., but I do not know where I am.

These words were his last and were dated 7 July 1803, the day on which Susannah gave birth to their son, a child Nicolas never knew she had conceived.

# 11

# Bligh's Second Mutiny

Later that year another American ship brought news: after the brief peace England and France were again at war. To Susannah it meant nothing. The world meant nothing to her. In Sydney, a man condemned for burglary was three times suspended from the gallows. The first time the cord separated in the middle and he fell on his face, the second time the rope unravelled at the fastening and he again fell to the ground, and when he was a third time launched the rope snapped short. The lieutenant of the New South Wales Corps in charge of the execution ordered the criminal to be taken back to barracks, and himself petitioned the Governor for a pardon, which was instantly granted. The Governor congratulated the officer on his humanity, and the pity of the situation took his mind for the first time in many months out of a torpor which had become habitual to him. A small bear of the kind the natives called Koala was found in Sydney, its first discovery by white men. The Governor nodded, but did not go to see the beast. An insurrection of Irish was rapidly suppressed, and the Governor took reports of it at second hand from the military and questioned none of the Irishmen himself, as he would once have done. In France, Napoléon was proclaimed Emperor, but the Governor, the day he received the news, did not even speak of it at his dinner table, where he and Susannah now ate unspeaking and alone. The tremor of a mild earthquake shook the town, but Susannah said nothing even then. She was walking upstairs when the movement was felt. She stopped and watched a chandelier sway and jingle, but then, when it came to rest again, continued upstairs as if she had seen and heard nothing. Jane Bryant was behind her, carrying the little boy, and it was then that Jane at last spoke sharply to her. It was a year since Susannah had known of Baudin's death, more than a year since Robert's birth, and in that time Jane, not Susannah, had been the child's mother. She said, 'I will be straight with you ma'am. When this child was born, and they strewed rushes, and oiled locks, and bound up the knockers, you ordered it all undone, so that you could hear the noises of the house going on. Now the ground rocks and you will not notice it. You do not know your child, and all this is not good. It is a year now, ma'am.' She put the child in Susannah's arms and went off to her cottage. For the first time in a year, Susannah took her own child on to the lawns and talked and played with him, and then afterwards, at dinner, she did ask her father about the earthquake. There was little damage. For two days she dressed herself briskly, and took the child at times from Jane, but then she relapsed into her long melancholy.

Redmond tried to treat her for this condition. She submitted to tepid baths to drive the blood from the head, and consented to have cold water poured upon her hair to promote the easier diffusion of the humours congested within the head. She swallowed a medicine he prescribed of cephalic and nervine herbs – vervain, sage, plantain, and white maidenhair. He told her the ingredients and their purpose.

'Maidenhair for the loss of a lover?' she said. He did not understand.

It was John Easty who fetched the herbs from the gardens he tended, and he and Jane took Susannah frequently into the Domain to divert her mind. They showed her the proper season for planting and transplanting seedling trees. 'The roots of a tree,' said Easty, 'when planted, should spread like a man's open hand.'

He placed the seedling in her hand.

'And plant the creature not more than three inches below the ordinary surface of the ground.' He dug a shallow hole with his hands, for her to set the tree in.

'And when the hole is filled up,' he said, scooping earth around the roots as she held the tree erect, 'tread the earth gently round the plant.' They planted many trees, and next

month he showed her how to dress strawberries, how to cut off
the runners, loosen the ground, and place fresh earth between
the rows, to make the plants strong and grow large fruit.

Her father, all the while, was as afflicted with grief as she was.
John Easty knew this, but less could be done for the Governor.
He could not be shown how to plant trees. Jane knew it too,
and took care to bring the child to him often. He saw what she
was doing, and was grateful. The boy was a great consolation
to him. One day he called her into his study.

'You have done so much for my daughter,' he said, 'and so
much for me.'

'I have done what any woman would.'

'No, much more. And I am ashamed that I have not done
what I promised when first you came to Susannah. But I have
remembered now.'

He took a parchment he had prepared, the form of her free
pardon, signed it in her presence, and gave it to her. 'It is a
small thing enough,' he said. To the girl it was not a small thing.
She embraced him with pure affection, and ran from the room.
The Governor turned back to his desk and stared at the mass of
papers, some signed by him and some still unsigned, but all
unread. He was letting the colony go to the dogs, and the dogs
were Major Johnston and most of his fellow officers of the Corps.
He no longer checked their open monopoly not only of rum but
of all trade, so now it went altogether unchecked. The Governor
was weary. He began to write for the fourth time to London
requesting his own recall. The Governor's loss was not so great
as his daughter's, though his grief for her was great, but he did
have to live every day with the knowledge of something she did
not know, which he would never tell her. He knew why the
water on board the *Géographe* had been foul, though he could
prove nothing and do nothing. He took the blame heavily upon
himself that he had not thought to ensure that those casks were
well charred. It rarely left his consciousness that but for that
foul water, Baudin might still be alive, and his daughter not
bereft.


Back in England, not in London but on a man o'war off Torbay,
Captain William Bligh was defending his honour at a most

peculiar court martial. He was charged with grossly insulting one of his lieutenants on the quarterdeck of the *Warrior* by calling him a rascal and a scoundrel and by shaking a fist in his face, and with at other times acting in a tyrannical, oppressive, and unofficer-like way. It emerged from the evidence that Bligh often called his officers and men damned blackguards, vile and shameful lubbers, Jesuits, and vagrants. He once called the gunner a damned long pelt of a bitch. His defence was original, consisting of a contention that these were expressions commonly used in the navy, and that any officer zealous in his duty was occasionally given to such 'ebullition of the mind'. He candidly and without reserve admitted that he was not a tame and indifferent observer of the way in which officers placed under his orders conducted themselves in the performance of their duties. He cross-examined witnesses himself, asking one officer, 'Is it usual for me, when any duty is carrying on, to use a great deal of action, with my hands, without having any particular meaning in it, but being merely a custom, without the least intention of insulting anyone?'

To which the officer replied, 'A considerable motion of the hand, frequently swearing at the quartermasters or men of that description who were standing around. A great deal of action with the hands, as if to knock any person down – but I never considered it done with the intention of personally insulting any officer.'

Bligh was happy with this answer, as he was with that of the boatswain, who said Bligh had shaken him and torn his shirt, and was very hot and hasty and given to swearing, but that he believed the words no sooner escaped him than his passion ended. For himself, the boatswain never attached any particular interpretation to what was said. He would just as soon sail with Bligh as with any other captain he knew.

The officers of the court were amused to hear so much vilification sworn to in evidence, but found the charges proved and admonished Bligh to be more circumspect in his language. Outside the court he announced to all and sundry that he would get rid of the officers who had spoken against him, as soon as might be, since they had turned out to be the worst of serpents.

In Sydney, King was beginning to use language which if not so inventive was as intemperate as Bligh's, but with the Governor it was not out of natural impatience of mind but because he was at the end of his tether. He publicly called the Corps officers damned thieves and infernal scoundrels, and on one occasion ground his boot into a basket of eggs. The Corps was establishing a monopoly in eggs too, and when he learned this in the market place he was overtaken by anger. But the spectators were not to know what the reason was. Then a woman, unable to pay the price demanded by the rum monopolies, ingenuously came to the Governor himself to ask for rum. He did not understand why she had come, only heard her ask him for rum, and roughly asked what the hell her name was.

'Bridget, Y'r Excellency.'

'Bridget? Bridget? No other name?'

'The men call me Pony, sir.'

'Pony? Trot then, you hussy, trot.' And he took her by the shoulders, turned her round, and made her trot. Susannah saw this.

That evening, when the servants left them, she said, 'That was not like you, Father.'

He accepted the rebuke. 'I am glad to hear it was not. I am not inclined to put it so charitably myself. But, we shall soon be home. At last we are going home.'

'Home?' She had not known.

'My recall came this afternoon. A despatch from the *Hercules*, which has just put in. We go home as soon as I am relieved by the new governor.'

She said softly, 'I am sorry, but I will not go.'

He did not comprehend her. He did not believe her. But she would not be moved. She would not go because Sydney, and Government House, and the Domain, were the places where she had met Baudin, and taken him for her first lover, and borne his child. She did not explain all this. She only said that all the high moments of her life had been lived in that place, and she would not leave.

'And all the grief?' said her father. 'Not that too?'

She shook her head. She did not know how to put it in words,

but her grief was deep because her life there, even after she
knew of Baudin's death, was spent in a constant recollection and
re-creation of those high moments, which made her loss the
more painful but still tied her to the place. She had almost
forgotten England. Going away meant to her only the going
away of Baudin, and he had gone to his death. She would not
go, nor would she explain further. Her father began to understand. He half understood. Would she take time to consider?
She said she would consider, but her answer would be the same
because her reasons could not change. The Governor, staring
out of the window on to the darkened Domain, said her loss
would be very heavy to him. She knew it, and if anything could
have changed her mind it would have been that. But she would
not change her mind. The Governor was too proud to say that
the loss of his grandson would be dreadful to him. She knew that
too, and would have done anything not to hurt her father so
badly.

That night he did not sleep, and, long after midnight,
watching at his bedroom window, he saw his daughter walking
in the moonlight on the Domain. She stepped on to the lawns
from the east wing, walked a straight path slowly away from
the house, and then stopped and half-turned as if to face
another late-walker across the length of the lawn. He then knew
for sure that she would not come with him, but would stay, and
he knew why.


When the Secretary of State in London looked for a new
governor to replace King, he stated that he was seeking a man
capable of drawing on his own resources in difficulties without
leaning on others for advice, not subject to whimper and whine,
an officer of integrity unimpeached, and civil in deportment.
This tactful post was offered, two weeks after his court martial
for the use of inventively insulting language, to Captain
William Bligh. He was not at first sure that he wanted it. He
was not certain even after he was offered £2000 a year, twice
the salary of previous governors. He did not wish to be separated
from his wife Betsy, whom he loved, and she could not come
with him because she, a sailor's wife, feared the sea and could
not face the long voyage. But it was Betsy, who had been his

wife for thirty years, who eventually persuaded him to go.
Gently, she told him it might be his last chance of high office,
and that she wanted it for him. Bligh was fifty-four. He knew it
might be his last chance. Reluctantly, he went. In early 1806,
less than three months after Nelson won the Battle of Trafalgar,
Bligh left England. By August he was in Sydney.

This was Bligh of the *Bounty*, who was already a legend. But
the legend was not then what it has become. There were
certainly those who thought he was a tyrant. Some thought him
an outright villain. But it was also remembered that after the
mutiny on the *Bounty*, when he and eighteen members of the
crew were abandoned in mid-Pacific in an open boat, Bligh
navigated the boat for forty days across 3000 miles of mountain-
ous seas to Timor, from where he wrote to his wife, 'Know then,
my own dear Betsy, I have lost the *Bounty*.' It was a feat of
courage and navigation. He had never lacked either courage or
ability. He had gone with Captain Cook on his last voyage, and
was commended by him. He was there on the day in 1779 when
Cook was murdered by the natives of Hawaii. He fought at the
Battle of Copenhagen and was praised by Nelson. Such was
Bligh, a man commended and praised by the two greatest
sailors of his day; a man who loved his wife tenderly; but a man
given to ebullition of the mind. He was also a friend of Governor
King's. They had served together as young men. So King, when
at last he admitted to himself that Susannah would not return
with him, took his old friend aside, told him everything, and
asked him to cherish and protect Susannah and the boy Robert.
Bligh gave his word, and invited Susannah to remain at
Government House. With men he was at times an undoubted
bully, but with women he was gentle.

The day came for King to leave. A governor cannot depart
without a ceremony of honour-guards and brave music. On the
quay, Susannah stood by his side through all this. It was
intolerable for both of them. When the last military compliment
was paid, and King had saluted the Union flag still flying from
the residence in which he and his daughter had lived together
for so long, he turned to his daughter and held out one hand to
her. He led her a few yards from the drawn-up ranks of the naval
establishment. Every man could see and hear, but all looked
straight ahead, determined to appear unseeing and unhearing.

'Bligh will look after you,' said King.

Susannah could not meet her father's eyes.

He took her head in his hands and raised her eyes to his. 'Come with me, Susannah.'

'I cannot, but how I wish. . . .'

He released his daughter's head, so as not to see her tears.

She saw his hands drop by his sides, and saw that he clenched his fingers into his palms.

She raised her head, faced him again, took both his hands, and threw herself into his arms.

Then he knew it was hopeless. He held her and rocked her, and then gently released her.

'Goodbye,' he said. 'Susannah, I am not sure I can be brave much longer. Goodbye. God be with you.'

He walked rapidly to the jetty where his cutter was waiting, and did not look back as he was rowed out to the transport. Bligh took Susannah back to Government House, and left her alone as she stood on the lawns, with Robert in her arms, looking out to the cove. She heard the crash of the thirteen-gun salute for her father, and watched his broad pennant disappear round the headland.

Bligh, standing on the verandah behind her, gave her a few minutes after the ship passed out of sight and then walked over to her. 'Miss King,' he said, 'we must begin to teach your son the art of navigation. One cannot begin too young.' She liked the plain way he had called her Miss King since they first met, not fumbling around with a hesitant 'Mrs King' as many of the officers, and particularly their wives, thought it proper to do. He held out his arms for the child, and she gave it to him. He called out for Easty, and told him to make the boy a small yacht, a foot long, to sail on a pond. Jane made a red ensign to fly at the stern.

Bligh had been sent out with firm instructions to cleanse the colony of corruption and suppress the rum monopoly, and he did this with vigour. He tore up the licences of half the grog shops in Sydney and, when they were re-established elsewhere within a week, sent his sailors to impound the casks of rum. This was his duty, but it did not endear him to the New South Wales Corps, who owned the rum. The Corps officers transferred the ownership of the rum shanties to their mistresses, who set up

business afresh. Bligh's sailors called again, and this time stove
in the casks with marlin spikes. When the officers protested,
Bligh mildly pointed out that their women appeared to be
convicts on ticket-of-leave, which was so, and that convicts
could not by law traffic in rum. He wished to be clear in his
mind. They had themselves informed him that the rum was the
property of the women, had they not? The officers withdrew.
Bligh pulled down three brothels, walls, roofs, gilded mirrors
and all, but that was more a gesture than anything else. It was,
as he well saw, a trade that would thrive however many houses
he destroyed, and thereafter he left it alone. But with the rum
trade he was merciless and persistent. For a while the Corps
officers were reduced to living on their salaries.

'Which,' Bligh remarked to Sir Harry Browne Hayes, 'they
find an outrageous imposition. I say it is they who impose. I
would not pay them one-quarter of their salaries. They are the
sweepings of the British Army, and that is the sweepings of
sweepings.'

'Ah,' said Sir Harry, who had prospered and built himself a
house, and came to Bligh's dinners as he had come to King's,
'I was once a captain in the Cork militia, and I will not say
there was not a keg of French brandy for each man at Christmas,
washed up on the shore, unknown to the vigilance of the excise-
men, for there was a keg for them too, but we were not a
pestilence to the people.'

'Serpents,' said Bligh mildly, and this reminded him to ask
if Sir Harry's cargo of Irish peat had yet arrived from the bogs.

Sir Harry said it had. He had built his house in snake-
infested country, but had seemed unconcerned and done
nothing except order his cargo of peat. This had now arrived,
and he had encircled his house with a peat moat.

'And since then, not a brown snake has been seen, not so
much as an adder. It is the property of the peat to charm away
the snakes. It is a property well proven in Ireland.'

'There are no snakes in Ireland,' said Bligh.

'And doesn't that prove the property of the peat and its
undoubted efficacy? I have some left over, Captain Bligh, which
I should be glad for you to have. To build a moat against your
own serpents of the Corps.'

Bligh declined. He had other ways in mind.

For a week or so Bligh occupied himself ordering improvements to Government House. He prowled round the house with the government builder, the government mason, the government carpenter, and a foreman of works. At the end of the week he insisted on taking Susannah on a tour to show her what needed to be done.

'Wants new doors,' he said, 'new windows, window shutters, linings, and frames.'

Susannah thought the doors were still good enough. Perhaps if they were just repainted?

'New doors,' said Bligh. 'New shingling, flooring, whitewashing, plastering.'

Susannah made no further objection. She saw he was determined.

'In so rotten a state,' said Bligh, 'that the whole house wants being new.'

But after the repairs were done, Bligh returned to the colony's public affairs. He shot all the stray cur dogs, which was his undoubted duty, but unfortunately he shot Major Johnston's wolf-hound as well, by mistake. But he could also be marvellously bland. When there were protests, he replied that he was doing his duty in upholding the law, as, surely, all officers of the Corps would themselves wish to do?

One day John Macarthur called, and found Bligh in the gardens with Susannah, showing her son how to launch his toy yacht across the newly dug pond. Macarthur had come a long way in the world since King had sent him home to face court martial after the affair of the duel. In England delay had followed delay, and, when Macarthur resigned his commission, the impending court martial was forgotten and never held. Macarthur then turned everything to his advantage, and, presenting examples of undoubtedly fine merino wool from his sheep in New South Wales, he gained the interest of merchants, manufacturers, and the British government. It would be convenient if wool of such quality could be shipped from New South Wales rather than got with difficulty and expense from Spain. The Privy Council in London made him a grant of 5000 acres in the colony, to which he had recently returned.

The morning he appeared at Government House he wanted to talk about sheep, and to ask for fifty convicts as shepherds.

It was an entirely reasonable request, but Bligh knew that Major Johnston and his crew, deprived for the moment of the rum trade, were taking to farming and particularly to sheep, manipulating their way to a monopoly in mutton, leaving wool to Macarthur. On this understanding, Johnston and Macarthur were setting up sheep stations together. When Macarthur began to talk of sheep, Bligh found that his blandness had run its course. But at first he showed nothing. He walked on the lawns with his hands behind his back, and still kept his temper with Macarthur.

'You have royal sheep, I understand?'

Macarthur replied that he had been given fifty of the finest sheep from the royal flocks in England, and had brought them out. They were at present grazing his pastures. He asked for the convicts.

'Convicts? You have the king's sheep; why should you have his felons too? What have I to do with your sheep, sir? What have I to do with your cattle, which you have besides? Are you to have such flocks of sheep and such herds of cattle as no man ever had before? No, sir.'

Macarthur replied civilly that perhaps the Governor did not know he held his land by direct grant of the Privy Council. Furthermore he had been promised another 5000 acres if his first venture proved successful, and he hoped soon to ask the Governor for those extra acres. It was all to the benefit of the colony, which could become rich on wool.

Bligh took his hands from behind his back. 'I have heard of your concerns, sir. You have got five thousand acres of land in the finest situation in the country' – here he gesticulated violently towards the horizon where those lands lay – 'but you shan't keep them, let alone have another five thousand for the asking. By God, sir, you shan't keep them.'

Macarthur was still cool. He had his land by direct grant of the Privy Council, by direct order of the Secretary of State, and he presumed his right was indisputable.

By then Bligh's arms were flying about in full passion.

'Damn the Privy Council. And damn the Secretary of State, too. What have they to do with me? You have made a number of false representations respecting your wool, by which you obtained this land.'

'I beg you to come and see my sheep, sir. It is the finest wool.
If you will see them, I am sure your opinion will be that of the
Secretary of State.'

'Damn the Secretary of State. He commands at home. I
command here. And damn the Privy Council.'

Macarthur thanked the Governor for his patient understanding, and left.

Susannah could not help hearing all this.

In the afternoon, Bligh asked her to help choose two brooches
to send home to his wife. A jeweller from the town brought a
case of brooches to Government House, and it was laid on the
walnut table in the ball room. Together Bligh and Susannah
held the brooches in their hands, and up to the light, and when
they had found four they liked, two of silver and two of mother-
of-pearl, Susannah held them against herself so that Bligh could
see.

After a while, she said, 'No. My dress is white. Mrs Bligh, in
England, will not often wear white.' She sent Jane for a blue
silk shawl, and gave it to Bligh. He looked at it.

'Well,' she said, 'drape it round my shoulders. I will wear it
so that you shall see the brooches against it. That will be better.'

He put the shawl round her as he would have put it round a
daughter, and she pinned on the brooches one by one until they
found the two that most pleased Bligh. He had an emu's egg
which he was also sending to his wife, and insisted on packing it
himself, so that it should survive the voyage. Susannah watched
him as he made up the delicate package.

'Captain Bligh,' she said, 'in the town they are calling you
Caligula.'

He finished the package and sat opposite her. 'So I have
heard. And Major Johnston is putting it about that I propose
giving my horse a commission in the New South Wales Corps.
He is mistaken. I would not give my dog a commission in that
Corps. It is a dangerous militia.'

'I do not think all the officers are bad. Major Johnston and
Mr Macarthur did trouble my father very much. In his last
year here he aged five years on their account. I have no reason
to love them, but. . . .'

'My dear, but what? They are a parcel of damned rogues.'
Bligh was being very moderate. He would listen to Susannah.

If one of his own officers had said the same, he would have kicked the man down the steps of Government House.

'Mr Macarthur. . . .'

'What of Macarthur?'

'He will take your words to him this morning and spread them all over the town, and use them against you. And he will write to the Secretary of State.'

'Damn the Secretary of. . . .'

Susannah leaned forward and took his hand. 'Those words will be all over the colony by now. Mr Macarthur has a literal mind. But his wool is good. I have been told his wool is good.'

'Oh, I am sure the man is a hero of the fleece. A hero of the golden fleece. The Spaniards have an order of the golden fleece. a sort of knighthood. I once met a Spanish admiral at court, Don Faustino Espinosa de Urquijo y Bourbon if you please, who wore its emblem, a sheepskin, a sheepskin emblazoned on a medal. With feet attached.'

Susannah smiled at this picture of the decorated Spanish admiral.

'A sheepskin,' said Bligh, 'with head and feet attached. I shall have a medal struck for Macarthur, with head and feet attached.'

'Go and see his flocks,' said Susannah.

'Some day,' said Bligh. 'If you will come with me?'

She nodded.

'Caligula,' said Bligh. 'If they think I am Caligula they must delude themselves that this place is Rome.'

Two weeks later Macarthur was complaining bitterly to Johnston of the visit he had received from Bligh. 'When he moves it's like a great planet. Nothing less than his coach and four in waiting, six or eight light horsemen with a sergeant, three footmen outriders, and he himself riding in a small sulky with a canvas awning over him, and the side of this vehicle stuck around with pistols and a blunderbuss, so much is this great man afraid of his beauteous person.'

'And I hear old King's daughter was in company with him,' said Johnston.

'She was.'

'And the Frenchman's boy with her?'

'Also. And Bligh being sweetly civil. He is sometimes civil when she is with him. I cannot bear the man's civilities. He viewed my best merinos and "Oh," he says, and "Ah," he says, feeling the wool, and he could not have told if I was showing him a goat. And he lifted the boy to ride on a sheep, as if it was a side show.'

Major Johnston said little. That day Bligh had revoked with contumely no fewer than fifty-one liquor licences, impounded a stallion running loose which belonged to Johnston, and caused two dozen newly landed casks to be stove in. Over many months Bligh continued to be firm. He reprimanded his Judge Advocate for passing sentence of death while he was drunk with contraband rum. The Governor so frequently acted lawfully, and so persistently hacked at the concerted interests of rum, sheep, and a corrupt militia, that these interests finally found themselves obliged, of course for the greater common good, to go above the law and appeal to natural justice. Which meant that they took matters into their own hands and usurped the power of the Governor, persuading themselves that, unless they did so, insurrection and massacre would follow, so great was the people's loathing of Bligh.

This was nonsense, as even Johnston saw.

'God's teeth,' he said. 'What am I to do, Macarthur? Here are these fellows advising me to arrest the Governor.'

At which Macarthur sat on the barrel of a cannon in the square of Hyde Park barracks and concocted a petition in proper form, stating that the present alarming state of the colony, in which every man's property, life, and liberty was endangered, induced the inhabitants – whose signatures, he assured Johnston, could easily be procured later, when the deed was done – most earnestly to implore Major Johnston, as commander in chief of the Corps, instantly to place Governor Bligh under arrest, and to assume command of the colony.

Johnston hesitated. Macarthur took up the petition again, and added this sounding sentence: 'And we, His Majesty's loyal subjects in the colony of New South Wales, pledge ourselves, at a moment of less agitation, to come forward to support with our fortunes and our lives the actions taken in our name'.

And so, on 26 January 1808, the twentieth anniversary of the

colony's foundation, Major Johnston proclaimed martial law
and, asserting that he was acting to protect the civil order which
he was in fact about to overthrow, assembled his troops at the
barracks and gave them a little rum and then the order to
prime and load. The cannon on which Macarthur had sat to
draft the unanimous petition of the inhabitants, one of only two
field-pieces in the colony which would fire, was trained on
Government House.

Bligh, hearing the tumult and learning its cause, came from
his study, ordered a man to bring him a decanter of the best
Madeira, filled his own glass, and drank a toast to the portraits
of George III and Queen Charlotte. As he did so he heard the
whole body of troops marching from the barracks with bayonets
fixed and colours flying and the band playing 'The British
Grenadiers'. In five minutes 300 men surrounded the residence
and burst in, kicking down the doors. Bligh retreated upstairs.
It was half an hour later, and the whole house had been
ransacked, before he was found crouching under a feather bed,
something he always afterwards denied as reflecting on his
honour, explaining that it was his duty to escape in whatever
way he could. He was taken to the ball room, where he faced
his accusers with contempt.

'Johnston, I see troops stationed all round this room, like a
Robespierrean party, like a revolutionary tribunal.'

Johnston did not reply. Bligh stood facing him. He had put
on the full dress uniform of a naval captain, and was wearing
his Copenhagen medal. 'This is mutiny,' he said. 'The world
knows there was a mutiny on the *Bounty*, and the world knows
the consequences. Johnston, you are a dead man. This is
treason.' It probably was.

It is generally recorded that Bligh was arrested 'in the
company of an unnamed lady'. That phrase has often been used
against him, and very falsely. He may have been intemperate
in many things, but he was chaste. The unnamed lady was
Susannah, the daughter of his friend, almost his ward, and she
stood with her son Robert, then aged five, in the ball room with
Bligh, surrounded by bayonets.

# 12

# The Generous Heart of the Countess d'Estaing

Mme la comtesse d'Estaing had never seen the young boy Robert, and, living in Europe, never could have done, but she fervently wished to see him and had four times written to Susannah, each time asking that the boy might for a while be entrusted to her so that she could attend to part of his education, and to his establishment as a gentleman. To write from London to Sydney was in itself an adventure. The letter could miscarry. The ship bearing it might be wrecked, or stay revictualling at Cape Town for two months, or the reply might easily lie six months in Canton on the homeward passage while the master of the ship in which it was conveyed waited for a cargo, for to find a profitable cargo, of tea or silks, he would almost certainly have to sail home from Sydney by way of a Chinese port.

The Countess had been born Françoise Vouvray, in Rouen, the daughter of a substantial merchant, and it was she who had for so long lain on the conscience of Baudin. Hers was the wound that scarred his mind until Susannah, in the last months of his life, brought him peace, or something very close to peace. In his last days, feverish, a week out from Batavia and knowing in his heart that he would never see either woman again, he wrote not only to Susannah but also to Françoise. We have seen the letter to Susannah. It was written in the very hours of his death and was of love and gratitude. His letter to Françoise asked forgiveness from a woman he had not seen for years, and whom he believed to have greatly wronged him. He asked her forgiveness for having thought this, and for having told her – in a violence of despair, loss, and rejection – that she had ruined him.

She had been the occasion of his ruin, but he had brought it upon himself. He had known that for a long time. He also remembered her many acts of love towards him, which had been recalled to his mind by those of Susannah. Françoise had betrayed him? What he began to see, and with certainty, was that he had driven her to it, and he was ashamed.

He had met Françoise in his twenty-fifth year. She was a few years younger than he was, a Normandy woman, some of whose distant ancestors crossed to Hastings with the Conqueror. She was tall for a woman, almost Baudin's height. She was fair, and her eyes were Norman blue. Baudin was an officer of promise. He adored her. But he was rash. Because he could bear her absence no longer, simply so that he could meet and be with her when she returned with her father from a spring holiday of a month at Baden, he declined the offer of his first command because it would have demanded his immediate departure, certainly for many months. It was the offer of an extraordinary command, a first-rate ship of the line of one hundred guns. He was not an officer of birth, fortune, or even genius, just high talent. He had been a very young first lieutenant of a first-rate in the Caribbean, and his reputation as a navigator was already unquestioned. But the command of a first-rate was beyond his greatest hopes. Still, he did not think for a moment before doing what he did, though his refusal of so splendid an offer was tantamount to a resignation from the service, the more so since the offer came, indirectly, from the throne itself. Bougainville, who was Baudin's principal mentor, had the ear of the Minister, and the Minister had the ear of the King. When Louis XVI was told of the refusal he shrugged. Here was an officer whom great merit and greater luck had brought to his favour, and he chose to throw that favour away. Baudin was betrothed to Françoise. His rash act ended that betrothal. At first he made nothing of what he had done. His brother officers wondered at it, but he told them nothing. He told Françoise nothing, though she was distressed at his distraction. 'Do not ask me,' he said. 'Do *not* ask me.' When it became apparent that there were now no commands for him at all, and that he would very likely remain unemployed and on half pay for the rest of his life, he did tell her, in a passion of disappointment and rage at himself. When she tried to comfort him, and to blame herself, he railed at her. He did not recognize himself. One day, in tears of despondency, she at last defended herself, saying, 'I did not do it. I will not be harried for something I never wished and would never have asked,' and he hit her, something he had never done, something unthinkable to him, and disgraceful. When she shook this off, and still tried to rescue him from his despair, he shunned her in silence and resentment. They could no longer marry except on her money, his prospects being quite gone, and in his pride he railed at this too. She was faithful for a long time, for a year, but then she did a deed of self-preservation, and at last accepted the repeated offer of a young nobleman. Françoise still half-loved Baudin, but she had been pushed too far. No one could have endured more. She had hoped for Baudin's children. She became instead the mistress of M. le comte d'Estaing, a favourite of the King, a man who could open all the society of Paris to her, and of Versailles. At a brilliant court, at the brilliant last burning-out of the last court of the last French king before the Revolution, she shone.

Nevertheless, she was at first uneasy. There was even a time when, having returned from a visit with d'Estaing to the court of Venice – Venice also at the end of its glory and in its last years as a sovereign State – where d'Estaing had been sent by the King on a brief mission to the Doge, she wrote a note to Baudin saying simply, 'Memories and regrets,' and giving a time and place. Baudin came, listened to her oblique account of two months in Venice. She had been fêted. And yet. . . .

'What shall I do?' she said.

It was the moment of all moments which Baudin afterwards regretted. Why should his courage have deserted him? But what courage he had left was defeated by his pride. He could not begin to give her what the Count could: he could not offer her Venice. He was angry and humiliated. If he could have brought himself to say, 'Please come back,' she might have done. There were several times that evening when a single gesture might have changed both their lives, but both were too proud to make it.

The Count, who knew of this meeting, was a rational man. He did not want to lose Françoise. He had the sense and tolerance to wait, and to be kind to her. His feeling for her was real, and hers for him. She continued to be his mistress. Baudin took it badly.

And then one day, a year later, a cousin of hers came to him, Jeanne, whom he had met through Françoise. Jeanne knew their whole history. She came ostensibly to enquire about the memoirs of his travels, which she had heard he was writing. She knew a bookseller who published nautical books, and offered to help with an introduction. Baudin was touched by this. He had written very little, but he thanked her and looked strangely at her. She rose to go, and, as she did, she asked, 'You have heard the news of Françoise?'

'What is it?' he said. Something in the way she spoke made him afraid. He thought Françoise was ill.

'What is it?' he asked again.

'She married, yesterday.'

'D'Estaing?'

Jeanne did not reply. Baudin could only stand and look down. He never knew what his face showed.

An astrolabe is a representation, a model, of the heavens. The afternoon of the second day after he knew, Baudin stood in the shop of a marine instrument-maker near Nôtre Dame holding in his hands a planispheric astrolabe of brass engraved with the names of the days and months, and of the known planets. An astrolabe makes the grand assumption that the earth is the centre of a spherical universe, and with it a mariner could, after a fashion, navigate a ship. To hold, it is a thing of beauty. Its use is as a calculator. Set it to show the positions of the sun, or of the stars as they can be observed, and then make computations comprehensible only to a sailor or an astronomer, and it will reveal the length of day in any latitude. It will show when the sun will rise over Paris on a given day of the year, or at Madeira, or in the frozen latitudes of the North Cape. Perhaps the Greeks invented it in the second century before Christ. Since the fifteenth century the Portuguese had used it in more refined form as an aid on their voyages of discovery. It was never more than an aid. The instrument Baudin held in his hands was made in Paris as late as 1700, but it was even then archaic and by the last decade of the eighteenth century was no longer of any practical value. Baudin, in all his voyages, had never used one, though he knew its use, but now, in his distraction, he was consoling himself, hardly knowing what he was doing, with a representation of the heavens of which he knew very well neither the earth, nor any man, was the centre. The instrument-maker knew Baudin, to whom in previous years he had sold a sextant and many charts. That afternoon, Baudin held the universe in his hands for two hours. He stood motionless. He was offered wine, which he refused. Then he computed the time the sun rose on 1 December, over Rouen, the day he first met Françoise. He computed the hour of sunset two days later, the evening she became his mistress, and the hour of sunrise the next morning; he had woken before her and watched the day at first reveal and then illuminate her sleeping face. He calculated the position of Saturn in the heavens over Paris on the evening she asked him for the last time, 'What shall I do?' And he was overcome.

In the shop, the instrument-maker's boy lit more candles. Baudin looked up to see that it was dusk outside. He gave the astrolabe into the boy's hands and went out into the street. That night he left his lodgings. No one knew where he went. Two months later he found a merchantman at Havre which needed a first lieutenant, for the Caribbean. From there he drifted into the distant service of Austria, roaming the South Seas for botanical specimens, envious of the better fortune of others, contemptuous of himself for his envy, and loving his lost Françoise with a hopeless love.

So, at the last, it was to her also that he wrote, asking forgiveness, and telling her of Susannah – because, to the mind of the dying man, what had at last eased his soul would, he thought, solace Françoise too. When she received the letter she had a large enough heart to see this. By that time her husband was no longer an envoy of Louis XVI. That King had gone to the guillotine, and so had the Count. The Countess fled to exile in London. By the kindness of one of Baudin's brother officers, who commanded the French port where the *Géographe* and *Naturaliste* at last put in, and who knew nothing of Susannah but did know the history of Françoise and Baudin, Baudin's effects, because he had no close family, were transmitted to the Countess by a neutral ship. So was a letter from Sydney which

some months later came to that same port addressed to Baudin.
This was the letter in which Susannah told him that she was
carrying their child. The Countess made enquiries, and slowly
the news came to her that the child was a boy. The Countess
had no children of her own. When Governor King returned
from New South Wales in 1806 she called on him and learned
more. He could hardly do other than welcome any interest
which might help the son of his daughter, and the Countess,
though in exile, was still a woman of means. Susannah was
petitioned by her father, by the Countess, and, through her
father, by Bligh, to accede to the Countess's request. Would it
not be better for the child to go to England for a while; or,
better, would she not go there herself, taking the child with her?
Susannah declined every proposal. The Countess's reply to her
denials was always the same – that the offer remained open for
her to accept if she should ever wish to do so.

# 13

# From a Coalition of Bandits, a New Rome

On that evening of the mutiny, in the ball room of Government House, Bligh glared at Major Johnston and then motioned Susannah and her son to take seats at the long table behind which they had been standing. He took the Governor's chair himself.

'Now sir,' – he addressed Johnston – 'you have your bayonets. I see them, sir. You will need them to strike at me, because you shall have nothing from me except you take it by massacre and secret murder. But will you murder a woman? And a boy?'

Johnston nodded to his sergeant that the men should order arms, so that the bayonets no longer pointed at Bligh. 'In the name of the King . . .,' he began, but got no further.

'The King?' said Bligh. 'You have no King. You have put the King's protection away. You have a rebellion. You have your rum-rebellion. You will have your rum again, and your rum-shanties again, and an intolerable profit from felons whom you will then be enabled to flog for their intolerable drunkenness. In short, sir, you will soon have all your fortune again.'

Bligh looked around, recognizing those officers who were standing with Johnston. 'I shall remember you all, gentlemen. But where is the hero of the fleece? Where is Mr Macarthur? Abiding with his flocks, gentlemen; hiding behind sheepskins, gentlemen, and hiding behind you, gentlemen. Will you all hang for Macarthur's fine fleece?'

Neither Johnston nor any of his officers replied.

Bligh took from the table the Great Seal of the colony which had recently been sent out from England and received with much ceremony. On its face it showed convicts landing at Botany Bay. Their fetters were removed and they were welcomed by a female figure representing Industry sitting on a bale of goods with various attributes arranged around her – a distaff, a bee-hive, and a pick-axe. She was pointing with her right arm to a vista of ploughing oxen, rising habitations, and a church on a hill.

'There do appear,' said Bligh, 'to be no rum kegs on it. But take the Great Seal of New South Wales, sir, and hang it round your neck with its cord. You are a traitor and I will see you damned for it. But for the honour of the colony, I beg you to hang yourself first with the Great Seal.'

'You and the lady shall remain here,' said Johnston. 'But' – this to his adjutant – 'take the French boy and give him in charge of the orphanage.'

Susannah lifted her head and looked in the eyes of the man she had laughed at five years before at her father's table, when, half-drunk, he had railed against the French counterfeiter and insulted Baudin. 'No,' she said. 'Johnston, if you touch my son, I will have your eyes for it.' Those were the first words she spoke in the room. No one moved. The adjutant and the other officers knew her. Many of them were in the colony in her father's day. She had many times at Government House received them and their wives, or women not their wives, when the ladies of the naval garrison would not receive them. Some remembered Johnston's old hatred of Baudin. Not one would do anything so wretched as take Baudin's son.

'A rabble,' said Bligh, 'may make a mutiny and take a colony, and flog all the brutes in it, but it remains a rabble. Johnston, you already perceive the extent of your authority. Get out and govern, and live in fear of every British sail. Put your sentries and spy-glasses on the headland, and fear every report and every signal. You have taken the colony. Now you must govern.'

Bligh had risen from his chair and was gripping the edge of the table. 'Get out. Govern your colony. Govern. Govern.' He was shouting.

'Busy yourselves, gentlemen,' said Susannah, and it was she who dismissed them.

Johnston did govern. He declared that Bligh was under house arrest. He declared himself Lieutenant-Governor, an office to which he had no possible title, and posted up a reckless proclamation.

## SOLDIERS

Your conduct has endeared you to every well-disposed inhabitant in this settlement. Persevere in the same honourable path and you will establish the credit of the New South Wales Corps on a basis not to be shaken.

God Save the King.

By Command of His Honour the Lieutenant Governor.

This was nailed up all over the colony, and was the first that many well-disposed inhabitants knew of what had been done in their name. Johnston's soldiers, pursuing their honourable path, burned Bligh in effigy in the town and at outlying settlements. The government printer ran off caricatures of Bligh being dragged out from beneath a bed, smothered in feathers. Johnston, coming to a realization of what he had done, was uneasily writing confident despatches to London. They arrived at a time when the Secretary, who was in charge not only of colonies but also of the War Department, had graver things on his mind. Napoléon had invaded Spain. The Secretary cursed both Bligh and Johnston.

Bligh veiled the portraits of George III and his Queen with dark gauze, so that they should not see the infamy around them in the colony. He wrote copious despatches, and some of them reached London. When Johnston learned of these smuggled letters he took Bligh's writing paper from him. When Bligh still wrote on scraps of paper, he had the ink removed from Government House. He took Bligh's telescope from him. Despatches addressed to Bligh were intercepted. Only one letter and one box were allowed to reach him. The box came from his wife and children who sent him two coats and the material for making another, three pairs of silk stockings, a portrait of his daughter Fanny, and some Canton tea. The letter, which came in the early months of the next year, was addressed to Bligh and placed on him the duty of telling Susannah that her father was dead. He had died less than eighteen months after his return, not having received any preferment, pension, or reward. His estate in England had been sold for £7000, which was Susannah's. The letter was from a cousin, who said that, a few days before his death, King had again been approached by the Countess d'Estaing, and that he had intended once more to ask Susannah, with all the force at his command, to come back herself or, if she would not do that, to send the child for at least a few years to the Countess. That had been King's dearest wish, and his last.

Bligh asked Susannah to walk with him on the lawns, to tell her. An escort of two soldiers of the Corps, ordered by Johnston to follow Bligh everywhere at six paces distance, walked behind them and, when the Governor and Susannah sat in an arbour, stood as if mounting guard over them. Susannah knew Bligh well enough to realize he had something to say which touched her. She saw him glare at the two men and knew that in a moment he would shout at them to go to hell, and that would be useless. She told him to stay, and went up to the two men herself.

She knew one of them, though not by name. He made a half-gesture of salute. She spoke to him. The man said, 'We must keep in sight, ma'am, but we will go further off.'

The two men retired so that they could hear nothing, but only see. They saw that the Governor spoke for a moment. Susannah sat up and looked away. Then he spoke to her again. She sat motionless. They saw Bligh take one of her hands in his. Then she lowered her head on to his shoulder and wept. The soldiers looked down at the grass at their feet.

In the arbour, Susannah recovered herself. 'Captain Bligh,' she said, 'I have never asked you. Why did you come here?'

Bligh looked at her, and understood. She had to talk about anything but her father. So he answered her gently, and continued to talk, to take her mind off what she could not bear.

'Why did I come here?' he said. 'My daughters. Harriet, Mary, Elizabeth, Fanny, Jane, Ann. Six daughters on the half-pay of a captain? Now I shall be able to marry them off well. I was crossing Berkeley Square, on half pay, with no thought in my mind of the South Seas. And there I met the Secretary of the Navy, who proposed it to me. But if I had stayed at home that day; you see?'

'Six daughters and no sons?'

'There were two sons, twin sons. We were living in the Lambeth Road. A small house. They would have been fourteen a few days ago. I remember the date. They were christened before they died. William and Henry. It is strange to give a child your own name and know he will die within the hour. I shall have no more sons. The house was near the Archbishop's palace, and the church where they are buried lies under the palace walls. The grave is near the tomb of two king's gardeners, father and son, gardeners to Charles I. He was a monarch who lost his head; as I, my dear, may lose mine.

'Though I do not think so,' he said, shaking himself out of that fear. 'I do not think so.'

'And I do not think so,' said Susannah.

'After the interment,' said Bligh, his mind going back to the churchyard of St Mary, Lambeth, fourteen years before, 'I had to go to Plymouth, to do with some duty, and could not in any way keep my mind from my two dead boys, until I was desired by Mrs Netherton, who was a friend of many years, to stay with her and her family – we were eight or ten in the party – at her house on Exmoor. I do not remember exactly where, but it was a very good country house with two good parlours below and a drawing room upstairs, and good plain furniture, and a hundred and twenty acres around it and a very good garden which she managed as an amusement, and employed her mind, and kept her health. Our dinner was fish from their ponds, and ducks and green peas and vegetables from their farm. She talked about her daughter who was in London, whom she called a tigress. I preferred it all to any other conversation, and had not laughed since I left home, and before.'

Susannah listened. She could no longer remember an English country house.

'My dear,' said Bligh, 'you must go home. I urge it. A hundred and twenty acres and a country house make for a cheerful good living. I came here for my daughters. If you will not go home for yourself, you must for your son.'

Susannah did not reply, but nor did she forget what he said, or what her father wished.


Robert's sixth birthday was approaching, and Bligh made a great event of it. Susannah was aware of preparations going on but did not enquire, guessing that she too was meant to be surprised. The Domain servants had been left undisturbed by

Johnston, and she saw Jane and her husband George Bryant conferring busily the day before, and knew that Easty and Bligh spent a whole afternoon together in the library, after which Easty emerged with a casual air intended to demonstrate that nothing unusual had been discussed. She noticed that Bligh's full dress uniform, which he had not worn since the night of the insurrection, was taken out by his servant and vigorously brushed, and the buttons polished.

On the day, Bligh appeared in uniform, Easty in his old regimentals, and Bryant in the borrowed clothes of a coxswain, carrying a great number of tiny ships which he had spent the previous two weeks carving in pinewood. Jane made the sails. Bryant's blue cloak, with its silk lining ruffled to represent the swell of a moderate sea, was spread out on the walnut table and most of the ships arranged upon it. Bligh supervised everything. When he gave the signal, Jane entered the room bringing Robert. He wore the tiny uniform of a midshipman, which Jane had also run up.

'Now,' said Bligh to the boy, 'you are six, and, since you will one day be a naval officer of the first water, no time can be too early for you to hear the tale of a naval commander who gained the entire admiration of the whole world.'

'Was it you, sir?' asked the boy.

'As good a man as me.'

And Bligh, with the assistance of Bryant and Easty, then demonstrated not the battle of Copenhagen, in which he had played a part, nor even the battle of Trafalgar which had assured the Royal Navy its mastery of the northern seas, but an action in the Indian Ocean in the year 1804.

'Canton,' said Bligh. 'And a fleet of East Indiamen are in convoy, sailing for England with a cargo of tea, silk, spices, and other rich merchandise.'

The sixteen East Indiamen were arranged on the cloak in line abreast.

'And with them sailed fourteen other merchant ships, and a brig.'

These too were put in place behind the Indiamen.

'Now,' said Bligh, 'there was in Île de France, across the wide Indian Ocean, far to the west, many weeks' sailing, a French fleet of five ships-of-the-line, splendid vessels, under Admiral

Linois, a bold Frenchman, who flew his flag in the *Marengo*, seventy-four guns.'

The five French vessels were placed on the table, but well over the horizon of the blue cloak.

'The French admiral had notice, how I never knew but he had notice, that the Indiamen would be in that Ocean. The fleets converged. The Frenchmen came near.'

The French ships-of-the-line were disposed on the cloak, facing the English fleet.

'But there are only five French ships,' said the boy.

'But five ships-of-the-line. Any one could destroy those merchantmen one by one. The Indiamen carried cannon, but only against pirates, not against a ship of war. But the French admiral did not attack. He hesitated. He was puzzled.'

'Why was he puzzled?'

'Because he had been told to expect sixteen Indiamen, not a fleet of more than thirty craft. And because the commander of the Indiamen was a very great sailor.'

'Like you?'

'Well now, the English commander was Captain Dance, and he knew that if he ran, his fleet would be torn to splinters. Or he could strike his flag to the French admiral, and surrender his fleet, and Napoléon would have all that tea, and all those silks, and all that was in those ships. But he did not run, and he did not strike his flag. Before he left Canton the Indiamen had been new painted with white bands on the black hulls, so that from a distance they could be taken for men o'war, and Captain Dance had wooden cannon made, and when he saw the French fleet he turned the sixteen Indiamen broadside on to the French, as if to protect the merchantmen behind him, and then ran his wooden cannons up to the gun-ports, and made many signals as if for a battle. And he waited. And the French admiral waited. And Dance ran up the red ensign, the flag of a King's ship, a man o'war, and waited, and still the French admiral did nothing, but hove to.'

On the cloak the French ships hove to.

'And all that night they waited, and Captain Dance lit blue fires on the decks of his Indiamen to keep them plainly in sight of the French all night.'

'What happened? What happened?'

'Come the dawn,' said Bligh, 'and the French admiral in the *Marengo*, ashamed as well he might be of his timidity, slowly approached and fired one bowshot. At which the Indiamen commenced a cannonade with every gun they had. They had nothing that could touch or scratch *Marengo*, nothing that could even reach *Marengo*, and not a shot grazed *Marengo*, but a vast deal of smoke was made and a vast deal of noise, and the Frenchman fled and took his five ships-of-the-line with him, and never did they stop running until they came back to Île de France.'

The French ships ran across the walnut table and fell over the edge.

'And what did the English ships do?'

'Made a good passage to England, and Captain Dance was given a dinner by the Lord Mayor of London and a knighthood by the King. And Napoléon could hear the laughter floating over from the white cliffs of Dover.'

'Will the King knight you too, sir?'

Bligh grunted. 'And the great thing, apart from the dinner and the knighthood and Napoléon raging, was this. If the French admiral had attacked he could have taken not only those ships but also, if he chose, the port of Sydney and the whole colony of New South Wales.'

At this moment the door of the ball room opened and the Domain blacksmith was conducted in, carrying a miniature sword and scabbard which he handed to Bligh, who drew the sword.

'Hold out your hands flat,' he told the boy, 'because the steel is sharp.' He gave the sword to Robert. It was inscribed, 'Robert King, midshipman, on his entering the King's service.' Glasses were filled and Susannah, with Bligh and the servants, toasted her son.

That night Susannah lay in bed very troubled. The day Bligh told her of her father's death, he had tried to comfort her by talking about the peace of mind he once found, in a grief of his own, in an English country house. He had urged her to go back. But her father's death had removed the last possible reason for her return. Then she thought of the day just passed, her son's birthday, when she had appeared gay. But she alone

in the house that day knew two things which no one else
guessed at.

First, her son's birthday was also the anniversary of Baudin's
death. Only she and her father had known that. She had never
even told Jane, and the others, though they well remembered
when news of Baudin's death reached Sydney, had never known
the day he died. He had died at sea. That was all they knew.
So the day just gone had been, for her, also a day to remember
Nicolas more especially than any other day. He had died, six
years before, many thousand miles away.

Then there was the second thing which no one else knew, and
the fact that they did not know said a great deal about the
nature of the matter. Redmond, the surgeon, had been sometimes with her. The visits of a surgeon to the Governor's house
went unnoticed. Perhaps the child had a cough. Perhaps Bligh
had a twinge of gout. Redmond had attracted no attention to
himself by expressing opinions for Bligh or against him. He
seemed interested only in his own prosperity, and he had
prospered. Susannah had not noticed his visits, though she
supposed, when she came to ask herself, that he had over the
past year come at least once a week. On one visit he asked her to
marry him.

There had been nothing in their conduct which was intimate,
not a word or a touch. He was present at the birth of her son,
but that was as a physician. She still thought of him as her
physician, not even as a close friend. She was unaware of
Redmond as a man. So when he asked, she felt only surprise at
a proposal unforeseen and unlooked-for. She did not reply
immediately. She was wondering how on earth the words could
have been spoken to her. He took her silence to mean that she
was considering her answer. Then she said, 'No, Mr Redmond.
How could it be?' But as she said this she saw that he thought
it could very well be, and that he hoped it might be. So she tried
to soften her refusal, which in her mind was complete, by
repeating the word 'No,' but this time more quietly. Then
she left him. That was before her father's death. And then,
on the morning of Robert's birthday, he brought a gift for
the child and proposed again. He could not have chosen
a worse time to ask her than the anniversary of Baudin's
death, and she said, 'Mr Redmond, never.' But she did not

speak vehemently. He could not stir her even to an emphatic rejection.

The despatches Johnston received from London were icily formal. He received no word of commendation for having, as he never ceased to inform the Secretary, restored and maintained a perfect order among His Majesty's subjects. He began to doubt, and resolved to get rid of Bligh, whose continued presence in the colony served only as a reminder to the inhabitants of his deposition, which appeared more and more clearly to have been a mutiny. He tried to ship him out on a transport. Bligh refused to go except in command of his own ship, the *Porpoise*, which had brought him out and remained with him at Sydney. Johnston hesitated, but then restored to Bligh the command of the ship, stipulating only that he should sign a paper undertaking to return immediately to England. Bligh signed. Johnston accepted the word of an officer and a gentleman. The ship was Bligh's.

'And will you go?' asked Susannah.

'Finesse, finesse,' exclaimed Bligh. She was no wiser. She was not sure of Bligh's finesse. She did not know what the word meant when it was pronounced in such exultant tones. Then he said that, whatever the appearances to the contrary, he was not deserting her and she would see him again after not many months.

He was animated. He buckled on his sword, kissed her cheek, and stepped briskly into his carriage. 'Finesse,' he called out once again, and then drove off. Why did she feel betrayed? She waited until Bligh's cutter put out from the jetty and then walked slowly towards the old orangery to watch his ship weigh anchor and depart. It was very hot, and at mid-day the sun shone directly down. She did not see the ship leave the cove because, for the first time in her life, she fainted.

When she regained consciousness the first thing she saw was the orangery. She had not entered it. It had not been entered for many years, since it had been hers and Baudin's. At first she did not recognize it. When she did, the beginning of a tear formed in her eyes, and she turned her head away. She was lying on a bench in the shade. She saw the figure of Redmond

standing watching her. He said, 'It is nothing. The sun. You
fell on the grass. Bryant brought you here and called me.'

He came over, took her pulse, and nodded. Then he withdrew again. He did not comfort her, as any man might have
done, by sitting beside her, or brushing her hair from her face.
He did not in any way touch her. But he was solicitous towards
her. He took off his coat and folded it for a pillow for her head,
but motioned Jane, who was hovering, to put it in place. He
was distant, and yet she was glad of his presence.

'Captain Bligh?' she said.

Redmond glanced back at the cove. 'The ship has gone. Lie
back for a few more moments. It is nothing. The sun.'

And it was nothing. In an hour she was herself again, but she
was not herself again. For the first time in her life she was alone,
except for her child. But even a much-loved child does not give
that company of an equal spirit which was life to Susannah. She
possessed a fierce inner spirit, but on its own it would wither.
Baudin had been an equal spirit. Her father had been an equal
spirit, and so, she now saw, was Bligh with his extravagances
and tendernesses. Now there was her son, whom she loved, and
Jane, whom she liked. But she was alone. She was not a woman
who could easily be alone. She could not remain for ever her
lover's widow.

A week or so later, Redmond suggested to Susannah that they
should take drives round the settlement. She first declined, but
then agreed. One day was happier than the others. Redmond
took her into town to inspect the shop of Mr Lane, which had
recently received by the arrival of the *Miranda*, out of Boston, a
shipment of clocks and fine time-keepers; an elegant assortment
of plain gold, pearl, topaz, and fancy spangled neck chains,
breast pins, and enamelled crosses; and a variety of children's
games and toys. She refused a topaz for herself, but accepted a
child's card-game for Robert, in which the cards bore the likenesses of Bonaparte, George III, Nelson, and the French
marshals. It was a game which, when played out, always ended
in an English victory. Mr Lane had also received by the same
ship a stock of English cotton prints, calico, checks, and muslins.
She spent half an hour among the fragrances and textures of the
new cloths, and ordered a length of calico to be delivered to the
house. When they drove back, the wind had got up a little so

that she had to hold on to her hat, and a warm breeze moved the
fabric of her dress against her body. She could not remember
when she had last been conscious of such a sensation. It had
become something she no longer noticed. Redmond had not
once in their acquaintance called her Susannah, not even so
much as offered to take her hand. That afternoon he asked her
again to be his wife. She shook her head slowly but smiled at
him. There was a steadiness about Redmond, and this ordinary
virtue spoke quietly in his favour. Had he been more a lover,
had there been any instant rapport between them, he would
have been less acceptable, as resembling Baudin. That
would have been unthinkable. He bowed, a formality he
still used with her, and said the afternoon was one he would
remember.


The nature of Bligh's finesse was not at first clear. He had
remained for several days outside the harbour. It became likely
that he was not intending to sail for England. Then he made
towards Hobart, tried to raise the garrison there against
Johnston, and ordered the Lieutenant-Governor of Tasmania
to print a proclamation denouncing the usurping serpents of
Sydney. His order was not refused, but, just as the ink had been
removed from Government House in Sydney when Bligh began
to scatter denunciatory despatches, so in Hobart, when he
demanded the proclamation, all printing ink disappeared from
the government print-shop. In Sydney, Johnston denounced
Bligh as having broken the solemn word of an officer, though
he would not say gentleman.

Then, just when Bligh was at his weakest, when he was
aimlessly floundering around in the seas off Hobart, pacing his
quarterdeck, declaring that he was outlawed, Johnston lost his
nerve. He lost it very suddenly, one morning, when he happened
to pass *The Major Johnston*, a grog-house named in his honour
a week after the mutiny. The publican had erected a flattering
sign outside, showing Johnston in full regimentals with a fear-
some snake impaled on his sword, and a figure, vaguely
resembling Britannia, with her arms raised as if in benediction
of the noble saviour of New South Wales. Now the sign had
gone. He had the publican brought out and asked him why.

'Blown down in a gale, sir,' said the man.

Johnston could recall no recent gale. The truth was that the publican was a shrewd politician. The inn sign had been chopped up for firewood. Johnston looked hard at the man, and ordered his licence to be revoked. It was his last official act in the colony. Next day Johnston, taking Macarthur with him, sailed for England. They said it was to vindicate themselves, but really it was to escape what might be a sharper form of justice if a British squadron appeared over the horizon and they were obliged to stand trial in the colony. This was understood by everyone.

Johnston had lost his nerve just in time. Only days later, the force from England arrived – an infantry regiment commanded by Lachlan Macquarie, the oldest Lieutenant-Colonel in the British Army, who came bringing orders which should have amused him. But he had been born a Scots laird, and was a serious man. He anchored in the cove and waited. There was a scurrying back and forth of cutters as the remaining mutinous officers in Sydney sent their respects, and informed him, in reply to his questions, that Governor Bligh was no longer in the colony, and neither was Johnston. He received their answers grimly. They smiled uneasily and set about arranging a triumphal welcome for him, when he should come ashore.

At ten o'clock in the morning on the first day of 1810 Macquarie landed with the officers and men of the 73rd of Foot, who stood at attention in drilled rows, shining and sweating. The ragged troops of the New South Wales Corps fired three ragged volleys in salute and then, at the order of their officers, gave three ragged cheers. Then there was silence. The eyes of all men of the Corps were on Macquarie, and so were those of the respectable residents of the colony who had so lately signed their names to the petition against Bligh which now seemed, in the presence of the drawn up ranks of the 73rd of Foot, plain treason.

Macquarie let his glance move over the Corps, the settlers, and the felons assembled to greet him. He nodded to his sergeant major, and the bugles, trumpets, drums, and pipes of the regimental band played 'God Save the King'.

Macquarie summoned the senior officer of the New South Wales Corps.

'Is Governor Bligh returned and in residence at Government House?'

'No, sir.'

Macquarie unrolled a paper and in a quiet voice – so that the silence was deeper as they all strained to hear him, and the words carried to every man – began to read a proclamation expressing His Majesty's utmost regret and displeasure at the tumultuous proceedings in the colony and the mutinous conduct of certain persons, appointing Macquarie his representative, and commanding and requiring him to reinstate William Bligh, Esquire, in the office and situation of Captain General and Governor-in-Chief.

Macquarie paused, as if waiting for Bligh to appear. He did not. The officers of the Corps were at that moment miserably considering the prospect, which now seemed a certainty, of their own courts martial, and wondering how summary those courts martial would be.

Macquarie continued to read:

'His Majesty, through his gracious anxiety for the welfare and happiness of his loyal subjects of New South Wales, and for the complete restoration of quiet and harmony, and to remove every motive for future disturbance, has also been graciously pleased to direct me to signify to the said William Bligh, Esquire, that he should at the expiration of twenty-four hours after being so reinstated, receive us, Lachlan Macquarie, in the office and situation of Captain General and Governor-in-Chief.'

His Majesty's loyal subjects there assembled would have laughed if they dared. Bligh restored for one day! One man did laugh, but he was Irish, and he had the Celtic good sense to cut his laughter short.

Macquarie waited for silence, said he lamented extremely that Governor Bligh was not there, and proclaimed himself Governor there and then. A tactful sergeant of the New South Wales Corps stirred his men into another ragged cheer, and the gunner lieutenant fired off a salute of fifteen guns, enough for an admiral.

That night there were fireworks. Macquarie barely glanced at them through the library window.

'Miss King,' he said, 'I had thought you would be returning to England.'

'No, Colonel Macquarie.'

He was not sure how to treat this extraordinary woman. She had for months been the only occupant of Government House. She had lived there, through the governorships of her father and Bligh, for nine years now. He would anyway have treated her with courtesy as an Englishwoman of his own rank and as the daughter of a predecessor, but there was more than that, which he did not quite understand. When the Secretary of State in London gave him his commission as Governor he remarked, by the way, that the Prince Regent had signified that he would wish all consideration to be extended to the daughter of the late Governor King. She was believed still to be in residence in the colony and perhaps at Government House. The Colonel waited for an explanation, but the Secretary said nothing more. This was because he knew nothing more. It was not for either man to question the reasons of the Prince Regent. What neither could know was that the Prince Regent knew nothing either, but was passing on a request of his father George III, who was now ill and often mad. The old King remembered his conversation of long ago with a young lieutenant whom he afterwards made Governor, and he remembered the man had a daughter who had stayed in Sydney. George III was by nature kind. So he said to his son, 'I knew the man. I did not know that he died without a pension, almost in want. We talked of Virginia. He had a daughter. If you please, look to the girl.'

So when Macquarie met Susannah he was uncertain. He imagined that for some reason she enjoyed the Prince Regent's favour. He discovered she had a son. He assumed she would be going home, and was ready to offer her a return passage in what had been his own quarters aboard the ship that brought him out. It had not crossed his mind that she would stay.

She would have stayed in any case, but there was now one more reason for her to do so. Three days before, after many months of Bligh's absence, and after many months alone, she had at last agreed to marry Redmond. 'Yes,' she said, 'but not yet.' She would keep her word. Her pride, if nothing else, would ensure that. She told Macquarie she would remain, and marry. He asked after her fiancé, and she told him.

'But, ma'am, will you form an alliance with a man who came here as a felon?'

'He was soon pardoned, and my father always said that when a man was freed, he became a free man. Colonel Macquarie, most of the men in the colony who know any law, all the police, and the government printer, were convicts. Mr Redmond has been the Governor's surgeon for many years.'

Macquarie nevertheless made discreet enquiries. He was told that Redmond was a fair surgeon, but unlikely to achieve any distinction in the colony. His advisers were mistaken. Redmond would achieve great things, and his acquisition of Susannah was only the first of them.

But perhaps Miss King was in Macquarie's mind when he made a speech the following day exhorting the upper ranks of society to hold out a pattern of good conduct to the lower orders. As to those lower orders, he pardoned seventeen convicts, issued to every soldier and felon an extra ration of seven pounds of beef and six ounces of sugar, and recommended regular attendance at divine service. A clergyman, one of those respectable inhabitants who had signed petitions in favour of Johnston, greeted Macquarie with a sermon on the text of Samuel I, chapter xvi, verse 12 – 'Arise, anoint him, for this is he.' The remaining officers of the New South Wales Corps were quietly informed that there would be no courts martial, though their men would be sent home. Peace descended. Then Bligh returned.

'Error, folly, profligacy, irregularity,' he expostulated, accompanying his words with much action of the arms.

Macquarie mildly offered him an honour guard of a sergeant, a corporal, and six privates, and ordered that at his appearance all sentinels should present arms and all drums beat a march.

'Infamous mutiny. Outrageous convulsion.'

Macquarie offered him an immediate passage home, assuring him that on his departure no single circumstance would be omitted that could convey the respect entertained for him by all ranks of Sydney society.

'Then, sir,' raged Bligh, 'I see I have no other resource but my patience.'

A farewell dinner, which Macquarie had been hoping to arrange for some time, was given for the departing Governor. A hundred guests sat down at table. Sideboards were covered with wine, fruit, and delicacies. Bligh was despatched with a banquet, fireworks, loyal airs from the band of the 73rd, great ceremony, and the greatest relief.

The Attorney General, in a farewell speech, declared that the polished nations of the world should not look with contempt upon a new colony whose enterprise was not, as was theirs, debilitated by the indolence of apathy and refinement. ('Hear, hear' and applause.) Looking into the future, he beheld the southern continent, superlative in arms as in the arts, giving laws to the world and regarding with proud superiority the effete nations of the northern hemisphere. 'In this loyal city of Sydney,' he said, addressing a gathering largely composed of lately mutinous officers and magistrates, while the pigs sniffed round in the streets outside, and 4000 convicts in the jails shifted in their rags or in their chains, 'in this great city I behold arising, from a coalition of bandits, a new Rome.'

They danced until three. At noon Bligh sailed for England. Susannah, her son, and the man who would soon be her husband, remained in their new-found Rome.

# PART TWO

# 14

# Robert Goes to Europe

In Europe, after Jena and Austerlitz, there seemed no battle
Napoléon could not win; and after Vienna, Rome, Madrid,
and Warsaw, no city he could not take. They were grave times,
so that in London the court martial at Chelsea Barracks of a
colonial major for overthrowing a colonial governor would
hardly have been noticed, except that the governor was Bligh,
and if ever there was a man who could put Napoléon out of
men's minds for a few days it was Bligh. His evidence against
the major lived up to the expectations of all. He fumed,
complained bitterly that he had been burned in effigy (laughter),
vigorously repudiated the very idea that he had been found
lurking under a feather bed (laughter), and insisted, as further
evidence of the villainy of the usurpers, that lampoons of him
had been published at the Government Printing Office in
Sydney (laughter) showing him in his shirt tails (loud laughter).
Here the officers of the court smiled too, but they found Major
Johnston guilty of mutiny and ordered him to be cashiered,
dismissed the service. The Prince Regent, who as commander-
in-chief had to confirm the sentence, thought it inadequate to
the enormity of the crime. He considered Johnston ought to
have been tried for treason, and had to be persuaded that the
law would not allow this, since the events had taken place not
in England but in New South Wales.

'A nonsense,' declared the Prince Regent. 'Even New South
Wales ought to be subject to the King's Peace. The Lord
Chancellor of England told him respectfully that it was not.'

'No, neither in law nor in fact,' retorted Bligh, when he was told of this. He felt himself hard done by, and was appeased only when he was promoted Rear Admiral of the Blue, with the pay of that rank back-dated six months, the date of his arrival in England. He was surprised to find how distant New South Wales came to seem even to him. As for the Government and its Secretaries of State, they were concerned with far greater things, and not only with Napoléon. The United States, tired of having its ships stopped at sea and its sailors impressed into the Royal Navy, declared war on England. 'Rebels everywhere,' roared Bligh, and wanted to burn New York, but no one at the Admiralty listened to him and he was forced to explain his grand strategy at home to his daughters and to his beloved wife Betsy. He was exalted when the British did burn the White House at Washington, but loudly deplored the order sent by the Admiralty to all English frigates on no account to engage single-handed the American frigate *Constitution*, which had already sunk two British ships.

Susannah's world, in Sydney, was very remote. Bennelong, not having been seen for many months, crept back one day from the bush badly beaten and old, and died in his hut on the Domain. She remembered the first time she saw him, making legs in London when she was a girl of twelve. Susannah's maid and friend Jane Bryant gave birth to a daughter, Mary, and Susannah rejoiced for her. Susannah herself, after two years of marriage to Redmond, and at about the time Napoléon was at last in retreat, from Moscow, gave birth to a son, John, and Redmond, when he first saw the baby, kissed his wife warmly on the cheek and thanked her. Her son Robert was now nine years old. She was more in his company than in her husband's.

And at about this time the new governor bought 100,000 Spanish dollars and put them into circulation in the colony. To make 200,000 coins of them, he had the middles punched out. The centres were called dump dollars, and the outer rings, with the hole in them, holey dollars. They supplemented, but did not immediately replace, the assortment of Venetian ducats, Indian rupees, South American moidores, French crowns, and English guineas, and the odd silver coins brought in by sailors from all the ports of the world, which had previously been the colony's only currency. Convicts had been thought not to need coins, and, while they were in the chain gangs, they did not. But by now many were emancipists, having served their sentences. Settlers too were coming, though at first very few. A currency was needed, and apart from the rag-tag of odd coins, that currency had become rum. Now there were dollars. Spanish dollars were thought not to be quite the same thing as pounds sterling, but this coinage of a dying civilization was as internationally accepted as sterling later became. Anyway, in early New South Wales the words *sterling* and *currency* were not generally used in any ordinary sense. Currency was the name given to those children born in the colony, almost all of convict parents, and there was by now a whole new generation of such children. Those free settlers born in England, who had come out of their own accord, called themselves Sterling. The Sterling liked also to be known as Exclusives. These rancorous divisions, between Currency and Sterling, Emancipists and Exclusives, haunted Australia for decades.

Sir Harry Browne Hayes came to visit Susannah after the birth of her son. He picked up the baby, patted it, rocked it, sang to it until it cried, sang to it again until it stopped crying, and then gave it back to Susannah and turned to Robert, with whom he conversed as if with a grown-up. Susannah gave the new baby to her nurse, and then she, Sir Harry, and Robert, walked in the gardens.

'My neighbours,' he said, 'have taken to calling themselves the Ancients. I called on them the other day.'

'The ancient what?' asked Robert.

'The Ancient Nobility of Botany Bay.'

'How ancient is that?' asked Robert.

'Not really so ancient as me even,' he told the boy, and then went on, to Susannah. 'Perhaps you know the people. The man ran a day-school in England, never prospered, never made a living, came out here, failed once more at the teaching of children, and turned to raising sheep instead – many sheep, with convicts to do all the work, and so he got a fortune.'

Many families had done this. Susannah thought she might have heard of them, but was not sure.

'Their daughter;' said Sir Harry, 'getting married. They put a notice in the *Gazette*. . . .'

'Ah.' Susannah remembered. It was not then the custom to advertise engagements. The notice had been smiled at.

'Now you remember,' said Sir Harry. 'And what should the notice say, do you recall, but that a marriage in "high life" was soon to take place. Well, they're my neighbours, and out of neighbourly kindness – and I can see you're thinking neighbourly curiosity too, and I won't say you're wrong – well, I called to offer my congratulations. The girl's marrying an attorney who came out from England a year past. A fair match, so I offered the family my civil congratulations, and what did the girl's mother reply? What did she say? "I assure you," says she, "I don't feel complimented a bit by my daughter's marrying such a one as an attorney. I endeavour to bring up my family with different ideas, to give them a proper notion of their rank and consequence in society here, for I consider my family and a few others to be quite the same as if you were to speak of the Ancient Nobility of England, the Dukes of Bedford and Devonshire and Norfolk and so on." So she said.'

'That,' said Susannah, 'is a tale improved by you in the telling.'

'Susannah, I improve it very little. A little, but very little. A natural little. And really, what could I, a poor knight and an Irish one at that, say to all that ancient nobility? And I do believe she did not wish to receive my congratulations, poor as they might be, nor to receive me neither.'

'Ah,' said Susannah, 'how can you be received into high life, having received a free passage here, at His Majesty's expense?'

'I was thinking that would be it. I do not,' said Sir Harry, looking down at himself, 'appear to belong to high life. It must be that I dress too plain.' He was wearing striped trousers, a flared blue jacket with brass buttons, and two conspicuous watches dangling at the ends of two chains. The first did not keep time at all, though it chimed the hours, or mischimed them, striking twelve several times a day. The second, which he had only lately taken to wearing, was set at Cork time, ten and a half hours behind Sydney time, so that, he said, he should not forget time past.

'And what,' said Susannah, 'was *she* wearing?'

'Oh, a gown, a high-life gown, a brocaded gown, and all in the heat of the day.'

He did not tell Susannah that afterwards, in a conversation which he had cut short, the woman asked familiarly about

Susannah, whom she did not know at all, and after Robert, calling him the French boy.

Susannah knew some of the more respectable settlers called him that, but she did not care what they thought. Redmond knew too, but he did care. He was becoming a big man in the colony, and minded what was said. He had almost entirely given up his medical practice and taken to sheep-farming, which was one reason why he saw little of Susannah. He spent days at a time on his sheep station. He saw even less of Robert, but always treated the boy well, and tried to play the part of a father. And to Susannah he was a kind husband, in the sense that he was not unkind. They never quarrelled. Now they had a child of their own. Their marriage looked ordinary enough, and ordinary is what it was. It was a marriage which, apart from the new baby, was quite without event. Susannah would not have allowed herself to be seen unhappy, and would not have admitted even to herself that she was. But her days did not flower as they had flowered before. She never spoke of this to anyone, but Jane saw it, Sir Harry saw it, and anyone who knew her at all saw the change in her.

Susannah and Redmond lived in a house on the edge of the Domain which Governor Macquarie, remembering the oblique advice offered him before he left England to do all he could for the daughter of Governor King, had given to her for her use, without rent. So the house was Susannah's, held by the Governor's grace and favour. Redmond was most conscious that it was her house and not his. The income deriving from her father's estate went to Redmond on their marriage, as was the law, but the house was held by her and not him. This is something difficult for any man's pride to take. It was also difficult that their dinner parties were hers. He liked to entertain the more prosperous settlers, and to please him she asked them. He did not like to be seen in the company of Harry Hayes and therefore, again to please her husband, Susannah rarely asked Sir Harry to dinner, though they remained fast friends and he often came to see her in the daytimes when Redmond was away. But Redmond knew that without Susannah he could never have entertained some of those who did dine at his table. He could never have presumed to ask the Governor and his wife: Susannah could and did. He knew the officers of

the naval garrison came because of Susannah. He knew that
though they were in name his dinner parties, they were given
in her dining room, in her house, in her way. She did nothing
to make him feel this: she was loyal to him in that sense as in
any other. But everything was done in her way. She was not
extravagant, though she was to his mind over-generous and
careless of cost, and once or twice he hinted as much. She
replied that she never thought of it, and that of course was what
he meant.

The affair of the candles was a tiny incident. It was an
ordinary dinner party, and, as usual, after the roast, the servants
changed the candles before they had half burned down, taking
the candelabra from the table and immediately replacing them
with others in which burned tall, new candles.

'What happened to the old candles?' he asked afterwards.
She supposed the servants had them. She never enquired. 'But
why change them at all?' he said.

'Shadows,' she replied.

'What shadows?'

Susannah was faced with having to explain something that
had been second nature for so many years that to put it into
words was not easy.

'Oh, William,' she said, 'it is just candles. Let me do it as
I always have, and leave it at that.'

He insisted.

So she explained about shadows. It did not matter to him,
she said, and it hardly mattered to her, or to any young
woman. But some of their guests were not young, and then it
did matter.

'How?'

She walked over to the table, picked up a five-branched
candelabrum, and showed him. If the candles were long, then
the light fell from above on the forehead and hair and face of a
woman sitting down. That was a warmer and softer light,
gentler. If the candles burned down as far as half way, then
they were at eye-level, which was too direct a light. If the
candles burned low, then the light came from below, shadowing
and hardening the line of the chin and flickering in the wrinkles
of the neck.

'And so,' she said, 'I shall change the candles.'

He was a little graceless about this. She affected not to notice.
She continued to entertain his guests and hers. At these gatherings, most of her friends called her Susannah, but Redmond
always addressed her as Mrs Redmond.

Their first real crisis came because Sir Harry Hayes had a
fine daughter back in the old country, and because Redmond
heard Susannah laugh.

Sir Harry was going home to Ireland at last, and of course
he came to tell Susannah and to make farewell gifts to her and
to Robert.

'Now my daughter,' he said, 'is beautiful, and though that is
by her own account, by what she has achieved she surely must
be so. It was at Carlton House in London, where the Prince
Regent was holding a great ball, adding to his own and the
national debt, at Carlton House as I say – though it may have
been at Kensington Palace – but wherever it was. . . .'

'But you said your daughter wrote and told you?'

'She wrote twice, lest one letter should miscarry, though both
letters came by the same ship. And in one letter it was
Kensington Palace and in the other Carlton House, the very
same ball. When I saw her last she was a little girl, but even
then she had a rich memory, a various recollection. Not a
narrow remembering. She gave a man a choice. A man could
select from what she said and believe what most pleased him.
So then in London she saw the Prince, danced with the Prince,
and, being a daughter of mine, asked permission of the Prince
to approach him later; and the Prince, I suppose liking the look
of the girl, or being won by the promise that appeared to be
wrapped in her dutiful request – for as I say she had that gift,
she always gave a man a choice to make what he would of what
she said – gave his gracious permission to be approached after
the ball, upstairs, and it was there she told him the sad story of
her father's unfortunate wooing. I can see her pleading for her
father, and the good Prince's generous heart touched by her
filial words, and I can hear him saying, "Let Sir Harry be
pardoned. Let the Irishman go free." And so it was. The pardon
is with the Governor now, having come in the same ship with
my daughter's letters, and tomorrow I am promised I shall have
it in my hands, and I shall see the old country again.'

Robert said, 'And if you go, we shall not see you again?'

'Only when you come to Cork. And I shall be sorry to leave you, and to leave my house on the bay that is as fine as the bay of Cork, or very nearly. And I shall grieve for my friends here, and most of all for your dear mother. But I have longed for Cork, and you know I have kept Cork time on me for the last two years. I suppose it was in hope. Now I shall be there again.'

At this the other watch, that kept no time at all, chimed twelve, although it was only four in the afternoon at Sydney, and half past five in the morning at Cork, and Sir Harry un-hooked it from its chain and held it out to Robert.

'Will you take this to remember me by? It is no good for time, but it is gold, and I should like something of me to remain with you, as a keepsake.'

Robert was delighted. As he took the precious watch in both hands it half-heartedly began to chime again, and Susannah laughed.

'And my dear Susannah, this is for you.' He took from his pocket a silver locket containing, as she very well knew, a tiny likeness of himself on one side and a lock of hair on the other. She had always assumed the lock of hair to be from his abducted love, the girl who was a fine wanton but lacking in the deeper things, the girl who had cost him many years in New South Wales, but now he told her the lock was of his own hair – at which she laughed aloud, and, promising to keep it always, kissed him on both cheeks.

At this moment her husband appeared.

She began to tell him what was happening. 'Sir Harry,' she said, 'is leaving. . . .'

'So I hear,' said Redmond.

'Mr Redmond, sir, I was making my farewells to Susannah and the boy.' Redmond said nothing. His manner did not encourage Sir Harry to continue.

He addressed his last words to Susannah. 'Then goodbye, my dear. I do not forget your father. I do not forget. . . .'

She knew he was about to say he did not forget Baudin either, but he did not say it.

'Goodbye Susannah. Goodbye Robert. Good day, Mr Redmond.' Susannah kissed him again, and he left.

Redmond did not see that she was deeply touched. He had

heard her laugh as he approached the house, and it did not please him. She never laughed with him.

'I am not sorry he is going,' said Redmond.

'But I am,' said Susannah.

'He was a great deal with you.'

She lifted her head. 'He was, too.'

Redmond saw the watch still in Robert's hands.

'What is that?'

'He gave me his watch, sir, to remember him by. It chimes.'

'He was altogether too much with the boy,' said Redmond. 'It was not an influence I liked.'

'I am sorry that you did not like it, but I am not sorry in the least that Robert knew Sir Harry.'

'To associate with convicts,' he began, but she stopped him.

'William,' she said, 'that is absurd.' And so it was. Redmond himself, though he had been pardoned very early because he was a surgeon, had been a convict. He had chosen to forget it, and had done more than forget it. He had willed it out of his consciousness. It had meant nothing to Susannah, as she had very well shown by marrying him, and she would never have said a word but for his objection to Sir Harry.

Redmond should have left things at that. He was not blind. The nuances might evade him, but he could see Susannah's spirit was up. But when Robert went to show his watch to Jane, Redmond said that his having found Susannah and the boy with Hayes had brought to mind a matter he had been meaning to raise for some months. Such influences as Hayes's, whether Susannah admitted it or not, were not good for the boy, and Sydney was full of them. Would it not be better if he were sent to Europe? The Countess, he knew, had renewed her request that the boy should be sent. Surely, he said, it would be better?

Susannah said, 'No. No. No.'

He repeated himself. But the reason he gave for wanting Robert to go, though it had some force, was not the real one. He really had put it out of his mind that he was ever a convict. Few people in the town remembered, and it was a town which connived in forgetting the past. Redmond was now almost rich. He was acceptable to the new settler aristocracy. Susannah, though she did not care, would most eagerly have been wel-

comed into that society. But her son by Baudin was an impediment. Not to her, because as her father's daughter she could do
what she pleased. But to Redmond, the French boy was an
impediment. Redmond did not see this as a mean reason,
merely a rational one, for wishing Robert in Europe. All the
same, he thought it unwise to tell Susannah his real reason,
and he was right to think it unwise.

He told her he had returned early to say he would be away
for the night, with his foreman, up country.

She nodded.

Susannah missed Sir Harry. The older people, who had
known her father, or herself as a girl, were becoming fewer and
fewer. She saw less and less of Redmond, but occupied herself
with Robert and with her new son. He had Redmond's eyes.
Susannah and the Governor's wife were friends, and took long
walks round the Domain. Mrs Macquarie was a great walker,
and paced out the perimeter of the grounds at 3 miles and
377 yards. On the eastern side of the Domain, down by the
inlet known as Farm Cove because there the first furrows in the
colony had been ploughed, she sat for hours in the shade of a
hanging rock, often in the company of Susannah and Robert.

'He is a fine boy,' she said, when Robert had bounded off.
'But my dear, how are you going to educate him in this colony?'

'I teach him myself.'

'You can teach a ten- or eleven-year-old boy, but when he
becomes older there are some things a woman cannot teach.'

'The naval officers teach him as much trigonometry as they
know. He already has the beginnings of a competent navigator.
He could go to sea. And he handles a dinghy as well as any boy.
Easty has taught him that.'

'He could go to sea if the colony had a ship in which he could
serve, but we have a couple of coasting brigs and a schooner.
If the sea is to be his profession, he cannot pursue it here.
Susannah, you can bring up a boy, but not a young man. You
must send him away for a while.'

'Perhaps,' said Susannah. She knew the arguments were
strong, but she put them out of her mind.

'My dear, you are stubborn,' said Mrs Macquarie. Susannah
agreed. She knew, in all reason, that Robert ought to go, but
she did not want to lose him. For the moment, she did nothing.

Susannah had many friends, and found a new one in an impetu-
ous young man called Greenway who came to the colony about
a year after Hayes left, also as a convict. She concealed this
harmless acquaintanceship from her husband. It was the first
thing she ever had concealed from him.

Francis Greenway had forged a note of hand to obtain £200
which he contended a man rightly owed him but refused to pay.
He was transported but given a ticket-of-leave as soon as he
arrived, because he was likely to be useful. Sydney needed
buildings. He was an architect, and an architect who had
practised in the noble cities of Bristol and Bath. He also claimed
a friendship with the great Nash, who was at that time just
beginning his grand schemes for Regent Street in London.
Whether or not he knew Nash, Greenway was as much given to
grand designs as that great man. He was a ruddy West-Country-
man, very impertinent, who as a ticket-of-leave man wrote to
the Governor as an equal, suggesting grandiose schemes for a
new Sydney. He was lucky, because Macquarie also had such
dreams in his head, for which he needed an audacious architect.
Greenway was audacious. Within a few months of his arrival he
was urging plans for a bridge across Sydney Harbour: he was
told a bridge there would inevitably collapse, but this did not
discourage him from bringing forward plans for churches,
barracks, forts, court-houses, hospitals, a fountain, and a
stables. It was the stables which above all recommended him to
the Governor. Macquarie, agreeing in that one thing with
Bligh, considered Government House a ruin and wished to
rebuild. London told him he could not. But London did not
concern itself with stables. Macquarie therefore welcomed
stables which were far grander than the new house he had been
refused for himself. If he could not live decently, then his horses
should. The stables were built – a stone, castellated, Tudor
edifice, among the grand stables of the world. But Greenway
was at heart not a builder in the Tudor style. He was a neo-
classicist, as, coming from Bath, he would be. Susannah also
knew Bath, having lived there as a girl. She was amused by the
young man's panache. One day, when he had already been
appointed civil architect, he took her and Robert to the site on

which he was building a cathedral. The walls of Sydney sandstone were already rising. Twenty masons were at work,
chipping and smoothing the blocks. The master-mason
escorted the architect and his guests.

- 'Brush them, ma'am,' he told Susannah.

'What?'

'Brush the stone with your hand,' said Greenway, and showed
her. She moved her gloved hand across the block and found that
Sydney sandstone, though a good building stone, will
yield a fine dust to the pressure of a hand moved across its
face.

The cathedral was being built near the Hyde Park barracks.
It was unlucky that Susannah and Robert were there the day
Tyrone's man was exhibited in the town.


Flogging was so commonplace in Sydney, so much a part of
ordinary life, that children at play practised on the trees. They
made scourges, drew the strands through wet, red soil, and left
blood-red stripes on the white bark of the eucalypts. Captain
Tyrone was a quiet-spoken man who commanded a penal
settlement where convicts were sent who had offended again in
the colony. He was a diligent man, concerned at what he called
the diminution in the force of the cut when the scourge was
made of home-grown flax.

'And the use of this flax,' he told a missionary, 'creates a great
disparity in the punishment, according to the different stages of
the use of the scourge.'

The missionary did not comprehend, so Tyrone explained
that one lash with a new cat was equal to three when the strands
had lost their firmness, which could happen as early as the
twentieth stroke. The missionary came to the opinion that
Tyrone honestly believed he had a disinterested concern that
supposedly equal punishments should fall equally on the backs
of offenders, and that Tyrone considered it an injustice that one
man, receiving fifty strokes with an old cat, should suffer less
than another receiving fifty with a new instrument. Tyrone
liked to call a cat an 'instrument'.

'You consider it an inequitable disparity?'

'Yes, to which must be added another cause of disparity

which no amelioration in the cut can prevent; I mean the different qualifications of the scourgers.'

'The different strengths of the scourgers?'

'Yes.' Tyrone had not considered another inevitable disparity, which was the different strengths, of body and mind, of the men scourged. That difference would not have occurred to him.

'Furthermore,' said Tyrone, 'being anxious to do my duty, I have ensured that fifty lashes under my superintendence is equal to a thousand under any other man's before in the colony.'

'How is that?'

'Before, the scourgers rarely broke the skin, but when I have the lash inflicted, I have never seen a case where I did not break the skin in four lashes.' Tyrone had worked this improvement by making the handles of his scourges longer, and by ensuring that there were nine separate strands instead of the five which the laxness of some officers had allowed, that along the length of each strand six or seven knots were tied, and that the scourgers, if they relented in the application of the punishment, or if disparity between one flogging and another was observed, were themselves flogged. Dogs licked blood from the triangles where Tyrone's prisoners were tied to be flogged. Ants carried off the scattered fragments of the flesh of men's backs. A deep hole was worn in the ground by the scourger's foot as he pivoted. The most telling result of such diligence was the exhibition in Sydney of a prisoner who over the previous year had received 2000 lashes. He was walking quite well because it was some weeks since he was last chastised and he was recovering his strength. He was a strong man who had tolerated well the loss of blood, body fluid, and the surface skin where repeated lashes had flayed him. Tyrone made it a rule to offer a man water after the infliction of every fifth stroke. The man had served out his sentence at the penal settlement and returned to Sydney, where the soldiers let him remain at the barracks because although he could walk he could do little else. They fed him and gave him a blanket. They did this largely out of kindness, but also because he was a curiosity. It was unusual for a flogged man to be a curiosity in Sydney, but he was. The soldiers called him Tyrone's man.

Robert, too, was discovering how to brush sandstone when three redcoats marched past, escorting Tyrone's man to the

west end of the town to show him to the regimental sergeant
major, who disbelieved what he had been told..

Susannah did not see clearly to begin with, because she
thought that the white glare must be the shimmer of sun on the
man's back. Then she cried out. Tyrone's man had been so
flogged that the bones of his shoulder blades shone through
the flesh like polished ivory horns.

It was not this sight in itself that was most terrible to her, but
rather that Robert did not exclaim, and was as curious as the
soldiers. She saw that her son, brought up by her, was already
at the age of twelve inured to a violence that revolted her. She
remembered Mrs Macquarie's kindly-meant words about her
son's upbringing. How could a young man enter any sort of
gainful profession in the colony? How could his spirit survive
intact the sight of such commonplace brutality? That evening
she made up her mind, and wrote both to Bligh and to the
Countess. When eight months later she received replies from
both, she summoned all her courage to send her son away. She
did not tell her husband until she had told Robert. The boy
was delighted at the prospect of a great adventure. He needed
to be a little brave to part from her composedly, but only a
little. He was old enough to welcome the adventure, but too
young to put himself inside his mother's mind and discern the
wrench of parting which she concealed from him. Soon after
the news came to Sydney that Napoléon had finally been defeated at Waterloo, Robert sailed for England. He was thirteen.
Susannah did not watch his ship weigh anchor and make sail.
She had watched too many ships leave the cove. She said her
goodbyes on the quay where, having embraced her son, she
told him – and the words were heard clearly by the sailors in
the ship's cutter as it waited – 'Robert, wherever you go, and
whatever you do, remember who you are, and where you come
from.'

Then she told Redmond she wanted to be alone for a while
and walked from the jetty towards Bennelong Point where she
stood on a high outcrop of sandstone. Her mind was full of her
son but she did not look back to the cove but inland, over the
growing city. She heard the chip, chip, chip of the masons'
chisels as they worked on the stones of the cathedral.

# 15

# Bedford Square and the Bois de Boulogne

It was on a winter morning in November, in a fog so thick that it shrouded the maintops, and the cry of the look-out that all was well came out of the unseen air, that the ship *Constantia*, bound for London out of Sydney, brought Robert at last into the Thames estuary. In Sydney there was mist, but he had never seen such fog. At Greenwich the fog lay oppressively on the river. The smoke of 100,000 coal fires of a city Robert had never seen, held low under the heavy clouds, obscured all but the massive outlines of the Greenwich Hospital, the most magnificent group of buildings in the whole of the kingdom.

On the south bank of the river lay Deptford, where kings' ships had been built for centuries, and then, another mile upstream, on the north shore, the bonded stores and narrow houses of Limehouse and Wapping, whose foundations rose from the water on wooden piles. 'That house is mine,' said the master, pointing to what was only a dim suffusion of yellow light floating by a hundred yards away. 'They will know I shall dock this afternoon. Even in this fug, we shall have been sighted at Gravesend in the estuary, and the post will have ridden to the Pool of London faster than we have sailed.'

'Should I know of Deptford?' asked Robert. 'I have heard the name.'

'I cannot say what you know, sir. But Captain Cook set out from Deptford.'

In the flat calm of the fog the *Constantia* was no longer under canvas, but was towed by her own longboats. The sailors sweated at the oars in the chill. And then, as they came into the Pool, the fog lifted, revealing to starboard the Tower of London, and before them London Bridge. But the sky was still leaden. Robert had never seen such a sky. He had lived all his life in light. Then it snowed, and the master swore, and said this was a freak. It was not a heavy snow, but in the freezing cold it settled where it fell, fringing the rigging of a hundred ships in the Pool, icing the decks, and tracing the bare branches of trees on both banks.

'All the trees are dead?' said the boy.

'Dead?' echoed a sailor. 'Dead, sir? No, sir, they have lost their leaves for the winter, and will grow again.' Apart from a few fruit trees planted in the Domain, Robert had never seen a tree that lost its leaves for half the year. In New South Wales a leafless tree was dead.

When the ship moored, he said goodbye to the master and his mates, gave a guinea to the captain's servant, who had also acted as his on the long voyage, and was greeted on the dock by a liveried steward who removed his hat with a sweep and conducted him to the Countess's coach.

'It is four miles to go, milord,' said the steward, 'and icy for the horses, so we may be some time.'

'I am not my lord,' said Robert.

The steward bowed as if this were not to be believed, but merely an expression of an eccentric desire he would humour.

They passed by St Paul's Cathedral, a gigantic wonder, descended the cruel gradient of Ludgate Hill, where one of the horses fell and had to be heaved to its feet again, continued west along Fleet Street, cut north through narrow and filthy streets, then skirted great squares, and finally entered Bedford Square, where the coach stopped. The steps were lowered, Robert descended, and while his portmanteaux were lifted by four footmen he stood on the stone pavement, wrapped the collar of his great-coat more closely round him, and gazed in wonder up and around. He had seen wonders. It was a day he would never forget. He had never seen such fog, or felt such cold, or seen trees without leaves. He had never seen so many masts as he had seen at anchor in the Pool. He had never imagined the vastness of St Paul's. He had never seen snow. It now lay half an inch thick on the pavement and he bent to touch it, and took a handful. It did not feel like salt. It melted.

'Milord,' said the steward, and conducted him to the door-way, by each side of which a blazing torch flared. Before Robert entered he looked up at the five storeys of the stone façade. He had never seen so high a house. He looked back round the square. In Bedford Square alone there were more, grander, and taller houses than he had seen in the whole of his life before. He ascended the three stairs to the porch and was immediately divested of his great-coat, hat, and gloves. By the hallway fire a glass of hot punch was offered on a silver tray. The steward waited while he first sipped it, and then drank, and then asked if he would care to enter the library. He had never seen so large a room, never gazed at so high a ceiling, never stood on such rich carpets, never felt the warmth of so grand a fire. He was standing facing the fire when the double doors behind him opened, and he turned to see, thirty feet away across the room, a woman as beautiful as his mother but dressed more richly than he had ever seen a woman dressed. Françoise, Comtesse d'Estaing, was a woman of great elegance. She was then in her late forties. Her hair was very fair, with strands of grey which she let show. Her gown was of yellow silk, but in Robert's eyes it was cloth of gold.

She walked to the centre of the room and waited for him to come to her, but he did not know. So she crossed to him, extending one hand.

'*M'sieu*,' she said.

He took her fingers, and bent over the hand.

'*Madame*,' he replied.

She smiled, and thought he did that well.

She said, 'We will have much to talk about, but later. You will be shown your rooms. Your clothes will have been unpacked for you. Then we shall take supper in an hour's time. But first, your rooms. You will already have done much for one day.'

He said, 'I have seen wonders in one day,' and the words so struck her that she raised a hand to her neck. She rang the bell, and when Robert was taken upstairs she remained facing the fire, and said, 'Oh, Nicolas.'


At supper he sat on her right hand. There were only the two of them at the long table. 'We shall not usually eat alone,' she said, 'but this is the first evening.' He was bronzed from the voyage across the world. The *Constantia* had taken the Great Circle route, south from Sydney, across the Tasman Sea, south of the South Island of New Zealand, in the low latitudes across the Pacific, round Cape Horn, and then north east across the Atlantic to Europe, putting in only at Rio de Janeiro for water and fresh food.

'So you have crossed the world,' she said, 'like your father.'

He said, 'My mother has told me that you were a friend of my father's, and that this is why you have been so kind as to . . .' The boy wanted to know more about his father, whom he knew only from Susannah. He was curious why the Countess should, as he put it, be so kind.

'Your father,' she said, 'was a very great friend. It was in another world. I will tell you about that world later, when you are older, and when you have seen something of Paris.'

He was content.

'What shall I do?' he said.

'What will you do now you are in Europe? In a week, you will begin to be taught those things that a young man should be taught. I do not know what they are, but tutors will come who will tell you. That is arranged. After this evening, whenever we are together we shall speak French, and one of your tutors will converse with you in Italian. I did say that I did not know those things that a young man should be taught, but you must forgive me that I have already made a decision on your behalf, which is that a gentleman can perfectly well do without a knowledge of German.'

Robert nodded, but did not understand.

'I am French,' she said. The Prussians, wherever they touched France, had devastated the country.

He still did not comprehend, but nodded as if he perfectly well did.

'And we shall live half the year in Paris. I am luckier than many. I have lived here for twenty years, and London is my first home. Most of my friends are English now. But my husband the Count, of whom your mother will have told you . . . ?'

'Yes.'

'After his death, I gave up all hope of a great deal that he possessed in France, and indeed the greater part of it has gone, but his Paris house had the good fortune to be seized at the end of the war by the Duke of Wellington, for his staff. I did not believe it when I was told that the English soldiers had not looted it but had even repaired the depredations of the previous occupants, who were my own countrymen. And then they went to the great trouble of finding me, and restoring it to me, and sending me an inventory they were anxious I should check. It is strange. The French fought for twenty-five years for the dignity of man and succeeded only in stripping away all dignity, but the Duke's English soldiers gave me back a house I had forgotten.'

'I have heard it said in Sydney,' Robert solemnly remarked, 'that the French these days are given to an excessive admiration of the English. An Anglomania they call it.'

The Countess laughed. 'That,' she said, 'is a rebuke I gladly accept.'

A few minutes later, after she had said nothing for a while and he had not interrupted her silence, she said, 'Will you come by the fire? I have something to show you.'

Over the fire was a full-length portrait in oils of a nobleman in court dress.

'The Count, my husband,' she said. 'It was done at about the time I first knew him.'

By the side of the fireplace, at eye level, was a framed engraving. It was the head and shoulders, perhaps three inches in height, of a French naval officer, hatless, with the single epaulette of a lieutenant. The eyes and the half smile took the attention of everyone who looked at it.

'Have you seen that before?' she asked.

'No. But it is my father.'

'Yes. In the last year that I knew him.'

'Captain Bligh told me he was a good sailor.'

'Had he been fortunate, his name would be remembered with that of Bougainville. He did as much as Bougainville. But now I think you will want to go to your bed.'

She stood still looking at the engraving, so he said good night, and went to the door.

'Robert.'

He turned in the open doorway and she waited. He did not

know what she wanted, and when she saw this, she said, 'God
bless you and keep you. Good night.'

The boy was fourteen. He did not know what was required
of him. But he had the divine good sense to realize that some
ceremony was expected. He returned to her, she put her hand
on his head, and it was done. The Countess had no children,
and had known no children. She had lived in England for
twenty years, but she was French. As a child she had always
done what any French child did, asked for her parents'
benediction before she went to bed. It had not occurred to her
that Robert would never have done such a thing. But he had
come back to her, and she was grateful. While he was with her,
he would be in the place of a son.

The boy slept. Françoise d'Estaing lay awake, seeing Robert's
face and the engraving of his father in the last year she had
known him. The eyes were the same, and the brow. His instincts
were the same: he could not possibly have known what she
wanted, but had returned to her by the fireplace. And most of
all, she remembered the boy's reply when she asked if he had
not seen many things already in one day. His words were, 'I
have seen wonders in one day,' and those had been, almost to
the letter, the words of Nicolas Baudin to the girl Françoise
Vouvray, at the end of the first day they spent together, so
many years before, in Rouen. As they parted, he said to her,
'*J'ai vu, aujourd'hui, de grandes merveilles.*'

Next morning they went to see Bligh.

'He remembers you well,' she said. 'He talks of you very
much, and of your mother. How long is it since you saw
him?'

'Since he left New South Wales. That is seven years.'

'You will find him changed. Try not to show that you do. His
wife, Betsy, is dead. He is very ill. I have seen him often. He
made me promise to bring you the day you arrived.'

Bligh was lying on a sofa in his small house at Lambeth, and
did not try to rise. 'Françoise, Françoise,' he said. 'I always
know you when you come.' His sight was almost gone, but he
always recognized her.

He did not recognize Robert. All he saw was another figure.

'I have brought you Robert.'

'Robert?'

The boy came nearer. 'I am Robert King, sir. You gave me a word when you were Governor.'

'Susannah's boy?'

'Yes, sir.'

'Robert, then. You are Robert?'

Bligh held up a hand, which was emaciated. The Countess watched Robert as he hesitated, and then took it.

'I made you a midshipman. Now you are here. You have gone to sea?'

'No, sir, I have come to stay with Mme d'Estaing, and to go to Paris.'

'Greek and Latin, and Paris and Rome. I was at sea when I was thirteen. How old are you now?'

'I am fourteen.'

'And Susannah? Susannah wrote to me. Was it about you? How is your mother? I never did like Redmond. I told her. How is Susannah?'

'She is well, sir, I believe.'

'I never did like Redmond.'

The Countess said quickly, 'And now Robert says there are cathedrals in Sydney.'

'Castles? Macquarie is building castles?'

'A cathedral, sir.'

Bligh sat up straighter and looked brightly at Robert, as if he were much revived. 'It was a Robespierran party, bayonets all around. And I said a rabble could seize a colony, but could not govern it, and they were all afraid.'

'They were all afraid,' said the boy.

After that visit, Robert saw Bligh twice more, but was not there with the Countess on the day he died. Bligh talked of going to take his first command, which was the *Bounty*. He talked of provisioning the *Bounty* at Tahiti, in Matavai Bay. In his dying hours he sailed the South Pacific, but he never talked again of New South Wales, except that in his very last hour he called out to the Countess by her own name sometimes, but mostly as if she were Betsy his wife, and twice, very near the end, as Susannah.

He died in the rank of Vice Admiral of the White. The Blue, Red, and White had once been the squadrons of the Royal Navy, but had long since ceased to have any real meaning. The

men had difficulty carrying his coffin down the narrow stairs
He was buried in the parish church of St Mary, Lambeth, in
the same vault with his two sons who had died aged one day
twenty-two years before, and with his beloved wife Betsy. The
inscription described him as Vice Admiral of the White, and
Fellow of the Royal Society, an honour won for his botany, but
there was nothing to show he had been Governor of New
South Wales. The Countess planted round the vault the herb
phlox, commonly known as White Admiral. After the service
Robert took her arm but did not lead her straight to the carriage
but a few steps towards Bligh's old house, which was very near

'What is it?' she said.

Robert could remember Bligh only as a great man. The
Governor of New South Wales was a great man. To Robert, the
rum rebellion against Bligh was as if it were the whole French
Revolution. 'I was thinking,' he said, 'that the men had trouble
carrying the coffin out, the stairs were so narrow. It is so small a
house for a great man to die in.'

'Great men matter,' she said. 'Houses do not.'


After Bligh's death the education of Robert, which was to have
been undertaken by the Admiral and the Countess together
fell wholly on her. The house in Paris, next to the British
Embassy in the Rue du Faubourg St Honoré, was a palace
The very inside walls were faced with marble. In the suite of
drawing rooms, where the walls had been papered in the zeal
of the Revolution with tricolor paper, the scrupulous English
had removed this paper and restored the Gobelin tapestries
What they could not replace of the looted Sèvres china they
made up with the best of Wedgwood, and offered their apologies
for this shortcoming. A boy soon learns to live in a palace
though it was true that it never seemed to him so grand as the
house in Bedford Square. That was by comparison an annexe
but he had seen it first.

A defeated Paris insisted on its glory. Robert was taken to
view the half-completed immensity of Napoléon's Arc de
Triomphe. It was still a dummy, but French pride insisted that
the appearance of the arch should be completed with scaffold-
ing and painted canvas. The opera maintained its splendour

Robert often went, in the company of the Countess and her many friends, and vigorously applauded the new operas of Rossini.

The Countess leaned over to him. 'Robert, I am inclined to applaud too much, or so I was often told. Perhaps you ought not to follow me in that.'

M. le duc de Grisaille, who was often with them, waved this idea away as if it were a nonsense, but did say, 'There is now such difficulty with applause. There never was.'

'Why? said Robert.

'Because in the old days one knew what to do. One never applauded until the King chose to applaud. There was always silence while one waited for His Majesty. That has gone. Then a man could end an opera quietly, not as this fellow Rossini does, with dominant chord after dominant chord to whip up the claque. But what Italian ever disliked noise?'

They saw a lot of Grisaille, who was constantly with Françoise. She said to Robert, 'The Duke cherishes old ways, although he half mocks them. The Revolution fell very unequally. He was a Duke when I was the daughter of a merchant in Rouen. Now I have all this, and he has lost everything. I know he does not appear to you to have lost everything, but he has very little. Some people, when they look back over those twenty-five years, notice only that nowadays the men dance with their hats off at a ball, whereas before they kept them on. To so many others, those years were the end of everything.'

By the time he was seventeen Robert, when he was in London, was an English gentleman. When he was in Paris he could pass, in speech, dress, and manners, for a Frenchman. He was more than competent in five languages, two of them dead, but that was then expected. He rode. He hunted. He was a handsome young man. When he was seventeen he was introduced at a *levée* to Jacqueline Brie, an actress at the Comédie Française, by the way a courtesan, and above all a woman of agreeable warmth and wit. She was an indiscreet gossip but was still received everywhere because of her vivacity and because her indiscretions were on the whole without malice.

She took to Robert. She taught him, in one evening, how to flirt. She showed him how to offer her little flowers of courtesy and compliment.

'Perhaps we shall meet?' she said. 'Do you ride in the Bois?'
He said he did.

She called to Grisaille, who was playing *Écarté* with the
Countess and another couple. 'Duke, will you lend me one of
your mares tomorrow, for the afternoon? I mean to show
Robert the Bois.'

Everyone heard.


They rode out along the Avenue de Neuilly, then south into
the Bois de Boulogne, skirting the oak woods which had been
stripped for firewood by the occupying armies of England and
Prussia in 1815, through the newly planted chestnuts, sycamores,
and acacias, with their lighter foliage, and southwards for
another mile. They began at a walk, broke into a trot, then
cantered along the ridings until she reined up sharply, letting
him canter past. He circled her at a gallop while she waited.

'Bravo,' she said softly, and turned her horse's head into the
dark wood of mature, spreading oaks, until she reined the mare
in again.

Robert would have been insensible if he did not feel that a
woman sitting side-saddle in a black riding habit on a summer
afternoon in the Bois, and now holding out her arms to him,
was one of the more splendid sights of life. He flicked the reins
of his own horse over a bough, walked to her, and put his head
in her lap. He had forgotten, or he did not know, that a woman
sitting side-saddle conceals beneath her skirts the pommel she
sits astride, and so his ardent head encountered this leather
pommel and not the softness he had expected. She laughed, and
took his head and moved it a little to the side, finding him the
softness he wanted.

'Take me down.'
He did, and they stood facing each other.
'Do not let the mare stray.'
He secured it.
'Now let me down again.' She took his hands and, as if
curtsying, lowered herself to the bed of leaves. She let her hair
fall back.
'Come here then.'

'So,' she said, half an hour later that afternoon, as she lay lazily back, gazing upwards at the sky between the oak branches, and watching Robert as, ten yards away, he leaped upwards trying to catch a low oak bough, to swing on it in great high spirits, 'I see a young man greatly pleased with himself.'

He was abashed and came back to her. 'Jacqueline, I did not mean that.'

'But why not? I am happy to have pleased you. It is some years, I tell you, since I saw a man frisk so happily.'

He sat beside her and helped her retrieve dry leaves from her petticoats.

'They are everywhere,' he said.

'Then take them from everywhere.' She pressed his hand to her waist beneath the riding habit and the petticoats.

They hunted leaves.

'I have heard,' he said, 'that you knew Napoléon.'

'Say what you mean. You have heard that I was his mistress.'

'And that the Duke of Wellington, when he was in Paris. . . .'

'You are a proud boy, and put yourself in exalted company.'

'Yes, and that is insufferable, isn't it?'

'No, not from you. It is a tale often told, but none the less true. To sleep with Napoléon, oh, you slept with the conqueror of the world. But Wellington was far and away more of a man.'

The boy stroked her hair.

'And now,' she said, 'you are thinking how to enquire about yourself. Yes?'

'Yes.'

'Well, I have never known anyone else try to swing on a tree. Thank you for that. And you were not ungentle. And that is enough for any man to be told.'

He took her in his arms and said, 'I would do anything for you. Anything.'

She released herself. 'I am afraid that you might. You might take after your father in that. But, Robert, you shall not, because I shall not let you. I shall not let you begin. I will tell you this now, while we are both happy, but we shall not come here again, I shall not seek you out again, and I forbid you, and I ask you, not to try to see me. I have made you a little gift, because I wanted to. Of course we shall meet occasionally, in company with others. Let us be affectionate friends. You will find other women.'

'They will not be the same.'

'You cannot conceivably know that. And I tell you that you are wrong. Now, we shall ride back, and we shall ride back happily.'

'What did you mean about my father?'

'Nothing. Now, help me up.'


When he returned, the steward handed him a note which said, 'When you have changed, come to my sitting room.' He found the Countess reading. 'There was no point in telling you before,' she said, 'but I will tell you now. Last night Mlle Brie asked the Duke if he would lend her a horse to go riding with you this afternoon. He did once have many horses but that was many years ago. Now he has none. This morning he borrowed money to buy a horse to lend to her this afternoon. Tomorrow he will sell the horse at a loss he cannot afford.'

'I did not know that.'

'How could you, though I did once tell you he had little? But it would be kind of you to accept no further invitations, and to offer none yourself. I say nothing against Mlle Brie. She ought very well to have known, but she is thoughtless.'

'I give you my word.'

The Countess had not expected matters to be resolved so easily. She was gratified, but she looked sharply at Robert, and asked herself in what intangible way he had changed so suddenly. He *had* changed. The evening before a woman had taught him how to woo. That day she had given him, in an afternoon, the beginnings of an understanding of the nature and quality of the relationship between a man and a woman, of longings and fruitions, which he had never begun to guess at. Above all, by forbidding him the desperations that often follow, she had opened to him a comprehension of much that had before only dimly entered his consciousness. Her reference to his father had opened the door of this comprehension further still. He began to see for the first time the power a man and a woman had over each other.

'May we speak?' he asked.

She assented.

'When I first came to you in London, you said you would tell me, when I was older, about what you called almost another world.'

'Yes.'

'I have been told you were presented to the Doge.'

If the Countess had been a woman of artifice she could have smiled away the inconsequentiality of this question. But it was not inconsequential. It went to the heart of the matter.

She was back in the great Venetian palace, at the banquet, which she had attended as mistress of the emissary of Louis XVI. She was a young, supple girl curtsying so low that her high wig touched the red steps before the throne. She had murmured, '*Serenissimo*,' as she had been told, and the old Doge told her in careful French that she was a beautiful woman. She had been so surprised that he should acknowledge her at all, let alone say such words, that she stumbled over the hem of a petticoat, which tore. Probably only she felt it tear, but it was something she had never forgotten. That visit had been golden, and yet unhappy.

'I was presented to the Doge,' she said.

'And you were at Versailles too?'

'After my marriage. I was presented to the Queen, but not to the King. The ball was always on a Sunday. You will think of it as very grand. It was very grand. My court dress cost what my father earned in a year when I was a girl. He was a woollen merchant. Do you know, it was not the magnificence that most awed me. D'Estaing was very kind. I was touched by his gifts, not magnificent gifts, but silver. You see, before the Revolution, as a *bourgeoise*, I could by custom wear nothing made of silver, and no plumes in my hat.'

Robert looked past the Countess at the two likenesses which were taken from England to France and back again whenever the household moved – the life-size oil of d'Estaing and the tiny engraving of Nicolas Baudin.

'Why am I here? What was my father to you?'

'Your father and I were to be married.'

'He loved you?'

'And I loved him with my whole soul.'

'But you married d'Estaing.'

'I married d'Estaing.'

'This afternoon, in the Bois, I told Jacqueline I would do anything for her. She said she was afraid I might. She said I very well might, like my father. She forbade me to see her again. What was it that my father did?'

She told him the whole story of the declined command, the broken engagement, and Baudin's broken career.

Robert asked, 'And that is why I am here?'

'Yes.'

'You and my father were all that to each other,' said Robert, 'but you married d'Estaing. Forgive me, but you once told me that men mattered and houses did not.'

Françoise looked at the boy. 'Robert, we brought out the best in each other and the worst in each other. We tore each other apart. Why is it that those things inspired at the start with the greatest generosity and love, end so often in havoc?'

There was a long silence.

'My mother does not know?' he asked.

'Not unless Nicolas told her, and I do not think he would.'

Robert embraced Françoise as he never had before. There had never been any constraint between them, but now it was as if they were at the same time mother and son, and the dearest of old friends. When they returned to London, Robert enrolled at Gray's Inn and began to eat the twelve dinners a term which was the only preparation then required of a man who proposed to make a career in the practice of English law. He and the Countess never again alluded to the conversation of that evening in the house in the Rue du Faubourg St Honoré.

# 16

# The Lemon Tree

Thirteen thousand miles away from Bedford Square and the Bois de Boulogne, the criminal court of Sydney was working routinely through its business of theft and murder. Robert Duncan stood charged with the murder of Abel Hughes in the penal colony at Newcastle, seventy miles north, where both had been serving sentences of one year's hard labour for the joint theft of a pig in Sydney. Before that theft both were ticket-of-leave men. They were originally transported from Norwich eight years before, also for the theft of a pig.

Duncan did not deny the capital charge. He neither defended himself, nor was he in any way defiant. He stood awaiting the inevitable sentence.

But the Judge-Advocate was new from England and was not satisfied to write down, 'Death', and see the man taken away.

'Was there a quarrel?' he asked. 'It was revenge?'

'Revenge, sir? He was my friend.'

'Let me be clear. If there is any defence it is my duty to hear it. So let me be clear. You and the man Hughes were felling a tree together?'

'Yes, sir.'

'And so that it should fall in the direction you wished, you had on one side undermined the roots. There was a large hole, so large as a man could climb into?'

'Yes, sir.'

'And when this man got in to the hole, to look at the roots, to determine how much more work remained to be done before the tree fell, you struck him in the head with a hatchet. And yet you say he was your friend?'

'He was very weary of his condition. I too was weary of my life. He dropped like a log of wood. Oh, sir, if people knew how easy it was to take a man's life, things of this kind would happen oftener.'

The Judge-Advocate was a very young man, in his twenties, and he was a Christian. He was badly troubled because, in spite of the enormity of the act, he did not think he saw evil in the wretch before him.

'You say you were both weary of your life. Had you been much flogged?'

Duncan had been speaking indifferently, almost inaudibly, but now he raised his voice and cried, 'Let a man be what he will, when he goes *there* he is soon as bad as the rest. A man's heart is taken from him, and he is given the heart of a beast. Sir, if I have been bad, what has been done to make me good?'

The young Judge-Advocate, and all those in court, were abashed by this outcry. For the first time the murderer met his judge's eye.

'No, sir,' he said, speaking again in the voice of indifference, 'we was not flogged. That has lately been given over a little. There was the box, sir. That was enough.'

'What box?'

'It is a dark box in which a man is put. He is given water but no food. He cannot properly stand, nor properly sit, and he cannot see the air. Men do not dread it for a day or two perhaps, but after three days a man is not in his mind.'

Duncan was a Roman Catholic. Father Massey, the priest who shrived him before his execution three weeks later, was the same missionary who some years before had listened while Captain Tyrone quietly explained the methods by which he would ensure that fifty lashes inflicted under his superintendence should be the equal of a thousand under any other man's. After the display of Tyrone's man in Sydney, that officer had been admonished that no man ever again was to receive at his orders more than twenty-five lashes without the written approval of the Governor. Because he was an officer who loved his duty, he obeyed, and had instead devised the box. In this he was only a little ahead of penal fashions. Solitary confinement, often in the dark, was soon to be the guiding principle of the Philadelphia system of imprisonment, which was thought to be marvellously reformative and would spread throughout the larger cities of the United States. Tyrone's diligent ingenuity was, however, entirely responsible for making it impossible for the prisoner either to stand or sit.

The priest who shrived Duncan very much wished to see Tyrone's penal colony, and first approached the Judge-Advocate, who declined to give his authority because, although he was a Christian, he was also a Protestant and did not wish a Romanist to circulate in a settlement where many of the inmates were Irish. The English fear of Irish insurrection was always great, and priests were considered to provoke rebellion. Having been refused in that quarter, the priest then considered whom else to approach.

At that time Sir Thomas Brisbane, Macquarie's successor as Governor, moved from old Government House in the cove to his much larger country residence at Parramatta, fifteen miles upstream from Sydney. He came into town once a week to discharge his duties, and spent much of the rest of his time cataloguing the 7385 stars visible in the southern skies, which he plotted from a new observatory he built at Parramatta. It was the most complete study ever made of the southern sky, and won Brisbane the Gold Medal of the Astronomical Society of London. He was an amiable man who had got the governorship because he was a friend of the Duke of Wellington. Brisbane thought to make Parramatta the Richmond or Versailles of Sydney; was pleased that the approach road was wider than Pall Mall; liked the house, whose portico had been erected by Greenway; liked horse-racing, of which he became a great patron in the colony; and was the only man who ever called Susannah Sue.

'Sue,' he would say, and he told her this tale often, forgetting he had told it before, 'the Duke said, when there was first talk of my being sent here, that the Secretary of State demurred, objecting that he wanted someone to govern not the stars but the earth of New South Wales. But they appointed me all the same.'

That afternoon he had sent for her to see the effects of an electric fireball which that morning, between nine and ten, after an immense burst of thunder, had struck the Parramatta house. He met her carriage in the driveway, waving his arms and exclaiming, 'Sue, Sue, the observatory is safe, untouched. Praise be.' His wife and son were also safe. They had all been taking breakfast in the only room in the house that was unscathed. He showed her the wreckage with the enthusiasm of scientific detachment. He had never before seen the results of such a visitation. He scrambled around with his foreman and Susannah tracing the path of the fireball. 'You observe,' he said, pointing at the solid wall of his office, 'that it made its exit there, making a hole rather larger than a musket ball.' The celestial and terrestrial globes on either side of his fireplace were unharmed, but the papers on his desk were singed. He showed her the skylight in the roof through which the ball had entered, the ruined ceiling of his and his wife's bedroom through which it had passed, and the lobby where the doors had been wrenched from their hinges and hurled across the flagstones, and the fanlights over the doors shattered into a thousand glass fragments. There had been no fire, though the smell of sulphur hung everywhere. But his observatory was safe, and Brisbane rejoiced. He was already measuring the exact calibre of the cavity through which the electric fireball made its exit. He showed no apprehension of the danger in which he had stood. He was, after all, a man who had served in the carnage of India, Canada, and the Peninsular Wars.

Into this sulphurous mess, with the carpenters and glaziers already scurrying around measuring up for repairs, with Brisbane absorbed in his own observations, and Susannah awed by the nearness of the escape, came Father Massey. His visit was unannounced. He came to ask access to the penal settlement, where he knew thirty-one convicted men were awaiting execution. On the face of it, he could not have chosen a less likely moment to get what he wanted. But God was with him. The singed papers on the desk were the death-warrants of those thirty-one men. At first Brisbane listened to Massey as the priest followed him around. Then he sat at his desk, motioned Susannah to the sofa, and heard Massey out. He picked up the singed papers and glanced through them. Five were for murder. He signed these. The rest were for theft or forgery. He rang for his secretary and directed him to draft pardons for those twenty-six men, and a *laisser-passer* for the priest to see whatever he wished at the settlement.

The priest fell on his knees and gave thanks. The Governor affected not to notice this, and the secretary got the man to his feet.

'I wish to go too,' said Susannah.

'No,' said Brisbane.

'I very much wish to go.'

'Sue, Sue, Sue, it is just no place for a woman.'

'Since I was a girl, I have repeatedly been told this entire colony is no place for a woman.'

'But what for?'

'I once saw an example of Captain Tyrone's work and have never forgotten it.' She told Brisbane about the man flogged to the bone.

'But Sue, I have never even seen the place myself.'

She did not reply to this, but let the obvious retort go unspoken.

'Very well.' He directed another pass to be made out, and later, after Susannah left, gave orders to his secretary to make sure that if she insisted on going – and he heartily hoped she would not – she was to be accompanied by an ensign and six troopers, whether she liked it or not. Then, before he retired to bed, the Governor, who could not bear to see a man kneel because one's inner emotions were not something to be shown outwardly, confided this to his journal: 'Sunday. Had inexpressible satisfaction in sparing the lives of twenty-six fellow creatures condemned to death. If I may have been the instrument of saving one soul from death, may I have that soul for my reward.'

Susannah did insist on going. Two weeks later she and the priest set out. Redmond was as usual up country, and she merely sent word to inform him that she would be going to Newcastle for a few days. It was a desolate place, with huts only for the guards. The three hundred convicts had only rotted canvas for protection from the heat of the day and the

cold of the night. They had not a blanket between them. They
fed at dawn and at dusk, from troughs, and worked through
the day without break and with only muddy water from a foul
well to sustain them. They worked chained together in gangs
of six.

'Assemble the felonry,' ordered Tyrone, and, when they
were paraded by his guards, who were themselves mostly convicts utterly dependent on Tyrone's good will, and the more
savage therefore to their fellows who were still in chains, he
told them that a Romish priest and a lady would be coming to
amuse themselves inspecting the sweepings of the colony, and
(very quietly) that if one man so much as uttered a whisper
that he was discontented with his lot, which would of course be
a calumnious lie, he (Tyrone) would have to ensure that such
a lie was properly punished.

This was received by the convicts with a broken smile,
because these were men with whom life had gone so wrong
that even the common words of speech, and the word *life* itself,
had taken on new and perverse meanings. Life signified to them
the various cheats and deceptions practised to sustain existence:
life to them had been theft, beatings, waylayings, and the
seizure by the stronger of the weaker man's share even of water.

'Christ,' said one, 'a judy and a milestone come to taste the
steel.'

'Maybe they're right go-alongers,' said a second. 'Work 'em
up to the arm-pits. Gammon the coves.'

A judy was any woman. A milestone was any fool, and
therefore any clergyman, country-bumpkin, or other gullible
creature. The steel was prison, from the Bastille. A go-alonger
was anyone simple-hearted enough to swallow a line, any hard
luck story. Such a go-alonger could be worked up to the arm-
pits, that is to say taken for all he was worth before he woke up
to the fact that he was being taken for a ride. To gammon was
to deceive. Most of the inmates had manifestly failed to gammon
the twelve; that is, they had failed to deceive a jury into finding
them innocent. To croak was to die. To be done was to be
convicted. Bunce was money, and a bit was a small coin. To be
cleaned out was to lose everything. With these people it was a
language of despair. Almost all had been chanted, that is to
say had rewards offered for their arrest. Almost all had been

bridged, betrayed. Almost all had been unpalled, that is deprived of pals or friends, by the gallows. Most terrible of all, a bad man was called a good man and a good man bad. It was as if they had to adapt their words to the complete subversion of their hearts, and could not bear to speak anything outright.

Tyrone received his visitors with courtesy. He let the priest stand, but for Susannah found a chair, an awning, and some tea. He was surprised to see the escort. For the day he had released from chains those men who would not instantly murder him if they had the chance. But their debility spoke for itself, and so did the weals and sores where the fetters had only that morning been removed from their ankles. Not a man among them dared lift his eyes to the visitors.

'The condemned men are in there,' said Tyrone, indicating a windowless shack with barred doors. 'Perhaps,' he said to the priest, taking the pardons from his pocket as he spoke, 'you would care to reveal to them their fates before you console them?'

'You have had those reprieves for a week,' said Susannah, 'and you have not told those men who is to live and who is to die?'

Tyrone shrugged, 'They will know soon enough.'

The priest said, 'And those who are to die?'

'Will be taken to Sydney and there hanged,' said Tyrone.

'And those who are reprieved?'

'Will remain here as my guests.'

Susannah got up and began to walk towards the prison shack, but Tyrone touched her arm. 'It is dark inside,' he said, 'and in spite of all care, the felonry stink.' So thirty-one pale wretches were led chained into the light. The sun blinded them. They could not easily see to walk, and as one man stumbled he brought down two others, who cried with pain as the chains cut into their shrivelled flesh. The ensign escorting Susannah glanced at her. She showed nothing.

'Gentlemen,' said Tyrone, addressing the bones and rags assembled before him, 'here is a priest who will comfort your immortal souls, after first telling you what is to become of your mortal bodies.'

The priest loathed Tyrone. He took the paper from the man's hands. On it were written the names of all thirty-one men, in alphabetical order. The priest looked rapidly over it, crossed himself, and said: 'I see most of you are Irish, and of my faith. Some of you are not. Your own priest is not here. I will read this list, with joy for some and sorrow for others. I will first say "Our Father", in which all may join, because I shall say it in no spirit of faction.'

He said the Lord's Prayer, putting into English, in his own words, the Latin of the Roman missal.

Half of the men mumbled some of the words. Tyrone briskly joined in, only his words were those of the English prayer book. Susannah thought he made the words a mockery.

Then the priest unrolled the list and began to read.

'John Andrew. Your sentence is commuted to five years in this settlement.'

The man, who had been weeping, continued to weep.

'You are reprieved,' said the priest.

The man still wept.

'Patrick Barry. You are reprieved and your sentence like-wise commuted.' The man bowed his head.

'John Connell.' The man looked the priest square in the face.

'John Connell, you are to suffer the full punishment of the law, and may God have mercy on your soul.'

Connell laughed. He fell on his knees, embraced the fettered ankles of the man next to him, and laughed, and gave thanks.

The priest thought him distraught, but then saw that he was elated, and rebuked him for the blasphemy of thanking God for his death.

'No, Father,' said Connell; 'I know I shall not be in Heaven, but I shall no longer be here.'

And throughout the calling of the thirty-one names, this was the pattern. Those condemned to be hanged rejoiced to be free of their earthly oppression, and those reprieved wept. The priest was a brave man, but needed all his courage to carry through the grotesque litany of welcomed death and lamented reprieve. The ensign, who had seen enough service to be familiar with the pain and torment of mortally wounded men, swore to himself and thought he had never witnessed anything so horrible. Susannah stood motionless and a tear ran down each cheek. As the naming ended, and after the priest said a blessing, at which the soldiers of the escort spontaneously knelt, Tyrone came over to Susannah and bowed. The man was of course quite mad. She saw through her tears that he was smiling. He was carrying a rattan swagger-stick with which he flicked at one of the condemned men who was half lying on the ground at her feet. Susannah did not know what she then did. She held out both gloved hands, palm upwards. Tyrone, still smiling, placed his rattan in her hands, where she let it lie, and then with a rapid upward sweep slashed him across the forehead.

Tyrone fell dazed. The ensign half drew his sword and kept his eye on the assembled prisoners, but not a word came from them and not a movement. The privates of the escort rose slowly to their feet, lest any sudden movement should precipitate the riot they all expected, but no convict moved. The ensign glanced at Tyrone, left him where he had fallen, and, taking Susannah's arm, led her briskly away. As he held open the carriage door for her, she found she was still grasping the rattan, and gave it to the priest.

Though it was only seventy miles by sea from Sydney to Newcastle, the chances of wind and weather and the difficulties of the short journey inland made it six days there and back, and Susannah returned to find Jane overtaken by disaster.

Jane's husband George had a friend, Francis Daley, also an emancipist, who had borrowed money, obtained a small grant of land, and started a market garden and orchard on the north shore. He grew peaches, oranges, pomegranates, and apples. He had no lemon trees, but his neighbour, a settler arrived from England three years before, had many. One day Daley stole a single lemon tree, which was conspicuous because in his orchard it was alone. The settler's bailiff saw the lemon tree, recognized it by a grafting mark as his master's, and went to fetch a constable. Daley saw the bailiff inspecting the tree, and, while he was gone, uprooted the tree, which was only three feet tall, and smoothed back the soil into the spot where it had been planted. Then he threw the tree into the harbour, so that when the bailiff reappeared with the policeman there was no lemon tree. It then became Daley's word against the bailiff's, and there the matter would have ended. Except for one thing.

The constable was going through the formality of questioning
Daley when by an evil chance Bryant appeared, having taken
the ferry across the narrow channel from the cove to north
Sydney. Thinking to help his friend, he told the constable that
on each of the three previous days he had visited Daley and had
on no occasion seen a lemon tree. Therefore a lemon tree could
not have been there. This was a foolish lie, kindly meant, but
disastrous. It took the constable an hour to discover that no
ferryman remembered carrying Bryant on any of the previous
three days. It took him another hour to visit the Domain,
where Bryant's fellow gardeners, thinking in turn to help him,
insisted innocently that Bryant had been at work in the Domain
at all times in the preceding days. There was now enough suspicion to create at least a case to answer. Daley was summoned
before the magistrates. Bryant was unaware what his own
friends and the ferryman had said, and took his oath that he
had visited Daley on three separate days and seen no lemon
tree. Daley was acquitted of the charge of theft for lack of
evidence. Bryant, after the unwilling evidence of the ferrymen
and his fellow gardeners, was convicted of perjury. The magistrates, wishing to be lenient and not caring to flog a man of
fifty-five, but unable to overlook a perjury, sentenced Bryant
to one month in a penal settlement. Short of letting him go it
was the lightest sentence they could have imposed. They did
not stipulate which settlement he was to be sent to. A clerk,
filling in the committal form, wrote in, 'Newcastle'. It was all
very summary, and by the time Susannah returned Bryant
was on his way northward and Jane was beside herself with
fear. Susannah found herself implored for help at a time when
she was least able to offer any assistance at all.

    She had already received a brief note from the Governor
asking if she would like to explain herself. She went to see him,
contrite and defiant, contrite that she had abused his trust and
embarrassed him, ashamed that she should so have lost command of herself, but not at all regretting the results of that lack
of control. Tyrone deserved to be struck as contemptuously as
she had struck him. The Governor kept her waiting for half an
hour, and when she was summoned to his room she passed in a
corridor the ensign who had accompanied her to Newcastle.
He was just leaving after a long interview. 'I am sorry for this,

ma'am,' he said. 'I had no alternative, and I could not stop my men talking. It is all over Sydney.'

'You were kind,' she said, 'and I did not make things easy for you.' He bowed. He was a boy of nineteen.

'Well,' said Brisbane, not sitting or asking her to sit.

'Nothing excuses what I did,' she said.

'No, it does not. And here,' he said, tossing a folded paper on to the desk, 'is a demand from Captain Tyrone for an apology, which I imagine you will not make.'

'Never. Though I do to you.'

'And what was that damned young officer doing, the one I sent with you, that he should let this happen?'

'I think you have just seen him, and if he would not tell you himself, then I will: he could not have behaved more properly, and he could not conceivably have foreseen what I did. I did not know myself until the cane was in my hands. I did not know what I did until it was done.'

'That does not help.'

'The man is mad, sir.'

Brisbane nodded. 'That was the opinion of that young man, too. He spoke up for you with some courage.'

'I would not wish this to hurt him.'

'It shan't. But I take all this very badly from you, Sue.'

'The man is mad.'

'That is now my concern. I will tell you this. I have a letter from my Judge-Advocate, which concerns some box in which Tyrone has been incarcerating his prisoners. I have that young officer's report. I have a letter from that priest. Tyrone has no commission to run a hell-on-earth. I will bring the man here and he shall answer to me, but this is no concern of yours and you will not meddle further.'

She did not reply.

'Look, damn your eloquent silence, Sue. It is nothing to do with you, and you will leave it alone.'

'How long will it take to bring Tyrone to Sydney?'

Brisbane showed a flash of anger and struck the desk with his fist.

Susannah said, 'Sir Thomas. . . .' He looked round. She never called him that. And her voice had changed.

She said, 'I know I have disgraced myself. I am not proud

to have made such use of the kindness you have always showed me. But now there is something I must ask you, if you will hear me.'

There were times when Susannah's heart was in her voice.

Brisbane was angry, but when she spoke as she did then he could in no way refuse to hear her.

'Tell me.'

She began, 'There is a man . . .,' and she told him briefly the long story of George Bryant.

'And he is gone to Newcastle?' said the Governor.

'He will be there now.'

'Sue, I will do what I can for him. I am sorry it is perjury. A month is very light, you know. But I am sorry it is Newcastle. I will recall Tyrone as soon as I can replace him, which will be a week. In the meantime I will send orders, today, that no unusual punishment shall be inflicted on Bryant. He shall not be flogged. You can reassure your maid.'

'She is my friend too.'

'Very well, Sue. I will do what I said. But I would do the same for any man, because it ought to be done; you understand that?'

'I know you would. Thank you.' She left him.


By then George Bryant was at Newcastle, and Tyrone was overseeing his labours. The committal papers that came with all prisoners, young and old, said that they were to be put to hard labour, and Tyrone carried out his orders. The work for a man of Bryant's age was terrible. Twelve hours a day, under a sun that seemed to remain for most of the day vertical, these 300 men felled timber and dragged the logs to the river to float them downstream. Bryant worked with five others. The six were joined at the ankles with light chains. Bryant had worked in the fields, or in the gardens of the Domain, all his life. He was as strong as the others, and after a few days would in spite of his age have toughened and become stronger than them, because he had been for so long better nourished. They were half starved. But Bryant was one of two men in that gang of six who were desperate. The first was David Hirst, who was desperate because he was ill. He said he had a cold, but a low

fever had been with him for months, his soft cough was that of
tuberculosis, and he was very weak. He was not desperate from
the knowledge that he would very likely die within the year,
because he did not have that knowledge. He was desperate
because he could not keep up with the others, and went in fear
that this would be seen and he would be punished for his idle-
ness by being thrown into the box where a man could neither
sit nor stand. His mates knew he was weak, and they concealed
this by taking an added burden on their own backs. Among
300 men, Hirst had so far escaped notice but knew he would be
found out one day soon. The other desperate man was Bryant.
His torment was that of the mind. He did not think himself
unfairly punished. He did not regret his spontaneous and useless
lies to help a friend, but his false oath sworn upon the Bible bit
deeply into him. He was harsher on his own perjury than the
bench of magistrates had been. They saw perjury every day.
But Bryant had never before sworn a false oath. And the
separation from Jane was unbearable. Theirs was the steadiest
of marriages, having none of the fire and lustre that had been
life to Susannah and Baudin and would have sustained their
marriage, but possessing a firmness of comfort, faith, and love.
They had never been separated until a few days before when –
all between morning and evening – Bryant was seized, sentenced, hustled to the quay, and thrown on the transport to
Newcastle. He would have left with no possessions at all except
that one of the ferrymen went to the Domain cottage and
gathered up two shirts, a Bible, and some bread and fruit, and
tied them all in the blue cloak, loosely knotting the ends. He
used the cloak because he could see no bag in the cottage.
Besides, the nights at Newcastle would be cold, and the cloak
was warm. The ferryman hesitated to take these things because
Jane was not at home. She was scouring the town looking for
her husband in the wrong places and not finding him. The
ferryman paid a sailor a dump dollar to give the bundle to
Bryant, which he did. When he arrived with his bundle at
Newcastle, Bryant had more than any other man there. The
guards took the apples but tossed him back the stale bread, the
Bible, the shirts, and the cloak. Tyrone ruled by the book. He
made a felon's life a misery, but a felon's property was sacro-
sanct and God help any guard who stole it. The guards had

been thieves themselves. There is no honour among thieves,
particularly not among thieves who have risen to be guards,
but they feared Tyrone, and, besides, had no use for a tatty
cloak. One of them knew its story, and amused himself by giving
Bryant the nickname of Bishop.

'Here y'are, Bishop. Take your cloak of office, Bishop.' For
three days Bryant worked to exhaustion in his chain gang, from
dawn to dusk. When night came the men, still in their chains,
fell into exhausted sleep, except Hirst, who coughed and could
not sleep.

Tyrone had not become more savage after Susannah's assault on him. He knew she had harmed herself more than him.
To strike an officer in front of convicts was an outrageous af-
front, but he took comfort from the sure knowledge that condign
punishment would be visited upon her. He had written the
Governor a reasonable letter – and its tone *was* one of sweet
reason – requesting an apology. When he received an order to
present himself before the Governor, he assumed that it was to
receive this apology. He had the assurance of madness. He
never doubted.

So on the morning he received the Governor's letter, which
was Bryant's fourth day in the settlement, Tyrone was in good
humour. He harboured no unusual vindictiveness in his mind
when he left his hut to deal with a gang that had downed tools,
and refused to continue.

'See to it yourself,' he first told the corporal who came to
him with the news.

'I have seen to it all I know, sir.' The corporal meant that
he had kicked three of the men as they lay, and promised one a
flogging, but the fellow had not seemed to care and had
answered nothing at all. 'They are taking their ease on the
ground, and will not work.'

Hirst had collapsed, and the others, also very weary, refused
to go on. Bryant was one of them. The six men sprawled on
the sandy scrub, waiting for Tyrone. They had no doubt they
would work again. They had no doubt they would be punished.
They were of two minds towards Hirst. They would continue
to support him until he was beyond support, but they knew that
could not be much longer now, and they would be relieved
when he died.

Tyrone appeared and the guards kicked the men to their feet. Hirst found the strength to stand, and to Tyrone's glance looked no worse than the others. Tyrone also saw Bryant. 'And the Bishop?' he said. 'Are you leading your colleagues out of the paths of righteousness?' He did not know this was Susannah's man. He had no especial animus against him.

Hirst found his tongue, 'No sir. The Bishop does not lead. There are no leaders.'

Tyrone was even disposed to be generous. 'I lead,' he said. 'Get back to work and there's an end to it.'

The men stood with lowered eyes. Another moment and they would have turned listlessly back to the timber they were dragging, and carried on. But from Hirst there came an unearthly croak.

'Never no more. We will destroy ourselves first.'

'And then,' said Tyrone, all affable and tapping the sides of his breeches with his rattan, 'you will be in Hell.'

'What is Hell?'

The gang was twenty feet from a canal dug to float the smaller pieces of timber to the river. Tyrone tapped the sides of his breeches again. 'Have these men double-chained,' he said to the corporal. It was done.

'March them to the canal.'

It was done. They stood on the edge.

'To the very brink,' said Tyrone.

They were edged up to the brink. The bank was sheer.

'Gentlemen felons,' said Tyrone, 'how could I wish to stand between you and your desires? If you are disposed to destroy yourselves, here is the opportunity. The canal is deep, and the chains heavy. You are on the brink. You would undoubtedly sink immediately.'

He walked behind them, flicking his rattan. It was a show. The corporal, seeing this, whispered to a guard who fetched Bryant's blue cloak.

'What is this?' said Tyrone. He was told.

Tyrone smiled. 'Well then, life is barren enough without its trappings. Let us be cautious therefore how we strip these trappings away. Give the Bishop his cloak. Put it on.'

'Put it on.' Bryant heard the words of the Judge of so many years before, and felt the cloak placed round his shoulders.

'Well?' said Tyrone.

Hirst jumped. The corporal and two guards leapt to prevent him, but they were too late. The six men were on the brink, and Hirst dragged them in. All the other men but Bryant were weary of life, but only Hirst had wanted death. They struggled. Bryant was the last in the line of chained men. He clung to a root in the side of the bank. The two guards frantically supported his shoulders. The corporal fumbled in panic for the iron key that would unlock the fetters, but it was useless because the chains were not at the wrists but at the ankles. When the guards could no longer hold him, and when he could no longer cling to the root, Bryant drowned in terror.

'They are not dead,' said Tyrone when the bodies were dredged up fifteen minutes later. He was active in their resuscitation. He laid the men in the scorching sun, for the heat to revive them. He caused the bearded ends of feathers to be introduced into the oesophagus. He wrapped the men in canvas, and ordered that their heads should be kept in constant motion by being tilted side to side at the hands of fellow convicts. 'Put the solid parts of each man in motion,' he cried. The dead men's arms were rotated vigorously. He proceeded through each certain remedy. He ordered rum to be forced into the men's mouths, and while the guards ran for this he made do with warm urine, which he had read to be efficacious. He ordered his own snuff to be blown through quills into their nostrils, and tobacco smoke to be blown through long reeds into their stomachs and, as he imagined, into the intestines. Finally, to drain the fluid from the men and restore their vital functions, he hung them upside down by the ankles. 'They are not dead,' he said. But the six men had drowned in chains. As they hung downwards in Tyrone's last certain remedy their ankles were still chained. In the panic no one had thought to remove the fetters.

Tyrone went to his hut, 'They are not dead,' he said. 'Tell me when they stir.' Half an hour later, on his own initiative, the corporal had the six men taken down, and covered the bodies with the canvas which had unaccountably failed to revive them.

After the men sank, the blue cloak still floated over the spot where Bryant was dragged down. To Tyrone, property was sacred. He had the sodden cloak retrieved, and that too was laid out in the sun to dry. He intended to restore it to Bryant when he revived. He did later ensure that it was returned to the widow.

# 17

# Manly Cove

In Sydney, Susannah's striking of Tyrone with his own rattan had for several days been a fable, but the death of the six men in chains was still unknown. One morning, when it was ninety in the shade, but the heat was tempered by a southerly breeze, Susannah, her son John, and Jane's older daughter Mary, took a walk down to Bennelong Point to view the harbour and talk to the Governor's waterman. Now that Governor Brisbane spent so much of his time at Parramatta, the man had little to do in Sydney and was ready to earn a few dollars on the side. Susannah taught John as she had once taught Robert, preferring her own judgement to that of the various pedagogues who, having failed in London, came to Sydney and put advertisements in the newspapers offering to teach Latin, Greek, French, Mathematics, Physiognomy, Trigonometry, the Elements of Calculus, and in short to give a thorough grounding in all the knowledge thought necessary to prepare a young gentleman for the Professions, Commerce, etc., all to be taught by new and improved methods. Susannah was a thorough and determined instructress, but that day she had promised John that if the weather was favourable she would see if the waterman could take them to Manly, a fine beach reached by crossing the open waters of the harbour, sailing through the heads, and then bearing north. It was six miles from the town, too far to row, and the trip therefore depended on the wind and on the waterman's judgement of how it would hold throughout the day.

The waterman came out of his hut to greet them. 'Good morning, ma'am. Good morning, sir. Good morning, Mary.'

'So, Mr Smith, do you think we have a fine day for it?'

Susannah knew the winds and currents of the bay almost as well as John Smith, but he sailed those waters every day.

He surveyed the cove, and the harbour beyond, and the sky – as he had already done twenty times that morning – and said they could have a worse day for it if there were no change, and he foresaw no change.

'And you, ma'am, were of the same opinion?' he said, looking at the picnic hamper she carried. 'Or you'd not have brought that.'

They set off in the Governor's fifteen-foot cutter, and just over an hour's easy sailing in light airs brought them to Manly. It is a beach of magnificence. The bay encloses a semi-circular sweep of sand. Apart from one stone cottage there was no building in sight. Sydney could have been a thousand miles away. As they went ashore, Smith scanned the beach for signs of tracks but there were none. He scanned the brush for signs of dead fires, but saw none. He helped Susannah and the boy ashore.

'We shall be alone, ma'am,' said Smith, 'except that if I know Wilkinson, he'll be here by this afternoon.'

'Who is Wilkinson?' said John.

'You will see,' said Susannah. Then she turned to Smith and told him to give Wilkinson her compliments, and to say that if he wished to come he would be welcome but that any demonstration he wished to give she would rather he kept within his pen.

'And my voice goes with that too,' said Smith, and off he went to tell the man. He returned to say that nothing would keep Wilkinson away, but that he promised to keep within the pen.

'What pen?' asked Mary.

'You'll see, young miss.'

'And Smith,' said the boy, 'when we landed, why did you look around? Are there savages?'

'Here?' said Smith. 'Not any more, sir. Years ago, yes. But all you see now, and I've seen two or three in, oh, the last five year now, is a poor outcast. Once in a while.'

'Why are they cast out?'

'There was a man called Bennelong, who died about the

time you were born. He was a famous black, and they gave his name to that far western point of Sydney Cove that you know. He was a famous black that went to Europe and bowed to the King.'

John looked to his mother for confirmation.

'I saw him,' said Susannah. 'I knew him.'

'But when he came back, sir,' said Smith, 'why, he was cast out. He drank liquor, and put his women in petticoats, and forgot how to hunt, and when they cast him out he died.'

'Did you not give him food, Mother?'

'Most of the time he hid,' said Susannah. 'And no one knew where to find him. It was pitiful.'

'It *was* pitiful,' said Smith. 'I have seen men leave food for him that he would not eat.'

'Why would he not eat?'

'He would not eat what he did not catch himself, and in the end he could catch nothing, and so he ate nothing. Then the soldiers gave him rum to see him drunk. They meant well. I gave him rum. I did not mean badly. But he died.'

'Will all the blacks die?' John asked.

'I don't know about die. But it is true they have mostly gone, no man knows where.'

'I shall help them,' said Mary.

Smith looked at the girl. 'No, Mary. Best helped by being left alone. They were not always pitiful creatures. Take this beach. Why was this beach so named?'

'After the man who found it?' John suggested.

'No. No more than Lord Sydney came to find Sydney for himself. I do believe that noble lord's name was given as a compliment to the city, but, since he is long dead and longer forgotten, the city instead will be an everlasting compliment to the family. Which is an irony, Master John, since that lord's son has never yet been heard of, or nothing that he ever did anyway; and that lord's father was Member of Parliament for as rotten a borough as ever existed, a borough with two Members and four men to elect them. Winchelsea it was, and I know Winchelsea because my father came from there.'

'Was he a waterman too, like you?'

'He was not. There was no being a waterman at Winchelsea, because by the time my father lived that fine port was so silted up it had no more sea in it. As I remember, sir, it was a mile's walk from Winchelsea to anywhere near the sea. So, as I say, to call so fine a port as Sydney after them, does the family too great honour.'

'But what about Manly?'

'I had forgotten that was the story I started with. Why, it was the first governor that ever came here, who saw some blacks on the shore, and they did not run, as they often ran, or crouch and gibber and throw spears and then run, but they all approached him like men; and spoke to him, it was said, as if they were the owners of a great estate welcoming a chance visitor and offering to show him the grounds. So he gave the leader a hatchet, at which he bowed, and offered the Governor in return a throwing stick – which he showed him the use of as if it was something beyond the wit of a white man, but showed him very civilly, and when the Governor failed to throw it at first, retrieved it civilly and showed him again. And they were gentle to their womenfolk, which the blacks are often not, and so the Governor said, "Seeing you are so manly, I shall call this Manly Cove." '

'But perhaps the blacks already had a name for it before that?'

'If they did, they were too polite to disappoint the Governor out of his intended generosity, and took the name as a gift.'

Susannah opened the lunch hamper.

'Join us, Mr Smith,' she said, but he made excuses not to, saying he needed to remain near the cutter. He accepted a leg of chicken and ate that, propped up against the side of the boat, with the bread and cheese he had brought with him in a handkerchief.

After midday, a figure left the cottage a quarter of a mile away, crossed the dunes, and walked along the shore towards them. As he came nearer they could see he wore trousers of thick dun-coloured canvas, a shirt of the same thickness buttoned down to his wrists, gloves, and what showed the man not to be the beachcomber he might have been taken for, a stout pair of much-patched leather boots reaching to his knees. His face was burned mahogany by the sun. He nodded to Smith and then approached Susannah, making as if to remove his hat.

'Wilkinson,' she said, when he was still ten feet off, 'stand where you are a moment.'

He stood grinning. This was a request he was used to receiving.

'If your hat contains what I think it does, then do me and Mary the courtesy of *not* removing it.'

'I did promise there should be nothing but in the pen, ma'am, and so it shall be. But I see you remember the hat. Lord, ma'am, there nothing there but so familiar a creature as would be lost if I did not bring her.'

'What creature?' asked John, and would have run to the man, except that he slowly put up a hand to halt him.

'Watch then, young man. Watch, young miss.'

The hat stirred on the man's head, as if the headband were tightening of its own accord, and from the broad brim a tail emerged to curl over his brow like a love-lock. The child did not see what it was. There were four spectators, all with their eyes on the man's brow and his hat. Susannah sat very still. The boy innocently gazed with open curiosity. Smith sat apparently as he had been, but his right hand was on his belt, at his knife handle.

Then John saw. 'Snake,' he whispered. A boy not an Australian would have shouted in fear. John was afraid, but he remembered what he had been told, again and again – that if ever a man saw a snake he must kill it, but if the snake was within striking distance of another man, then he must whisper a warning, *never* shout. Mary held her breath.

'Oh, snake is it?' said Wilkinson, and he gave the tail a good pinch, at which it retired to join the rest of the animal in the brim.

'Well done, boy,' said Wilkinson, 'and well done those who taught you. It's not every boy that remembers not to shout.'

'He might have hurt you?' said the boy.

'Might, but he wouldn't. He's no king-brown, boy, because I'm no hero. A king-brown I would not allow, leastwise not on my head.'

'And as for you, John Smith,' said the man, 'how many's the time you've seen this, and never a time yet when your hand did not go to your knife.'

'And always will,' said Smith.

'Ah. That's fair. Each man to his trade. I daresay I'd be a poor man to be with in a squall.'

They followed Wilkinson across the beach to a spot near his house where a pen stood, ten feet square, made of wattle. In each corner rested a metal rod three feet long, with a hooked end. In the centre were a sack and a smaller bag. Wilkinson smoothed back the gauntlets of his gloves so that they protected his wrists, and then removed his hat and twirled it round. As it twirled, a yellow snake unwound from the brim, and, finding itself on the ground, came straight for the man. He deflected it with a flick of his leather boot, caught it by the tail, and fed it into the mouth of the small bag, all in a second. Then, taking up one of the metal rods with one hand, he picked up the sack with the other, loosened the knot at its mouth with a motion of his thumb, and tipped on to the earth around him three snakes, two only a foot each in length, and the third six feet long. The large snake slid lazily to a corner and he did not watch it at all. The two smaller ones came at him rapidly from two directions at once, each biting a boot. John heard the impact of each snake against the leather, and saw what he had not known before, that a snake bites with open jaws, and does not softly penetrate, as he had imagined, with its forked tongue. As the snakes came at him again, Wilkinson leaned down and picked each out of the air with his leather gauntlets as they struck and tossed them one after the other into the neck of the sack which he held open with the rod. This was barely accomplished when the large snake launched itself from its corner at Wilkinson. This time John did shout, and so did Mary, but the man knew it was coming and, as it struck at him, not at his boot but higher than that, he deflected its head away with the hooked rod, catching it at the throat and flicking it by its own momentum to the corner of the pen farthest from which it had come. It attacked again. Once again Wilkinson deflected its drive in the same way, but this time flicked it high in the air, and, as it passed him, he caught its tail and slipped it, again by its own momentum, into the mouth of the sack, which with a quick twist he knotted.

Susannah and the waterman had seen all this before. John and Mary had not. They now knew snakes did not move up and down like sea-serpents or like woodcut illustrations from the story of Adam and Eve. Snakes propel themselves with a sideways undulation. They bite with open jaws. And they are very fast. John would have said as fast as a galloping horse, but that was an illusion because the pen was small; but as fast as a cantering horse.

Wilkinson earned his living from those snakes, giving sideshows on holidays, existing on the pennies thrown into the ring. For the past few years a renaissance of Christianity had hurt his business. Holidays were almost all Sundays or saints' days, at any rate holy days, and the clergy of Sydney had forbidden him to perform in town on the days when he was most likely to draw crowds. Besides, one clergyman had been bitten, and though he had recovered, and the snake died, that had been enough to make the clergyman's colleagues thunder out from their pulpits that the serpent was the symbol of anti-Christ, and so on. Now Wilkinson lived as best he could by giving sideshows at villages outside the city, and by entertaining the few visitors to Manly.

'Are they all poisonous snakes?' asked John.

'All.'

'And you left the poison in them all?' said Mary.

'Ah,' said Wilkinson. 'There you have me.' They had already given him a dollar, and he felt it unfair to withhold a secret of the trade from them, though one secret he did not tell was that he had to train the snakes to attack. So he said, 'There are four snakes which all run at me. Never at the same time, as you saw. But there is no saying they might not. Now, they do say, and I have never seen it shown otherwise, that to confine several in a sack together, as I do before I release them, lessens their appetite for biting. But all the same, four is too many, and I have drawn the venom of three.'

'Which one is still poisonous?' asked John.

'The big one. The king-brown. He is a certain killer.'

'But why,' said Mary, 'have you not drawn his venom?'

'Because my father once tried, and did not live to tell me why he failed.'


It was only two o'clock, but Smith was watching the sky and the way the sand blew. They must be getting back. It was a placid passage. Even the water between the heads was calm. But Smith kept the lugsail half furled, and watched the tops of the trees on the north head for any sign of movement, though there was none. They were well into the shelter of the harbour, within half a mile of the Sydney Cove, and within sight of any watcher in Farm Cove or on Bennelong Point, when they were struck by what Smith had known might strike - a sudden squall known as a southerly buster. It was as well that the canvas of the cutter was of Australian flax, and therefore frail, and that the sail, half furled though it was, split from end to end with the force of the gust, otherwise the cutter might have been dismasted and capsized. As it was, the boat shipped water before Smith recovered it, and then, again in the most deceptive of calms, rowed it to the Domain jetty. Redmond, from the grounds of Susannah's house, saw the useless canvas flapping as the cutter made fast, and the sodden skirts of his wife as she stepped on to the jetty. The boy and girl were drenched too. He waited for them.

As Susannah and the children left the jetty they passed a gang of fifteen convicts building a wall under the easy super-intendence of a sergeant and three private soldiers.

'That's her,' said one.

'Who?'

'That's the one that gave Tyrone what for.'

The word ran along the line of men, and they waved their trowels and cheered the woman. It was not a ragged three cheers, not a matter of hip, hip, hip, hooray, but a roar of cheering gratitude. Men in faded yellow prison uniforms jumped up, waved their arms, and cheered. And what could Susannah do? The sergeant yelled at the men to keep a respectful silence, but they did not hear him, or took no notice. The three soldiers, who had been leaning on the wall smoking, roused themselves and stood to a sort of attention, and the sergeant, seeing that order was not to be preserved, and moreover heartily sym-pathizing for the first time in his life with the rabble he could not restrain from cheering, saluted Susannah. He would have saluted her anyway, but the convicts took his salute as approval of their cheering, and cheered the more loudly. Susannah nodded to the sergeant and walked on towards the house, where at the open door Redmond stood in silent anger. Mary

bobbed to him, and ran off to her mother's cottage. Redmond
took no notice of her, but stared at John's clothes.

'Go and get out of those things, and leave your mother and
me.'

John glanced at Susannah, who motioned him to do as he
was told.

'And now, madam,' Redmond started, 'I come home to
find. . . .'

'William,' said Susannah, 'I too am wet. I see you have
something to say, but it will wait until I am dry.' And she went
to her room.


Throughout dinner he said nothing. John went to bed, and still
Redmond said nothing. He went to his room across the hallway,
and for half an hour she heard nothing. She read in her sitting
room. Then he called her. He had left the door of his room
open. But he called out, 'Come here.'

'I am here,' she replied, and continued to read.

He called again. This time it was almost a shout, but she
waited. After ten minutes he appeared in the doorway of her
room with a glass of brandy in his hand. He was not drunk.
Redmond did not get drunk.

He said evenly from the doorway, 'I came home this afternoon to find the house empty. When I went to look for you I
was in time to see you and my son, and your maid's daughter
whom you seem to like to take as well, very nearly overturned
into the harbour, by a squall a child could have foreseen, let
alone Smith, who should have had more sense.'

'You can thank Smith's sense that we are safe. He knows
those waters better than any man.'

'What were you doing?'

'I took them to Manly.'

'And after I arrive, in time to see you, and my son coming
ashore from the adventure. . . .'

'John is my son as well as yours.'

'That is something you should remember. I arrive back, and
what do I see? As you come ashore, you are cheered by a gang
of convicts, and you acknowledge those cheers graciously.'
Redmond's voice had little animation, and therefore he could

not be said to sneer, but the word 'graciously' was not intended to please.

'I acknowledged the sergeant's salute. I know him. And whether I knew him or not, I should have done the same.'

'And John waved.'

'Boys do wave.'

'The matter is, Mrs Redmond, as you very well know, that during my absence you have made yourself, and me, the talk of Sydney by interfering where you had no business to interfere, in the administration of this colony – and by striking an officer, so that convicts cheer you.'

'What I did, I think I would very likely do again. I have accounted to the Governor for what I did. He is bringing the officer back from Newcastle. I suppose there will be an enquiry. I will account to him but not, William, to you.'

'You discredit me, Mrs Redmond, by what you do in my absence.'

Susannah was not at that moment going to tell him to call her by her Christian name, but once again it struck her as absurd that the man could not bring himself to do this, but called her Mrs Redmond as if to emphasize that she was no more than an appendage to him.

'Anything I do,' she said, 'whether it pleases you or not, is likely to be done in your absence, because you are never here.'

'I have work to do,' he said. The work was increasingly that of his sheep station.

Redmond was still standing in the doorway, as he had been throughout this conversation.

'Please sit down,' she said.

He remained where he was.

'Well,' she said. 'What is that black armband you have been wearing today?'

'For Johnston.'

'Major Johnston?'

'He died three days ago.' Johnston the insurrectionist, having been cashiered, had been allowed to return to New South Wales on condition he took no part in the politics of the colony. He had given his word, and kept it. He returned and flourished on sheep. He had been one of Redmond's intimates. Susannah had not seen him for years. He had kept very much in the company of sheep-men. One of them was Macarthur, who had also been allowed back, though not until nine years after the mutiny he had encouraged. He was now the biggest of the graziers.

'I am sorry about Johnston,' said Susannah.

'Hypocrisy,' said Redmond. 'You hated the man.'

Johnston brought back to her mind so much that was vivid in her past – her father, Bligh, the mutiny, her defiance of the man across the ball room, and Baudin.

'You hated the man,' Redmond repeated.

'No. I think my father did, and I never knew why. I never knew him hate anyone else. But I did not hate him, though I very much disliked him. And when I say I am sorry, I am sorry, at least for the death of a friend of yours.'

'He was one of the great sheep-men,' said Redmond.

'And, William, I suppose you are very nearly one of those great sheep-men now?'

'And if I am, then you will see why I cannot have my wife meddling in affairs which will upset the colony, or reflect on my credit. This must not happen again, and if it does, I shall go and I shall take John with me.'

He had previously been so content to leave the child to her that she had never thought of this. No one had ever threatened Susannah since Major Johnston in the ball room. She rose and met her husband's eyes with as much defiance as she had faced Johnston. But Redmond left her standing there, and went back to his room. He was the father of the child, and in an infinitely stronger position than any insurrectionary major. He was beyond her power.

# 18

# Susannah Alone

At eleven the next morning the Governor drove into the carriage drive of Susannah's house, descended alone, ordered his escort to dismount and wait, and was received by Redmond himself, who expressed delight at the unexpected visit.

'Good morning, Redmond. I'm afraid my business is with your wife. Could she be told?'

Would the Governor take some refreshment first?

He shook his head and waited silently, which Redmond took for displeasure, and expressed the hope that Mrs Redmond's recent conduct had not been such as. . . .

'No, man. But let me see her.'

This sounded more peremptory than the Governor intended, but he hated what he had to do and was in no mood for niceties with Redmond.

Susannah appeared.

'Alone, Sue,' said Brisbane, but then thought this discourteous and turned to her husband. 'I'm sorry, Redmond, to ride rough-shod into your house like this, and then demand to take your wife off on her own. I beg your pardon, and I hope you'll understand.'

Redmond withdrew. The Governor and Susannah were left alone in her sitting room. She saw this was no visit of ceremony. There was no ceremony in Brisbane's face.

He said, 'What I have to tell you is the worst news, Sue.'

'Bryant?'

'Where is his wife?'

'At her cottage, with her two children. You are telling me he is dead?'

'He is dead.' He told her that Captain Tyrone had presented himself at Parramatta the previous evening with a fantastic story which placed great emphasis on the methods untiringly applied to revive the dead men.

'Sue, I would not have believed him, but he came with a corporal. It was impossible to see the two of them together without coming to the conclusion that the corporal practically had charge of Captain Tyrone. Certainly he was the more rational of the two. And his story was the same as far as the story mattered, which was how those poor men died.'

'Which men? How many? How?'

Brisbane told her. She covered her face in her hands, and repeated, 'Jane, Jane, Jane, Jane.'

'Sue, I do not think she should be told exactly how.'

'Oh yes she shall.'

'That would help no one. I was thinking to keep a little pain from her.'

'It will come out. It was seen by too many. Where is that corporal now, and where is Tyrone, and what of his trial?'

'The corporal is on his way back to Newcastle. Tyrone is under close arrest, and if I could shoot the man I would. But he is mad. You told me that, and now I have seen for myself. The corporal will say nothing. The two guards who saw it will say nothing. Tyrone will never see the outside of a mad-house again. The six men are dead. Bryant is dead. My only concern now is with his widow, and I have come to you because you first came to me. I am proposing what in my judgement is right; or, perhaps, what is kinder to the only creature to whom any kindness in this wretched matter is now possible, and that's Bryant's widow.'

'I never thought you meant otherwise,' Susannah said at last.

'Then, will you take half an hour for thought, and tell me if you think what I suggest is right? I do not know the woman. I do not know her needs.'

'She had a husband. She has two young daughters, one aged ten, and one two years old. And what of the other five men? Had they five wives?'

Brisbane opened his hands helplessly.

'What of them?' Susannah demanded.

'Of the six men,' said the Governor, 'the corporal tells me that even the names of four were uncertain, and that the fifth, who was dying, was unmarried. The sixth was Bryant.'

'God have mercy upon us.'

'Sue, if you will show me to Mrs Bryant, I will myself tell her that her husband died. I shall lie, and may God forgive me for that, and tell her he fell into the canal. There shall be no chains.'

'No. Go home. When was the widow of a man who died in a prison last told by the Governor himself? That would not help. Your presence would show you were lying. But,' she said, touching his shoulder, offering some consolation, 'few men would offer to do it. It is good-hearted in you. But let me tell her. Then, God help me, it will be believed.'

Brisbane thanked her. Then he explained the matter of the cloak, which Tyrone had returned to Parramatta dried, pressed, and neatly packed. He had brought it with him, and would place it in the front hall.

He left. Susannah prayed, and then went to tell Jane. Jane told her elder daughter that her father was dead, and her younger daughter that her father would not be coming back ever. She fetched the blue cloak from the hallway where Brisbane had left it. Carrying it in her arms, she walked slowly over the Domain lawns down to the water's edge. She gazed across the cove towards the north shore, facing the plantation from which the single lemon tree was stolen. Then she turned her eyes towards the open water of the harbour. She stood for five minutes, hugging the folded cloak to her breast. Then she walked rapidly into the town and visited four friends. She had formed an intention of great heroism, which she carried through to its uttermost.


Jane called on John Smith, the waterman. She met Nathaniel Lilley and William Allen, who worked as fishermen in Rush-cutter's Bay and sold the fish in the town. She talked long into the night with William Moatham, who had once been master's mate aboard a frigate. Jane was a free woman. Governor King had signed her pardon many years before. Her two daughters

were born free. John Smith, the same waterman who had taken
Susannah and the children to Manly Cove, was a ticket-of-
leave man. He was the Governor's man, and his position,
among that community of felons, was one of great privilege.
Lilley and Allen were convicts, but worked for an easy master
who left them very much alone and even let them keep a tenth
of the proceeds of any fish they sold on his behalf. Moatham
was the only man whose situation was in any way hard. He
was a convict, who could not expect a ticket-of-leave for another
two years, and he was made to dig ditches. Of all the group he
had suffered the greatest fall in being sent to New South Wales.
He was born in the southern Cornish fishing village of Mousehole, which its natives pronounce Mowzell, had gone to sea at
ten, by fourteen knew the English Channel, on its French and
English shores, as well as any man could, and in 1800, when
there was a real fear that Napoléon might invade Britain, was
taken into the Royal Navy straight away as master's mate.
The sailing master is not to be confused with the captain of a
ship of the Royal Navy. The master has no command and no
commission. He is responsible to the captain or commander of
the vessel for its handling and navigation. He may advise the
captain how to manage the sailing of his vessel, but the decision
is the captain's. An exceptional master, or a master in time of
war, may reach commissioned rank, and then the way up is open
to him. Captain Cook served many years as a master and did
not receive his lieutenant's commission until he was a few months
short of forty. Bligh, in his turn, once served as master under
Cook. But those men were exceptional. A master is a sort of
maritime sergeant major, and likely to remain so, but it is an
honourable rank, as is that of master's mate. A master's mate is
likely to be promoted master after a few years. At the age of
nineteen Moatham, because of his intimate knowledge of the
coasts of Normandy and Brittany, was guiding sloops and
frigates through the inlets of northern and western France by
night, searching for craft which might mount the invasion that
never came. Master's mate, of all ranks, is perilous, poised
between up and down. Once a man is master, he will not be
broken thoughtlessly. But while a man is master's mate, it needs
only one slip and he is back to ordinary seaman. A bad commander, an irascible commander, an uncharted rock, and he

is back in the fo'c'sle. In the running aground of the frigate
*Hecate* in 1801, Moatham saw two of his friends swept overboard and perish, and he swore at the incompetence of the
lieutenant of the watch who had disregarded his urgent advice.
Next day he was back in the fo'c'sle, and from the day of that
injustice the fall of a capable and brave man could almost have
been foreseen. He sank to transportation.

Moatham, Smith, Lilley, and Allen listened to Jane Bryant.
All had known her husband. She had the ready sympathy and
fellow-feeling of all. The only man to hesitate was Smith, perhaps because he had the most to lose, or perhaps because he
was the most level-headed of them all and saw the risks more
clearly. But he also saw that he was essential to the whole
enterprise, and that without him it would fail before it started.
So he consented.

Next day, Moatham visited Nathaniel Charles, the skipper
of an American schooner out of New Bedford who had put into
Sydney with the usual speculative cargo of cloth, canvas, spirits,
and New England manufactured goods. Trading between
British colonies and the United States had barely been interrupted by the War of 1812, and several governors of New
South Wales, such was their need, turned blind eyes to Navigation Acts which restricted trade with foreign, and therefore
American, vessels. If a cargo was needed, it was bought. This
gave the Americans the raffishness of habitually successful free-
booters. The Americans had also never forgotten 1812. In that
war their seamanship was superior. Free men made better
sailors than pressed men. Not that life on board an American
vessel was really any more free than on board a ship of any
other nation. An American captain, like any other, was at sea
second only to God, and that was only because of a technical
matter of seniority. But the Americans were honestly infected
with the idea of freedom. There is no better place in the world
than a ship to demonstrate with conclusiveness, and within an
hour, that no two men are created equal, but the power of an
idea survives all demonstration that it is nonsense. The
Americans believed, and their belief made them strong.
American skippers personally got on very well with their Royal
Naval counterparts in Sydney, but this did not lessen their
contempt of a colony which was no more than a jail. It did not

lessen their contempt for what they saw as a hard slavery of the
greater part of the people there. The French thought the same,
but the Americans were more vigorous, and had a missionary
zeal and a missionary good faith. Captain Charles listened to
Moatham, agreed to what was proposed, and sold him a compass, a quadrant, and the necessary charts. He then waved
away further money, and gave enough good Yankee canvas to
replace twice over the split lug-sail of the Governor's cutter in
which the escape was to begin. Everything was agreed, and
Captain Charles was a man who would keep his promise.

They gathered at Jane's cottage. Lilley and Allen, the two
fishermen, brought two seines to fish with and a gaff to spear
larger fish, and eight gallons of fresh water in leather bottles.
Moatham brought the instruments he had purchased, two
makeshift spears, and a handsaw. John Smith had from nowhere found two ancient blunderbusses, and powder for them.
Jane bought and begged fourteen pounds of salt pork in a barrel,
a hundredweight of rice, and the same amount of flour. There
was also some sugar, tea, and coffee. The waterman had two
lanterns in the cutter, a barrel of tar, and a cask of rum. For
warmth they had the clothes they wore, four blankets, and the
cloak. It was nine in the evening, twenty minutes after a summer
sunset, and they would leave at nightfall. A dozen souls who
had helped them to collect supplies must have known what they
intended, but no whisper of it got out. Jane wrestled hard with
herself and then was unable to face Susannah. It hurt her to
leave for ever without saying goodbye to a woman she loved.
She asked the advice of the others. John Smith was for telling,
but the others would on no account trust Susannah. So it was
settled.

It was an uneasy evening for Susannah. That morning she
had been to see how Jane was. Jane had thanked her again and
again, and at their parting was in tears. Susannah thought the
tears those of grief for a dead husband, and that the thanks
were offered for what she had so lamentably failed to achieve.
She found such thanks hard to bear. Next to Jane, Susannah
felt the death of George Bryant more than any human being.
That evening Susannah twice put on her shawl to go to Jane,
but twice thought it more merciful to leave her in peace. The
next day she would suggest that Jane should come to live in the
house and leave the cottage.

But still, she was so uneasy that at half past ten she did go to the cottage. There was no answer, and she entered. The cottage was dark and empty. Where were the children? On the kitchen table, she found a note Jane had left. Susannah read it, and hurried down the path to John Smith's jetty. The cutter was gone. On the path back, she found a scattering of rice where one of the bags had leaked as it was carried to the boat. She returned slowly to the house and to her room, where she again unfolded the note. It was in pencil, on grocer's paper, and it said:

Dearest Susannah – who next to my George and children I always loved as My Life, and Shall never forget the goodness of you. We are gone without Farewells because the Others were fearefull and would not tell any Person, though I spoke against their Feare and would have told You before any one. We are Gone to America, having plenty to carry us there, where Mary and Elizabeth will Prosper, and the Others be Free Men. God be with you for All you Did, and We shall surely meet one Day in the Lands of Promise.

Susannah sat and thought fiercely. Jane was a free woman, and had Susannah known she wished to go home, or to America, she would have paid the passage for her and the children. And who were the 'others'? Jane was free but if she was assisting convicts to escape she was again a criminal. They had plenty to carry them there? Spilt grains of rice did not suggest plenty. To what vessel had Smith's cutter carried them? She might still be able to help. If she could find them aboard any ship in the harbour she could at least make their passage easier. She knew there were only two American vessels in port. She knew the captains of both. She harnessed the sulky herself, and, near midnight, observed by the sentries, called on both. Neither had passengers. Captain Charles did say to her, in parting, 'If I see your people, I will do my best for them.'

When she returned to the house Redmond was waiting, demanding an account. 'There is nothing,' she said. 'It is nothing.'

Next day, when the hue and cry was up, Redmond kept silence, not for Susannah but for the sake of his own reputation. When the port officer came to ask why Susannah had visited two American vessels the night before, she told enough of the truth. She was looking for her maid Jane Bryant, who was

missing. She pointed out that Jane was a free woman. The port
officer remarked that three convicts and the Governor's waterman were also missing, and so was the Governor's cutter. He
said every vessel in the harbour had been searched. They could
only have escaped in the cutter.

'The cutter?' she exclaimed. It was the cockleshell that had
nearly overturned bringing her back from Manly. 'And Jane
has her children with her?'

The port officer concluded that Susannah knew nothing, and
he was very nearly right. She said nothing of the letter. She
feared terribly.


In the carriage drive, boxes were loaded on to Redmond's
travelling coach. Susannah ran to his room and found he had
taken nearly all his possessions. Through the window she could
hear John and Redmond's chief stockman talking about the
sheep station they would reach in two days' travelling. Redmond met her as she ran down the stairs. He said, 'I am doing
what I said I would do. The port officer may believe you had
no part in this escape, and I suppose the Governor will believe
you, but I will not. I am taking the boy. I have taken him for
visits before, and I suggest you allow him to believe this is
another. I shall allow you enough to keep the house up.'

'I had nothing to do with this escape,' she said.

'But I do not believe you. Now, will you say goodbye to
John? You will need to be cheerful.'

Susannah lifted her head, walked slowly down the stairs and
into the yard, and made conversation with her son while he
instructed the coachman how to secure the cases containing the
sporting guns Redmond had just bought for him. They said
goodbye as if it were for a week or so, kissing each other on the
cheek. The escape had evidently been kept from him, because
he called back, as the coach began to move off, 'Tell Jane next
time she shall come to see the station. And tell Mary too. She
thinks she is too young for the journey, but she is really the same
age as me.' They waved while the coach was in sight.

Susannah walked into the empty house, and through the
empty rooms, and was alone.

# 19

# The Escape around the World

For two days and two nights, in mercifully fair weather, the four men, the woman, and the two children, sailed northwards, passing on the second night the lights of Newcastle. They were not pursued. On the orders of Sydney, a lookout was kept to the south west, but not to the north. To the north there was, except Newcastle, nothing. To the east stretched the Pacific as far as Cape Horn. The day after the disappearance of the cutter, the American schooner slipped out of the cove, bound for Tahiti and Valparaiso. The port officer, feeling uneasily that he was acting irrationally, searched her again before she weighed anchor, found nothing, and took a farewell drink with Captain Charles.

'Would they steal the Governor's cutter to come aboard my vessel?' asked the captain.

The port officer said he thought not. 'God help them wherever they are, and those children.'

'Amen to that,' said the captain.

Susannah watched the port officer's boat return, and by the pilot sent a last message to the captain of the schooner. She remembered Jane's assertion in her letter that they were going to America. Susannah's note to Captain Charles said, 'I have no reason to suppose that you may, but if you should be at any charge on account of Jane Bryant, her children, or the others, I will repay it when you next call at Sydney.' As far as the coast-guard could keep her in sight, the schooner sailed due east, for the Society Islands, Tahiti, and Valparaiso.

On the third night north the seven fugitives slept ashore, in the lee of a sandbank. The two fishermen caught enough fish to enable them all to eat well. Jane cooked some rice. They found no water, but allowed themselves a plentiful ration from the supply they had brought. North of Newcastle they found enough coal, in an outcrop, to keep them warm, which was as well because there was little scrub-wood to make a fire. The men kept watch two hours turn and turn about through the night. All the ammunition they had for the blunderbusses was a mixture of shrapnel, grit, and old nails, but they hoped that this far north the blacks would be so unfamiliar with firearms that the noise of the powder alone would be enough to ward them off. No blacks were seen.

The cutter sailed well. On the fourth day, when the wind dropped, they rowed easily. They had six oars, but men for only four. They sang. No one watching these seven creatures on that ocean could have said they were desperate. No one would have said, watching them, that their water was reduced to six gallons. No one could have thought Jane a recent widow; but that was her courage.

On the fifth day they came to a cove, and Moatham nodded. The breakers at the mouth were deceptively rough, and they made an easy passage into calm waters, beached the cutter, collected brush, and made a fire. The wood was green. 'Smokey Cove,' said Moatham, 'taken possession of in the name of us.' They made a meal of more rice and fish, and even a little salt pork. They brewed coffee. A sane observer would have said it was mad. They could not stay there. There was no water. Their provisions must be running out. If the weather broke, there would be no shelter. No one knew where hostile blacks might be. And yet the fugitives lit a fire. All that night they kept the fire blazing. At dawn they all went to the farthest point of the cove, looked out to sea, and returned, and all that day and the next night kept the fire burning. It was at dawn the next day that Jane and the men looked hard at each other and said what they had at first not given one thought to say, and then, for the last day, had been afraid to say.

'He has left us,' said Moatham.

'No,' said Smith, 'we do not know that.'

Lilley and Allen mended their fishing nets. Lilley said to Moatham, 'It was you who dealt with him. Why do you say he has left us? You were sure of him?'

'I say it because he knows these shores. And because any vessel must have seen our smoke. If he were here, he must have seen it.' Jane said nothing. Smith resolved to search further north.

'But if he should come when we have gone?' said Jane.

Moatham knew that was impossible. The American schooner, whose captain had promised to meet them in this cove and then take them across the Pacific and round Cape Horn to America, would have made better time than a cutter, even leaving a day later. If he had not come already, he would not come at all. And yet, said Jane, he might have been delayed at Sydney. That was indeed their only hope. So they left in plain view on the headland a cross six feet high, and another in the cove, and messages at the foot of each, and then they sailed slowly north, examining each cove. The ration of water was halved.

Only Moatham was sure they had been deserted. The others hoped. Moatham was wrong, but it did not matter. Two days later, after they prospected first north and then south again, they found the schooner wrecked and broken-backed on a headland they had previously passed in the night. She had been there before them, and been driven ashore in a storm that blew itself out before they arrived. Some of her crew had the good fortune to drown. The dismembered carcases of the others were scattered over the beach. Here the blacks were cannibals. Moatham recognized the features of Captain Charles.

They salvaged four floating barrels, one of rum, two empty, and one, pricelessly, half-full of fresh water. Smith and Moatham also dragged two spars from the surf. To approach the wreck more closely was dangerous. The seas that were smashing her to pieces would smash any man. If they stayed, more casks might wash ashore, but they could not wait for fear of the blacks. They could not bury the bodies, but heaped them over with sand. Then they sailed the cutter north again, back to Smokey Cove, but lit no more fires.

The men were then generous. They knew that to go back was almost certainly to hang. But they knew that if the children went on they would probably die. They offered to return, and Jane declined their offer. They had to go on. If they remained where they were they would undoubtedly starve. Only Moatham knew what lay north and west, and he told them.

He had never sailed those waters. The chart he had from the American captain took him no further north than the rendezvous the schooner had never kept. But Moatham had seen the old Dutch charts, and the charts of Cook. A chart and its features remain long in the memory of a man who was once a master's mate. He said that to the north was the Great Barrier Reef, the greatest coral reef known to man, stretching for 1200 miles up to the northernmost point of New Holland at Cape York. He did not know this reef. No navigator did know it well. They would have to negotiate the channel between the reef and the shore. They would have to sail by daylight and beach the cutter by night. He knew nothing of the natives. He knew there were harbours. Captain Cook had once repaired the *Endeavour* in one of them. The climate was tropical, and the rains those of a monsoon. Further North lay New Guinea, where no white man would survive. They could not go there. Once at Cape York, they would set course west across the Gulf of Carpentaria, and then across the Timor Sea to the Dutch East Indies. Their destination, said Moatham, was Kupang on the island of Timor. It was agreed. Moatham spoke with authority. Only Smith, the Governor's waterman, comprehended the magnitude of what was proposed.

They sailed northwards across the Tropic of Capricorn. The monsoon set in. The rain came. For eight days they had no hot food. But they caught the rainwater in the sail, and filled the casks they had salvaged and the leather bottles they had started out with. In turbulent seas, no fish were caught. They chewed the rice grain by grain. When two fish were washed aboard, Lilley gutted them with his thumb and made the children eat them raw. 'Suck them if you can,' he said. To encourage them, he did so himself. The children stomached them. The children were not seasick, and the men not severely. Jane was badly seasick, and could not take food or rum. To be wet to the skin was the natural condition of them all. They shivered themselves warm. They never lost account of days, which Smith notched in the gunwale with his sea-knife. Then the rains ceased, and water ran low. When they came to the barrier reef they had to find a landfall each day before dusk, and one night, in exhaustion, were all but murdered. None of the men saw the blacks. A child screamed, and Smith fired a

blunderbuss into the air. In the powder flash they saw a
hundred faces within ten yards. The savages did not attack
again that night. Next morning the footprints of seventy and
more could be seen in the sand, and the cask of rum was gone
from the cutter.

They were saved many times – by luck, by courage, by a
change of wind, and, later, by rain which fell when they were
down to their last pint of water. They were saved so often that
after a while they never thought of it. They only knew they
survived. On one occasion they were undoubtedly saved by an
island. It was a coral island in the barrier reef. They had ample
water, because it had again rained incessantly, but they were
exhausted. They knew they could not make the mainland
before darkness fell. Providence was with them. They ran
through the small reef surrounding the island, though if they
had been dashed to either side it would have been their death
on the coral. Then, when they were safely through the reef,
they saw breakers only 200 yards ahead. The breakers were too
severe, and they all knew it. And then, through the breakers,
a way through the surf appeared, and the breakers did not
smash the cutter, but only drove it safely up a fine beach of
black sand. If the breakers had not driven it so far they would
not have had the strength to drag it themselves to a safe distance from the shore. Then the rain stopped and there was an
hour's hot sun to dry their clothes and the blankets. Two
blacks appeared, an old man and a woman, the first natives
who had been friendly. They carried a firestick. For the first
time since any of them could remember, they lit a fire. They
accepted the fish the blacks offered, ate, made coffee, and all
slept. That was the only time they ever slept on land knowing
there were blacks but keeping no guard. They were too exhausted to care. Next day the blacks returned with another,
younger man and his woman, who made signs with a stick in
the sand. It was the children who understood that they were
drawing a turtle. The two fishermen followed the blacks.
Smith and Moatham, now recovered enough to stand guard
again, remained with the cutter and Jane and the children.
An hour later the fishermen returned, each with a turtle
enough to last for a week. They cooked turtle flesh, and drank
turtle soup. Apart from the fish, this was their first hot meat

since they left Sydney, and the first ample meal since they knew
the schooner was wrecked.

For three days they rested.

Then Smith came to Jane. 'We must go, and you must tell
them.'

'*I* must tell them?'

'They will do for you and the children what they will not do
for themselves. Jane, they would die here.'

She glanced at the two fishermen sprawled on the beach,
and thought perhaps they might. But then she looked at
Moatham, who was gazing out to sea as if laying a course.

'Him?' she said, 'I believe he could navigate us to Portsmouth.'

'I believe he could. And I believe if any man can get us to
Timor, he will. If you tell him. But I have watched him for
two hours, and what I see is the reef-stare. Listen to me, Jane.
I have spent my life among sailors, and I have heard tell of
it. When a man is driven as far as he can go for the moment,
when he is at the end of his resources, he goes into himself.
Many good sailors rot on coral islands. A man, when he is
weary, gazes at the surf breaking on the reef, and hears the
sound, and if there is drink to drink, he drinks, and then
gazes at the reef, and drinks, and gazes again, and his spirit
is so lulled that he looses all activity. Men lose their will that
way. If he should lose his, we are all dead, Jane.'

'Then,' she said, 'take the children along the shore.'

Jane went over to the man staring at the reef. 'Good
morning, Mr Moatham.'

He nodded without looking at her.

'Mr Moatham,' she said, 'I have wondered. What is
coral?'

He spoke almost straight into the air. 'There is noble coral,
so called, and that is richly red. And then there is your rose
coral, and your mushroom coral. I have heard it is nothing but
the old skeletons of the smallest sea creatures, which when
alive are like tiny anemones. But when it is coral it is dead, and
I have never seen it alive.'

'I had a coral necklace, that was given me in England,'
she said.

He smiled. 'Those reefs are the dead necklaces of many

sailors. We were fortunate to come through that as we did, so easily.'

'And we shall get out easily enough?'

He did not reply.

'Walk a little with me,' she said. She took his arm, and led him away from the two fishermen, who were too apathetic to glance up, and away from the children, whom Smith was engaging in a hunt for fire-wood.

'It is warm,' she said. 'Shall we sit?' They sat on the beach. Again he sat facing the reef, a little in front of her, not speaking. At the nape of his neck his grey hair was long. She put out a hand and stroked it, and continued to stroke it. He turned his head and she feared that his eyes were hostile, but they were not. They were red with long gazing at horizons in hot sun, and they were helpless. She held out her arms to him and he put his head on her breast. Then he talked. Over many years, Moatham had receded into himself. When he talked it was not so much to her as to himself, saying aloud what he had over and over again said silently in his thoughts. His words were incoherent. Only Moatham and any God in whom he confided knew that he was reliving the capital moments of his life. He spoke the names of Marazion, Truro, Mousehole, and Bodmin – the geography of his life as a boy. Then there was Plymouth, and the *Hecate*, and two names Jane could not catch but which were those of the two men lost when the *Hecate* struck. That was the running aground of one of Her Majesty's frigates, which had floated clear with the tide, but the wreck of Moatham's life, which had never since found a tide to float it. Then there was one joyful recollection, none the less incoherent. To Jane's ears came the date of 28 February, repeatedly, and the words, 'I am back'. She thought they were the words of a woman, to Moatham, perhaps written as the only three words of a letter, on some long gone 28 February. She did not know, and she did not ask, and Moatham never spoke the woman's name. When he stopped for a moment she held him tight in her arms, and then let him speak again, and then once again held him, until he wept openly and bitterly. She rocked his head like a child's. It must have been two hours. Then he raised his head, and shook himself.

'That I should let myself go so,' he said. 'It is very weak.'

Jane said, 'You are as strong a man as I know. And if you wept, do you not think a woman is proud to hear a man weep for good reasons?'

By early afternoon they set sail, making only for the mainland that evening. They had left the island that had saved them but which, to save themselves, they had to leave. They had eaten. They had rested. They had salted down a cask of turtle flesh and filled another with turtle oil. They had despaired, but because they had despaired they had renewed their hope, and they went on.

They were in peril of their lives every day, but on two occasions in particular came very near to death. Once, in the Gulf of Carpentaria, they were chased by blacks of a kind and of a ferocity they had never seen before, not the blacks of the south-east coast of New Holland who never went to sea at all and took to water only in bark canoes, but by warriors in canoes of thirty oars. By then they had been six weeks on the passage, they had reached a weariness they did not realize until they tried to pull at the four oars and found they were too feeble to keep in unison, and they were saved only by a change in the wind. The Governor's cutter, flying before the wind with her lugsail, outran two canoes of thirty oars. Beyond the gulf they found the estuary of a river, rowed upstream to replenish their fresh water, and were working their way out when they were hit by squalls and all but swamped. The cutter began to leak so badly they had to throw two barrels and their blankets overboard to lighten her. Jane wrapped Elizabeth in the blue cloak and refused to part with that. They beached the cutter at last and spent two days paying the seams with the barrel of pitch they had brought from Sydney. And then, after ten weeks, they came to Timor and the Dutch port of Kupang.

They were Europeans. They were in distress. They did not need to recount their much-rehearsed tale of a shipwreck, because they were evidently shipwrecked. The barrels they had on board, and two spars, were plainly from a Yankee schooner. They were those recovered from the wreck of Captain Charles's vessel. They were fed, clothed, and housed without the least suspicion. The Dutch Governor promised them a passage to the Cape of Good Hope on the next East Indiaman. After a week there was an incident which they feared might give them away. The Governor asked them to sign an order on the British Government to repay him for the provisions he had supplied. The four men and Jane were in the room with him, and he asked the senior to sign.

They hesitated, as no sailors ever would. There is a hierarchy on board any ship which is very plain. Moatham, who was known to have navigated the cutter, would have been the obvious man. The Governor pushed the paper towards him. But Moatham, having done all he had done, hesitated to commit what he thought of as a forgery. Smith hastily signed. When the men were together later, they were apprehensive, and for a day feared arrest. They need not have worried. The Governor had noticed, but thought either that Moatham could barely write, or that they were simply confused after an exhausting passage. He could not have suspected what they were. The truth would have been the wildest and most unlikely of all speculations.

Then they were unlucky. The first vessel to put in was not a Dutchman, but a British frigate. This was the foulest and most unlikely chance. Commander Redvers was told of the English survivors and asked to take them to Cape Town. He interviewed them, guessed that they were convicts, and put the men and Jane in irons. On the expostulation of the Dutch women of the colony he released Jane from fetters, so that she could look after her daughters. Then he set course for the Cape. The first weeks of that passage are through the filthiest of tropical climates. The sailors, seeing the vapour rise from jungles of the islands of the Java Sea, said the whole land gave off a poisonous miasma. Four weeks out, the elder child, Mary, died not from any miasma but from exhaustion assisted by scurvy. The men of the lower watch committed her decently to the sea, though the commander would not heave to for the burial. Jane was permitted to be present, but the four men, who begged for this indulgence, were not. The commander gave as his reason that he did not dare to risk mutiny. The five, seeing no point in further deception, told the sailors they were from Sydney. Redvers was told with some awe by his sailing master that Moatham had navigated the cutter from Sydney to Timor by means of a quadrant and compass. The commander immediately confiscated these instruments. He was an unusual officer, and at Cape Town received his deserts at the hands of the Port-Admiral.

Commander Redvers submitted a formal report, and next day was summoned to the flag-ship. Admiral Sir Julian Cunningham, Knight of the Thistle, was a very senior and undistinguished admiral, whose last command this was. He was returning home to farm in Scotland. He had spent all his life at sea. In many wars it had been his misfortune never to be where the battle was, and scarcely to fire a shot at an enemy. He had borne this with patience, and was loved by almost all the officers who served under him, one of whom had been Nelson. He was a man of honour. He also had a reputation as a mild man.

'Redvers,' he said, 'I have your report.'

'Sir.'

'You kept these people in irons from Timor?'

'I thought it necessary.'

'So that four skeletons should not rouse a mutiny among your own crew of, what, one hundred and eighty men?'

'I judged them likely to be seditious, sir, from their previous conduct.'

'You discovered they had navigated from Sydney to Timor, in a fifteen-foot cutter, in an open boat?'

'Yes, sir, they stole the Governor's cutter; which I took on board.'

'Redvers, I am a sailor, and that is your profession too. Let us consider. Of what length would you estimate the passage to be from Sydney to Timor?'

'Of three thousand miles, sir. And above.'

'Rather above. That is, shall we say, comparable in distance to a passage from Portsmouth to Boston? Forgive me, I was familiar with that second port in my youth. You will not be; but you know its position?'

Redvers said he did, but really he did not yet follow the drift of the Admiral's remarks.

'That,' said the Admiral, 'is a feat of courage and seamanship which I have never in my life approached, and which perhaps you have not. At a quick computation I would say they sailed further in an open boat than Captain Bligh when his mutineers put him off the *Bounty*, and Captain Bligh, you will recall, had

a crew of eighteen seamen, not two fishermen, a waterman, a
woman, and two little girls.'

'I think so, sir.'

'Then, man, you are beyond praying for. Have you no
admiration for excellence in your own calling? Can you not
understand what these people have done? I see you cannot.
Very well. I say nothing, Redvers, of the death of the girl on
the passage here from Timor. There is enough death in those
waters. But to keep those men in chains was unconscionable,
and not to see what they had achieved was insensible. Put them
aboard my flag-ship by this evening. They will return to
England with me. Restore to that man his quadrant and compass. Good day.'


Moatham was brought to the Admiral's stateroom with a guard
of two marines.

'What are you?' said the Admiral.

'Moatham, sir, a convict.'

'And before you were a convict?'

'Master's mate, sir. *Hecate*, thirty-four guns.'

'Ah. Moatham, did you bring that cutter from Sydney to
Kupang?'

'It was a fortunate passage, sir.'

Cunningham told one marine to fetch the master of his own
flag-ship, and charts of those waters. The master's name was
Robert Strong. When he appeared, the Admiral dismissed the
second marine too.

Cunningham rose, walked round to the chart table, waved
the two men near him, and said to Moatham, 'Show me how.'
Cunningham and Strong listened for half an hour.

Cunningham said, 'Moatham, for what crime were you
transported?'

'Theft, sir.'

'You do not hedge, do you?' said the Admiral. 'Then tell me,
were you an habitual thief?'

'It was only once, sir.'

The Admiral left the two men at the chart table and gazed
out of the stern quarterlights. 'Moatham, what I can do for
you when we return to England I have no means of knowing.

It may be very little. But you have my word I will do what I can.'

He swung round. 'Mr Moatham, on the passage home it is my pleasure, as I feel it will also be Mr Strong's, that you should mess with him and the other warrant officers.'

'Sir?' said Moatham, utterly confused.

Cunningham repeated himself, and said that Mr Strong would see to it.

'Sir, there is one thing I must say.'

'Say it.'

'God knew more about that passage than I did, sir.'

'I fancy God needed your assistance at times.'

'And, sir, without Smith, we would be dead. And without Jane Bryant we would never have started, nor continued, nor ever finished. It was she that did it, sir.'


No one who knew Sir Julian Cunningham was surprised at this act of generosity. It was part of the man. He was a good sailor, who throughout his life encouraged in others an excellence he did not see in himself. He valued and rewarded in others a courage which had never been demanded of him, and which he could never be sure he possessed. What his act of generosity meant to Moatham was not to be calculated. His bitterness departed. He messed with his equals, whose admiration was not so openly expressed as the Admiral's, but was still evident. His equals thought Moatham a good and modest man. The generosity, kindness, and above all justness of an Admiral made up, as much as any action could, for the bloody-minded injustice of a careless lieutenant that night on the *Hecate*.


Sir Julian's flotilla was three months at the Cape before it sailed. News of the arrest of the seven at Timor and of their being sent to England had reached Sydney. Susannah was astonished and delighted at their survival. The news of the death of the older girl had not yet arrived. Susannah and Robert often corresponded. She knew he had taken to the law, and now wrote asking him to do all he could for the prisoners when they arrived.

Three months in the warm climate of the Cape was a splendid restorative for all of them, and the passage home was miraculously smooth. It was Sir Julian's last passage home, and the sailors said the South Atlantic was showing its respects to a well-loved sailor. Only the English Channel was rough. Sir Julian's ship paid off at Gravesend, he was piped ashore, and then he did a last quixotic thing. He ordered his own barge to take the prisoners downstream to London Bridge, flying his broad pennant. The flotilla had dispersed in the Channel, some ships to Plymouth, some to Portsmouth. The news of the Botany Bay people was in London days before them. When they landed at London Bridge a thousand men and women waited to greet them at the Monument, the Doric column 200 feet high erected to commemorate the Great Fire of London. The tipstaff met them, and from there they were conducted to Newgate. It is a mile to walk, and it became a procession. Jane came ashore first, with Elizabeth wrapped in the blue cloak; then Moatham, in a suit of broadcloth, the gift of his fellow warrant-officers and made by the ship's tailor; then Smith; and then Lilley and Allen. There was no cheering, everywhere a silence, but when the procession began, the men with one movement doffed their hats. Billingsgate fish-porters, cabmen, clerks, and the brokers of City of London banking houses, all uncovered.

It was the duty of the Sheriff of London to be there.

'This,' he said to his tipstaff, 'is a strangely silent demonstration.'

'And a very firm one, sir,' said the tipstaff. 'The firmest I ever saw.'

Next day at Bow Street the five adults were arraigned before the Metropolitan Magistrate. The charge against the four men was that of escaping from a sentence of transportation, and that against Jane Bryant of aiding the escape. Jane was allowed to carry Elizabeth in her arms. The court was full. The Magistrate, old Bond, addressed the prisoners.

'Will you listen to me? In a moment my clerk will read the indictment aloud, so that you may know with what you are charged. But before we do that I will tell you as simply as I can what course these proceedings may take. When the indictments are read you may deny the charges, or you may say nothing.

I am not your judge. Whatever happens today, it will be my formal duty to return you to Newgate, and you may later, if the Crown so decides, be brought to face a judge and jury at your trial.'

The court reporters and hangers-on, who knew very well how this stuff was commonly rattled through, to the near-incomprehension of the prisoners, looked at each other and grinned.

'Now,' said the Magistrate, 'at this or at any subsequent proceedings, you may say nothing, or you may speak for yourselves, or you may address the court through counsel who has already communicated to me an offer to represent you, without expense to yourselves. You might think yourselves wise to accept his services, but the decision is yours.'

The prisoners looked at each other, and, seeing their confusion, the Magistrate said, 'If it helps, my advice to you would be to accept the gentleman's offer.'

They nodded.

'All of you?' said the Magistrate.

They all nodded again.

The Magistrate turned to the barrister's benches. 'Mr King, you have seen the indictments and do not demur at their form?'

Counsel stood to say he did not. Jane Bryant looked in the face of the young man she knew and yet did not know. He knew her. The indictments were read, the Magistrate recited the formal committal to Newgate, and, before handing the prisoners over to the Sheriff's officers, gave them a purse of forty guineas subscribed by some gentlemen known to him. The Magistrate called King to him. 'Mr Attorney has been in court, as you may have noticed.' Robert had not, but glanced up in time to see the Attorney-General leave through the side door. 'He will see you in my chambers.'

Robert bowed. Old Bond, a good lawyer, a man who spent forty years as an advocate before he accepted the stipendiary magistracy at Bow Street once held by Sir John Fielding, said, 'King, you won't mind if I suggest you listen to the Attorney and say as little as possible beyond, "How d'you do?" and "Good morning"? I've known Sir Charles for many years. He listens well to silence.'

Sir Charles Bankes, Attorney-General of Great Britain, after the Lord Chancellor the principal law officer of the realm, head of the legal profession to whose members he was known simply as 'Mr Attorney', surveyed Robert King.

'How d'you do, King? Your people are plainly guilty, you know.'

'How d'you do? sir,' said Robert. He did not really know where he stood. He had seen the Attorney only once before, in court, when as a student he had watched him prosecuting two men for treason. They had hanged. He knew very well that the Attorney would himself prosecute in only the gravest of cases, and beyond that he knew little more. It was only two months since Robert had been called to the Bar at Gray's Inn, and in those two months he had appeared in court once, as junior counsel to a much more senior man, and he had said not one word in court, having been called on only to watch.

The Attorney kept silence. King's people were plainly guilty as could be. Very well. But transportation was hated. The escape had been heroic. Three of the prisoners, the woman, Moatham, and Smith, had a natural dignity which would distinguish them anywhere. And if the woman was going to stand in the dock carrying that child of two years' old. . . . Then there was that silent demonstration when they landed. The Sheriff had plainly told the Attorney that he had seldom seen anything like it. There also lay before the Attorney, on the table, a letter from Admiral Sir Julian Cunningham, in which he wrote, 'I confess that I never looked at these people, without pity and astonishment. After having combatted every hardship, and conquered every difficulty, they had miscarried in an heroic struggle for liberty.' He had no doubt the Admiral would say that in court if given the opportunity. The Admiral also offered to employ on his Scottish estates all the prisoners, should they be acquitted. The Admiral did not say, but Mr Attorney very well knew, that he owned, at a rough guess, a tenth of the more arable parts of Scotland, which gave him a certain influence even in London. The Admiral also returned, from all those Scottish acres, sixteen Members of Parliament, a number useful to the government of which the Attorney was a member. Then Mr Attorney looked at King. No barrister ever has his wig cleaned, so the length of a barrister's experience can readily be determined from the state of his wig. King's was

the whitest he had lately seen. A new man would have the
jury's sympathy. He might be competent. Or, which from the
Crown's point of view would be much worse, he might be useless, in which case the Judge would by tradition help him in
every conceivable way, perhaps to the extent of conducting the
defence himself. These were the thoughts that ran through the
Attorney's mind. Robert had only the faintest glimmer of all
this, though to get that glimmer from the impassivity of the
Attorney showed the beginnings of a legal instinct.

'Who will pay for the defence?'

That was none of the Attorney's business, but Robert replied,
'There are sufficient funds, sir.' It was a lucky answer, because
the Attorney's mind went to those Scottish acres, and assumed
a connection between them and the young barrister which did
not in fact exist.

The Attorney leaned back. The young man said nothing.

'King, the prisoner Jane Bryant seemed to know you in court,
and you to know her?'

'My grandfather was Governor of New South Wales, sir, and
Jane Bryant was the midwife at my birth.'

The Attorney covered his face with his hands, and for the
first time in legal memory laughed, and laughed. He already
knew what sort of a case he had, but now there was this too.
All it needed was for this piece of information to be volunteered
in court, and the jury would be in tears and the prosecution in
rags, if it weren't in rags already.

Robert stood silent.

'Beg your pardon, King. A man's birth is no laughing matter
to him, eh?'

The Attorney picked up the indictment, took a pen, and
scrawled across it, *Nolle Prosequi*. The Crown was stating, in the
person of Mr Attorney, that it did not wish to pursue the
indictment. It was all done with. The prisoners would go free.
That was that. He passed the endorsed paper to Robert, who
read the two words.

'Good morning, sir,' said Robert.

The Attorney called him back. 'King, if that was the first
case you have ever argued, and I think it was, you did it un-
commonly well.'

Robert said it was only fair of him to admit that his conduct of the case had been exactly that advised by Mr Bond the Magistrate.

'I knew that. But you see, King, you managed to carry out his advice, which few men do. It says a lot for you. You will do well. Good day.'

# 20

# The Last Benediction of Françoise

Robert took Jane, her daughter, and the four men to Bedford Square. The four men had accepted the Admiral's offer and would be going soon to his estates in Scotland. Jane did not yet know what she would do. They were all bewildered. Their release seemed more a miracle to them than their magnificent passage. They looked on Robert as a saviour. It was useless for him to protest that he had done almost nothing, and that any man could have done as much for them. It was useless for him to explain that, had they not been represented at all, the result would have been the same. It would have take a couple of weeks rather than a couple of days, but that was all the difference his presence could possibly have made. They did not believe him. It seemed insulting to tell them the truth, which was that their release was a simple matter of policy. He did tell them that the interest of Sir Julian had mattered a great deal more than his advocacy. The most they were prepared to believe was that the two men had played an equal part.

Their release became an event of the Season. Members of both Houses of Parliament, various duchesses, and idlers of other descriptions, left cards at Bedford Square. The Countess looked at the second afternoon's collection, heaped in a silver tray, and told Robert it might be simpler to give a once-for-all reception. 'Will it be all right for your people if we do?' she asked. 'It will be given for them.'

'I'll see that it will be all right for them,' he said, and asked Jane to come to see him in the library.

She curtsied.

'Jane,' he said, 'there are some proprieties to be observed, and the first is that you will never curtsy to me again. Now, you have seen the newspapers? You, and Elizabeth, and Moatham, and Smith, and the others, are famous people. In London, fame may last for several weeks. The Countess is going to give a reception, and we shall ask those people who've already called and left cards, and some others. And any one you would like to ask as well.'

'We do not know anyone in London, Mr Robert.'

'Very well. But this is a reception in your honour, the five of you, and the little girl. You must all be there. The Countess will receive the guests, and so will you, Jane. That is the way we will do it.'

'I don't rightly know how, Mr Robert.'

'When they come into the great room the steward will call out their names, and they will come up to the Countess, and then to you, and you both say, "How d'you do?" or some such thing, and that's it. The Countess will tell people who you are, they will say a few words to you, and you smile. You've seen it many times at my mother's house.'

'But it's not for me to do. I can't do it.'

'Yes you can, Jane. I will stand the other side of you. You do exactly what the Countess does. If she curtsies, as she will to anyone who's very great or very old, or both, you do the same, but to nobody else. If she shakes hands, you do the same. And I'll be next to you and be doing the same as well, except that since I'm a man I mostly just nod and say, "Good evening." Jane, if the King comes, which he won't, do what the Countess does, which will be to curtsy and say, "Good evening, sir." '

'What about Moatham and the others, sir?'

'The others will be at the end of the room, and after a while I'll break away and look after them. Now, will you do this for me?'

Jane considered, and then saw he was smiling, and smiled broadly back at him. 'I will.'


At the party, Jane received with a dignity which charmed everyone who came. Afterwards the Countess kissed her on both cheeks and hugged her. The greatest man to appear was

Viscount Castlereagh, His Majesty's Secretary of State for Foreign Affairs, an old Tory, who looked at her and said, 'More than I could have done, Mrs Bryant. You know ma'am, when I was at the Colonies I used to write despatches to New South Wales, or put my name on to 'em anyway. Was reminded of New South Wales the other day in Cabinet. Blacks massacring convicts; well six or seven convicts.'

'It is true, sir, but white men have killed the blacks too, and more than six or seven.'

'I dare say, ma'am. I dare say. Yes, I remember it well, despatch after despatch to New South Wales. In my day the trouble wasn't the blacks or the convicts; always the military. Officers always getting above themselves. Yes, despatch after despatch to Sydney. Signed them all.'

'I'm sorry I never saw any of them sir.'

'That's the thing, ma'am. You put your name to despatches, and send them off, and nobody ever does see them. And suppose they do reply? Ma'am, I'm still putting my name to despatches, and I shan't be still in office to see the replies, even if they ever come. You're a brave woman.' And he wandered off into the crush, where Robert presented Moatham, who was told he was a good fellow.

Across the room Jeremy Bentham was making a reforming harangue to Admiral Sir Julian Cunningham, but Bentham broke off when he saw Castlereagh and hurried over to accost him.

'I know you as a tyrant, sir,' Bentham began civilly.

'Very likely, very likely,' replied the statesman. 'Nobody has a good word to say for anyone these days. I know of you as a political economist. Good evening to you.' Castlereagh mellowed wonderfully in the last months before he cut his own throat. To the Countess, when she found him again, he remarked, 'Fellow Bentham, much more entertaining than I'd thought. I'd always heard he was a great man except that he would talk constantly about happiness, as if he were an American. He's said to believe any action's good if it produces happiness. Rot. Suppose a pickpocket were to make himself happy by picking Mr Bentham's pocket?'

Castlereagh had come because he was an old friend of the Countess's, and also out of curiosity because his had been one of the voices which had told Mr Attorney it might be politic to be generous with the Botany Bay people. Bentham had invited himself.

'I once met that man Jefferson,' said Castlereagh. 'The American. Can't remember where. Can't remember what we were talking about. Perhaps we'd stopped a few American ships. Can't remember. Decent fellow. Knew where to draw the line. Didn't go on too long about liberty and the pursuit of happiness; but I tell you, Countess, for a while there we were batting inalienable rights back and forth, across the dinner table. And all it was about was a few ships. I remember now. It was ships.'

'I once met him,' said Françoise. She had been a girl, with d'Estaing. Thomas Jefferson was American Minister in Paris. It must have been 1788 or '89, a world away.

'I was a girl,' she said, 'and he was kind.'

'Even American ministers are kind to girls, my dear. What'd he have to say for himself, though? That's another matter.'

'All I had to talk about was inalienable rights too. It was all I knew about him. It was at the Tuileries. He said he'd changed the words. It was originally life, liberty, and the pursuit of property, and he changed property to happiness in his Declaration of Independence, and either nobody noticed or nobody dared to object to happiness.'

'They wouldn't, would they?'

'He sent me a lace shawl the next day.'

'What's sending a girl a lace shawl but the pursuit of pleasure? I've done that, Countess. Often. In Ireland.'

'I remember he said another thing. That you ought not to confuse the pursuit of happiness with the pursuit of pleasure.'

'That, my dear, is evidence of an agile mind.'

The steward came over to the Countess, who nodded. He gave three raps on the table. 'My lords, ladies, and gentlemen, I ask your silence for Mr Moatham.'

In a quiet voice, at times almost inaudibly, and encouraged by Smith, Moatham got it out that from the purse presented to them at Bow Street they had purchased two watches, which they had had inscribed, and which, with the permission of those gentlemen, they wished to present to Admiral Cunningham,

and to Mr Robert King, as thanks for doing more than any
men in the world could have done.

It was a surprise to both men. The Admiral was never so
gratified by anything as by this unlooked-for gesture. Robert
remembered the watch given to him many years ago by Sir
Harry Hayes, and told that story, and said he would treasure
them both.

When the chatter began again, Jeremy Bentham was soon in
full flight to Jane Bryant.

'Think of me as one of His Majesty's judges,' said Bentham.
'Think of me as that. And a poor man is before me for what –
the theft of turnips, invaluable turnips, priceless turnips. And
what is my sentence? I say, "I sentence you to transportation,
but to just what I know not. Perhaps to storm and shipwreck,
perhaps to infectious disorders, perhaps to famine, perhaps to
be massacred by savages, perhaps to be devoured by wild
beasts. Away with you, take your chance, perish or prosper." '

'There are no wild beasts, sir,' said Jane.

'And when a man has endured the length of his sentence,'
said Bentham, 'as it may be seven or fourteen years, tell me, is
he a free man?'

Jane said, 'Mr Robert's grandfather, the Governor, always
said that New South Wales was a free land, and that in a free
land there could be no slavery, and therefore no slaves.'

'But is a man free, after his sentence has been served? Is he as
free as a man who comes out free from England?'

The whole assembly was now listening.

'No,' said Jane, 'he is not.'

Thus was the central issue of a whole continent put in a few
words by Jane Bryant in a drawing room in Bedford Square.
Her adventures, known to everyone in that room, and the way
her words were spoken, heard by everyone, and the nature of
that gathering, because the men in that room possessed between
them a great deal of power, ensured that Jane's words were
infinitely better heard than if they had been addressed by any
Member of Parliament to a House of Commons in its natural
state – that is to say with a bare quorum present, and half of
that quorum asleep.

'And,' said Bentham, 'if such men are not free, then by whose
authority are they not free? Not by the authority of the

Secretary of State or by Lord Castlereagh's – even though I do call him a tyrant, because he will recognize that word for what it is, a mere offer to exchange political compliments. He would not say such men were not free.

'If I were a young man,' Bentham continued to Robert, 'a young man starting in the law, I would say that there was my great issue, and I would return to the country of my birth and seize that issue. If I were you I should return to New South Wales. And,' he said, addressing Jane, 'if I were younger and a woman of your courage and plainness of speaking, I would take myself also back to New South Wales. You have work to do there.'

At which he bowed in rapid sequence to Jane, Robert, Castlereagh, and the Countess, and left in a silence which lasted until he disappeared through the doorway. The old radical knew how to make the most of an exit. *The Times*, the *Morning Post*, the *Edinburgh Review*, and a hundred other newspapers, reviews, and pamphlets, were full of it all.

Three days later Françoise said, out of the air, out of a conversation which had nothing to do with return or parting, 'Dear Robert, you are going back, aren't you?'

'Yes. I was in any case.'

'And Jane and her daughter?'

'Yes. She told me yesterday. I asked her why. I said it was a long way to come in order to go back. I said she ought not to be swayed so soon by Mr Bentham. I said he was an habitual swayer of minds.'

'I think he might be pleased that you should think that.'

'She said that, with respect to Mr Bentham, it was not he who had done the swaying. She had swayed herself by what she heard herself say out loud, which she knew was true but had never thought to say before. Then she said a strange thing. She said when they escaped they started out first for America, which I'd forgotten. And she told me about a letter she left for my mother. She had never expected to meet her again on this earth, but had said they would meet in the Lands of Promise.'

'And now she thinks New South Wales may be the Lands of Promise?'

'Françoise, I think she may now believe that people can have a hand in creating their own Lands of Promise. But I think that is a reason that must take its turn with others. I think Sydney is home to her, which she now sees the more clearly now she is away from it. She now knows no one here. I think she also loves my mother, which she feels more clearly now she is away from her.'

'So you will take her?'

It was arranged. Jane wanted first to see again the Dorset villages where she had lived as a girl. An older sister, an old aunt, and a grandmother were still living; and Jane herself was aunt to children she had never seen. Robert reckoned with the possibility that once she was in Dorset she might want to stay there, and, if she did, he would wait a while to see that she was settled in her determination, and then leave. Otherwise, they would go on to Weymouth, take passage along the coast to Plymouth, and take ship there for New South Wales. Within two weeks the others had gone to Scotland and Jane and Robert were ready to leave too. The Countess's coach would take them to the West Country. While the boxes were loaded, on the pavement in Bedford Square where he had first arrived years before, Françoise d'Estaing and Robert stood facing each other in the same room where they had first set eyes on each other that evening.

She smiled and once again extended one hand.

'*M'sieu*,' she said.

He took her fingers and bowed over them.

'*Madame*.'

So they laughed, and went out to the coach. The Countess kissed Jane, and held Elizabeth tightly and kissed her too. Then there was no getting away from the goodbye to be said. The others were already in the coach. Robert stood and looked into the blue, Norman eyes of Françoise d'Estaing, Françoise Vouvray, whom his father had loved, and who had become to him as much a mother as his own mother. She held herself very straight. It was he who cracked, holding out his arms to her, and she ran into them. They separated. It was still unbearable. He was an Englishman in an English square, watched by passers-by who were English, but he went quickly down on one knee, and she said the familiar words of the benediction she had spoken to him every night since he arrived in her house. Then it was all right.

# 21

# In the Morning, It was Leah

In three days' easy driving they reached the Dorset of Jane Bryant's ancestors and of her husband's. They came to the country of the villages near Dorchester which all begin or end in 'puddle'. There are Puddletown, Tolpuddle, and Affpuddle, and Jane's remaining family lived in and around them.

Robert left Jane with her aunt at Tolpuddle, and went on the few miles to Dorchester where he took a room at the King's Arms. His was a very grand equipage for Dorchester, and it was assumed he would take the grandest room, which was on the first storey at the front, a room with a fine bow window, generously glazed. It was an old posting inn where coaches changed horses on the way west to Exeter and Plymouth, but the porch with its Tuscan façade, and the rooms at the front, were new. While his two coachmen and the inn servant lugged the baggage, a girl from the inn bobbed at him in the lobby, flew up the stairway in front of him, waited for him on the landing, and chattered round him as she showed him his room. She was dark and lithe, with the brown face of a country girl. She spoke a soft Dorset dialect that he could at times hardly understand. Would he come and look out of the window? Now see, there to the left, as far as a man could see, that was Grey's Bridge. He must have crossed that coming into the town. Didn't he recall that, sir? And there to the right as far as a man could see – and she stretched herself as far out as she could, leaning forward from the waist with her bare arms on the window sill, urging him to do the same – at the top of the hill, was where the soldiers were, in barracks. And then swiftly she was gone, all life, leaving Robert smiling at the brief remembrance of her. She was both chambermaid and kitchen girl. At dinner she appeared briefly, standing in an apron holding the dishes of meat, carrots, and peas from which the waiter served Robert. He looked up at her. She would not catch his eye, but knew very well she pleased him. After dinner he smoked for a while, and then went to his room. He was sitting in the bow window, doing nothing in particular but observing the High Street, when, with a light knock, in she came, bobbing again and asking if she should turn the bed back. She chatted again. The men said his horses were too fine for Dorset roads, good turnpike roads though they were, and she thought the men were right. Not shod for those roads either.

'What is your name?' said Robert.

'Leah, sir, because . . .'

'Leah? But surely that's a Hebrew name, and you're from Dorchester?'

'I'm not from Dorchester. I'm not a town girl, sir. I'm from Puddletown. And as for me being Leah, sir, we're all named from the Scriptures, my brothers and sisters and me, and Scripture names aren't Hebrew, are they, sir?'

Robert reflected that the only Leahs he had known were Jewish, the daughters of City bankers and merchants in London.

'In London,' he said, 'there are plenty of Rebeccas and Ruths, but I don't think they are named from the Scriptures. The custom is going out in London.'

'If that's so, sir, then folk lose the chance of naming children right.'

'How's that?'

'Well, sir, I was expected at night, and was to be called Rachel. But I was delayed, sir, and was not born till morning.'

'Ah. Yes?'

' "In the morning, behold it was Leah." *Genesis*, sir.'

'You know your Bible better than I do,' he said.

'You're an educated gentleman, sir.' That put it so exactly that Robert smiled.

'But that wasn't the end on it, sir.'

'No?'

'My father was so set on calling me Rachel that he gave me that name too, even though I did come in the morning. So he called me Leah Rachel, and when at the christening the parson asked him why, he spoke up at the font and said he never had thought the Scripture story was fair-dealing, and that him giving me both names made amends for it. The parson said if a learned man said that, it would be blasphemy, but seeing as it was my father, it wouldn't be counted against him.'

The girl stood watching Robert, put her hands on her hips, and said, 'You don't rightly follow it at all, do you sir?'

'I'm afraid I don't.'

'Well 'twas an old swizz, sir. I always thought that story was an old swindle soon as ever I could read it. You know Jacob, the one that had the dream where there was a ladder with angels going up and down it, and at the top was God and he said to Jacob that he and his tribes after him should have all the land they could see. The Promised Lands, see?'

'The Promised Lands,' said Robert. 'Go on.'

'See, Jacob went on a journey and came to a well, and there were flocks of sheep belonging to his uncle, and one of the girls tending the sheep was Rachel, and she was his uncle's daughter. Jacob took to Rachel and said to his uncle he'd work seven year for him if he could have Rachel to marry. So they struck the bargain, like a hiring fair on Lady Day. Well, after seven year he asked for her, and they had a wedding feast, and I daresay he took a bit of drink, and they sent Rachel to him when it was dark, leastwise they said it was Rachel, but in the morning he sees her's not Rachel at all. "In the morning, behold it was Leah." Leah's her older sister. Well, there's an old swizz if ever I saw one, and Jacob tells his uncle so, and the uncle says he can have Rachel too if he works another seven year, and so he does, and has them both, but he should rightly have had Rachel in the first place. There's more to it than that, but that's what matters. Anyways, my father speaks up at the font, and he says there won't be no short-changing when he gives me in marriage – as he hopes, God willing, he'll live to do – seeing that he'll be giving away Leah and Rachel both at one time to the same man. So I s'pose when it comes to the wedding, Parson will say, "Leah Rachel, do you take this man?" But nobody calls me anything but Leah in the ordinary way of things, nor ever has.'

She chatted on. She said she couldn't help hearing him talk

with Mr Brigges the waiter, and asking about Puddletown, and
the church there, and the monuments of old knights lying there.

'I shall go there tomorrow,' he said.

'I come from there, sir. I always say the stone creatures in
the transept are my monkeys, only they aren't monkeys, they're
apes. Shall I show you, sir? It's my free day tomorrow. I could
tomorrow.'

'Show me, Leah.'

She bobbed and was gone. Robert slept very well.

After breakfast he walked into the High Street and she was
there.

'I'll rest the horses today,' he said, 'so tell me where I can
hire a gig.'

'Lord, sir,' she said, 'it's no more than a walk.'

'How far is it?' he asked.

'A mile or two, sir.'

It was six. After one or two it became plain she was much
more used to walking than Robert. He was no better shod than
his horses for the Dorset roads, but he covered the six miles in
two hours. She got him some ale, and then showed him the
church, unaffectedly holding out her warm hand to him as he
climbed the gallery stairs behind her. It was the gallery where
the fiddles and serpents played for hymns, and the choir sang.
For nearly two centuries, fiddlers and choristers had carved
their initials in the wood of the gallery. The oldest date was
1635. The gallery was one of the newer parts of a medieval
church. 'There's mine,' said Leah, showing Robert the carved
characters, 'L.M. 1636'.

'1636?' he said.

'Well, sir, I reckon any letters ought to be old or they'm not
worth the carving, but I didn't want to be first, because
'twouldn't be believed, so I carved mine a good year after the
first.'

She showed him the Norman fount, where her father had said
*Genesis* was a swizz.

In the transept they saw the knights, the old knight and his
lady lying side by side in stone, and the brasses of Christopher
Martyn, died 1524, and Nicholas Martyn, 1595. Then there
was the fine Martyn monument with canopy and carved
creatures.

'My monkeys,' she said. 'Only they're apes.'

They could have been either.

'No,' she said, 'Parson says they're the Martyn apes, since apes are that family's creatures, only they look like dogs because the man that carved them never saw either ape nor monkey. I've seen a monkey, at the fair, so I call them my monkeys.'

'You carved your name L.M.' said Robert. 'What is the M?'

'Martin. But all the real Martyns, the old ones, went from hereabouts centuries ago to the Crusades, and never came back save as monuments. Parson says so. All the Martins now living never owned so much as a field, or a stone in a field. I'm no knight's lady, sir. I'll never lie by the side of a stone knight.'

It was her church. She was at home in it. She was not awed, but she was not irreverent. She led him by the hand to the three-decker pulpit. She would not go to the top deck, from which the parson preached, but on the second storey a heavy folio Bible lay open on a lectern, and she mounted the stairs and faced it, with her eyes closed.

'I must Point the Book,' she said, 'to see what it says for you.'

Still with her eyes closed, she touched the open Bible with her forefinger, and then looked to see where she had touched.

'It don't matter,' she said. Robert could have sworn there was a tear in her eye, and that this happy girl had become unhappy.

'What is it?'

''Tis nothing but the old Apocrypha.'

'What does it say?'

She answered bravely. 'It is *Ecclesiasticus*. "Put not thy faith in a light woman." '

She came down. This time it was he who took her hand. '*That*,' he said, 'is *not* you.'

But it had taken the sun out of the day for a while. She did not chatter to him now. He insisted on hiring a fly to take them back to Dorchester, and at Yellowham Wood on the way back, when she asked him, he pulled up, and she got down and gathered a posy of primroses, which she gave to him.

'Leah,' he said, 'I should have done that for you.'

'It is for what you said.'

The ride back restored her spirits, and when he handed the fly to the groom, to return to Puddletown when he could, she jumped down, bobbed at Robert, and ran away into the inn and upstairs. Half an hour later, long before dinner, when he was sitting in his bow window writing, she knocked softly, came in, and did not chatter, or ask to turn down the bed, or make any pretext for her presence, but stood with her back to the closed door.

Robert was twenty. Since the day with Jacqueline in the Bois de Boulogne he had met, and pursued, and been pursued by, many women – all of them older than himself, all without exception worldly, all of his own rank. As a result he was an assured young man. He had felt affection for all of them. But none of them had been vulnerable, none of them younger than himself. This girl, he thought, was perhaps only sixteen. She was in fact fifteen. He would be gone in two days. He had seen her face in the pulpit that afternoon. He owed it to her to care for her. Yet how was he, without bruising her, to tell her to go? Besides, he did not want her to go.

What passed between them was the most solemn of regards.

He said, 'Would you consent if I were to ask you to come to me this evening?'

She shook her head stubbornly. 'No. Now.'

He walked across to her. But it was she who, without looking, bolted the door behind her. She threw back the bedclothes with one sweep. She stretched up to kiss his face. She drew his face down to her breast. She gave to him a warmth which, when she saw with what affection he received it, she redoubled. No woman had ever been so sweet to him. And she was as assured as he was. She embraced him with her warmth and encircled him with her brown legs.

Then she talked. Then she chattered. And Robert, from the candid generosity of Jacqueline Brie in the Bois, and the ingenuous warmth of Leah Martin at the King's Arms, formed an early expectation of the goodness of women, which is one of the most fortunate beliefs a man can hold.


That evening Jane came back from seeing her sister, her grandmother, her aged aunt, and her nephews and nieces. Elizabeth, who was a sweet child, had been made much of. But Jane had been away for nearly thirty years. She was recognized by no

one, and those who did remember her when their memories
were stirred were themselves so changed by age that she did
not recognize them. Not one. Not her sister. Now that she had
come home to Dorset, it was New South Wales that seemed
home to her. In Dorchester she walked up High East Street, and
then up High West Street, asking after anyone who remembered
George Bryant, but her husband was forgotten too. She went to
Robert and said, 'I will be coming home.' He told her they
would set out the next day.

That evening she wanted to see one last part of the town, the
West Walks, where she would remember the avenues of trees if
they did not remember her. Robert went with her. They walked
in silence.

On the way back in the dusk she pointed out Yallop Bros. in
High West Street, the shop where as a girl she stole those two
lengths of silk, and, opposite, the court where she was transported for that high crime.

'What is a wedding dress made of?' asked Robert.

'Whatever a girl can afford, sir. Cotton. Muslin. Satin. Silk.'

That night Leah tapped on his door very late, when he was
already in bed, and slipped in beside him, curling round him.
As the clock of St Peter's struck two, he watched her asleep.
Once she stirred and made little noises as if dreaming. Then he
fell asleep himself and when he awoke, at eight, she was gone.
On her pillow was a note, in pencil:

> YOU NEAD MORE SLEAP THAN I DO I SHALL BE GONE
> TO MARKET TODAY REMEMBER MY MONKEES AS I SHALL
> ALWAYS REMEMBER WHAT YOU SAID —
>
> YR AFFECTNTE LEAH

At eleven o'clock Robert went to Yallop Bros., Drapers to the
Nobility, Gentry, and Citizenry, and commanded two lengths
of silk to make two wedding gowns.

How much was required, asked the shopman. Of what height
were the ladies?

Robert held up a hand to show him.

'Both ladies the same height, sir.'

'Both.'

What quality silk did he require? Silk of Italy, or of the
Levant, or the silk of Piedmont?

'Such as a knight's lady might wear.'

The shopman was used to humouring the nobility and gentry, and bowed gravely.

Robert carried away from the shop two lengths of the finest Piedmont, and left them for Leah. 'Here,' he wrote to her, 'is one wedding gown for Leah and another for Rachel, whose husbands will be fortunate in them both. I shall remember your monkeys. What I said was true.'

They left for Weymouth at noon, and a week later embarked from Plymouth for New South Wales.

# PART THREE

# 22

# Susannah Recovers Her Dreaming

Jane Bryant, her daughter Elizabeth, and Robert returned as heroes. London newspapers had reached Sydney before them. The magistrates, the free settlers, and the principal sheep-owners, Redmond among them, made representations to the Governor that to preserve the Peace and prevent any tumultu-ous gathering the three should be made to land discreetly at a cove a few miles west of Sydney. Brisbane was by instinct sympathetic to the settler interest, but put aside these sugges-tions. First, he had no power to do what he was asked. Second, he could think of no better way of provoking a tumultuous assembly than to forbid it. The woman Bryant would be wel-comed as a heroine because everyone knew she had acted heroically. He felt so himself. Though he could hardly con-gratulate a woman who had led an escape from the colony, he knew it would be idiocy to try to prevent a triumphal return. He proposed to do nothing. He would rely on the good sense of Jane Bryant and Robert King. Despatches from London said they had behaved there with good sense, and he trusted they would again. So no extra guards were mounted, and the police were told to turn a blind eye to a reasonable festive drunkenness.

Jane was received with bunting, drums, a string band, a brass band, and the cheers and exultation of more than a thousand emancipists and ticket-of-leave convicts. She was chaired to her old cottage which had been preprared for her, and Elizabeth was carried head-high by her side. Robert ap-peared with Jane on the quay but when she was chaired away he slipped back on board ship and in the rejoicing was not missed. Hundreds accompanied Jane to her cottage. Her friends went inside with her. The others sang and cheered around the cottage, until they were told that rum would flow freely at the Black Dog and the Sheer Hulk, public houses in the district known as The Rocks, the other side of the cove from the Domain. The rum was supplied by Robert, who made a brief speech and then left others to make longer speeches. It was reported next day that some of the drinkers became so saturated with rum that when they lit their pipes a blue flame came from their lips, and that became a legend. But it all went off very well.

Susannah did not go to the quay, but half an hour after the roisterers had left Jane to go off to The Rocks she went to the cottage herself and the two women embraced. Above all, Susannah and Jane were happy to be together again. There were other things to be talked of, but they could wait till the next day.

'And where is Robert?' said Susannah. Jane told her of the plan to supply rum in convenient places, a plan contrived between Robert and the port officer, when his cutter met the ship at the headlands, and that Robert would soon be back.

When Susannah returned to her house he was there waiting for her.


There were practical matters to be settled. Jane was to leave her cottage, with its memories of her husband, and live with Susannah, though certainly not, Susannah insisted, as her maid. Jane suggested that a housekeeper was needed, and that is what she became. She insisted that one duty should remain hers and not the maid's. She should dress Susannah in the evenings, and brush her hair at nights. These were the times when they talked most closely together. This was understood by them both. It went without saying that Elizabeth would come with her mother. It was then that Jane asked after John, and was told that Susannah had not seen her second son or her husband, since the day after she last saw Jane. They were prospering greatly up country. Redmond came occasionally to Sydney and was sometimes accompanied by John, but never brought the boy to Susannah. She had asked to see him, and this had been denied her. She asked again, and received the reply that her insistence could only hurt the boy. She did not ask again.

The affinity between Susannah and Robert was strong and deep. It always had been, but now it was different. They parted as mother and son, and as mother and son they were reunited. But the parting was six years before, when Robert was a boy. Now he was a man. Susannah saw him as a man, and he saw her as a woman. Like the Countess, she saw Nicolas again in him. Father and son were very alike. Robert was taller and broader, but his features were his father's. His eyes were the same. But in her son, Susannah saw not only Nicolas but herself.

There were gestures of the hands which had not been there six years before in the boy, but were there now, and they were hers. He could not have imitated them from being in her company. It was heredity showing itself in like gestures expressing like feelings. For instance, they were discussing where he should live. She naturally said her house was his. He said he would soon be starting to practise law, and would engage his own chambers in the town. She understood. There was no contention between them but both mother and son, making a point, said at the same moment, 'You see . . .,' and found themselves accompanying the words with identical gestures. Both sat resting their elbows on the arms of wooden chairs. Both were leaning forward with both hands raised so that each saw the other's palms, with the fingers half apart and half curved. Both saw the same gesture at the same moment, both held it for a second, and both smiled.

Susannah looked at the hands. 'It is as if we were two heraldic lions in conversation,' she said.

And they held their heads in the same way. He had her directness, whereas Nicolas always had a diffident look. Susannah wondered if her son had her own sudden wilfulness.

Robert asked about Redmond and John. Why had she not written to tell him, if not straight away, then after a while? She was not sure. Perhaps it was because she had continued unconsciously to think of Robert as the boy he had been when he went away. She said she could not realize, from such a distance and after such a time, how much he would have changed. Robert understood this. Did he not see his mother in

a completely new way! A boy of thirteen or fourteen knows
that his mother is beautiful. But Robert at twenty saw for the
first time that Susannah was a woman of rare vividness and
life and wondered how she lived alone, if she lived alone. It
seemed she did. Robert lived in the house for a month or so
while he found chambers. Susannah presented him to Brisbane,
and they got on well. Brisbane took his duties in the leisurely
way Robert had seen in the men he met at the Countess's in
London, who seemed to run the British Empire from Whitehall,
or from their clubs, with the same urbane ease with which they
ran their country estates. Those were the days when young
gentlemen in the Civil Service – the Home Office, the Foreign
Office, the Colonial Office, or whatever department – drifted
into their offices at ten, drifted off to their clubs for a leisurely
lunch at noon, and then, having drifted back to Whitehall,
stayed there until four and no later. Their masters, the Secretaries of State, demanded no more of themselves. The House
of Commons sat half the year if that, and the Lords a great deal
less. It was assumed that if a man did not have the capacity to
bear the burden of high office with ease, he did not have the
capacity to bear it at all.


Soon after Robert's return it became known in Sydney that
Mr Commissioner Wyndham was coming out from London
with full powers to summon witnesses, enforce their attendance,
take their evidence, and to enquire in any manner he considered necessary into the late outrages committed by and
against the natives of New South Wales, and thereafter to
advise His Majesty's Secretary of State in any way he thought
fit; and the Governor was requested and required by His
Majesty to give all aid and assistance to James Wyndham, Esq.,
in the performance of his duties.

    Governors do not like commissioners sent out to watch them
governing.

    'You don't know the man, do you?' the Governor asked
Robert. 'Not at the Bar, is he? Not a barrister? With respect,
my boy, a prying barrister is the curse of the governing classes.'

    'I don't know him. I've heard of him. Well liked. The last
thing he did was on Irish workhouses, much thought of. Much

reported in *The Times*, as I remember. He said something about awful consequences if the potato crop should ever fail, but it was dismissed as too fantastic. Far-seeing, they said, far-seeing and fantastic.'

'What's potatoes got to do with workhouses?'

'That's what he was asked at the time. He said a quarter of the whole population of Ireland was in workhouses, that even in workhouses they had to be fed, that in Irish workhouses nobody was ever fed anything but potatoes, so it was very much his business to enquire what would happen if one year there were no potatoes.'

'What came of it?'

'Nothing,' said Robert. 'But it was highly thought of.'

'Not at the Bar, is he?' asked the Governor, returning to his first anxiety.

'No, not a barrister. A good classicist. His edition of Horace's *Odes* is much admired.'

The Governor thought the man was altogether excessively admired, but was relieved he was not a barrister. A good classicist he could take. Excellence in dead languages was universally thought to be a quality that fitted a man to play his part in the government of Empire, and perhaps it did. It was at any rate a lot better than being a barrister. Wyndham was in fact at the beginning of a long and brilliant career in the Civil Service, though moving from the Irish poor law to New South Wales was, as the Governor put it, no more than moving from one workhouse to another. He was glad the man was not at the Bar, but would rather he was not coming at all.

At first meeting the Governor was gruff and the Commissioner cautious. Wyndham formally presented his Commission, which the Governor formally accepted, and then, with the document lying on a low table between them, the two men made what can only be described as small talk, which neither knew how to bring to an end. Eventually the Governor said, 'You know, Wyndham, Mrs Redmond's got some paintings of blacks. Might help you.'

'Indeed.'

'Done by her father. Her father was Governor here, you know.'

Wyndham did not know, nor did he think there was much to

be learned from the paintings of a former governor, but he
could not say so. The Governor for his part was anxious to
bring to an end this interview at which neither man wished to
commit himself by saying anything, and so he seized a pen,
dashed off a note to Mrs Redmond, and placed it affably in the
hands of the Commissioner. This gave Wyndham a pretext to
express his thanks and take his leave.

The Governor brushed away the thanks, 'Not at all, not at
all,' and Wyndham departed, relieved to get away but knowing
that, little use as he felt the introduction would be to him, he
could not fail to present the letter since it had been the first
accommodating gesture of the Governor. Commissioners are
as uneasy about governors as governors about commissioners.

So he called to present the letter to Mrs Redmond, and both
were utterly surprised. The Governor had sent word to her that
Mr Commissioner Wyndham might be calling, but she had
expected, as far as she expected anything at all, a brief conversation with a man of whose presence in the colony she knew
her friend the Governor to be nervous. She had not expected a
man so young. Wyndham was thirty, younger than her. But
that was a triviality. What was not trivial was that the instant
she saw him she knew that for too long her days had been
deserts, and would no longer be. Wyndham had expected a
Mrs Redmond, and saw instead Susannah. Both, at the moment
of meeting, thanked the gods.

They stood facing each other for only a few seconds before
Susannah collected herself, asked him if he would sit down, and
said she would show him the water colours she had.

'There are only three,' she said. 'My father sent the others
to London as he did them.' The first showed a naked aborigine
full-face in an attitude of dance, with both arms extended, the
right hand clenched and the left held with the open palm displayed. The second showed a group of three blacks, a woman
cooking fish over an open fire, a man eating a fish, and another
man standing waiting. The third showed a family going walk-
about, the man leading, the woman following with spears and
fish in her hands and a child on her back, and a boy bringing
up the rear carrying more spears and a glowing firestick.

'The third sketch was always thought the best,' said Susannah,
'but I prefer the second. I have seen them eat fish like that,

holding the head and tail and eating the middle out, nibbling along the bone. They eat with delicacy, and pick the bones clean.'

'I like that one too,' he said, 'but I have seen the third, the one with the family, or something very like it.'

'You may have done. There was a set painted of that family, and Mr Blake the poet had an engraving done from one of them. I do not possess a copy of the engraving, but I think he made them very noble savages indeed, and lost a great deal of the life. Or so I thought.'

She was right. The Blake engraving is not so revealing as the original, done in his spare time by a governor making a record of what he saw to send to his superiors in London.

'They are very living,' said Wyndham, 'and done with love.'

'He would have been surprised to hear you say that, but it is true. Everything he did, he did with love.'

She put the tinted sketches back on the table, sat facing Wyndham, smoothed her gown over her lap, and smiled at the man.

'Thank you,' he said; and then, 'I was awed by your king and queen in the hallway.'

So he might have been. George III and his Queen, eight feet high in vast gilt frames, confronted the visitor from either side of the entrance to the drawing room.

She said, 'There is no room for them anywhere else. They are too big. Captain Bligh gave them to me, intending them I think as a parting gift, though in truth I believe they were not his but my father's. I know he had them brought from England. But they are the portraits which Captain Bligh loyally toasted the night he was deposed.'

'You were there?'

'Yes, I was.'

She said no more about that, but went on, 'So, you have come to see about the blacks. They do not often come into the town any more, so perhaps you have not seen a single one yet?'

'I have seen two,' he said, 'and one was dying. It was the afternoon after I came off the ship. As soon as I went to my quarters I was told there were these two natives, under a tree very near the house, and I went to see them. There was an old man and his son. The son had lain under the tree for three days, and was dying. No one knew of what. Every few moments the old man spread himself on the boy's body, trying to revive him with his warmth. Or else he would have him in his arms, rocking him. He lifted up the lids of his eyes, so that he could see the day. But the young man died.'

Susannah leaned back in her deep chair and regarded Wyndham, and he, not looking into her eyes, which would have been too direct a communication, but at her hands which lay in her lap, thought her grave and lovely. Each had said something which confirmed to the other the instant rapport both had felt. His compassionate observation of the man and his son touched her, as her statement that all her father had done, he had done with love, had struck Wyndham as a shining and splendid thing for a daughter to say.

'Mr Wyndham,' she said, 'if you care to come, I think I can take you closer to some of the natives than you might otherwise get at first acquaintance.'

'I think you know them well?'

'No. No one knows them well. But I know some of them, through my father. Bligh treated them well, too. They have long memories. They will still receive me. In a few days' time there is to be a *corroboree*, and, if you wish, we could attend. It will be within a few miles' drive.'

He would have gone anywhere with her. He said that if she would send word when, he would send his carriage, and left with a greater sense of hope, and of delight to come in her society, than he had ever known before.


The *corroboree* began at sunset. The clouds on the western horizon changed from white to gold, and then to orange and to deeper and deeper reds. In the eastern sky the heavens became at first, by an illusion, more blue, and then sank through gradations of blue into greens and greys. Susannah and Wyndham watched from a place of honour, on a knoll. As the stars rose the blacks gathered in greater numbers, appearing unseen from the out-back until there were many hundreds. All were men. No woman of their own race was there. To say that they danced is too feeble a word. Fires were lit, and as the men swayed they flickered with light, out of the light of one fire into darkness and then into the light of another fire. Then they enacted the hunt, and their spears and throwing sticks glistened in the air and in and out of the light. Susannah and Wyndham followed the flight of one spear which rose high in the sky out of the light and into the stars, and then fell out of the stars.

'It came out of the Southern Cross,' she said. 'Look, follow those two pointing stars upwards.' She took his hand, raised it, and moved it so as to demonstrate to him the pattern of the constellation. 'Trace them with your hand. After the two pointing stars, there are the four stars of the Cross. I knew some of my father's sailors, who needed no more than to glance at the sky, who still did this. They called it touching the stars.'

She released his hand.

'The blacks say that those two brightest stars in the Cross were two brothers who went hunting, and were trapped by a bushfire, and escaped to the sky.'

In front of Susannah and Wyndham the men leaped like silhouettes across the glowing red of an outcrop of sandstone illuminated by the fires. The long yellow grass showed gold in the light. The men's skin glistened. They were anointed with seed oil and painted with charcoal, red ochre, and blue clay. Men became lizards, kangaroos, and trees. Other men, the hunters, sang a chant.

Wyndham said, 'I have heard a *corroboree* called a speaking pantomime. Whoever said that had seen and heard nothing.'

'When I was a girl,' said Susannah, 'when I first came to the colony, my father's gardener, John Easty, who is still gardener in the Domain, was taking me into town one day when we met two blacks who knew him. He had given them an axe head. He said to me, "I will show you two things, one now and one later," and he moistened his finger with his tongue, and then, while the black man stood still, not at all minding, he rubbed his finger on the man's shoulder so that I could see that he was covered in a caking of dirt, a crust. Then Easty told me to do the same, and I did. I felt the caked dirt, and then, after a lot of rubbing, the skin beneath it. The man submitted, making no protest. Easty said, "Remember by that, that these men are savages; but I will show you another thing too." Then he took me to a *corroboree*, like this, and I felt probably as you now feel, and Easty said to me, as we watched, "They are savages, and

it is foolish for learned philosophers, who have never encountered them, to say that they are not; but you must also
see, as you watch this, that they have souls; and even if not
Christian souls, souls as good as ours." '

'I think you do know them well,' said Wyndham.

'No. But in this country I have felt in myself something
which I think they feel, and if this is so then I have something
of the beginnings of an understanding. These fables of theirs,
peopled with lizards and stars and memories of ancient events,
may seem nonsense, but my own world has been peopled with
stars, and with the memory of events that were once events
but have become so changed in my mind that they are now as
much myths as any myths of these men. They are the legends
of my own history. I think legends are the spiritual side of
events, events changed by long remembering. I could never
explain the spirit of the cove, where I have lived since I was a
girl, but I know I would never for long leave that place.'

'I would have asked you why you stayed.'

'I do not *know*, but I feel that the place, because I have lived
there, and because others I knew lived there, is now part of my
consciousness of everything. And that *is*, to me, everything.
The spirit of that place is as real to me as my present consciousness of this moment.'

'As real as what you see now?'

'As real as what I feel and hear and see now. And part of
what I feel is what I think you may feel. The presence of others
is part of ourselves.'

'That,' said Wyndham, seeing her side-face in the flickering
fire, 'has been demonstrated to me undeniably this evening.'

'I know.'

While they were talking, the black women had come into
the light, joining the men.

'Oh,' said Susannah. 'Mr Wyndham, you may want to
leave.'

He took her meaning. 'Or I may feel later that I ought to
have left?'

'Yes.'

'Do you wish me to take you away?'

'Stay,' she said.

The women too were painted, but differently. A broad charcoal line encircled each breast. Vertical lines were drawn between and above the breasts. On the back of each woman, curved lines represented the boomerang of her lover, and between the maidenhair and navel of each was painted the phallus of her lover.

A woman called Kunnunurra stepped forward, and the man Toongabbe with her. She sank to the earth as if in a faint, and he knelt by her, seeming to whisper in her ear, and then to breathe in her ear, and then to whisper to her breasts.

'Do you know what he says?' Wyndham asked out of the dark.

'He is invoking the spirit, which will become a child.'

'His child and hers?'

'We would say so. They would not.'

'Tell me.'

'For them, a child does not come from the joining of a man and a woman. The man does not beget a child with his body. They see no connection between the joining of a man and a woman and the birth of a child.'

'How can they not see?'

'It is not a creation, but an incarnation, or a reincarnation. The spirit has always existed, and always will exist, but does not at this moment live in the embryo form of a human being. They do not get the child. They prepare the way for it. If a spirit enters the woman with the man, that is fortunate, but incidental. If a child is born, it will be the incarnation of a spirit that was waiting to be freed.'

'And when a spirit dies, it passes into another?'

'It will continue to exist until it is freed again, and embodied. The blacks are very good at time. Everyone will tell you they are very bad at time, but that is not true. If they say they will come on a given day, or even in a certain month, they may not. They are careless in that sense. They will say, "I did this tomorrow," or "I shall do this yesterday," because the past and the future are all included in the present.'

Wyndham said, 'They say that if nothing exists but what a man perceives, then at any given moment, for any man or woman, his past and his future must exist in the present?'

'That is it. They call it the Dreaming. There is a continuity of existence. Sometimes, if they are driven from all the places they have known or their tribe has known, then they lose their sense of the knowledge of the past, and their sense of the place around them, and then they are lost souls. They can will themselves to die. The Dreaming is everything.'

The woman and the man were now standing, facing each other, swaying with a slow rhythm.

Susannah said, 'The woman is "singing the man". That is what they call it, though she does not sing, or utter any sound. If she fixes her gaze upon the man's brow, she is said to be singing his brow, and whatever she sings becomes hers. If she sings his hands, they become hers. Whatever she sings, becomes hers.'

The other blacks, who were watching, began a slow chant.

'What do they say?'

'They are describing what is happening. I think it will become evident.'

Susannah did not translate, but this was the sense of the chant.

> Man's prick,
> Long one,
> Grow long,
> Think of her, come into her,
> Grow long, open the legs of the woman on the bed of leaves,
> And having grown long,
> Quicken,
> Let the quick semen enter her,
> Making a way
> For the spirit
> That will enter her.
> Prick, grow long, grow long.

All the spectators were chanting. The standing, moving couple alone remained silent.

'You see, she is singing the man,' said Susannah again.

But that had become, as she said, evident. It was at first a simulation, not an enactment. That was part of the ritual. Kunnunurra and Toongabbe did not at any moment touch.

The eyes of the woman were upon the man who, as she sang him, did grow long, and erect, and did in spirit enter her, thrusting with rhythm into the air until, to a sigh from those who watched, the spirit left him and ejaculated into the air,

rising shining, rising among the stars, falling in flickering rib-
bons against the firelight, and then falling to the earth.

So far as that is plain, it is a true account of what happened:
so far as it is exalted it reflects the exaltation of the participants
and of the watchers.

The members of the *corroboree* slipped away into the darkness
to perform the enactment, of which this was the simulation. In
the dark Susannah gave Wyndham her hand and said, 'Shall
we return?'

On the way back in the carriage she broke the silence only
once, and said, 'They say, that the man who loses his Dreaming,
or the woman who loses hers, is lost.'

Susannah had not known what they were to see, until the
women appeared. The men usually danced alone, enacting the
hunt. The women rarely appeared too. But when Susannah
had known what was going to happen, she said, 'Stay.' She
found, on the way back, that she had lost her shawl. She did
not say so, but Wyndham understood from her quick glances
around. He said nothing either. When the carriage stopped at
her door she said, 'Good night, Mr Wyndham,' and he handed
her down.

Jane undressed her.

'Mr Wyndham will be here again, ma'am?'

'Yes,' said Susannah. 'Yes.'


Wyndham spent much of that night and the next morning
fighting against Susannah. She had taken him utterly outside
his experience, and beyond. He ached to go back to Susannah,
but he knew that if he did he would not be in command of
himself. For a man who, since he was a boy, had been sure of
the sovereignty of intellect, this was an extraordinary realization.

His servant shaved him.

'Richardson,' he said, 'the lady lost her shawl last night.'

'Yes, sir,' said the man. Richardson had accompanied his
master the night before, sitting in front with the driver. While
Wyndham and Susannah watched the *corroboree*, Richardson
stayed with the driver who, being a ticket-of-leave convict who
had spent many years in the colony, told him a great deal more
about Susannah than Wyndham knew. The story, as the driver

told it, was in the main true, though enhanced. Baudin had never been an admiral. It would have been incorrect to call Redmond a bloody wife-destroying villain. But the story of the French Admiral and the French Admiral's boy was essential to any understanding of Susannah, and so Richardson, for the moment, understood her better than his master did. The servant was much older than Wyndham. This was his second generation in service with the family. He had been with Wyndham's father twenty years before when that gentleman was a cavalry colonel in India. The older Wyndham was now dead, but Richardson had seen him made very happy by a woman, unexpectedly met in Simla, who had showered him with love throughout one last summer before he returned to England, his estates, and his family. Richardson had never told the son, because to do so would have been a breach of confidence even though the father was many years dead; but he remembered that summer.

So when Wyndham said, 'Richardson, the lady lost her shawl last night,' the scenes of that Simla summer passed across his mind in the few moments before he replied, 'Shall I attempt to recover it, sir?' It was a considered reply, and when Wyndham signified that he might if he wished, he did.

In the afternoon Richardson appeared with the shawl. 'I had it from a black, sir.'

A nod.

'To whom I thought fit to give a half-guinea, sir.'

'Which you shall be reimbursed,' said Wyndham. He understood very well that Richardson had given perhaps a shilling to the ticket-of-leave driver who took him back to the place of the *corroboree*, and two-pence to the black who had the shawl. But Richardson, although he was prepared to accept a reasonable profit on his enterprise, would have taken good care not to find the shawl unless he thought the finding of it might be to his master's advantage. And Richardson did not suggest, as he might have done, 'Shall I see that it is returned, sir?', because he knew that if he had, Wyndham would have felt bound to say, 'Of course,' and left himself without the means to see Susannah again.

Wyndham was a scholar and a man of the greatest probity, but does it follow that the impulse of life may not run strongly

in such a man? At that moment it ran strongly in him, telling
him, 'Go to her again.' Even so, it was three hours before he
wrote a short note to Susannah saying he had the shawl and
asking if he might take occasion to return it.

She said she would be grateful if he did. He called on her
again. For an hour they talked about the colony, his childhood
in Camberley, hers in Bath (where he also had briefly lived),
his preferences in foxhounds, and her preference for China over
India teas, before at last he got up and began the phrases of
leave-taking. He supposed she must have other business to
attend to. He was glad to have seen her again. Was it not
strange they both knew Bath? She listened to these phrases
with the smile with which they are customarily received. He
had retained the shawl, and now held it out to her. She looked
him directly in the eyes; he failed to meet hers, which told her
again what she already knew.

As soon as she received Wyndham's note, Susannah had
decided she would, if necessary, herself make more than the
first move. She thought it unreasonable that the man should
always have to run the risk of rebuff. It was not that she thought
Wyndham lacked the courage to say what had to be said, but
rather that he might not know how to say it. She was right.
When he failed to meet her eyes she got up. When he did look
at her again and, as if remembering himself, offered her the
shawl, she took one end of it and no more. They were left
standing, each holding one end of a silken, Indian shawl.

'Mr Wyndham, say candidly what you wish to say.'

He looked up, and then she said the words which gave him
nothing to lose.

She said, 'I think I shall very much regret it if you do not.'

But she was not really asking him to say anything, only telling
him that she knew there were things he wished he had the
words to say, and so she kissed him swiftly and, taking his hand,
put it to her cheek. At which he put his hand on her shoulder,
and then held her by the waist, and everything was very plain.


Susannah crossed from the bed to the window. There was only
a crescent moon. She looked back at the bed. His voice said,
'I think you are amused?'

'I am happy,' she said. 'I am fortunate.'

Susannah, while Redmond continued to live with her, even when he was indifferent to her and more often away than at home, remained faithful to him. After he went, taking John with him, and she was alone, she could no longer live without lovers. There were two. But for her, unless there was wholeness of heart, there was nothing, and with those two men she found that there was nothing. The affairs were brief. But with Wyndham, she knew from the instant she saw him that they would be worlds to each other. So she said, 'I am fortunate.'

So was he. He was a great deal more fortunate than her. Wyndham had never known well any women but his sisters. He had never before found himself in a woman's bedroom. He was fortunate that Susannah rapidly discovered this without showing she discovered it, and then led him without showing that she led. He did not know he had found a woman who was both bold and gentle. By the laws of any reasonable expectation he should at that moment have felt a remorse born of a conviction that he had sinned. He did feel this later, when he was alone. But because she had led him so assuredly to a contentment of body and mind, he felt no remorse at the time. Beyond anything he ought to have been grateful for that. He would have been had he known.

She came back to the bed. 'I read in this morning's *Gazette*,' she said, 'that Mr James Wyndham was due to dine at the barracks tonight with the colonel and his officers.'

'Will it seem too terrible, and presumptuous, and tell you too much about my hopes, if I say that I sent my apologies this afternoon?'

She laughed.

'But,' he said, 'there is something which greatly worries me. I do not know your Christian name.'

Of course, he would not. He knew her only as Mrs William Redmond.

Susannah told him her name.

# 23

# Waltzing Matilda

Beyond the western foothills of the Blue Mountains which divide Sydney from the inland continent, mountains which for twenty years defied all attempts to cross them, lay fine pasturage and most excellent sheep country. There were few gulleys and no swamps, but healthy hills on a gravelly soil. At times it was like a gentleman's park in England, for carriages could be driven over the fine sward between the trees. In other places there was more and lusher grass than in an English meadow, grass two and three feet high. In this country, Redmond had acquired, by successive grants and by purchase, a sheep station of fine grazing land, as large as an English county. If an observer had been able to survey the whole of that kingdom, on an early evening in late autumn of the year that Jane Bryant and Robert King returned to Sydney – on the evening in fact that James Wyndham discovered Susannah's name – he would have seen at the furthest eastern extent of the land the new mansion of William Redmond; at almost its furthest western extent, at Tongala, the rum shanty known as the Abandon Hope; and, ten miles to the north of this shanty, a solitary man on the plain preparing to eat a solitary supper.

The man had tramped forty miles that day. He camped near a creek which irrigated the meadows that stretched as far as he could see. On one side of the creek a bank rose, and the man was making camp there on a patch of sandy gravel between two eucalypts. He filled his billycan from the creek, and brewed tea over a fire built from the bark and twigs of the eucalypts. He sipped the tea from a tin mug which held a quart, and then

returned to the creek to refill the billy, in which he boiled his
supper, bacon of the coarsest and saltiest kind. He ate it with a
tasteless, hard ship's biscuit. He was on the tramp. He knew he
would find a week's work the next day at the station to the
south, and then he would be on the tramp again. That was how
he had spent his life since his emancipation two years before.
Since his last work he had tramped for seven days, and had
seen no human soul except two blacks, whom he would not
have counted as human souls. He had not seen a white man for
a week, or a white woman for three. A man becomes used to
solitude, but never to the sudden loneliness that comes upon
him at times from out of that solitude. He threw more bark on
his camp fire. Then he removed his neckerchief, put it on the
ground, took the pistol from his belt, and placed it on the
neckerchief to prevent sand getting into it. A man on the tramp
carried all his possessions in a kit-bag tied at the neck. The bag
was called his matilda. A man on the tramp, carrying his bag,
was said to be waltzing his matilda. That was the plain meaning, but there was another.

When he had eaten, the solitary man on the plain took up
his matilda, held it as if it were a woman, and danced silently
round the fire he had built. When a lonely man did this, in the
outback at the end of the day, then in another sense he was
waltzing his matilda.

This was long before the words of the song were written,
though the haunting tune was already known and played. It
was an old Scots air which Gordon Burns knew because he was
a Scot, from Perth. He would have no trouble finding work the
next day because in the old days in Perthshire he had been a
shepherd, and such men were rare. As would later become well
known, Burns was a man of ruddy complexion, five feet eight
inches tall, well-built, bearing on his left cheek a small scar in
the shape of a star, and speaking with a Scots accent.

At the other extreme of this sheep kingdom, at the same time
as Burns found the creek by which he camped, a quarter of an
hour before sunset, William Redmond was bringing to an end
the hour which he devoted every day to the instruction of his
son John in the art of shooting. Sunset is very late in the day for
that kind of instruction, but Redmond was thorough. He told
his son that a man, when it came to it, would not be able to

choose the time of day or the state of the light. So he taught
John to shoot in full light and half light, in true light and
treacherous light. The boy was eleven years old, and already a
good shot with a carbine. In the fading light he had just hit
four bottles out of five at thirty yards. His father then hit the
fifth with a pistol shot, which at that range was luck, but much
applauded by the boy.

'Father, why won't you let me use pistols?'

'Because your wrist and your arm are not strong enough.
Another year. You will soon handle a carbine as well as I do.
Pistols later. Now, in.'

They gave the weapons to a bearer, and walked across the
lawns to the house. It was a two-storeyed Georgian house,
grander than all but two or three in Sydney, and grander than
the Governor's at Parramatta. Redmond had been lucky. The
small grants made to him by Macquarie prospered. Very early
he sank two wells and struck water, which saved him in the
drought of 1815. He sold fine crops of wool while his neighbours
had to slaughter their flocks for mutton. Redmond bought out
three neighbours. His prosperity then qualified him for yet
larger grants, which he had received in time to enable him to
thrive by satisfying an altogether new demand from England
after the war. Redmond benefited indirectly from Napoléon
who, as part of his plan for One Europe, shipped Spanish
merinos to France and Germany. By the 1820s England was
unable to compete with the woollen products of those two
countries. The only other wool so fine came from New South
Wales. In the previous years, Redmond had shipped four times
as many bales than ever before into Hull and Liverpool. He
was a rich man, and his mansion was grand. Of all the sheep-
men, probably only Macarthur was richer, but he was showing
early signs of madness.

As Redmond entered the hall he glanced at the table, with
inserts of Sèvres porcelain, on which his letters were placed.
There was a note from his foreman about the next day's journey.
He and the boy stretched out in leather chairs in the drawing
room. The mantelpiece was of marble from Italy. Over it was
a portrait of the boy done six months before by a Frenchman
in Sydney who had introduced himself as formerly of the court
of Louis XVI, and, whether or not that was true, had produced

a good likeness of John in European hunting dress holding aloft by the legs a pair of dead quail. On a pedestal rested a bust of Redmond by a German sculptor, also resident in Sydney. For dinner, Redmond and his son ate not quail, because there were none in New South Wales, but trout bred in the fish ponds and lamb raised on the station. Redmond's house, like that of a few other big sheep-men, had its own vineyards and made its own wine. It even made its own drinkable champagne, of which the boy was allowed two glasses.

'Father,' said the boy, 'what is a half-brother?'

Redmond answered slowly. 'Why?'

'Because I have been told that Jane has come back, and I should like to see her again. And that Mary is dead. I am sorry, because we once went to Manly together, with Mother. Mary was the same age as me. And I have heard that Robert King is back, only they say he is my half-brother.'

'Yes,' said Redmond. He had told the boy nothing himself, but knew that it would all reach him sooner or later through the servants.

'I do not know what a half-brother is,' said John. 'I have never heard him called my half-brother before.'

'It means that I am your father, but that I am not Robert's.'

'I do not remember Robert. I remember Mother talked about him. He went to England. But she called him her son too, as well as me.'

'Yes.'

'So both Robert King and I are her sons, but only I am your son?'

'Yes.'

The boy did not pursue this, and by not making things clear to him there and then Redmond ensured that he would learn about Baudin from gossip too. But John did say, 'When shall I see Mother? We do go to Sydney sometimes.'

'Do you wish to see your mother?'

'When we go to Sydney.'

They were not going to Sydney the next day but to visit the overseer of the Tongala Section, five hours' ride away. And in that section, at the same time as Redmond and his son were dining, the residents for the time being of the rum-shanty known as the Abandon Hope were just settling down to mutton and damper.

There were ten of them in a hut ten feet by six. The walls were made of raw sheets of bark stripped from trees, and so was the roof. Mud was piled on top of the roof, making it almost waterproof when it rained, but for weeks at a time there was no rain, and then the mud dried and cracked so that in the daytime those inside could see the sky through the roof, and at night a man approaching the shanty would see light shining up from within. The table was a plank of eucalypt. It had been made when the wood was still green, and the heat of the cabin had curled and warped it so badly that a man had to be careful where he placed his mug of tea, or it would slide off. The chairs were tree stumps sawn off eighteen inches high. At the hearth, which ran the whole length of one of the shorter sides of the shanty, Joseph Halloran was kneading the damper. He took flour and water, kneaded it, flattened it out, placed the flat cake on hot embers, and then covered it with more embers. After half an hour it was uncovered and eaten straight away, hot. Cold damper is as soft as brick. The mutton was stewed, as always, and the whole washed down with quarts of tea.

Four men slapped down coins, which Halloran accepted, nodding. They were paying for a week's food. Four others offered nothing, and he made no remark. The last, a raw young man who had started work only three days before, fumbled uneasily in his empty pockets and then offered a handful of tobacco. Halloran shook his head. The customs and courtesies of being on the tramp were new to the young hand. Halloran made his profit on rum. You paid for rum. But if you worked in that section, or if you were passing by and came in for the night, nothing was asked or expected for food and shelter. If a man was known to be flush, as four of the men in that shanty were flush, then what he slapped down would be accepted. But if a man had nothing, nothing was required of him. There were shanties where even to offer was an insult, but most keepers would take money from those who could pay.

'Time to pig down,' said Halloran, and he and two others who were old residents rolled into bunks that lined the wall opposite the fire. Then sheepskins were flung on the floor, and the other seven men lay the length of the hut with their bare feet towards the fire, and the rest of their bodies covered in any clothes, blankets, or other skins they had, which they shared between them.

For a while they smoked.

All were Redmond's men. Two were convicts assigned to him. Six were convicts on ticket-of-leave, whom he paid. Halloran and another man were emancipists.

'I saw his kitchen in his mansion,' said Halloran. 'The vista from that man's kitchen.'

The kitchen, though Redmond never saw it, was the marvel of his house. The drawing room, the library, the reception rooms, and the ball room, were opulent. But the kitchen was a beautiful room and Halloran, a shanty keeper, knew this. It was the largest room in the house. The builder had given it space, width, height, and light from a clerestory of windows in the high walls and from a skylight too, and all this light reflected off white-washed walls and white-scrubbed flagstones. An iron spit which could roast an ox turned in a fireplace twelve feet wide and ten feet high.

'And there is a battery,' said Halloran, 'of copper saucepans, and broiling pans, and pans to fry in, and moulds for water-ices, and great ladles, and stirring spoons four feet long. I counted them as they hung on the walls, and there were one hundred and eighty-four, all copper, all shining.'

'And the vista.' Halloran had seen great houses in Ireland, and knew a vista when he saw one. From one end of the kitchen, with the whole room glowing in light reflected from white walls and from that battery of copper things, you could see across the flagstones, through the open door into the court-yard, across raked gravel paths, to the open door of the lobby at the other end, and in the lobby was a floor laid diagonally with squares of black and white Italian marble.

The fug in the shanty was by then very agreeable. It was the warmth induced by the wood fire, tobacco smoke, and rum.

'And the champagne cellar,' said Halloran.

None of them had ever tasted champagne.

'There is a shaking table for the champagne,' said Halloran.

'What of it?' asked a shepherd.

'It is not a table at all. It's an affair like a great revolving drum which is turned each day. Turned slightly. Every day.'

'And why's that?'

'So that the sediment, which is in champagne, gathers on the cork, and leaves the wine sparkling and clear.'

'You ever tasted it, sediment or not?' asked the sceptical one.

'I never did.'

'Nor ever will. We raise his sheep, and shear his sheep, and bale his wool, and that Redmond, because he's a free object, has his champagne, and all the country he can ride over in a day.'

Redmond was considered a free object. Not one of his men knew he too had been a convict. It was something by then unknown in the colony. Redmond was thought to be so aristocratically free an object that he had a nickname, which had stuck: he was known as Pure Merino.

At dawn next morning Gordon Burns scraped the previous day's mud from his boots, slung his matilda and his billy over his shoulder and began to walk south by the sun to the Tongala Section. Two hours later, Redmond, having breakfasted on chops, steak, claret, and coffee, set out with his foreman and John to ride there also. His visits of inspection were never announced. He liked overseers and men to be uncertain when they would see him next. Redmond was a tolerable master. He did not flog his assigned convicts for every loss of a sheep, as one of his insolvent neighbours had. One servant of that man, maddened by constant beatings, loosed a whole flock into the bush, and only half were ever recovered. The loss of 200 head hastened that man's bankruptcy and the sale of his land to Redmond. For himself, Redmond found it enough to threaten the return of a convict to Sydney, which generally meant an appearance before a magistrate who was a friend of Redmond's, and then the chain gang. He had sent three men back in the previous year and was feared for it. But he did not flog his men, and in that way was a great deal better than many. But he was not a man who was admired, only envied.

Burns reached Tongala before noon. The overseer, who knew him from the year before, took him on. Redmond's party arrived by mid afternoon. The overseer conducted a tour of sheep-pens, fences, barns, wool sheds, bullocks and bullock-drays, tools and tackle. Redmond inspected the wages books. He looked round the overseer's office, at the horse-hobbles, tin dishes, pannikins, stock-whips, guns, powder canisters, and a collection of pharmacist's bottles containing cure-alls for the diseases of sheep, who are delicate animals, forever ailing. He glanced at the overseer's room, where he and John would sleep that night before returning the next day. The overseer and the foreman would sleep in the bullock stables.

'Any new hands?' asked Redmond.

'Two, sir. One I've had four days now. Ticket-of-leave man from the town.'

'Not much use with sheep?'

'I keep him at fence-mending. If he stays, he'll learn.'

'And the other?'

'Came in today, just ahead of you, sir. A good man.'

'Seen him before then?'

'Last season, sir.'

'Why do you never keep good men?'

'It's always the best that are restless. Always the best that go off on the tramp, sir. This man's a shepherd.'

'We'll see the shanty.'

This was unwise. The shanty was Redmond's, like everything else on that land. Halloran was his hut-keeper, paid by him, though also allowed to take a cut of rum profits. But the men's shanty was their territory, and a wiser master than Redmond would have left it alone.

The overseer waited, hoping by his silence to encourage Redmond not to go to the Abandon Hope.

'At sundown,' said Redmond.

So at sundown they went to the shanty. The overseer, carefully preceding Redmond, knocked on the open door. Nobody ever knocked on the bark door of the shanty. Halloran, who was bending over a spit by the fire, did not look round but shouted, 'Whoever that is that knocks, the door's open.'

Redmond stepped into the fug of tobacco and roasting meat. No one stirred. The talk stopped. Halloran, half looking round, saw the high leather boots in the doorway, and straightened up.

'Good day, Mr Redmond. Would you be taking a drink with us?'

Redmond looked round at the ten men sitting on the tree trunks which did for chairs, or else lounging on the ground. No one stood up for him, not even his assigned convicts.

'And is that your fine son with you, sir?' asked Halloran.

Redmond said, 'This is my son. Which are the two new men?'

The very raw young man who had been four days at the station did get up. 'Me, sir.'

Redmond glanced at him. He evidently was not the shepherd. 'The man who is a shepherd,' he said.

'Here,' said Burns, from the floor.

'Name?'

'Burns.'

'Shepherd, Burns?'

'Aye.'

'Then,' said Redmond, 'you know a lamb from a ewe.'

The overseer caught Halloran's eye. The bolder men in the hut looked steadily at Redmond and said nothing. The less bold looked at the dirt floor. What the overseer had known within ten yards of the shanty, and what Redmond noticed as soon as he stepped inside, was that tonight the men were not eating old mutton. Ewes will bear lambs until they are old and stringy, and it was only then, when the flesh was tough and tasteless, that they were killed to feed the station-hands. For weeks the men had eaten old stewed mutton. That night of all nights there was not mutton but lamb, which was forbidden. Two lambs were roasting over the fire, and the aroma was not that of stewing mutton.

'Aye,' said Burns, 'I know a lamb from a ewe, mister.'

It was in part due to Burns that there was roast lamb that night. The year before, when he had passed that way, working his week or two weeks before going on, he and Halloran had become mates. When he had appeared that day, it was in the nature of a celebration that he and Halloran had gone and picked out two lambs.

Redmond surveyed Burns. 'Crawler?' he asked.

Crawler was a term of offence. A crawler was an assigned convict who absconded from his master and lived how he could, by petty theft if possible, by work if he had to. Burns, who was an emancipist, held his peace.

'Crawler?' said Redmond again.

Burns had got the scar on his cheek in a brawl in a Perthshire tavern. The other man had come off worse, and the assault had brought Burns to the other side of the world. By the time

Redmond came to the shanty, Burns had drunk his share of rum and water. He got to his feet.

'No crawler, mister. I crawl to no man, though that man be Pure Merino.'

Redmond put his hand to his pistol.

'The boy, sir,' said the overseer, putting himself between Burns and Redmond.

Redmond pushed his overseer aside, drew the pistol, and held it loosely, with the barrel pointing down.

'Out,' he said to Burns.

It had begun to rain. Inside, first drops and then rivulets fell from the roof bark, and spattered and hissed as they fell on the fire. Outside it was pelting.

'Out,' said Redmond.

Burns looked at the pistol, at Redmond, at the boy, at the overseer, and then round the shanty. He raised a hand in farewell to Halloran.

Redmond stepped aside. Burns stooped down, swung his matilda over his shoulder, put on his hat, and walked past Redmond into the rain. Six feet from the shanty he stopped, looked back at Redmond, and said, 'Purer Merino I never saw, mister.'

Redmond raised the pistol and fired over the man's head. Burns considered, spat on the ground, and walked away. Then, while Redmond remained fifteen minutes in the shanty to shelter from the rain, Burns walked to the stables and saddled the finest horse, which was Redmond's bay, and rode into the outback. He rode for three hours before the rain stopped. He rode on until he came to country where rain had not fallen at all and the ground was dry. Then he hobbled his horse, lit a fire, and stood by it in his soaking clothes, from which the steam rose. First he dried one side, and then turned and dried the other. His boots remained sodden. He brewed tea, drank the last of the rum with which he had filled his flask at the Abandon Hope, and then, huddled in an opossum rug which he took from his matilda, rode on. By taking the horse he had become an outlaw. Sun-up, which found him still riding, was the dawn of Gordon Burns's first day as a bush-ranger.

# 24

# Woman in a Lighted Doorway

'We, Jorgen Jorgensen,' said Jorgen Jorgensen in Susannah's sitting room, 'thereupon proclaimed that we did not hesitate to announce [laughter from Susannah] that the people of Iceland had thrown off the intolerable yoke of the Danish oppressor and had unanimously called Us to be Monarch and Head of State.'

Mr Jorgensen was a Dane who had once upon a time seized the throne of Iceland. It was a fact. It was for this and other matters of State – principally fraud and the amassing in London of most imaginative debts with no means or intent to repay – that he found himself a convict in New South Wales, in transit, on his way to the newer convict colony of Tasmania. In Sydney, since he was harmless, he was allowed ashore to pay social calls, the captain of the convict transport requiring only a written assurance, given on his word as a gentleman, that he would return. This he gave, signing the document, 'Jorgen, R.'

He was good company, took it very well when others found it impossible not to smile or even laugh at his adventures as he related them, and laughed himself. Without any doubt he had proclaimed himself King of Iceland and maintained the government until the captain of a visiting English frigate, lacking a sense of humour, took him under arrest to London.

'How,' said Susannah, 'was your unanimous call to the throne achieved?'

'By Ourselves,' said Jorgensen, 'with twelve men and a brace of pistols. We took the Governor's residence with ease. The

Danish governor, Count Tramp [a smile from Susannah, but that was the man's name], was resting on a sofa with a Danish lady.'

And how had King Jorgen maintained the government?

'In Iceland, ma'am, there are only the common people and the priests. I halved the taxes of the common people, and doubled the stipends of the priests.'

Jorgensen accepted more tea, and gave the briefest sketch of a career in which he had gambled in London, Lisbon, and the Cape of Good Hope, taken part in several revolutions, captained two ships, offered his services as a spy against the Americans to the British Foreign Office, and also – which was his reason for calling on Susannah – met the late Governor King in a London coffee house after his return from the colony. Jorgensen was a famous liar, but it seemed from the details of his narrative that the meeting with King was genuine. They had played chess. Jorgensen recalled a game his opponent won with a strategy known as the Queen's Walk, which Susannah knew was typical of her father's play. She was touched to hear him remembered.

Then followed more European escapades of Jorgensen's, the account of which he ended with this sentence: 'I will not attempt,' he said, 'to describe the amazing panorama of the field of Waterloo.' At which Susannah dissolved into laughter and Wyndham, who was just that moment entering the room, leaned on the doorpost and tried unsuccessfully to hide his.

Susannah introduced Mr Commissioner Wyndham to Mr Jorgensen, King of Iceland.

'Iceland?' said Wyndham.

Jorgensen inclined his head. 'We have,' he said, 'found Ourselves pushed to the front of affairs at both ends of the earth. But, Mr Commissioner, I would not mislead you into thinking Our career was all kingship. Monarch We have been, but also naval captain, revolutionist, British diplomatic agent, dramatist, preacher, political prisoner, gambler, hospital pharmacist, explorer, and commercial traveller; and the most demanding of these professions, We may say, was that of hospital pharmacist. An error by a monarch is generally retrievable, but one by a pharmacist sometimes not.'

'If,' said Wyndham, 'you are a competent pharmacist, I

could give you a note to the government surgeon in Tasmania which might get you a ticket-of-leave and employment.'

Jorgensen graciously accepted the offer and took his leave.

Wyndham asked Susannah, 'Shall we go out?'

She picked up a sketching block and pencils, and they left the house, walking in the direction of Farm Cove and Woolloomooloo Bay, half a mile to the east. She never walked with him on the lawns down to Sydney Cove. On the eastern shore of Farm Cove, very near the point where the waters of the cove met those of the harbour, she sat on a sandstone shelf in the shade of a hanging rock. Skirts were now much fuller, waists were at the waist, sleeves were long, necks high, and hats wide-brimmed. Susannah gave Wyndham the sketching block, arranged the skirts around her so that the folds of white muslin fell either side of her on the sandstone, waited while he sat on the grass and took up his pencil, and then turned her face towards the harbour. The place and the situation were familiar to them. Wyndham was much more than a competent artist with the pencil. He had not done the Grand Tour, as he would have done but for the war, but the galleries and museums and great houses of England contained between them, in objects that had been bought or looted from all over the world, as much as a man could see in many Italian cities. Wyndham was familiar with the etchings of Rembrandt and the drawings of Fragonard and Watteau. He knew life in a drawing when he saw it, which was why he had seen it in Governor King's water colours of aborigines.

Susannah did not pose for Wyndham. She just sat there, leaning back on her hands. She took off her hat and let down her hair, taking out the pins and then shaking out the hair with a toss of her head. When the sun fell lower in the west, the overhanging rock no longer gave shade, and her face was lit by the full rays. After a while she replaced the hat and shaded herself again.

Wyndham sketched quickly. He was not making one careful portrait but creating several figures on the same large sheet, and he was drawing her not only as she appeared before him, but as she appeared in his recollection and his imagination. It had begun a few weeks before, when he sketched her head and shoulders, caught almost a likeness, and was encouraged by this to draw her standing, sitting, and then lying. He had always drawn her in this place, and yet the first sketch in which he caught her to the life was one of Susannah full-face, with grave eyes and half smiling mouth which, when he showed her, she instantly recognized for what it was. He had drawn only her features, nothing else, but what she recognized was the moment and the place, which was not at the rock. It was herself looking up at him as she lay in her bed, and what was also present in that sketch was the woman's consciousness of the man looking down at her.

Wyndham had first drawn her reclining, dressed, and alone. Then reclining, dressed, while the figure of a man stood looking down at her. Then he drew the courtly pose of the man helping the woman to her feet. Then the man holding the woman by the hands as she lowered herself to the ground. The two figures then went through the progressions of a man with a woman. Susannah sitting upright on a sofa with Wyndham standing before her, as if talking. Susannah reclining on a sofa with his head in her lap. Susannah lying on that sofa half dressed, holding out her arms to her lover. Then there was Susannah lying with her lover beside her. Then there was Susannah entered and embraced by him. In all these scenes, the face of the man was never seen, but hers always. Over the weeks, as he drew, Wyndham showed her the sketches sheet by sheet.

She once asked, 'But do you separate yourself from us, do you stand apart as it were, to see yourself and me like that?'

'I do not separate myself. I could not. I am there with you. But I am also an observer. I suppose that is why I can never draw my own face.'

The best of the drawings without any doubt was that of Susannah's head alone, as she looked up half smiling. It was the best until that afternoon.

After half an hour she said, 'Now you must let me see.'

He had drawn her head and shoulders, with her hair up and with her hair shaken out. He had drawn her hatless and with the wide-brimmed hat. Then he had achieved two small masterpieces. The first showed Susannah lying on the bed by now so familiar to them, entered by her lover. What Wyndham had achieved for the first time was the absorption of the man as it showed in the lines of his back, and the intentness of the woman in the clasp of her arms round the man's shoulders, and in the raptness of her face. That was the first sketch. The second was an ideal – two lovers locked together, supported by nothing, lying on nothing, floating as if in air. It was all essence, and, for what it mattered, was technically the better of the two drawings. But the first had life and substance. Susannah passed the backs of her fingers lightly across the lines of the first drawing, and then, stopping her fingers at the representation of her own face, said, 'I love you for that. It is not as I have ever seen myself, but I know it is how I feel.'

Late that night they lay in bed talking. She lay with her back to him, and his right hand rested lightly on her hip. They had known each other for a few months, yet the gesture seemed as accustomed as that of a man to his wife, married many years and well beloved.

'Then the report on the blacks is done?' she said.

'Written and despatched.'

James Wyndham had sent to London a report which would, like his report on Irish workhouses, be very much noticed. He wrote that he doubted if more than a few of the white population of New South Wales understood the blacks, and that he had met no single black who understood the whites. Their conception of the soul, life, work, and property, was in every fundamental feature different from that of an English Christian. The state of being a Christian was almost enough in itself to disable a man from an understanding of the blacks, but all Christian benevolence was necessary if those blacks were not to die, and the race become extinct. Yet if anything could more than Christianity disable a man from an understanding of these poor savages, it was an adherence to Rousseau's doctrine of the Noble Savage. The blacks did show manliness and generosity in some circumstances, but nobility was an attribute of plenty – of a plenty of sustenance for both spirit and body. As to bodily sustenance, the blacks around Sydney were being driven from the richest of their traditional hunting and fishing grounds. As to the spirit, they were losing their Dreaming. He explained the concept of the Dreaming. The older and weaker civilization of the blacks would not withstand the impact of the newer and more vigorous civilization of the whites. Furthermore, the whites had resorted, sometimes in fear and sometimes from cupidity, to massacre; and the blacks, bewildered at every turn, had been guilty of treachery and cannibalism. Wyndham then made a recommendation which was condemned as impractically radical. A mixture of the races was impossible. Even an association was difficult and full of dangers for both black and white. He advised His Majesty's Government to segregate the two races, and to protect the homelands of the blacks. The alternative was a drift to disaster, and probable extermination. He was, with respect, His Majesty's humble servant, James Wyndham, Commissioner.

There was not a word in that report which was not written by Wyndham, or which did not express the convictions formed by his own mind, but the formation had been assisted by Susannah. In London the report would be debated in the Lords, Wyndham marked down once again as a man whose rise would be rapid, and nothing would be done.

In bed, Susannah said, 'And now I have something more to be grateful to Jane for.' She had. Wyndham would normally have returned with his report. But the escape of Jane and the others, and the reports in the London press of the reception at Bedford Square, had created a demand for an enquiry into the whole business of transportation, to which the Government thought it prudent to accede.

'Wyndham's there,' said the Secretary of State. 'Get him to do it.' The Prime Minister assumed this expressed the consensus of Cabinet? Very well.

'If he'll stay there,' said the Irish Secretary. 'It's asking a lot of a chap to swallow one dose of Ireland and now two of New South Wales.'

Consensus of Cabinet was that Wyndham was a good fellow who would do what he was asked. So he might have done, but he did not think about reasons. He stayed for Susannah.

So, that night, lying by Susannah's side, Wyndham said, 'I am grateful to Jane too. You know, when I start on transportation in a week's time, I shall have Jane as witness and Robert appearing before me as advocate for the emancipists.'

'That is proper?' asked Susannah.

'To hear Jane as a witness is proper. To hear Robert as

counsel: I have thought about that. He knows how things are between us?'

'Of course. He has seen us together.'

'If this were London, I should recuse myself. But it is Sydney, and there is no one to take my place, and precious few to take Robert's if he were to withdraw. Anyway, I shall not hear him as your son, but as counsel for his clients, and that will be understood by us both.'

Susannah said, 'But, James, you must be prudent. You are Commissioner. I must not compromise you. It did not matter with the blacks. But an inquiry into transportation will touch Redmond. Without transportation, what will he do for shepherds? I am still his wife, and if he knew of us, he could make a great deal of it.'

'I shall hear him as I would anyone else.'

'But be prudent. Do not be seen with me too much.'


But how far could Susannah herself be prudent? It is one of the graces of wholeheartedness that it is sometimes incapable of prudence. They had been so far secure because they were seen together only by those on whose loyalty they could depend. To prepare his report on the blacks, Wyndham had to travel. He was naturally away from his town lodgings for two or three nights at a time. He did not often stay the night with Susannah. There were the afternoons. But when he did stay, when he would not go or she would not let him go, this was known only to his man, Richardson, and to Jane, and Richardson was as loyal to Wyndham as Jane to Susannah. Susannah's new maid had met Wyndham early some mornings, but she stood aside and said not a word. Susannah was sure of her. They were safe.

In his first week of his inquiry into transportation, Wyndham went to hear witnesses at Newcastle, and to see for himself how the penal settlement there was conducted. It was now reformed. He was to return on the Saturday, but on Friday received a message from the Governor asking him to come to Parramatta at the weekend if he possibly could, on a matter of urgency. He wrote to the Governor saying he would come, and to Susannah that he would not now be back until Sunday or even Monday.

'Wyndham,' said the Governor, and the two men, after their first apprehension of each other, were now friends, 'you have received or you will receive an application from a man called Tyrone to give evidence before you.'

'Tyrone?'

'He is in the mad-house here.'

Wyndham, who had not remembered the name, did remember a letter from the mad-house.

'Wyndham, I don't know what that letter said. The superintendent would normally read any letter sent by an inmate, but thought it would be improper to intercept a letter addressed to you as Commissioner. That was my opinion too.'

'I do not remember that it was more than a simple application to give evidence.'

'Now,' said the Governor, 'it would be improper for me to make any request to you in respect of that application, so I shan't. I'm not sure it isn't improper for me as Governor to say anything at all to you in the matter, so if you stop me, there's an end to it. But I'd like to offer you some information which might save a lot of distress. I'll say nothing about the application, which is up to you, but I want to tell you about an event of some eighteen months or two years ago.'

Wyndham nodded. The Governor told him the story of the six men drowned in chains. Wyndham understood that if Tyrone, formerly a captain and now a lunatic, were to appear, he would probably tell the whole story, thinking in his mad way to exonerate himself. The colony would be inflamed, the whole affair of the escape would once again be opened up, and, most of all, Jane Bryant would know for the first time how her husband died.

Wyndham accepted some whisky. He began to see how the closeness of the colony led to corruption, the smallest of corruptions at first, but leading to who knew what? In London he would not have heard Robert as counsel: here he would. Now, in the graver matter of Tyrone, he knew that his judgement was swayed, and he knew that his mind was already made up, by consideration for Jane Bryant, a woman he knew. He fell back on a device of procedure, and prayed that he might be doing right. His commission gave him wide discretions.

He said, 'An insane man might by reason of that insanity be

incapacitated from giving evidence. That's one thing. Another
is that there's nothing in my commission which says where I
shall hear evidence. The man need not come before me. I may
go to the man and hear him at the mad-house.'

Nothing more was said. What Wyndham proposed to do was
in every way proper. Only he knew that his reasons for acting
in that way were those of policy. And there he was hard on
himself. In humanity to any woman whose husband had died
as Jane's had, he would have heard such evidence in private,
had he known what it was likely to be. He would visit Tyrone
in the mad-house.

He dined with the Governor. At nine o'clock, when they were
smoking and talking, a servant brought a note. Wyndham
broke the seal carelessly. Not until he opened it did he realize
it was from Susannah. Just as he had once not known her
Christian name, he still did not know her handwriting. She had
never written to him before. There had been no occasion. But
that night she could hardly bear his longer absence and she
wrote. The note said, 'Darling, please come back tonight if you
conceivably can. Please come back.' She signed herself with the
single initial *S*.

The servant said the messenger was waiting for a reply.

'Is there anything . . .?' asked the Governor.

'If I may,' said Wyndham.

The Governor waved him to the study. Wyndham took up a
pen and wrote, 'Susannah – I so much want to come, but it
would mean complicated excuses, and I don't see how I can.
I'll be back early tomorrow.' He sealed the note and sent it out
to the messenger.

He returned to the Governor, and they did not retire until
eleven, a late hour in a colony which rose with the sun.
Wyndham always slept well, but now he did not sleep. Just
past midnight he dressed, roused his clerk, and said he was
returning to Sydney. He would take the clerk's mare. The
carriage and the clerk could stay at Parramatta until Monday,
when he would return to see the man Tyrone. Wyndham left a
note to the Governor saying he had after all decided that he
should have returned in response to the message he had
received, and offering apologies. Then he saddled the horse
himself and rode to Sydney.

It was only fifteen miles on a dry, warm, moonlit night, but even so it was extraordinary to travel that road alone, so late. He was challenged by sentries as he left Parramatta, three times along the road, and twice in Sydney, once as he entered the town and the second time as he approached the Domain. Each time he answered with the single word, 'Officer,' – the response required from any gentleman, whether he was ensign or governor. The truth of the response was never doubted. It was two o'clock before he arrived at Susannah's. He led the mare into the stables, unsaddled her, threw a blanket over her, and fed and watered her. You cannot enter a stables silently. The other horses were roused, and by the time Wyndham walked across the courtyard to the house there was already a light in the hallway and in one of the upper rooms. He was seen. The door opened before he could ring, and there was Susannah.

She stood at the open door, in her nightdress and barefooted. He had seen her like that a hundred times before; and yet he had never once seen her like that. Susannah, in that nightdress, in her bed room, he had seen many times. But now the time and the place changed the nature of everything. Susannah in that nightdress in the doorway open to the Domain, and at night, was something else, and quite different. Susannah in her bare feet, there, was something else and different. Her appearing there expressed in that scene and in that moment all the hope, anxiety, longing, fear, warmth, and love that was in her.

She said, 'Oh, I did not think you would come.'

He enclosed her in his arms. Over her shoulder he saw a figure with a candle at the top of the staircase. It was Jane. She recognized who it was at the door, and vanished. Susannah held Wyndham. 'I did not think you would come,' she said.


Of course the sentinels at the Domain recognized that it was Wyndham who answered their challenge, and saw to whose house he rode, and they talked among themselves. But they thought it nothing to Wyndham's discredit. It showed that even Commissioners were human, and he was considered a lucky devil. Wyndham and Susannah were also seen by another observer as they embraced in the lighted doorway, but there was no talk of that at all, at present. The Governor, when he received Wyndham's note next morning, thought it no part of his duty to surmise, but, having nevertheless surmised, hoped for Wyndham's sake that he would be circumspect. Wyndham returned to Parramatta to see Tyrone in the mad-house alone, and heard again the story he already knew from the Governor. Tyrone was pleased that the Commissioner should come to him rather than summon him, thinking this showed the importance attached to the evidence he had to give. For a year Wyndham toured the colony, and heard anyone who wished to be heard. He heard Redmond as spokesman for the wool interest, and Redmond departed satisfied that he had convinced Wyndham of the importance to New South Wales of the wool trade, which he had, and that convicts were essential to the well-being of the colony.

Then it was time for Wyndham to go. He would write his report on the ship on the passage to England. He had been in the colony eighteen months. He had to leave Susannah. He did not ask her to come with him, not because he did not want to, but because he knew he could not, and that her reply in any case would be a refusal. It would be an impossible proposal. For him to ask her, for them to discuss it, and then for her to decline, would have done nothing but cause pain. She was still married to Redmond. Only kings and great dukes divorced: each single divorce required a separate Act of Parliament. Susannah knew she could never be Wyndham's wife. So, even between themselves, they never though of returning together. Everything made it hopeless. For Wyndham to return with the wife of a man who was principal spokesman for the colony's wool interest would also have vitiated large parts of his report. They had to part, and they knew this and faced it.

Wyndham was completely changed by Susannah. In eighteen months she had done for his instinct and spirit what his tutors, schoolmasters, the university, and the practice of politics had done, over nearly thirty years, for his intellect. Not that instinct and intellect can be divided. That is the point. In Wyndham they no longer were.

They walked together. He said, 'It will be spring now, in England.'

She said, 'You have missed the spring? Englishmen do here,
for several years. You have missed the trees coming into leaf all
at once, and the flowers coming into bloom, and the sudden
greenness?'

'I suppose I have. You put it more vividly than I have felt it.
But I have felt it.'

She stopped, and took a leaf from a young eucalypt. 'Oh, we
have brought in fruit trees from Europe. Some I planted are
now quite grown. And in the town there are plane trees, which
were brought in, and they lose their leaves in the winter, and
then come into leaf and give shade in the summer. But their
foliage now seems bright to me. I am used to the tints of greys
and greens which are everywhere here.' She turned over the
eucalypt leaf in her fingers, a narrow leaf, olive green above,
grey beneath, without gloss. 'It is subtle,' she said. 'The tints
are very gentle.'

She had told him something about Baudin, though never his
name. It had aroused in him a twinge of that most absurd and
destructive of emotions, a jealousy of past things, which he felt
and then dismissed. She had told Wyndham what she did only
to explain that, if she could, she would not grieve for him as she
had for Baudin. Not because she did not love Wyndham, but
because grief destroyed the spirit.

'And if you wish to please me,' she said, 'you will not grieve
for me, but remember me with happiness. I shall remember you
with happiness. You gave me back my Dreaming, and I shall
not lose it again.'

A few days before his departure, when they went to the
hanging rock for the last time, she asked him to give her the
drawing which had first caught her to the life – only a head
and shoulders, but the one that showed her consciousness of him
in her eyes.

Wyndham took the other sketches back to England with him,
and, at his death, which is many years after this story ends, they
passed with his other papers to his Cambridge college. His
career had been a brilliant one. He had ended by accepting an
earldom but declining the Viceroyalty of India in order to
become instead Regius Professor of Classics at Cambridge, a
sacrifice which, since the Chair was not even at Oxford but only
at Cambridge, was thought to be excessive. The Fellows of his

old college gathered one evening to consider a portfolio, found among his state papers, and marked 'New South Wales, Susannah'. As the first drawings were taken from the portfolio, a eucalypt leaf fluttered loose and dropped on to the table. None of the Fellows recognized it. They gazed at the sketches in silence. All the Fellows were bachelors, many of them clergymen, and most of them celibate. It was by then two-thirds of the way through Victoria's reign, and the instincts of these gentlemen should have been to destroy the portfolio. Not one of them made such a suggestion. The Master of the college, an aged man, looked long at one drawing and with a movement of his hand followed the lines of it almost as Susannah had when she first saw it the afternoon Wyndham drew it. Then there was another, which moved them all, which showed a woman in a lighted doorway, at night. The drawings were deposited in the college library along with the rest of the Wyndham papers, and the portfolio marked 'New South Wales, Susannah' took its place with others marked 'Soudan', 'Jamaica', 'British Columbia', 'Bengal', and with the names of other parts of the Empire where Wyndham became Commissioner or, later in his long career, Governor.

Susannah framed the drawing she kept, and hung it in her sitting room. It was only a head and shoulders but visitors often looked at it, and then returned to it, sensing that there was more to it than they could see.

# 25

# Great Oaks, and the Wild Colonial Boy

In the six years after Gordon Burns was driven out, and out-lawed himself by the theft of Redmond's mare, the Tongala Section greatly prospered. Where there were once ten shepherds and a hut-keeper, there were now thirty shepherds, each with 800 sheep. Halloran was still hut-keeper, but his shanty grew to be three times the size it was, and he had two men under him to serve up mutton and damper, and more mutton and damper, washed down with quarts of tea.

'Listen to this,' said Halloran, one supper time, holding up a copy of a Sydney newspaper three weeks old. 'Pure Merino has been lecturing the assembly again about Great Oaks.' Halloran was one of only two men of the thirty gathered in the shanty who could read, and his reading aloud was a large part of their entertainment. Redmond had become a member of the colony's legislative assembly, which, though it could legislate for practically nothing, certainly assembled and thundered away on mighty matters.

Redmond was reported at length. As the colony grew and prospered, he said, and as the day drew closer when they would inevitably govern their own affairs, when the assembly would be responsible not to the Governor in Sydney but directly to His Sovereign Majesty the King, it behoved them to consider what form the government of the newly independent colony should take. There would of course be an elected Lower House, for was theirs not a country of free men? ('Hear, hear.') Though the extent of the franchise was a matter to be decided. ('Hear, hear.') But there should also, as in the Mother Country, be preserved an ordered society, an hierarchy, the pinnacle of which should be an aristocracy. Aristocracy was that Great Oak – (here the Honourable Member was interrupted by cries of, 'Hear, hear,' from those Members who thought of themselves likewise as Great Oaks, and by howls of laughter from those other Members who had been harangued once too often about Great Oaks on pinnacles). Aristocracy, as the Honourable Member was saying, was that Great Oak which gave shelter to, and under whose shading foliage thrived, the honest commerce of their fledgling continent. (Cries of, 'Baa, baa,' from certain Members.) Honourable Members, said Redmond, might bleat if they wished. The assembly would notice that those Members who went, 'Baa' were merchants whose fortunes were based on the shipment of commodities other than wool, who had grown rich on whale oil, who had prospered on the provision of whalebone stays for ladies' corsets. He might call them the Members for blubber-and-stays. ('Order, order.') An aristocracy could be created only by His Britannic Majesty, whose loyal servants they all were, but he would dare to say that no finer candidates for a new House of Peers could have arisen than had done so from the sheep-men of this colony. (Cries of, 'Squatter,' and, 'Sheep-king.') Mr Redmond said he had been called both these things, and proudly accepted both titles. What were hurled at him as jibes he accepted, with humility, as compliments. (Laughter.) They might laugh, but had not the fortune of the colony been made from the world's finest fleece, and had he not advised settlers for years, many members among them, to put their money into four legs? The wool trade itself had indeed proved a Great Oak. (Laughter and further cries of, 'Baa.')

What the newspapers did not say, because the reporters were ordered not to mention it, was that at this point the blubber-and-stays interest began to sing, 'The Four-Legged Oak', to the hymn tune of 'The Old Rugged Cross'. But in the shanty, the thirty men were already bawling the song. Redmond was repetitious in his speeches, and the response of the blubber-and-stays men was well known.

It was in the middle of this uproar that Shaw, the driver of a bullock wagon, ran into the shanty and silenced them all by shouting, 'Johnny's shot. The poor sod's shot bad.' They brought him in and laid him on sheepskins. He was a shepherd, and still clasped the silver-headed crook he had brought with him from the old country. They took it from his hands. He was dying. One ball from a carbine had pierced his throat, making a neat wound as it entered, and a larger, ragged wound as it went out at the back of his neck.

'Bush-ranger,' said the driver. 'We was ambushed two miles out. A horseman. But when he rode up to us, after he shot Johnny, he never came close, but looked and turned away. He did it for nothing.' The driver was his mate, and stood with tears of anger in his eyes as Johnny died. He lived half an hour and, though he gasped and tried to speak, the blood bubbled in his throat and he could not say a word.

Halloran left the cooking to his two assistants, and with Shaw and two others carried the body of John Erskine to an out-house and laid it out. 'He was a good man,' said Halloran. 'He was a careful shepherd. You could tell that by the way he walked among his animals, without disturbing them. They never feared him or ran from him. It is a sure sign.'

The four men stood round the body.

Halloran told Shaw, 'Go back to the shanty and get some rum for yourself. We will come afterwards.'

After he went, Halloran looked at his two companions and said, 'Now, boys.'

Erskine had been an unusual man. He understood sheep. That was a gift possessed by perhaps six of the thirty men on that section. He had also been determined to have a sheep-run of his own one day, and that was a determination shared by no one else. The odds against an emancipist were so great they were impossible. An honest emancipist could hardly thrive. An ex-convict who made money generally did so at the expense of his former fellows, selling them high meat at high prices, or sozzling them with rum until they were too drunk to know he charged them for three times what they consumed. An emancipist who thrived most often did so by taking the week's pay of a man in one drunken night. Erskine had wanted to be a sheep-man. If he had been a settler, he could have had a grant of 3000 acres for the asking. An emancipist could hope for only 100 acres, useless for sheep. But Erskine had saved for five years and possessed £396 sterling. Although the currency was

the dollar still, accounts were made up and wages reckoned in
sterling and the equivalent paid in dollars, which, when paid
into a bank, were again converted back to sterling. By each
conversion the wage-earner lost a percentage, but Erskine had
sterling in the bank. He had meant to take up his grant of 100
acres, buy another 200 acres, borrow enough for 400 sheep, and
then take his chance. It was not much of a chance. He would
have had to buy newly-shorn sheep. It would have been a year
before he could shear them again, and then six months before
he got paid for the wool by the Sydney merchant. In that time,
a single drought, or a pack of dingoes, or an ordinary epidemic
of disease, could ruin him. Sheep were a rich man's game. A
rich man could wisely put all he had in four legs. If he had
capital, he would survive. If he survived, he could not help
becoming richer. A poor man had one chance in ten, or, if he
was truthful with himself, one in a hundred. But Erskine had
meant to try. Now he was dead, and his money was in a
Sydney bank. He had no known family. He had made no will.
His £396 would be forfeit to the colony.

'Well, boys,' said Halloran, 'it is up to us to find Erskine's will.
Shaw was his mate, and I know he left it all to him.'

'Bang to rights,' said the second man. The third nodded.

Halloran wrote a will. He had done this for men before,
though before their deaths. He had once been an attorney's
clerk in Dublin and knew a form of words. Then the dead man
had to sign.

'While there is still life in him,' said Halloran; and then, so
that he could, if it came to it, swear that the man signed while
there was still life in him, he caught a fly in his cupped hands
and put it into the dead man's mouth, which he closed. Then,
taking the stiffening fingers, he placed the pen in them, and
guided the hand so that by the side of the words, 'John Erskine,
His Mark,' the hand of Erskine made a cross.

'Now you must witness,' said Halloran. He had asked these
two men because he knew one could write and the other,
though he could not properly write, could copy the characters
which represented his name if they were written out for him to
copy. The will was made, signed, and witnessed. The fly was
released from the dead man's mouth. Halloran took the paper
and folded and refolded it back and forth until it frayed, and

then put it in Erskine's pocket to be found the next day. Then
they covered the dead man and left him.


Once a year for the previous six years, Redmond had suffered
a raid from a bush-ranger who was one of many celebrated in
ballads of the time as the Wild Colonial Boy. He broke into
Redmond's Sydney office and did not crack the safe but carried
safe and all away. In two successive years he held up wagons
carrying payrolls to the sections of Redmond's station, and took
the money, amounting to 3000 pounds in all, each time taking
the draught-horses with him, and, before he rode away, ordering
the driver and guard to remove all four wheels from the wagons
and smash the spokes. Twice he broke into Redmond's mansion,
once taking all the silver plate and a pack-horse to carry it, and
the second time drawing the bungs of all the wine-casks in the
cellar, so that two years' vintages spilled into the cellar and
flooded it. Each time, wherever the robbery took place,
Redmond found next morning the skin of a newly slaughtered
lamb nailed to the main door of his mansion.

The lambskin left Redmond in no doubt who nailed it there,
and so the description of Gordon Burns, alias John Henryson,
alias Robert Dunbar, alias the Perthshire Shepherd, alias the
Wild Colonial Boy, of ruddy complexion, five feet eight inches
tall, well-built, bearing on his left cheek the mark of a small
scar in the shape of a star, and speaking with a Scots accent,
became famous. Rewards first of £50, then of £100, and finally
of £200 were offered on posters tacked to a thousand trees. The
Wild Colonial Boy had killed two men. The first was a servant
of Redmond's who levelled a gun at him while he was escaping
with pack-horse and silver, but was himself shot before he could
fire. The second was one of the horse-police who pursued the
bush-ranger for five days, and was killed by a shot from a
carbine. When Redmond was told of the murder of the shepherd
at Tongala he resolved to get the man himself this time. He
took five armed men with him. Four were policemen, whose
services Redmond could command because he was now a
magistrate, and the fifth was his son John, aged eighteen, the
best shot of them all. Redmond was preparing to depart at
dawn the next day when he received a note from Robert King

asking if they could meet soon on a matter of business. Redmond replied that it would have to be later that day, or else when he returned. Robert came in the evening.

Redmond and Robert King had never spoken since Robert's return. They had seen each other a few times in the streets of Sydney, acknowledged each other, and passed on. There was no enmity between them. There was a certain estrangement. Robert felt that Redmond had treated his mother badly. But if the two men had moved in the same circles they would at least have been civil. They did not, however, move in the same circles. Redmond was almost always up country. Robert rarely left Sydney.

But there was no enmity. When Robert came, the older man offered his hand, which Robert accepted. They sat, and Redmond waited.

Robert explained that this was a difficult thing for him to do. He had received news of the death of the Countess d'Estaing, with whom he had spent several years in Europe, and who for those years had been a second mother to him. Redmond said he was sorry. Of course he remembered the lady who had often written to his wife. He had never met the lady, but he offered his condolences. But, further than that, he did not see . . .?

Robert said, 'The Countess appointed me as executor of her will in New South Wales.'

'Yes?'

'There are two bequests to persons in the colony. One is to me. The other is to my mother.'

'I see. To my wife?'

'Yes.'

'And what is the effect of this bequest?'

'The Countess states plainly in the will her intention to create trusts in favour of my mother, so that the income of her residual estate, after bequests to me and others, should accrue to my mother.'

'Yes?'

'I am the executor in New South Wales of those trusts. I have consulted three other members of the Bar, and the opinion of them all is the same as mine, which I have communicated to my mother.'

Redmond waited.

'The will,' said Robert, 'was made in Paris according to French law. According to English common law, which is the law by which the will must be construed in the colony, the trusts fail.'

'I see,' said Redmond.

'My mother instructed me to tell you this. If you will ask your solicitors here to approach mine, they will tell you how the will affects you.'

Robert got up.

'This has been awkward for you,' said Redmond. 'If I understand you, the effect of what you have been obliged to tell me is that because the trusts fail, the property goes as a simple bequest to your mother; and then, because she is my wife, the property falls entirely to me?'

Robert said, 'That is broadly the effect.'

'What is the amount?'

'About one hundred and fifty thousand pounds.' This was a very great fortune, much greater than Redmond had thought. He was one of the richest men in the colony, but it was more than he possessed.

At this moment John entered the room to ask about the next day.

He and Robert shook hands as strangers. What else could they do? Redmond had never permitted John to see his mother, even when the boy asked. Robert and John were half-brothers who had not spoken since Robert was fourteen and John five. They were sons of the same mother, and did not know each other.

Redmond said, 'I go up country tomorrow. When I return, I will attend to this matter. I do not envy you what you have had to do this evening. Will you tell Mrs Redmond – will you tell your mother – that she will be hearing from me? And will you give her my regards?'


Robert passed on this message to Susannah, who nodded. The loss of the money did not distress her. She did not think of it as the loss of a great fortune, because what could a fortune buy? It could buy more land and sheep. That is what Redmond would do with it. Since she came to New South Wales she had always had the leisure and independence to do as she wished. She had the house. She had enough. While her father was alive and Governor she did not think of money at all, and nor had she since. A governor's daughter does not need to think about money, and it is difficult to get into the habit afterwards.

In the week since the news had come, she was much more bothered about Robert. The Countess's death was a blow to him. They had written often. She had not told him she was ill. Now, a week later, he had done his duty as executor. The evening after he came back from Redmond, he told Susannah, 'That part of it is done.'

Susannah said, 'You loved her, didn't you?'

'Yes. She was generous beyond words to me.' He had never told his mother about the first evening he saw the Countess, the meeting in the drawing room, and the benediction before he went to bed, but he did now. He had never told her about the two portraits. Now he took a small package from his pocket and gave it to Susannah.

'It came to me,' he said. 'I prize it, but it will be much more to you.'

It was the engraving of Nicolas Baudin, with the one epaulette of a lieutenant.

She said, 'Nicolas.'

Susannah held the framed engraving cupped in both hands. She felt the sting of tears, and did not let Robert see her face. She went to the window. Nicolas was younger in the engraving than she had known him, but what came first to her mind was that the eyes were as she had remembered them throughout the many years when she had possessed no likeness of him. She had remembered well.

'I will go,' said Robert, and was opening the door when Susannah said, 'Stay with me.'

It was a long time before she managed to ask her question. Why had the Countess, whom she had never seen, tried to leave so much to her? By the will Robert received a bequest of £50,000. That made him rich. Susannah could understand that bequest. But why should three times that amount have been left to her? Robert explained that if the trusts had been valid in the colony, the property would have been hers for life, and would then have passed to her heirs.

'That is not it,' said Susannah. 'Why a life interest to me? Why anything to me? Why so much to me?'

'I think it was a way of leaving it first to Nicolas and then to me. I think perhaps she saw you as Nicolas's heir. You see, she and Nicolas. . . .' He had never told his mother or anyone about the conversation in the Rue du Faubourg St Honoré, and nor would he now, more than to say that.

Susannah said, 'I know. He never told me. But I should have been insensible not to know when she wrote asking for you. I have never admitted this before, but that was one reason why I would not let you go, for so long. Then I thought that was ungenerous of me, as it was. I am glad you went. You never saw your father. But in seeing her, you must have seen something of him.'

She came away from the window and put the engraving on the table. She smiled at Robert. 'Although,' she said, 'seeing him that way, you must have seen him as a younger man than I did.'

Halloran knew very well in his heart who had shot Erskine, but he could not understand why. At Tongala the career of the Wild Colonial Boy had been followed eagerly. The horse-police had ridden as far as that farthest section of the station, nailed 'Wanted' posters to a few trees, and asked questions which were always answered in the same way. No one knew Burns, or had ever known him, or seen him, or heard of him. The reports in old Sydney newspapers of his raids on Redmond's property were read aloud in the shanty. The spilling of Redmond's claret, so that two vintages slopped knee-high on the flagstones of his cellars, had them howling with laughter. When his career went from robbery to killing, well, the killings of a guard and a policeman were fair game. They all knew the meaning of the lambskin pinned to Redmond's door after each attack, because Halloran had told them about the evening Burns met Redmond, and of Burns's fine contempt for Pure Merino. But only Halloran of all the men in the Section had stayed six years in the one place, and only he had ever seen, met, and talked to Burns, and been his mate. Halloran had never seen him again, but he knew Burns had been around Tongala on several occasions. He found the remains of camp fires, and the tracks of a hobbled horse round the fires. Not all the sheep that were lost fell prey to dingoes. Dingoes maul a carcass. They do not gut it and leave the innards. He knew Burns had taken sheep. He had a fair idea that the tea, coffee, and sugar missing from his stores was taken by Burns. He said nothing. Burns had been his mate, and he knew how he was driven out. But to kill Erskine was not fair game. It was murder.

Redmond, his son, and the four policemen came at noon. Redmond's inspection was cursory this time. He had other things on his mind. Now it was John who demanded curtly to know why a flock had been let to graze too long in one place. Who was the shepherd? When the man appeared, John asked why the ground was puddled in one spot, why it was churned up by the feet of the sheep, showing they had been there all day. If they stayed still too long they crowded each other, and the weaker were lamed. If it had rained, then their feet took the wet-rot from too long standing. The man plainly had been neglecting his work. And why was that dog kept? He was too old to be useful. The shepherd answered that, though the dog might be old, he was wise; but he thought to himself he would take good care to keep that dog from John's sight on the next visit.

Redmond rested the night and then took off the next morning, breaking his force into three groups and sending them in three directions, fanning out over the section. He took one policeman with him and rode to the west. Two other policemen rode east. A third party composed of John, a policeman, and Halloran, rode north. Halloran did not wish to go, particularly not in a party with John in charge, but he could not refuse. He undoubtedly knew the Section better than any other man there.

It was to the north, near the old camp where he had passed the night before walking to Tongala the day before he first became a bush-ranger, that they first found traces of Burns.

'Do you know the blacks hereabouts?' asked the policeman.

Halloran denied that he did, but John did not believe him. He ordered a fire to be lit, and they waited. The fire was not for warmth. It was a summer's afternoon. After three hours two blacks approached cautiously, their heads and the tips of their

throwing spears showing over the crest of the shallow rise. They
did not attack. In that Section they would not attack, since
they knew there were many white men and retribution would
be bloody. They could also see that the three white men by the
fire were well armed.

'Walk towards them,' said John. 'They will know you, I
think.'

Halloran did as he was told. He knew the men would know
him, and they did.

John looked coldly at Halloran. 'Now tell them we want them
to track a man.'

Halloran told them in signs and a pidgin mixture of Tongala
dialect and English. John gave the blacks tobacco, and
promised them two lambs, and the skins, if they found the
man.

To track a man on horseback over meadowland is so easy
that the whites could have done it for themselves, but after the
meadowland there would be scrub, and then, if the trail led that
far, mountains. That night they found a camp fire. To a white
man the ashes seemed cold. The blacks held the ashes in their
hands and to their lips, and said they were two days warm.
Since the fire would have burned all night, the man was a day
and a night ahead of his pursuers. Then they came to the bush.
There a horse's tracks were still plain. At one point they lost
the trail in a creek, which was now almost dry but perhaps had
not been the day before. A man would water his horse at a
creek. He would fill his own water flasks at a creek. But Burns
had not stopped there. They could find no trodden ground, and
no fire. The horse was being ridden at a walk, but the rider was
not stopping. Furthermore, he had ridden along the bed of that
creek for half a mile. It took the blacks two hours to find the
track again. The rider had doubled back on himself. He was
expecting to be followed. This became a certainty when, an
hour further on, they found tracks carefully obliterated. For the
whites, that would have been the end of the trail. They waited
in a group, unable to do more than look for the most obvious
signs like crows circling. No crows circled, but after a quarter
of an hour two crows did appear, flying steadily westwards into
the unexplored interior.

The policeman said, 'Even the crows have lost their way.'

'But we have not,' said John.

Halloran waited for the blacks to reappear, as he knew they would, with a fresh trail to follow. They did. It began a quarter of a mile away, in a gulley, in what were now granite foothills. The blacks proceeded steadily, calling softly to each other when a new scratch was found which betrayed the passage of a horse. Once they called up John, whom they had readily recognized as the leader, and excitedly pointed to two scratches he could barely make out for himself. John asked Halloran what they were saying. It was that the man was now leading his horse. 'How far ahead?' asked John. The blacks could not say. But soon there were signs which did enable them to say. There was a squashed ant, but the body was not yet dry. The man was less than a day ahead. Then a broken twig, but the point where it was broken was still perceptibly moist to the blacks, though it had lain in the hot sun. The man was four hours ahead. Then, in a sparse patch of grass, a few blades were trodden. Three hours ahead. Then there were salt marks on the granite. These were drops of sweat from a man, which had dried. He was less than two hours ahead. Then they found salt drops not yet quite dry.

John, Halloran, and the policeman rode up on to a ridge, and there before them they saw the man. He was 300 yards off, on a plateau, walking his spent horse. The policeman looked at John, who estimated the range, and nodded. It was a long shot, and it would betray their presence, but then so would one glance back by the fugitive. The policeman drew his carbine, aimed carefully, and fired one shot. It cracked the silence of the mountains, echoed among the rocks, and missed. The startled man looked back, mounted, raised his horse to a trot, and tried to make off. John and the policeman led their horses 200 yards out of the gulley until they reached the dusty plateau and could mount. Halloran hung behind. John cursed him and shouted at him to follow. The policeman's mount and John's were not fresh, but they were not exhausted, and they bore down on Burns. The dust rose from the dirt. In the confusion Burns doubled back into the dust. John was a good enough horseman to wheel and pursue, but he was impeded by the policeman, whose horse carried him headlong on. The policeman reined in, and at a hundred yards hit Burns's horse with one shot from

the carbine. It fell. With a second shot he thought he hi
Burns, but the man staggered into a gulley, and in the mêlé
the policeman and John somehow lost sight of him. They coul
now take their time. Burns was finished. They walked thei
horses slowly up to Burns's horse, which John recognized as hi
father's old bay. The policeman went up to shoot the strugglin
animal, but John stopped him. 'You may need all you have fo
Burns yet.' The dust was settling and the two men moved t
cover, and waited. They had time. The first move, if there wa
to be a rapid move, could be Burns's. If not, they would g
slowly after him, in their own time.

Burns at that moment was lying in his own blood under
scrub half way up a gulley. His left arm was smashed wher
the policeman's second shot had hit him, but in his right h
still held his carbine. He was looking dully at Halloran, wh
was standing ten feet away.

'Well,' said Halloran. 'Old mate.'

Burns looked down in hopelessness at his arm, and at th
stones on which he lay, and then up at Halloran.

Halloran came closer and sat on his heels. 'Why did you ki
Erskine, the man back at Tongala? Why did it come t
murder?'

'I was coming to pay you a visit, mate; anyway, to visi
your stores.'

'But you shot the man. What for?'

'Who was he?'

'A shepherd, as you were.'

'I was riding in. Then there was the bullock cart. And in th
sun, there was this guard, and the sun glinted on his musket
I thought he raised it, meaning to aim at me. I saw the su
glint on a barrel.'

'It was no gun-barrel,' said Halloran. 'It was a glint on
shepherd's crook he always had with him. He brought it ou
with him. It had a silver head.'

Burns said nothing. Then he said, 'A man gets too quick, too
afraid. Then he shoots too easily.

Quietly John and the policeman came up from behind
Halloran saw them. Burns saw Halloran's eyes move, and
turned his head. It was true Burns had a carbine still in hi
right hand. It was also true that he could not have fired it, no

having the strength to lift it. It was true he did turn towards John, but he only turned his head. Whether or not John realized that the man was helpless only he knew. The fact was – and this was much talked over in the shanty later – the fact was that the policeman made no move to shoot, and did not even raise his carbine as he approached. But John shot Burns twice. The first pistol shot killed Burns, entering at the temple. A death mask was later sold in the streets and shops of Sydney. Like all death masks it was serene, and like most death masks it lied in being serene. As it happens, the mask was not of Burns at all, but of a hanged convict. Burns's head was too badly shattered by the pistol ball to allow any recognizable mask to be made. But the mask that was sold went into folk history, and then into scholarly history, as the death mask of the Wild Colonial Boy.

Redmond congratulated John. Back in Sydney he took legal advice on the Countess's bequest to Susannah, and was told, in an opinion which took an hour and a half to express, that because he was Susannah's husband the income from the amount bequeathed was certainly his for life, though after that it was a question whether the property would revert to his or to Susannah's heirs. His solicitor mentioned to him, drily enough, that as husband he was also liable to provide for the maintenance of his wife, according to the reasonable expectations of her station and his, even though they were separated. But there was no doubt the Countess's money was his for life.

Susannah and Robert no longer stood in Redmond's way to social advancement. He was the very personification of the Ancient Nobility. He had known of her attachment to Wyndham, and the Commissioner's report on transportation had not pleased him. It fairly summarized the evidence of Redmond and the arguments for the sheep interest, and said plainly that the large sheep-owners and graziers relied on convict and ex-convict labour, but it ended with the thundering words that transportation, though chiefly dreaded as an exile, was undoubtedly much more than exile; it was slavery as well. And with slavery, Great Britain, as a Christian nation, should no longer defile itself. Transportation should cease. But it did not cease. Wyndham's report was much noticed, and nothing was done. So, Redmond wished to be just. In matters of money he was hard but just. He wrote to Susannah offering her one-third of the bequest. She replied thanking him, but saying she did not need it. Redmond, who understood the uses of money, could not comprehend such an answer. He wrote a second time, offering at least an annuity. She replied, again thanking him, again saying she had no need. The house was hers, and, for the rest, she had enough. But she thanked him. Redmond remembered very well that the house was hers, by grace and favour and apparently in perpetuity. He still wished to be a reasonable man, and made a third offer, this time to Robert. Redmond said his enterprises would now be greatly increasing, asked Robert to work with him, and offered him an equal partnership in the sheep station with himself and John. Robert told Susannah. 'This is generous of him,' she said. Robert agreed, but he knew he had other work to do. He too declined, again with thanks. Redmond did not try again. The will of Françoise, Comtesse d'Estaing, leaving in effect the bulk of her estate to William Redmond, Esq., grazier, was admitted to probate in Sydney in the same court and on the same day as the will of John Erskine, shepherd, of Tongala, which left to Arthur Shaw, station-hand, his entire estate of £396.

# 26

# The Tolpuddle Martyrs

One day in February 1834, Viscount Melbourne, His Majesty's
Secretary of State for Home Affairs, the man after whom the
city was later named, found on his desk two letters which caused
him grave concern. The first was from the Duke of Wellington,
who informed Melbourne that half the agricultural labourers
of Hampshire, the county in which the Duke had his country
seat, were members of those dangerous bodies, the trade unions.
This was untrue. The Duke was misinformed. But nevertheless,
the Duke said so, and the Duke was a national hero and a
gentleman. The second letter was from William Ponsonby, a
Member of Parliament for the neighbouring county of Dorset,
who reported that in the village of Tolpuddle discontented
field-hands had been seen kneeling in white robes before a
death's head and reciting oaths of secrecy which ended with the
words, 'Remember thy end.' This was also untrue. Ponsonby
was mistaken. But Ponsonby was Melbourne's brother-in-law.

Thus it was that a new, reforming, radical government found
itself engaged in rigging a State trial. A State trial it was,
though it was held not in Westminster Hall but in the courtroom in High West Street, Dorchester. And it was certainly
rigged. It has the honour of being probably the last trial to be
so openly rigged by a British government. Successive adminis-
trations had feared insurrection ever since the French Revolution of 1789 set a bad example. The European revolutions of
1830 were tiny affairs, but the British Government went sniffing
round for sedition. Rioters burned Nottingham Castle and
Derby prison, and, in the countryside, a few hundred haystacks

blazed. So death's head oaths in Puddletown were to be made an example of. But what was the crime?

Miners had been imprisoned for illegal conspiracy when they threatened to strike, and shoe-makers for 'leaving work unfinished', but the Tolpuddle men had done neither of these things. Posters were plastered on the walls of Dorsetshire cottages threatening with transportation any man who joined a union, but they had not done that either. But they had formed what they called a Friendly Society. Six men were arrested and taken to Dorchester gaol. Their heads were shorn. The foreman of the Grand Jury was the same Ponsonby who was Melbourne's brother-in-law. The Judge was Mr Justice Williams, on his first assize. The Lord Chancellor, who on the Government's instructions appointed him one morning, was asked in the afternoon by his clerk to sign some trivial papers; he declined, saying that no man could be asked to do more in one day than make Williams a judge. On the day of the trial in Dorchester there was still some doubt what the indictment would be. The Judge, knowing that all the evidence the Crown had pertained to the taking of this death's head oath, directed the Grand Jury to find that a true indictment could be brought under the Act of 37 Geo. III cap. 123, the one hundred and twenty-third Act of the thirty-seventh year of the reign of George III, 1797.

Counsel asked for that volume of the statutes. 'But m'lud, if I have the Act to which y'r lordship was referring, it is one for the suppression of mutiny among seamen of the Royal Navy, at the mutiny of the Nore. We are not at the Nore, there is no mutiny, and there are no seamen. And anyway, if y'r lordship pleases, the Act's as dead as mutton.'

The Judge replied that, as to mutton, Dorchester was dairy country.

'And that is the substance of y'r lordship's reply to my submission?'

It was. The six men were tried under that Act. The chief witness of the oath-taking was a son of a man who worked as gardener for a Dorchester magistrate, and even he was uncertain.

'Can not you remember?' asked the Judge. 'I will give you a moment to remember.' The man remembered.

'Now,' said the Judge to one of the accused, 'what is the secret sign or signal by which the unions know when to meet all over England?' The man replied that there was no union that he knew of, and therefore no sign. He asked to read a statement of defence to the jury. The Judge said it could be read for him, and a clerk took the paper and muttered away to the jury.

'My lord,' protested the prisoner, 'it is so mumbled over, in such an incomprehensible manner, that although I know what is there, having written it, I cannot follow it.'

James and George Loveless, John and Thomas Stanfield, James Baine, and James Hammett, were sentenced to seven years' transportation, and heard their sentences pronounced in the same high, classical, austere courtroom, and beneath the same royal coat of arms, as Jane Bryant had heard hers pronounced more than a generation before.

In Dorset, family ties are close. The two Stanfields were both cousins of Jane's. Thomas Stanfield was nearly fifty at the time of his trial, and well remembered Jane's visit of eleven years before. The visit had been brief, but Puddletown is small, and the tale of Jane's sudden appearance was told and re-told. Stanfield's son John, now in his mid twenties, recalled the day the lady from London came in a great carriage. Those were the days when a Puddletown man could go all his life without seeing Weymouth, thirteen miles away, let alone London, and Jane Bryant was therefore remembered as a woman who came from London, and went to Weymouth, and then to the distant city of Sydney. John Stanfield particularly remembered the Countess's coach and its four horses.

So when the six Tolpuddle men were sentenced, letters were written ahead to Jane in Sydney. Robert had not the easy intimacy with Bourke, the new Governor, that he had enjoyed with Brisbane, but Bourke was approachable. He was said to be distantly related to Edmund Burke. The slight difference in spelling of the names did not diminish his belief in his relationship to the great statesman. So Bourke was amenable, and when Robert made representations on behalf of the Tolpuddle men the Governor was neither surprised nor ill-disposed. He knew Robert had represented many emancipists and convicts. Robert told the Governor that he ought perhaps to declare an interest, in that Jane Bryant, his mother's housekeeper, was cousin to two of the men.

'I see,' said the Governor. He knew Jane Bryant too. She had also appeared at many emancipist meetings. Nothing very much was said between the two men. The furthest the Governor went was to say that he would naturally consider any request from Mr King, and that so long as the Tolpuddle men behaved well he was sure their stay would not be arduous. As Robert was leaving the Governor called him back and told him the name of the transport on which the men had been shipped, and her probable date of arrival, and Robert saw that things were not going to be difficult at all. They were not. The Governor had already received despatches from London expressing the Secretary of State's conviction that the Governor would treat the men with proper humanity. The Secretary for the Colonies, like some other members of the Government, had been surprised at the flimsiness of the indictment. To get rid of dangerous unionists was one thing. To do so on such an empty pretext, and on a pretext which looked as empty as it was, was another. The rigour of the sentence should be mitigated if this could be discreetly done.

Jane and the older Stanfield recognized each other on the quay when the transport came in. The men were released on Jane's recognizance for their good behaviour, which the Governor had told her he would accept. She found the men lodgings, where on the second evening they all ate supper together. They asked Robert, who, as Jane told them, had already acted on their behalf. She said he was the man who had miraculously secured her own release in London. At Jane's suggestion, Susannah was also asked. So was Jane's daughter Elizabeth. The men were surprised to find themselves looked after and provided for, and forgot for the moment the misery of their imprisonment, exile, and sordid voyage in the 'tween decks with 200 other convicts. They had all conducted themselves at first with dignity, suffering their heads to be shorn in Dorchester gaol without protest, and holding themselves proudly when they were taken to Portsmouth in unnecessary chains. But the voyage exhausted them all. When they reached Sydney they were surprised to be greeted not with more chains

but with kindness. There were only five of them at supper, not
six. George Loveless, who had acted as spokesman for them all
in England, had been separated from them. They thought he
was coming out on another ship. Over supper, drinking beer
which, though not Dorchester ale, was better than any they had
tasted for many months, they told the story of their adventure
from the first. How, when they first saw the posters threatening
transportation, they had walked the five miles from Tolpuddle
to the great house at Kingston Maurward and asked the lord of
the manor for his advice, which helped them little. They remembered not knowing how to approach the Palladian mansion,
not wishing to go directly up the carriageway to the main
portico, but also not wishing to tread on the lawns which would
take them to a side door. They remembered how the lord of the
manor told them they had no recourse but to accept the wages
the farmers offered. They told him wages had fallen from ten
shillings a week to nine, then to eight, then seven, and finally
to six. They could not live on it. He said he could do nothing.
It was this recollection that made them at first hesitant when
Jane suggested they should ask Susannah to supper. They
imagined her as lady of the manor of Kingston Maurward.

'And if she were,' Jane retorted, 'do you think she would have
sent you away with such words?'

Susannah was the only one at table who had never seen
Dorset. It was as well she had not, because the men were able
to tell her, and in telling her they talked about home, recalling
to themselves the only countryside they had ever known. It was
very dear to them. They talked of meadows and rivers, of gorse
and tall ferns and heaths, of lanes and hedges, and of pine and
birch woods, and forgot their exile.

Until James Baine said, 'When we were coming in yesterday
morning, a seaman on the ship asked me what I thought of the
bay. And I told him it was the finest sheet of water I ever saw
in my life, only we were at the wrong end of the world.'

There was a silence which lasted too long, and Robert ended
it. 'I have often thought of Dorset,' he said. 'I have often
thought of Dorchester.' He had. That evening, meeting these
Dorset men, he had remembered the King's Arms, and Leah.

His interjection succeeded in taking them back to Dorset,
and away from the sadness of Baine's remark. They were all

drinking again, and Robert said, 'I once gave a girl in Dorchester two lengths of silk, for two wedding gowns.' He was going to continue, when Jane caught his eye. She was telling him to stop, but he did not take her meaning, and would have gone on except that she interrupted, saying, 'It was for two lengths of silk I came here first.'

The men laughed at that, but then John Stanfield leaned easily back in his chair and asked Robert, 'She was a Dorchester girl, then?'

'Puddletown.'

'Pretty girl?'

'A delightful girl,' said Robert. 'A *good* woman.'

Stanfield said, 'I have three sons back home, and a daughter. Reuben, Simeon, Joseph, and Dinah.'

'Ah,' said Robert.

'*Genesis*, sir,' said Stanfield.

There was an echo in Robert's mind. He was perplexed for a second, and then it came back to him, and he knew.

Stanfield said, 'I'll put you out of your misery, sir. Reuben, Simeon, and Dinah – the children of Leah. Joseph the son of Rachel.'

Around the table everyone except Susannah and Elizabeth understood. Jane had known, having been with Robert in Dorset. The rest knew because the story was a famous one in the villages of Puddletown and Tolpuddle.

Robert looked round at the faces of the men, and at Stanfield, and was about to offer whatever apology he could to the man for having inadvertently spoken of Leah, when Stanfield smiled widely and held out his hand across the table and shook Robert's.

'Lord, sir,' he said, 'she told me. How do you think a girl like her'd come by two lengths of silk, Piedmont silk she always said it was? Except' – this with a glance towards Jane – 'by lifting them from Yallop's shop. How'd she come by them? She had to tell. And why should I grieve for her good fortune? It was before I came along. And I tell you. You called her a good woman just now. When she first told me about you, she said you were a kind man. And she said you promised to remember her monkeys in Puddletown church.'

'I do remember them,' said Robert.

'She's a good wife,' said Stanfield, 'and a beautiful woman.'
He glanced at Elizabeth, who was trying to ask Susannah what
the story was, and said, 'That little girl there, Jane's daughter,
she'll be like Leah.'

Robert looked at Elizabeth and said yes, she might; so she
might.

'And I'll tell you something, sir. That silk is still dancing in
Dorchester. Or 'twas when I came away, and 'twill again when
I go home. 'Twasn't worn just the once, on the wedding day,
like the gentry do. A Dorset girl keeps the gown she marries in
and dances in it when she's a woman. At balls, and harvest
suppers. And on holidays. And Leah's got two of 'em. So you
see, you did well by her, sir, giving her the silk. For it will last
all her dancing days, and then go to Dinah.'

'Dinah?'

'Dinah the daughter of Leah. *Genesis*, sir.'

They parted in marvellous good humour. Robert could not
remember when he last liked a man so for his generosity of spirit,
and wished him and Leah all the joy in the world.

'Which I will tell her, sir, when next we meet.'


Robert went back to his mother's house that night. 'Silk?' said
Susannah, 'Two lengths of silk? Leah? Rachel? *Genesis*?
Monkeys?' He explained, and she was pleased.

'You said she was delightful.'

'She was.'

'Are you glad that your silk is still dancing?'

'I can see her dancing,' he said.


The five Dorset labourers remained in Sydney as ticket-of-leave
men. The Governor thought it most unlikely that they would
serve out their seven years or anything like it, and told Robert
so, adding, 'You realize, of course, King, that I have no
authority whatever to tell you anything of the sort?' Robert
told the five men all this, but one thing on which they most
required reassurance was the well-being of the elder Loveless,
George, who, as they now knew, had been sent to Tasmania.
This was 600 sea miles away, and by reputation had lately

become an even grimmer penal colony than Sydney had ever
been.

'Your man is there,' said Governor Bourke. 'But I had a
despatch from my Lieutenant-Governor there the other day,
saying he'd offered to let him bring out his wife if he liked, so it
seems it doesn't go too hard with him.'

But this suggestion that George Loveless should bring out his
wife caused no end of trouble. The Lieutenant-Governor meant
it to be a humane offer, and was astonished by Loveless's reply.

'But sir, I should be a monster to send for my wife to come
out here to misery.'

These words were not spoken contumaciously, but after
consideration, and thoughtfully, as if their truth were self-
evident. It brought the Lieutenant-Governor up short that any
man should tell him he was presiding over misery. Still, he told
Loveless to re-consider, and after some months he accepted, and
wrote to England asking his wife to come out. He did this before
he knew, by way of a letter from Robert, that his stay at the
wrong end of the world was not likely to be as long as he thought.
He replied, saying Robert could now imagine his plight. His
wife might already be on her way out to Tasmania. Robert
went to Hobart town to see him. It was a passage of three days.

By the time he arrived the situation was even worse. Despatches from London arrived one day before Robert. The Prime
Minister, wanting to be rid of the whole affair, had told the
Commons that the Dorchester Labourers would be set free and
sent home free of expense and with all comfort. The Lieutenant-
Governor promptly put down Loveless's name to go home on
the next ship.

Robert made a formal application for himself and his client
Loveless to see the Lieutenant-Governor.

'Damn it, King, every convict who's been put on short
rations for a week will soon be knocking on my door accompanied by counsel.'

Robert reminded him that Loveless was now a free man.
Loveless was brought in, and spoke eloquently for himself.
'Your Excellency knows that you persuaded me to send for my
wife. And for aught I know she may now be on the water, it
being nine months since the invitation left this colony. It would
be a dreadful thing for me to leave before I have heard from

my wife. You offer me the next ship or none, and I speak against that. Sir, it is not just.'

Loveless had been a lay-preacher in Dorset. Having pronounced this sounding speech, he stood with his burning eyes fixed on the Lieutenant-Governor as if on a sinful congregation. Robert saw that the man could have made a fortune at the Bar.

A pause. The Lieutenant-Governor said he had done what he had done out of humanity.

Another pause. Loveless said nothing, but did not take his eyes from the man's face.

Robert stood apart from them, looking out of the window, remembering the first case he ever argued, and the only one he ever argued in England, before the Attorney-General. He remembered how he had argued that case, with silence; with 'How d'you do?' and silence, and then one sentence.

So he maintained silence, and then allowed himself his one sentence. He remarked that the Lieutenant-Governor now had it in his power to resolve matters easily, by acting again with the same humanity he had shown when he let Loveless send for his wife: and he could do that by permitting Loveless to remain until it were known whether his wife was coming or not.

A pause.

'So be it,' said the Lieutenant-Governor.

# 27

# Don't Tread on Me

On the passage back to Sydney they ran into Iago. Iago was a pirate, whose name was shortened from that of the city of Santiago in Chile, from where he had come to New South Wales twenty years before. He was Spanish. He began his career as a privateer, preying on the coastal shipping of western South America, and making plundering excursions to Tahiti and Fiji. On one voyage he was driven by gales as far south and west as New Holland, where, having to careen his vessel to repair storm damage, he chose an obscure island in the Bass Straits, between the mainland and Tasmania, and found seals. The islands were alive with seals. They were an even easier prey than coastal shipping. For many years he made a living not principally from piracy but from clubbing these seals to death as they lay on the beach and bartering the skins with the shady traders, themselves little better than cut-throats, who visited the islands in luggers twice a year. He and his crew lived on kangaroo meat, and on the salt pork, biscuits, and rum for which they traded their seal-skins. They slaughtered or enslaved the blacks of the neighbouring islands. At first, out of instinct, they ravished and killed the black women, called gins, but soon found it wiser to keep them alive. A gin was better than no woman at all. A gin could also do all the work, allowing Iago and his companions to live a life of ease, from which they had to rouse themselves only to slaughter seals. Over the years most of Iago's Chilean seamen died, and were replaced by convicts who escaped from the penal settlements on Tasmania. Iago never quite forgot his original vocation, and attacked any vessel sufficiently small or helpless. He left alone the whaling ships owned by the men of the Sydney blubber-and-stays interest. The whalers were too well-manned and well-found, and the chance of reprisal too great. But he would attack anything helpless. There were half a dozen other privateers like Iago up and down that coast.

Robert was taking passage back to Sydney in the colonial schooner *Australis*, a forty-footer, new-built and a fast sailer. These are often turbulent waters. Twelve hours out of Hobart town she ran into heavy seas which carried away her jib-boom. By daybreak the storm had blown itself out, and *Australis* was lying hove-to while her hands made good the damage. In this state she was found by Iago's brig, the *Vallarta*. The *Vallarta* was probably fifty years old, having been built in Barcelona before the wars with France. She was a ruin of old age. Her hull was leaky and her canvas fragile. Even if her canvas had been sound, her masts could never have carried a full set of sails. But she had been built for life as a privateer, and carried six four-pounder cannons. She was still quite capable of taking a crippled schooner one quarter of her size.

The *Australis* saw her early, but too late. Her only hope was to run, but the wind at dawn had dropped to light airs, and was in the wrong quarter too. The *Australis* was armed. But all she had was a tiny two-pounder, a swivel-gun, and five muskets, one for each of her crew. The privateer brig was under-manned, but still carried a crew of twenty. Trevelyan, the skipper of the *Australis*, recognized the brig. He had never met her, or thought to meet her. He had never seen a vessel so old. He knew Iago's reputation. The skipper had been a boatswain in the Royal Navy. He knew what hope they had. He could not run. If he hoisted a white flag, Iago would murder them anyway. If they fought, they would have the slenderest chance, and that chance would depend on Iago showing an incompetence which was not likely.

At that moment the *Vallarta* put a ball across the schooner's bows. They were already within range of the four-pounders. The brig could stand off and pound the schooner to pieces, and they would all be dead. But Iago would not want to do that. He wanted the schooner, not a foundering wreck. So he would approach and board, and then they would be dead too. There was only one hope. It was a chance in a hundred, but the best they had. Trevelyan saw the state of the *Vallarta*'s canvas, then guessed that her crew were unseaman-like, and knew that the schooner, crippled as she was, could outmanoeuvre her. If he ran the schooner before the wind, sailing her straight towards the *Vallarta*, he could approach her bow-on so that he would, with luck, be out reach of her cannon, which were mounted broadside. Once the schooner was beneath the brig's bow, he could use his swivel. A swivel-gun fires canister, metal cans which scatter a rain of jagged bits of rusty metal. It is shrapnel. At close range a lucky shot could kill a dozen men, twenty men, cutting them to pieces. But that would be a brilliant action. The skipper knew he needed a hundred things to go right, and not one thing to go wrong. If the *Vallarta*'s crew had muskets, he was beaten. If they had canister, he was beaten. If they boarded him in the scuffle, he was beaten.

And before he could do anything he had to bring the schooner about, and for too long he would be broadside to the brig. He prayed they could not shoot. But he knew that at that range they could hardly miss.

They could not shoot straight, but one ball struck home.

If a cannon ball hits a man it will tear him in two. Even if it only glances a man, it may disembowel him. But to kill one man is the least damage one cannon ball can do in a sea-battle. If it strikes a mast squarely it will bring it down, and that would sink the *Australis*, capsizing her. And a ball, striking so small a vessel, carries with it such an impact that her timbers shiver, and her seams open. The ball that struck *Australis* took her high in the starboard bow. It shook her whole frame. But worse than that were the splinters. Most seamen who die in battle are not sheared straight in two, but pierced by flying splinters from the timbers of their own vessel. The schooner was built largely of Iron Bark, much harder than English Oak, and most sea-worthy. But its flying splinters are the more deadly for their hardness. When the ball struck, splinters killed two of the crew outright, piercing the head of one and the breast of the other, and wounded a third man in the arm. But still the schooner, having come about, made straight for the brig. Robert could not keep his eyes from the man who had fallen not two feet away from him. The splinter that entered his brain killed him,

ut twenty other, smaller splinters, had laid open his face and
are shoulders. Two feet away, Robert was untouched, but he
as deathly afraid. He took the dead man's musket and
rouched, like the other men, for shelter, though if another ball
ruck there would be no shelter from splinters anywhere on
oard the schooner. They ran straight for the brig as if to ram
er. Iago was astonished. The seamanship of his crew of seal-
illers was as incompetent as the schooner skipper could have
oped. The brig could not manoeuvre. As the schooner ran
nder her bows, the skipper jerked the lanyard to trigger the
wivel, and six men died on the brig's foredeck, torn apart by
agged bits of metal.

But then, as the two vessels slid past each other, almost hull
o hull, the jury rigging of the schooner's jib-boom fouled the
rig's main chains. The schooner's crew hacked her free. As they
id, one man was killed by a musket shot. When they did push
ree, they had lost all way, and were drifting in the brig's lee.
as soon as the brig could turn, however sluggishly, and train
er cannon, the schooner was lost.

And then, a mile away, from behind an island which had
een shielding her from view, came the vision of a full-rigged
hip, under full canvas, royal-topgallants, sky-sails, and all.
They did not know what she was, but Iago knew what she
aight be. A full-rigged ship of that size, for she looked to be all
f 800 tons, carrying that much sail, was very likely a frigate.
She was too deep hulled for an English frigate, but certainly she
vas frigate-rigged. It did not matter to Iago of which nation
he was. A man o'war of any flag would take his brig and hang
im. He ran before the wind, with as much sail as he dared,
eaving the schooner floundering. But he had no chance. The
rigate gave pursuit, hailing the schooner as she passed, and
hen, coming up to the *Vallarta* two miles ahead, put a broad-
ide of four balls into her at the waterline. It was enough. Her
imbers were rotten. She listed. The frigate put two shots into
er rigging, and her foremast toppled. As it did, she foundered.
The *Vallarta* had fired one shot in return, and that missed. The
hip circled the brig as she settled. Those of her crew who
urvived scrambled for floating spars. The frigate left them and
eat back to windward to the drifting schooner.

Only, she was not a frigate. She was built by the same yard

on the Charles River that had built famous frigates, and frigate
rigged was a fair description for even a seaman to use of he
She flew the Stars and Stripes, with the twenty-five stars o
twenty-five States in 1836, and, as a battle ensign, the forme
American Navy Jack, with its red and white horizontal stripe
the yellow snake sliding diagonally across them, and the mott
'Don't Tread on Me'. It was a battle flag she was not formall
entitled to fly. She was the *America*, 850 tons, Captain Cobl
out of Boston, bound for Sydney with a speculative cargo.


On the deck of the listing schooner, Robert and Trevelya
watched as the *America* approached. Both were exhausted.

'Oh, God be praised,' said Trevelyan. 'Oh, God be praised
He tried to rise to his feet to acknowledge the *America*'s signa
as she closed the schooner, but lacked the strength and fell bac

Robert said, utterly bewildered, 'A Yankee frigate in thes
waters?'

But Trevelyan by then knew what she was. 'No frigate, si
I did take her for a frigate. With that rigging, sir, any ma
might, but no frigate ever carried that much sail.'

By then the *America* was almost up to them, and Robert an
Trevelyan gazed at the ascending tiers of mainsails, topsail
topgallants, royal-topgallants, and sky-sails. Her crew wer
furling her main courses as she made to heave to.

'A merchantman, sir,' said Trevelyan. 'I've heard tell of them
but never thought to see one. Not in these waters.'

But there she was. Like any ship in those waters, she wa
armed. With that rig she was fast as any frigate. Like any shi
that could, she would, by a sort of freemasonry of the sea
destroy a pirate so that it should not survive to harry other
She was a beautiful American merchantman, at a time whe
American sailing ships were beyond question the finest in th
world. Even Englishmen admitted that. She was an astonishin
ship.


The *America* hove to, keeping the schooner in her lee, an
launched a boat with the first mate and six sailors. The *Austral*
was awash and listing. As the mate climbed aboard he slippe
on the tilting deck. It was slippery with blood. Three men wer

dead. The other three were hurt, one badly. Trevelyan and
Robert had come off most lightly. Robert, who felt himself
earlier to be unscathed, later found that his left shoulder was
full of a hundred splinters of shivered wood. His shirt and coat
were bloody and he was badly shaken. The American mate said
very little. He made a rapid survey of the schooner. He kept
two seamen with him, and told four others to take the three
survivors to the *America*, and then to return for the dead.
Trevelyan wished to remain with his schooner, but the mate
shook his head. 'I'll see to her, mister. We'll get her back to
Sydney.'

On board the American ship, Trevelyan collapsed. Robert
was conscious, but utterly weary, and shivering. He thanked
the captain.

'You saved our lives; those that could be saved.'

He did not know what the captain replied. Two men carried
him to a cabin and placed him on his side on a bunk. They
looked at his shoulder.

He recalled one of the men saying, 'Sorry, mister. Hold on,'
and then the man began to take out the hardwood splinters.
one by one. After an hour Robert half sat up. A man tried to
give him some coffee, but suddenly he was sick. The man
cleared up the mess, laid him down on the bed again, and then
a hand held his head and made him sip some liquid. It was a
solution of opium, and he slept for fifteen hours.

It was night when he awoke, and his first consciousness was
that he was looking upwards through a skylight at a clear sky
full of stars. His eyes rested on the stars, and then he recognized
a constellation. The stars of Aquarius winked above him and to
his right, high in the sky. Still lying down, he shifted his eyes to
the other side of the skylight, and there low on the horizon as
he looked left was the Southern Cross. He was not a sailor, but
a man in a continent of empty spaces gets to know the stars.
Besides, Susannah had taught him. So before he raised his head
from the pillow, and before he knew why he was lying where
he was or what had brought him there, Robert knew that he
was moving eastward. Then the movement of the vessel as she
cut easily through tranquil seas, told him he was on board ship.
Then his mind recalled the schooner, and the morning. He tried
to raise himself.

A voice said, 'Why not lie still for a while?'

It was a woman's voice. She must have been sitting near the cabin door. Now she moved across and he saw her standing above him. Then she sat beside him. 'Talk some, if you like.'

Her voice was American.

'The schooner?' he asked.

'We are towing her.'

His comprehension was still slow. He said, 'You are the American ship.'

She nodded.

'Then thank you.' He tried to raise his hand, but could hardly move it. She took it in hers.

'I have been sleeping.'

'Yes.'

'The men?'

'There are three of you,' she said.

He put his face into the pillow. Three other men, alive that morning, were now dead. He remembered that he had expected to die. He held on to the hand that held his. Then he slept again.

Next morning early a man came to him, gave him coffee, which this time he could drink, dressed his shoulder, and told him he would live a while yet. Robert drank more coffee, ate a bit, and was told to stay in bed. The captain would come to see him.

At mid morning he did. They introduced themselves. The Captain was James Cobb. He told Robert briefly how things stood. Trevelyan and the other survivor were mending. They had buried the three dead men at sea the day before, as decently as they could. The schooner was in tow. He hoped they would make Sydney with her, but her timbers were sprung, and she was leaking badly. He had two men aboard her, baling her out. If the weather held, she might make it. Another thirty-six hours should see them in Sydney Cove. Cobb was a strong, solid, bearded man. He suggested Robert should not attempt to get up before next morning.

In the evening the woman came to him again. He was sitting up when she knocked, and found himself staring at her as she entered. She noticed it.

'I am sorry,' he said. 'But, you see, we have spoken twice before, but I never really saw you.'

It *was* the first time he had seen her. She was tall, very tall for a woman. She was unbelievably slender. In profile she looked Persian, or as he imagined a Persian woman might look. He had never see a Persian.

There is little space in a ship's cabin to show natural energy in movement, but whatever she did, she did with a flexuous activity. Her very movement across that eight feet of cabin from the door to his side was all activity, and yet when she sat beside him she was composed. Her eyes, of so dark a blue as he had never seen before, looked steadily at him.

He admired the ship. She said the captain was half owner of the *America* and of her sister ship, which should now be in the China seas. She talked about Boston. He told her about Sydney, which she had never seen before.

At a break in their conversation he asked, 'Whose bunk have I taken for the last two days?'

'Oh, the bed is mine,' she said. 'No, no, no, do not thank me too much. I have slept in the saloon.'

'You saved me,' he said, 'and I have not even told you my name.'

'The captain told me,' she said. 'And I am Anna Cobb.'

'Oh, his sister?'

'His wife.'

Of course she was his wife. Why, Robert asked himself after she went, had he said, 'His sister?' Captain Cobb was a Boston man, and as plainly of English stock as a man could be. Trace him back three generations and you would come to Devon. Anna was not in the least English. She could not be Cobb's sister, only his wife.

The *America* came into Sydney harbour gently because of the schooner she was still towing. As they hit the swell between the north and south heads the schooner shipped more water. Cobb sent his second mate across to the two men aboard the *Australis*, to beach her if they could, or, if she foundered, to take to her jolly boat, which was still sound. The *America* hove to for fifteen minutes while the mate rigged a gaff sail and cast off from the ship. In that time the *America* signalled the gist of the encounter with the *Vallarta* to the semaphore station on the head, which

passed the signal to the cove. Robert was by now on deck with
Cobb and Anna. As they entered the harbour slowly, under
royals to catch the light breeze, Cobb flew the American Navy
Jack as his ensign at the stern. The only ship of the Royal Navy
in the harbour was the 20-gun sloop *Naiad*. Her young commander watched the three American sailors beach the half-
foundering schooner in Farm Cove, which was a feat of
seamanship. Then he took the telescope from his first lieutenant,
recognized the Battle Flag the *America* was flying, and smiled.
The engagements of the War of Independence and that of 1812
figured in the education of any English naval officer. As the
*America* came to anchor, the *Naiad* gave her a salute of thirteen
guns.

At government wharf, Captain Cobb, his wife, his first mate,
Robert, and the skipper of the schooner, were welcomed by a
crowd of hundreds, with the port officer and Susannah among
them. The port officer was an old, superannuated captain,
who had seen action in the war of 1812. He received
Cobb, congratulating and thanking him on behalf of the
Governor.

'Your ensign, sir,' said the port captain. 'I fancy *Naiad*
recognized it, and I remember it.'

'Well,' said Cobb, 'you thank the *Naiad* for me, will you, sir.
I don't rightly think your Admiralty would approve of thirteen-
gun salutes for a Yankee any more than the Navy Department
back home would approve of me flying the Battle Jack. But I'm
James Cobb III. I had it from my father, who was James Cobb
II, and he had it from his, who was James Cobb I and fought
under it in '78.'

Susannah, who had caught some of this conversation, left
Robert for a moment and came over. 'Captain Cobb?'

'Yes, ma'am.'

'A Captain James Cobb put into this port in 1803, master of
the *Columbia*.'

'My father,' said Cobb. 'But you couldn't have known him,
ma'am?'

Susannah had never known him. She had seen him once,
when he walked out of her father's study and passed her in the
hallway as she was kneeling over Robert, who was a child of a
few months. She asked her father who the visitor was, and he

told her, and told her also what the stranger's business was. It was Captain Cobb who had spoken to the French corvette and brought the news of Baudin's death. Now Cobb's son had saved Robert.

# 28

# The American Woman, and Map-Given Fear

Captain and Mrs Cobb, Robert, and Trevelyan were entertained everywhere in Sydney. The Governor gave a banquet in their honour, to convey to Captain Cobb the colony's thanks for saving the schooner and three of the souls aboard her, and for ridding the colony of a pirate. The sheep-kings gave an even more magnificent banquet, to welcome the largest American ship yet seen there, a ship, moreover, which was going to take a cargo of wool to Baltimore and might open an American market. At this banquet Redmond was the host and Robert introduced him to the Americans. Again Robert got on well enough with Redmond. They were more than civil. But between Robert and John there was a coldness which Robert tried to overcome but could not. John, who was now in his early twenties, was more aggressive than his father in defence of the wool interest. The sheep-men presented Captain Cobb with a medal, bearing on its face the arms of New South Wales with extra sheep added round the circumference, and on the obverse a representation of the *America*, correct in its glorious rigging, which very much pleased him. The third banquet was given by the emancipists. Robert had represented their cause for years, and they wished to show gratitude for his rescue. And, such was the spirit of faction, it was impossible for the emancipists not to give a grander banquet than the sheep-kings. They presented Cobb with a ship's clock inscribed, 'From the grateful citizens of Sydney.'

Sydney was a drinking city. The graziers drank deeply at their banquet, but this only made their speeches more self-congratulatory, which did not matter. But at the emancipist's banquet one incident struck Anna. They were well into the speeches when a Dr Malone rose to propose yet another vote of thanks and was immediately challenged by one of the 300 diners. The doctor was not one of them, said the challenger: neither he nor his forebears had ever seen the inside of a jail. To which the doctor eloquently replied that his maternal grandfather had been transported for no less noble a feat than highway robbery. The doctor was cheered and his challenger roundly booed.

'It was not highway robbery they were cheering,' said Robert later. 'They were cheering themselves if you like. Four out of five men here were once convicts themselves or are the sons or grandsons of convicts, and that is absurdly held against them by the new settlers. It is unjust, and they feel it.'

'I have seen it,' she said. 'It is a caste system. It is worse than that.' Her very first day in Sydney, she had seen chain-gangs of men emerging from the barracks and shuffling dispiritedly along the dirt roads. The broken spirit of the men, and the way it was broken, angered Anna. The chains, the yellow convict rags with broad arrows, and the public humiliation of their having to walk through the streets chained and dressed like that, deeply offended her. Robert had seen it almost all his life. She saw it with new eyes.

He took her to meet the Tolpuddle men, and she admired their independence. 'But they are quite different,' she said.

'Because they are from the English countryside and not from the squalor of a city,' said Robert. 'Because they know their cause is just. Because they know they were unjustly sent here, and know that is the opinion of most men. Because they have not been broken by privation while they have been here. Because they know they are going home.' So they were. They were waiting for the next transport, and would go as free men. George Loveless's wife had heard in time of the men's release and had written to Tasmania to say she would wait for her husband in Dorset, so he was going home too. It was a happy issue.

Captain Cobb was often up country with the graziers discussing cargoes of wool, and freightage, and at those times it was natural that Anna should see a lot of Susannah and Robert, particularly of Robert. He showed her Sydney and Parramatta, and one day they crossed to Manly. They walked together on the beach.

'You are very American,' he said. 'And yet the first time I saw you on the ship, the first time I was able to look at you, not just hear your voice as you told me to drink something, I thought you were Persian.'

'Every American was something else,' she said, 'not so long ago.' They walked on.

Then she said, 'Persian is not far wrong. I am Armenian. My grandparents were born there. It is all a legend to me now. My grandfather used to talk of home. He called it home. It seemed to me, as a child, that all the history of the world happened in that country. He talked about the Tigris and Euphrates, and Mount Ararat, and Aleppo, and Isphahan. He was not from Isphahan, but my grandmother was. Isphahan is in Persia, so you see you were near.'

'But I have never seen a Persian,' said Robert. 'Except in paintings on vases.'

'Then there are two legends. Your legend, from vases. And mine, from my grandfather. It seemed to me, as I listened to him, that Armenia had been overrun by every army in the world at one time or another. But they all went away afterwards, and we stayed. There were Greeks, Phrygians, Arabs, Tamburlaine himself. Did Tamburlaine have blue eyes? Maybe I have Tamburlaine's blue eyes. Or the eyes of some ancient Greek.'

They walked along the beach. Robert was quiet, wanting to hear her talk. She said Armenians were supposed to be the first Christian nation.

'Are you still a Christian?' he asked.

'Yes, that remains. I think much more remains too. I am probably more Armenian than I know.'

She stopped and looked out into the harbour with her back to him. 'All that water. I spend my life at sea. You know, the first Armenian king is supposed to be descended from Noah.'

Robert could not afterwards have said why it was at that moment, but he took her lightly by the shoulders, turned her round and kissed her on the mouth. When they talked about it later – the lovers' endless question, 'Why that moment?' – she told him she was surprised and pleased. She openly kissed him back. Then they walked to the boat, and he took her back to Sydney Cove.

It was in the best room of Edward Hargraves, hotel-keeper, that Robert and Anna became lovers. He did not wish to compromise her by suggesting his own chambers, which were too well-known.

Hargraves was an Englishman who had come out from Hampshire not as a convict but as a settler, though settler was the wrong word for Hargraves, who never in his life settled at anything but was always trying something new. At fourteen he went to sea. At eighteen he left the sea and became a runner for a lodging-house in Liverpool, at a time when that port was the second city of England and the Empire. It was his business to approach newly arrived passengers on the quays and persuade them that the lodging-house represented by him was the newest, cleanest, best-appointed, and most reasonable, where a man could eat good food, sleep between clean sheets, and probably not be robbed. This persuasion had to be carried on in competition with twenty other runners for twenty other lodging-houses. Hargraves was not dishonest, but he learned to be sharp. He reasoned that once he had a man's baggage he had the man. He worked on a percentage from the lodging-house. From this percentage he paid two strong men to assist with the baggage of the passengers he was persuading; that is, to carry it off rapidly in the direction of the lodging-house. The baggage was not taken by force. It was merely picked up smartly. It was done to help the traveller. No theft was intended. But Hargraves had discovered that a traveller infallibly followed his baggage. His career as a runner came to an end the day he failed to realize that a gentleman whose baggage he seized was a magistrate on the Liverpool bench. He went to sea again, and after one China voyage found himself at Sydney, where he saw that honest lodging-houses were badly needed. He founded one and called it Hargraves' Hotel. Robert conveyanced the land and property for him. Hargraves was anxious from previous experience to maintain an amiable acquaintance with a man who knew the law. He was always civil to Robert, and happy to let him his best bedroom, which had a dressing room adjoining. He

showed the room to Robert, asked no questions, suggested a
price lower than the going rate, and gave him the key. He
mentioned that there was also a side entrance which Mr King
might find convenient, since it led to a street away from the
quayside, which was often jammed with horses and drays.

'Just so,' said Robert.

The *America* was moored a quarter of a mile away, and Anna
could easily come into the town unobserved. She came in a day
dress of green silk, carrying a small bag. Robert took her to the
rooms. It was afternoon. They were cool rooms, but full
of light.

She asked him, 'Will you leave me for a while, and come
back?'

He waited for ten minutes and then returned, knocked, and
went in. He had been walking on the quay in the bright sun,
and at first could hardly see her in the room. She had closed
the shutters. She was standing in the doorway of the dressing
room, in white. As his eyes became accustomed to the darkness
he saw that she was in a nightdress with long sleeves, and had
brushed her hair out. Her eyes were lowered and she did not
raise them. She did not speak.

He locked the door behind him and went to her. She seemed
even slighter than he had imagined, but, though she was in her
bare feet, at the same time taller than he had thought. She
seemed as tall as him. He held out his arms to her. She took
one hand briefly, no more than a touch, and then slipped into
the open bed. He saw that she had folded the sheets back ready.
She lay with her face away from him, though with her eyes open.
He leaned across to touch her hair, and then went into the
dressing room. She had closed the shutters there too, but he
could just see that her dress was laid out on the sofa as neatly
as if left by a maid ready for her mistress to put on. Her other
clothes were folded on a chair. The three rings she wore, which
had been her mother's, were laid in a row on the dressing table.
He threw off his clothes, leaving them where they fell, went out,
and lay beside her. He held her shoulders through the linen
nightdress. Then with his right hand he held her at the waist.
He was naked, and she was warm as he lay against her. He
could feel that she was covered down to the ankles by the
nightdress. He kissed her mouth, and she kissed him back,

though not as she had at Manly, but much less openly. He raised his head to look at her and she made her first movement since she lay down, lifting her hand to his face and running her fingers across his cheek. He kissed the fingers. He caressed her and parted her legs, but only through the linen, letting his hand rest there. Then he found her ankles, and raised the nightdress to her waist. When he went to enter her she murmured something. He did not catch what she said, but something in the tone told him to wait, so he waited, penetrating her only a little, stroking her hair and lying still. Then he entered her a little more, but not fully, careful not to hurt her. She had kept her eyes closed, but now she opened them and looked into his. In her eyes was something he had not seen there before. He had almost always seen her active, but what he saw now was quiescence, and as their eyes met he ejaculated into her, sharply taking in his breath as if he were half saying, 'Oh'. She enfolded him in her arms.

They lay in this way for some minutes, until he moved away and lay beside her. He loved her closing of the shutters, her undressing alone, the nightdress that covered her, her silence, her whole chaste reticence.


After that they met often. One day she said, 'Is it always so easy?'

'Hush, sweet,' he said. She had no idea how delightful she was. No one had told her before. She still closed the shutters. She was always to do that. She had always been the sweetest, but now she was also the most pliant of lovers. She was, as he never ceased to wonder, so lightly made. She arched her back like the figures he had seen of Cretan dancers, raising her hips from the bed for him to enter her as he knelt before her. He held her to support her, but soon found she was no weight on his hands, and did not need it. She was tall, but so supple that the arching of the back came instinctively to her. He never knew a woman who gave herself so naturally. But in her most arched and supple moments she retained a decorousness pleasing beyond words. It said, without words, that she was a woman who would never give herself lightly, and that is a great thing for a lover to know.

She rarely spoke as they embraced. But she once said, 'This is abandoned and entire, and you have done that.'

'That is a huge thing to say.'

'I mean it to be.'

He never knew a woman so entire, or so decorous with it.

And she had a sweet gaiety too. Afterwards, she would put on his Indian silk dressing gown and sit cross-legged on the bed, sitting on her heels, and her eyes shone as he told her preposterous stories.

'There was a tiger,' he said, 'in Madras.'

She nodded, sitting very upright, listening.

'When I came out from England we touched at Madras. And at Madras there is an English club, a club for English gentlemen.'

'I too have put in at Madras,' she said. 'I found many English entrepreneurs and many English makers of good fortunes.'

'Those are English gentlemen. Well, in this club . . .'

'With pukkah wallahs to pull great fans back and forth, to cool the air?'

'At any rate to move the hot air round the club rooms. Well, there was a billiard table, with wooden cues brought out from England, and ivory billiard balls brought out from England, made of ivory shipped to England from Africa – which is the point of having an Empire – and billiard tables of green baize. And gentlemen played billiards in the cool of the evening.'

'You said there was a tiger.'

'He came in and wanted to play billiards. He was a large tiger. Man-eating. Striped.'

'All tigers are striped.'

'Wide stripes. The tiger came in, out of the jungle perhaps. . . .'

'Of course.'

'And sat under the billiard table to wait his turn. At which the two men who were playing said, "By Jove, there's a tiger," and one went for a gun to shoot it. There were guns on the walls. But the other man said, "Not cricket to shoot a sitting tiger. Not done." They paused to consider. "The fellow can't be a member," said the man with the gun, regarding the tiger. "No," said the other, "can't be, can he, seeing he's not English. Aren't any English tigers. Wouldn't say he was a member, would you?'' So, with reluctance, they shot him, though, since he looked a decent sort of tiger, not before they asked him to leave and he declined. There's a stuffed tiger's head on the wall now. They use it for the billiards trophy.'

Anna, still sitting up, spread out her slim fingers on the bed. 'We are like children,' she said. 'We play, like children. We talk about tigers with wide stripes.'

Anna insisted, after the first time, that she should bring food. There were cheeses and pâtés and fruit which she brought in a basket from the ship and laid out on napkins on the bed. She brought silver fruit knives from the ship, hallmarked with the crest of a Boston silversmith. It was as if it were a picnic, and their bed were a lawn.

'It is natural for me to wish you to eat,' she said. 'I would cook for you. I am an Armenian woman still.' Sometimes, on saints' days, she burned incense. She told him the Armenian church was very like the Greek Orthodox in its observances.

'My dear Anna,' he said. He loved her for it all.

'I told you my name was Anna,' she said. 'That is my American name. The name I was given by my parents was Anahita.'

'What does it mean?' he said.

She shook her head.

'What does it mean?'

'Love and fertility,' she said.

He kissed her hands. He had never before wanted children as he did from her.

She wrote her name for him in the Pahlavi script, and taught him to read the characters. He said they were quite like Greek.

Robert and Anna were lovers, and she was the wife of a man who had saved his life. It had just happened, but he knew it was indefensible and tried to forget it. With Anna he could forget it. They were happy lovers.

Sometimes they met Hargraves, and he asked Anna about America. Was it a good place for a man? Could a man like him flourish there? 'I think you would thrive anywhere,' she said. She told him he would undoubtedly do well in Boston or New York. 'Though,' she said, 'there are other men there who possess get-up-and-go. You would find plenty of others like yourself.'

'I shall go then.'

'Sydney could become another Boston,' she said.

'No. I shall go to America.'

Anna conducted the business of the ship. She dealt with the chandlers to replenish the *America*'s stocks of food and tackle. She dealt with the shipwrights to arrange the re-fitting of the 'tween decks, to take wool. It was she who paid the crew. Robert learned that this business had always been hers. She took to bringing the ship's ledgers to their meetings. When they fell asleep it was most often she who woke first, and he would find her reading, or writing, or adding figures. At first he was amused. Then he was puzzled. Then he was irritated. He thought to himself that the only time she let in the light was to see the ship's books. He told himself he must never say so bitter a thing to her, and then immediately said it. He said it more than once. One day he took a book from her hands and closed it. He could not explain it even to himself, but it seemed wrong. So soon after their most extraordinary moments together – which he knew were as much to her as to him – she wanted to be at work again, while he only wanted to lie and talk with her, or do nothing at all.

'It is not easy for me to do nothing,' she said. She said it was in her nature to work, that it had been in her parents' nature, and was in the nature of the Yankees among whom she lived and one of whom she had married.

'It is what you call American get-up-and-go?' he asked.

They laughed. They should not have laughed so easily.


Robert and Anna grew closer as lovers but drifted apart in other ways. Anna observed this. Robert did not, because he did not see what his heart did not wish to see. But the differences grew. Once when Cobb travelled inland, Anna stayed the night with Robert, which she had not done before. They lay in bed all evening, and Robert awoke after midnight to find her leafing through bills of lading by the light of an oil lamp. He took the papers from her hands and threw them across the room. She looked at him with coolness in her eyes, got up, walked in his dressing gown across the room, and picked up the papers. He had acted more impetuously than he meant, but her coolness drove him to another foolishness. He dressed rapidly, saying nothing and not looking at her, and left her. As soon as he walked through the door he knew he should go back, but he walked for an hour on the deserted quay. When he did return she was dressed and about to leave even at that hour of night. She appeared composed, though if he had come back five minutes earlier he would have found her crying.

'Robert, what did I do to deserve that?'

He said, 'I too have my work. But I should insult you if I brought a brief to bed with you, to work through some miserable claim for damages after you had fallen asleep. You must see that.'

He was very unhappy. The differences between them, which had previously delighted him, were now dangerous. She was American, and he had loved her activity of mind. She was Armenian, and he had admired her reverence for her ancestors and her dead parents, and her sureness in her faith. But Robert had come to see that Anna's certainty of faith carried with it an intellectual certainty which worried the liberal tolerance that had been educated into him. Still, and in spite of everything, he assumed Anna would remain with him when the *America* sailed. From their early days as lovers he had assumed this. They both had. They reached this conclusion rapidly. She had promised to leave Cobb. But now Robert did ask himself how this could be when she was still absorbed in the ship, its refitting, its taking-on of cargo, and its everlasting ledgers.

Susannah had seen very early what Anna meant to her son. She was apprehensive. She saw in Anna a woman as strong as herself, but profoundly different both from herself and from Robert. She did not say anything until one day when he came again, and talked about Anna.

'I have never known anyone so single-minded,' he said.

'And you are like your father, single-hearted.'

'If I am, so was she. And I trust her.'

'Robert, first of all she is the wife of the man who saved you. That is something you will never forget. But, if you could put that aside – and I know there are times when anything can be put aside – ask yourself how well you know her. You say you trust her. You trust her because you see, rightly, that she has a conscience. It is a conscience which will make her do what she believes to be right, whatever it costs her, or you. I think it is an American spirit. They will try to change the world. You do not understand her. She will never be feckless, but her good conscience will hurt you more than fecklessness, because you will have expected more.'

Susannah was perhaps right. Robert never found a more likely explanation.

Anna acted suddenly. One afternoon she and Robert walked in the grounds of the Domain, on the lawns and among the trees. She illuminated everything with her presence. He told her so. He admired and prized her, and thought her beautiful. When he looked back afterwards he thought there had never been a time when he was so conscious of her, of her movement, of the way her clothes sat lightly on her, of her scent, of her eyes, of the delicacy of her hands. He was very much in love with her. She discovered him looking at her with love. She led him to a high point where they could see the cove beneath them, and the *America* lying among the other vessels.

'Sit down,' she said. And still it was to come as a surprise to him.

She sat by him.

'Robert, I am going.'

He looked at her, and then down at the *America*.

'For him?'

'For him partly. I am his wife.'

'You have always been his wife. Why do you discover that now?'

'For him partly. But also because, even if I were not his wife, you and I are too different. We have seen that.'

Robert reasoned with her until he knew it was useless, and then he said nothing.

She too was silent.

'And what of everything else?' he said. 'Was that nothing?'

'You know it was a great thing to me.'

'You said it was abandoned and entire.'

'It was. It has changed. Other things have changed it. I could not say it was entire now.'

'I was sure you would be constant. I see I deceived myself.'

She tried to explain. 'Dear Robert,' she said, 'we are different. You expect too little.'

'I evidently expected much too much.'

'I mean that out here, in the colony, you expect too little. I am going because I know it is right to go, and I must. But there is also this – there is such a great difference. You do expect so little. You are afraid.'

'Of *what*?'

'When we came into Sydney harbour for the first time, do you remember I said this could be another Boston? You have heard me tell Hargraves that too. And do you remember, as we came in, I said there was a magic about the place? There is. But you have only to stay here a few months to hear nothing but sniping between those whose parents were once convicts, and those whose parents were not. Bickering will achieve nothing.'

'And what has this to do with us?'

'You are angry when I work.'

That was not an answer, but it was the essence of everything. And Robert was so lacking in perception of this woman who meant so much to him that he said, 'That is a big thing?'

'Yes. I once said something was a huge thing, and it was. This is another huge thing.'

'And if it is, what on earth has it to do with fear? You said fear. Fear of what?'

'You are afraid of distance. You do not know it, but it shapes your mind. I think you are all afraid of distance. You see that you are the farthest, most distant, most lonely. The distance is nothing. It is a few weeks' sailing, and what is that in a life-time? It is a fear that comes from maps. It is a map-given fear. Whenever you look at a map, you are underneath. The maps were drawn by Europeans. If I lived in Sydney, I would draw maps on a new projection, so that Australia was the centre of the world. London and Paris are still the centres of the world to you, and so long as you think that, so long will it remain true. You expect too little. You demand too little of the Cosmos.'

With that immense assertion she left him. If she had considered, she might have realized that, to him, a large part of the Cosmos was herself.

She rose from the grass.

The next day she sailed. She left a letter which was not unkind, or unloving. 'It was entire,' she wrote, 'as I have never known it before.' She wished him long life, and signed her name, Anahita, in Pahlavi characters.

Next morning, when the *America* rounded the headlands and disappeared from sight, Robert walked back to Hargraves'.

'She will be coming back?' asked the man.

'No.'

Robert went to their rooms. He picked up the silk dressing-gown, and a forgotten silver fruit knife that she had brought from the *America*, and he remembered the afternoons when their bed was a lawn and she had said, 'We play, like children.'

Her loss was very great to him. He had wanted children by her. Her name of Anahita, love and fertility, was now an irony.

Then there was her display of the power of will, which fascinated him. Robert had observed how little Man could achieve in the shaping of his own world. This did not surprise him, or cast him down. It did not mean that a man might not attempt great things, though to *expect* too much was hubris. Robert's reasonable European mind accepted that Man was only Man. Anna as a reasonable American could not swallow that word *only*. Man was Man. And she would say this although she was a Christian and Robert was not. As an American she believed that the pursuit of happiness was an inalienable right. No nation except America had ever dared to promise itself so much, but she never questioned the proposition. Add to this a belief in the virtue of work; and happiness may not only be pursued but also, by an exercise of will, achieved. And if happiness could be achieved, then what could not?

On the late evening of the second day Robert took the knife Anna had left and walked out across the Domain to Bennelong Point. It was an hour past sunset. A half moon sat high in the sky. To his right, in Farm Cove, he could just make out the hulk of the schooner, which had lain there since the *America*'s sailors beached her. Her timbers were too badly strained to be repaired, and she had been stripped and left to rot. Robert turned back to Sydney Cove and to the lights of the twenty vessels lying at anchor there. He took the knife with the hall-mark of the Boston silversmith and hurled it high and far. As he watched its flight his mood changed. He was no longer remembering what had been, but thinking of what might be. As the knife described its parabola against the sky, and then dropped towards the waters of the cove, it flew sometimes in darkness and sometimes in flashes of reflected light, caught by the moonlight or by the rays of the ships' lanterns as they rode, and it entered the waters of the cove with a long flash of light.

# 29

# A Marriage Blessed with Grace

The years that followed were a time of marriage, death, and, in public affairs, what was politely termed a fretfulness of society.

Sydney had the distinction of being regularly described – by visiting missionaries or by lady writers, generally of obscurely noble birth – as the most dissolute city on earth. Since the great ports of Liverpool and New York were also regularly condemned in the same words, this meant that Sydney was thriving. The city was building. Wide avenues were laid out. The Countess Ominskova – whose nationality was variously stated to be French, Polish, or Russian – was only one of the lady travel writers who was accosted by a dock-side tout who offered, for the price of a drink, to show her the one street in Sydney where no house had ever been broken into. This offer was always accepted, and the tout then conducted the lady to a length of avenue recently laid out by a speculative builder, a road on which, as the visitor would then discover, no single house had been broken into because no single house had yet been built. But the avenue had been built, by road gangs of convicts. Sydney was the only great city in the world where white men were still slaves. As the visitor leafed through his morning paper he noticed rewards offered for information leading to the return of stolen horses and absconded bondsmen. The usual reward for a horse was seven pounds, but for a man only two. It was easier to get another convict than another horse. But the refinements of life were there for the prosperous. One Saturday, John Redmond came into town to be fitted for his new overcoat of llama cloth at the establishment of Hayes and Co., late of Savile Row, London, and, while he was at the tailor's, his wife bought toys for their two young children, a humming-top for the boy and a doll for the girl.

Mrs John Redmond was the daughter of a grazier whose kingdom was not quite so large as the older Redmond's, but still a kingdom. The sheep-kings' families were already inter-marrying to strengthen their dynasties. John's was as political a marriage in its way as that of a Tudor prince to a princess of Aragon. The sheep kingdoms now stretched in a boomerang around south-eastern Australia, covering a territory that extended as far as from Boston to New Orleans. And Redmond's was the most powerful kingdom. Since Macarthur's recent death, after years of madness, Redmond was the emperor of the sheep-kings.

He had become milder with age, success and riches. He was not a man to whom women, or any woman, had ever intensely mattered. His passion had been to create a kingdom, and he had done it. So he did not see that, because of him, many years had lain fallow for Susannah. It was not in his nature to comprehend the depth of her distress when he took her son John away. But he was now sorry that he had acted unjustly towards her in never allowing her to see John again. He would have done, but for Wyndham. The night Wyndham returned from Parramatta and was embraced by Susannah in her nightdress in the lighted doorway, they were seen from the Domain by a groom who was woken by the sounds of the disturbed horses as Wyndham stabled his mare. The groom received a sovereign now and then from Redmond in return for such information. Redmond had not been envious or jealous of the scene in the lighted door which the groom described to him. But he had been very much in fear of anything that reflected on his good name. He did not wish it to be known that his wife had a lover. That is why he would not allow John to see Susannah. He would not let his son see a mother whose actions might bring the name of Redmond into disrepute. But that was all past. Redmond now thought he had been hard, and would have made amends if he could. But by the time he was assured enough of his own success and name to relent towards Susannah, and no longer to fear her, John had hardened. As a young man he would not

visit his mother. They had seen each other only twice, both
times in public places. He had raised his hat, and that was all.
When he married he did not ask his mother to the wedding,
and replied formally to her letter of congratulation. When the
children were born he told his wife they were not to see their
grandmother. Susannah bore this. She was used to the estrangement from John, and expected no more.

But she was more delighted than she could have imagined by
the events of the late summer of 1838. Young women in Sydney
could not 'come out' in quite the style of London. There was
no Eton *v.* Harrow match at Lord's cricket ground, no Royal
Ascot at which one watched not the horses but the society
gathered in the Royal Enclosure. There was no Queen whose
gracious nod in response to a girl's ceremonial curtsy signified
that young lady's formal entrance into Society. But in Sydney
there was a governor to curtsy to, and balls to dance at thereafter. When Jane's daughter Elizabeth was seventeen, Susannah
presented her to the Governor. She had come out. She was
escorted to balls by the young men of the colony, and sometimes, at his mother's request, by Robert. It was expressly at
his mother's request. He would not have thought of it himself.
He liked Elizabeth, but did not particularly notice her. She was
younger. When his mother asked him, of course he took
Elizabeth to this ball or that. Then it became a pleasure to him.
He was surprised. He had thought of her as the little dark girl,
two years old, whom he first saw on the landing stage at
London Bridge, and then next day in the dock at Bow Street,
wrapped in a blue cloak and held in Jane's arms. She was the
little girl who had crossed the world. He remembered her at
supper with the Tolpuddle men when they arrived in Sydney.
He saw her frequently around his mother's house, but that was
all. He still thought of her as the little girl wrapped in a cloak.

He was supposed to entertain her. He soon became aware
that it was she who entertained him. After Anna, looking for
too much, he had found nothing. Now he looked forward to
calling to collect Elizabeth, listening to her excited talk on the
brief drive to this house or that, and then dancing with her, or
watching her dance with other men. He saw that others thought
her beautiful. He looked at her again, and saw that she was.
She took such joy in whatever she did. She made life sweet for

him again. Afterwards, when he brought her home, if it was not too late and if the night was warm, they walked for ten minutes on the lawns of the Domain. She took his arm and chatted. She asked him about Paris and London. It was fifteen years since he had seen either city, but he told her what he remembered.

'More than *twenty* times the size of Sydney?' she said.

He assured her London was. And Paris.

Elizabeth had been brought up in Susannah's house very much as Robert had in the Countess's. She had become pretty well the daughter of the house. Susannah opened the society of Sydney to her as Françoise d'Estaing had opened that of Paris and London to the young Robert.

Jane was pleased to see her daughter so happy. She said, 'She thinks the world of you, Mr Robert.'

'And she is a great pleasure to me,' he said.

One night they returned from a ball given by James McDonald to celebrate the coming out of his daughter, Margaret. It was a grand house, almost as grand as the sheep-kings', overlooking the harbour from the heights of Vaucluse. The drive back took half an hour. It was past midnight. Elizabeth was in high spirits, it was still warm, and they walked a little before going in.

'Margaret says her father has more ships than anyone in the colony.'

Robert thought he probably had. He had half a dozen coasting schooners, a brig, and a three-masted barque which made voyages to India and China.

'She says that because she has no brothers, she will run the whole fleet when it comes to her.' Margaret was seventeen, the same age as Elizabeth, but young for her age. It was not that she did not love her father, but she still had the child's matter-of-fact acceptance of her parents' eventual death and her own sure survival. Once a few years before she had written a prize essay at school which began, 'When Mummy and Daddy died, Dr Smithson came downstairs and gave me thirty pounds.' From this beginning the narrator went very successfully to run the family's entire fleet of ships. She received full marks for imagination.

But Miss Margaret McDonald's imagined ambitions took

Robert's mind back to Anna's real ones. He was looking out at
the bay. The skeleton of the abandoned schooner was still
beached in Farm Cove. He could see it. He fell silent. Elizabeth,
who had been holding his arm, released it and walked a few
steps away. That season, fabric rosebuds were worn everywhere
– in the hair, as a corsage, at the hem of a dress. Earlier in the
day, before the ball, Robert had given Elizabeth a silken violet
to wear at her throat. She was dark-skinned and the violet
looked better than a rose. It was the first gift he ever made her,
except for the birthday and Christmas presents he had given to
the child Elizabeth – to the Elizabeth who had been a child to
him until so recently.

She preserved the silence. This was new too. The child he
had known was always chatting. The young woman he had
come to know in the previous two months also talked easily and
happily. He loved to let her talk. But now she held the silence,
and then she said, 'Robert, what is it that you want most?' It
was not a child's question, not an offer of three wishes. She
wanted to know his mind.

'Robert, what do you want most of all?'

He answered in one word, 'Children.' How he had wanted
Anna's children.

Elizabeth said, 'And I should love to give them to you.'

It is not possible for a woman to say more. It says everything.
He looked at her, and she met his serious eyes. She was no
longer the girl he had been escorting to a few dances. She was at
that moment Leah in Dorset, years before, looking at him
across the room with the bay windows, the time she came in
and stood by the closed door after they came back from
Puddletown. He saw Leah in her for the first time, though as
soon as he did, it seemed obvious. She was very like. Dorset
families are close. She was a Bryant. Leah was a Martin. The
Bryants and Martins had intermarried for years. She was Leah,
but more than Leah. She was a girl whom until so recently he
had seen almost every day, and yet not seen at all. And now
she said such words to him.

'Elizabeth,' he said, 'dear Elizabeth.'

He saw her to his mother's door. They said good night. Then
he went to his own rooms in town. He thought of her all
night.

Three days afterwards Robert was called in by the Governor and offered a judgeship of the Supreme Court of New South Wales, which he declined. That evening he told Susannah, who was not surprised.

'I said it was very good of him, but I was an advocate. Certainly I saw my work for the next few years as that of an advocate. He was decent about it, just nodded, said he'd rather see me a judge, but then, on the other hand, supposed he should be grateful for any reasonably moderate advocacy of the cause I seemed to have adopted. I said I was much obliged.'

The Governor was a believer in hierarchy, in order, in the keeping of one's station in life. It was the fashion of the times to believe in the virtues of the free settler. The Governor's masters in London believed in it, and so did the Governor. This did not mean that he was anti-emancipist. A British subject was a British subject, whatever his rank, whatever his parents might have been, and whatever his previous crimes might have been. The Governor believed in an English freedom under the law, even in an English equality before the law. He wished some of his judges showed a greater understanding of the principle, which was one reason why he had offered Robert the judgeship. The legal rights of the emancipists he would respect and even enforce. In a way he was a man of divided mind. Though he would ensure their rights, if he could, he was apprehensive that a too sudden acquisition and exercise of new freedom by the emancipists might lead to their too sudden political power. He was a man of his generation, and anything like democracy was anathema to him. Democracy meant the French Revolution and the mob, or, at least, the American War of Independence and rebellion.

It came down to this. He disliked excess. Democracy was excess. Though he believed profoundly in the virtues of the settlers, he rebuked their excesses too, and even those of the sheep-kings. He had recently declared null and void a deed – sealed and delivered, and signed by the marks of three un-doubted aboriginal chiefs – by which the younger Redmond had acquired about ten miles of land in exchange for the following valuable and legal consideration, viz.: eighteen Birmingham

knives, three colanders, one hundredweight of flour, three
coloured statues of the Virgin Mary, three tomahawks, thirty
axe heads of guaranteed iron, three candelabra, eighteen pairs
of red trousers, and thirty suits of slop clothing guaranteed as
worn by convict subjects of Her Most Excellent Majesty Queen
Victoria. That was the wording. The aborigines admired the
yellow of the convict uniforms. They had been unable to
explain why they wanted statuettes of the Virgin Mary, but had
insisted on them. The fact was that one chief had seen such an
effigy, three feet high, in the shanty of an English missionary
with High Church leanings, and had reasonably assumed it to
be a totem representing in one figure both the white man's
God and the white man's Queen. Three were demanded
because the three chiefs wanted one each.

When his deed was voided, the younger Redmond talked
darkly about executive interference with that freedom of con-
tract which was the right of all British subjects. His father, when
he saw the deed, called his son a fool and apologized to the
Governor.

So the Governor was an honest man, and one of the reasons
for his offer to Robert had been the wish for an upright judge.

'He asked me if I would think about it for a week,' said
Robert, 'and I said yes because to refuse him that would have
been uncivil.'

'Will you think about it?'

'No.'

His mother smiled. 'He knows that too. He only asked you
so as not to be (what was your word?) uncivil.'

They let the subject drop.

'Mother?' said Robert.

He rarely addressed her in that way. She sat up. He told her
about Elizabeth, Elizabeth's question, his reply, and then hers.

'You say she is like Leah? Is that all?'

'If that were all it would be a very great deal. But no, it is
not all, is it? But she is only seventeen.'

'I was only eighteen,' said Susannah.

Robert repeated aloud, but really to himself, the words
Elizabeth had spoken to him, 'And I should love to give them
to you.'

Susannah said, 'This time you will not need to ask Jane what wedding gowns are made of, as you did in Dorchester. But you must go and ask her for her daughter.'

Susannah gave the silk for the wedding gown, this time not from Piedmont but from Canton. It was a marriage blessed with grace. Within two years there were two children – a girl, Susannah-Jane, named after her grandmothers, and a boy, George-Nicolas, after his grandfathers. Robert was at peace. The colony was not.

But before the affairs of the colony erupted and embroiled the lives of them all, especially Susannah's, there were two private deaths, and both of these struck hard at Susannah too.

A new Government House was at last built in Sydney. As she saw the pile of quarry stone and marble rising in the Domain Susannah remembered Bligh's scathing inventory of the faults of old Government House nearly forty years before, ending with the growled phrase, 'Wants being new.' Since Macquarie's time there had been plans. She remembered that Greenway, the architect who showed her how to brush Sydney sandstone, had built such magnificent stables that successive governors, when they chose to live at Sydney rather than retire to Parramatta, were worse housed than their horses, a state of affairs which generations of convicts had thought only reasonable. Now at last there was to be a vice-regal palace worthy of the colony. It was designed of course by an Englishman. He was special architect to Queen Victoria. His list of works was formidable. He had patched up Windsor Castle and Hampton Court, and put the final heavy touches to Buckingham Palace. He had built country seats for the English nobility, and his masterpiece was an Oriental–Tudor–Jacobean folly for a Russian count in the Crimea. He was therefore very eminent. New Government House at Sydney lived up to his reputation. Its first ceremonial use was for a Queen's birthday ball in May 1843. The waltz, no longer considered indecent, riotous, and German, was danced by all the society of Sydney and the colony. There were the naval and military officers and their ladies, the blubber-and-stays men

and theirs, and, of course, most prosperous of all, the sheep-
kings and their queens, princes, and princesses. For the first
time Susannah saw her two sons at one gathering, Robert
dancing with Elizabeth, and John with Mrs John Redmond.
The older Redmond was there too. Half way through the
evening he beckoned to Robert and asked to be introduced to
Elizabeth, and, when they had talked for a while, asked Robert
to take him over to Susannah.

She saw them approaching.

'Good evening, William,' she said. She held out her hand.

He said, 'I am pleased to see you so well, and Robert and his
wife so happy.' They were the first words they had spoken for
twenty years. They said little more, but Susannah hoped it
would be the end of what had been first an enmity and then a
long estrangement, and that they would be friends. She asked
Redmond, 'Will you tell John that I should be glad to meet
him too, and his wife?' Redmond said he would ask, and he did
ask his son, who declined. He then told his son to do it, and he
refused. There was nothing to be done.

The Governor came over to Susannah, stood with her
watching the couples on the floor, and then said, 'Your son
dances with his wife as if he loved her.'

'He does, doesn't he?' said Susannah. Whenever people said
'your son' they meant Robert. It was natural, but at that
moment she could not help noticing it.

The Governor asked her to dance. She had never danced
a waltz before, but liked it. The Governor saw she liked it and
was pleased with himself. Well, he said, she must come and see
how her pictures had been hung. He meant the two portraits of
George III and Queen Charlotte which Governor King had
brought out, which Bligh had loyally toasted, which Susannah
had kept in her house for many years, but which she had just
presented to Government House. She thought them better
suited to the vast rooms created by a man who had built a
palace for a Crimean count. They had been hung well, with the
King on the left of the mantelpiece looking across at his Queen
on the right. Then the Governor took her into the great hall to
show her the coat of arms of her father, which were displayed
there with those of the other governors. Her father's blazon, and
hers for that matter, was a single golden lion rampant on a grey

ground. He had never used it in office. Susannah had never used it once either, and could barely remember it. It was by then getting on for midnight on an evening of late autumn, drawing near winter, and it was not warm. But there was no wind, so they stepped for a moment on to the terrace, and looked back at the house.

'What do you think of the palace they've given me?' said the Governor.

Susannah looked at the man, and then at the silhouette of his vice-regal palace. 'Crenellated,' she said, 'castellated, Gothi-cized, and superlatively bedecked.'

'Um. That's what I think. Turreted too. Superlatively turreted, for bows and arrows. Against the Russians, I should think.'

She was tired, said good night to a few friends, and then went to her carriage. When she got home, her maid said they had not sent for her earlier, not wanting to disturb her at the grand ball, but a man had come from the cottages to say John Easty was dying. Susannah turned sharply on the girl, but then said nothing. She could not have known Easty was worth a hundred grand balls in a hundred vice-regal palaces. She went straight away to Easty's cottage, to find one man watching over his body, and one candle lit.

Here was Easty, the man who had taught her to plant fruit trees to comfort her, the man who, when Bligh was Governor, had moved the toy ships on the blue cloak as Bligh told Robert the story of Captain Dance's famous victory.

He had come out as a soldier with the First Fleet in 1788, and now had died at the age of eighty-one, so far as she knew the last survivor of that fleet. Easty was also, though Susannah did not know it, the man who, on that October evening so long before, watched her as she stood waiting on the lawns of the Domain for the *Géographe* to come to her moorings and for Baudin to walk up from the cove. She was ashamed that for some time she had hardly seen Easty. He had not been in the gardens for a month. She might have asked after him. He was the Governor's gardener, not hers, but she might have asked, and found that he was ill, and gone to him.

She waited with him for a while, and then went back to the house and in the early hours of the morning wrote a letter to

the Governor saying he might wish to know what might otherwise escape his notice, that John Easty, lately dead, for many
years head gardener in the Domain, had come out to the colony
as a private soldier, had served for many years in the Army, and
to her knowledge had been a particularly loyal and trusted
servant to Governors King and Bligh. The Governor saw that a
flag was provided for the coffin, and a volley fired over the
grave.

Very soon afterwards Jane Bryant began to die. Susannah
did see this. Jane was not eighty-one. She had not reached a
great age like Easty. It was a rapid deterioration. Susannah
asked the Governor for his physician, who came. Redmond,
hearing of Jane's illness, himself recommended the best man he
knew, who gave a second opinion. Susannah was grateful for
this. But neither doctor could get near a diagnosis, let alone a
remedy. Jane did not die alone. Elizabeth, Robert, and
Susannah were constantly with her. But she said no last words
which were remembered, because she lost the power of speech
two weeks before her death. Another grave. Susannah stood
with Elizabeth on her left and Robert on her right as Jane was
buried. It was a fine day. The sky was unclouded. She told the
other two to take the carriage, and walked the mile back to her
house alone. She was in full mourning. Jane had been sixty-two.
Susannah was only three years younger. It was absurd, she told
herself. Her friend was dead and she could walk under a blue
sky back from the grave.

With Easty and Jane gone so close together, there was now
no one in the colony who had ever seen her and Nicolas together.

But she was alive. She was vigorous.

# 30

# The Clamour of a Summer Evening

It was in the name of liberty that the sheep-kings called the great public meeting whose real purpose was to further their own financial interests.

'I suppose,' said the younger Redmond, 'that it will have to be an outdoor clamour?'

His father replied that this was obvious. No hall in Sydney would hold the 3000 men confidently expected to turn up. 'Though as to clamour,' he said, 'the less clamorous the better.'

So the graziers held their assembly in Hyde Park. Since it was summer, and no crowd would stand long in the Sydney sun, the meeting was announced for an hour before sunset. More than 3000 came. There were benches for a few hundred, others perched in the lower branches of trees or sat on the roofs of carriages, and the rest stood. On a raised wooden platform sat the graziers who for this evening had turned into statesmen, for this was, as the posters plastered all over Sydney had proclaimed, *A Grand Meeting of Citizens to Determine the Future Conduct and Government of the Colony*. The Governor had been invited, but regretted his inability to attend. On the platform, William Redmond was chairman. His son John was to make the opening speech. By him sat his undoubtedly pretty wife.

He rose.

'Gentlemen,' he said, 'you will have thought it a large thing that we are all assembled here tonight to determine, a large thing that you have all come to determine. The future of this colony is a large thing, and we *can* hope to determine it, because

we are young. This is a young country. We are not hampered
by traditions. We are gathered here to make traditions.'

At this there was a first small cheer. The graziers had been
thoughtful enough to provide kegs of best beer for the refreshment of their guests, and most had drunk a pint or two already.

'Our country is young,' continued Mr John Redmond, 'but
do we love her the less for that? We all married this country as
each man here married his wife, in the pride and beauty of her
youth. . . .'

A cheer. Mrs John Redmond was undoubtedly pretty.
Applause, at which John modestly spread his arms in acknowledgement, and then continued.

'And as each man shapes the character of his youthful
spouse, so each man here tonight may shape the character of
the country which is also his bride.'

More applause. The crowd consisted almost entirely of men.

'Now,' said Redmond, 'as to the future government of this
bride, their beloved country . . .' But at that moment someone,
remembering the older Redmond's apostrophes to that Great
Oak, an hereditary aristocracy, began to sing 'The Four-
Legged Oak'. John took a chance. He listened, paused, but not
long enough to allow others to take up the song, and then said,
'I hear an old song; almost a traditional song? I was talking of
tradition just now. I am proud that my father has made that
contribution to the tradition of our country. I am sure he too
is proud.'

Applause.

But now, said John, they were almost at their coming of age.
The time was coming, as it came to every man, when he should
determine his own affairs, when the colony should determine
its own affairs. But what did they see? They in the colony were
taxed, but had no voice – in the colony itself, let alone in the
Westminster parliament of which he spoke – in the spending of
the revenue raised. It was another people, in another time,
which had raised the cry of no taxation without representation.
That was, he emphasized, another people, a rebel people. The
citizens of Sydney were Her Majesty's loyal subjects. (Hurrah.)
But the time had come when it might not be inapt to remark,
no more than remark, that New South Wales was now being
taxed by the mother country at ten times the rate which led the

American colonies to seize their independence in 1776. But that was another time. He would say no more as to that. He would talk instead of something with which they were all familiar. Wool. They would all know he was a sheep-man. He would assert that he was a sheep-man. But he would also assert that it was wool which enabled them all, all of them gathered there tonight, to live prosperously. It was wool on which the colony had prospered, and the prosperity of the colony was their prosperity, theirs to protect. Now was the time to call upon the Westminster Parliament, even if it dragged its feet on the great issue of independence, to act quickly to protect if not their prosperity, at least their means of livelihood. He would go so far as to say livelihood. Wool was the staple of the colony, and yet the price of labour had risen by one-half in the last year. Such was the plight of all connected with sheep – and he was a grazier but spoke not only for graziers but for all who earned their daily bread (Cries of 'Mutton and damper') very well then, their daily mutton and damper (laughter) from wool – such was the plight of them all that they might soon have to face the prospect of flocks and herds melted down for mere tallow. And that, he said, would be the melting down to mere tallow of the prosperity of them all. (Prolonged silence.)

In these circumstances, and in these circumstances alone, he proposed that this meeting should petition Her Majesty's Government to renew the transportation of convicts to New South Wales; those convicts who, as they all knew, had for the past few years been diverted to Tasmania. They would all know that the draft regulation to permit this continued emigration of exiles had been laid before the Secretary of State in London. That gentleman was known to be favourable to the interests of them all. He needed only to sign. But he must sign now.

Mr John Redmond considered, however, that he must allude to the moral arguments from which it would be unChristian to turn away one's face, arguments which he knew would be advanced against their proposal. He would only say in reply that the life of a shepherd or hut-keeper could often humanize and restore a fallen human being. He had often seen this effect. He would only say, and would leave this thought in their minds, that this was the system which had given birth to a new and splendid civilization, of which they were all members. It

had succeeded in this to a degree unparalleled in history. Here
John paused to pick up a tankard set before him, and then,
with the tankard raised high, he cried, 'Yours is the making of
tradition. Yours is the making of history. These things are in
your keeping.' Then, still standing, he drank.

It took much less of an invitation than that to induce a
citizen of Sydney to raise a tankard of beer. Thousands drank
with Mr John Redmond. He sat down, and the cheers were
great. Not all present cheered, but most did, and yet most were
themselves emancipated convicts. They cheered because the
beer had put them in good humour, because Mr John Redmond
spoke well, and, most of all, because they did not in their minds
associate themselves, or their former wretchedness and present
injustice, with the 'exiles' Mr Redmond wished to be shipped
out to herd his flocks. They had put their past behind them.
They were also all city men. Few had ever known the delights
of the pastoral life. So they cheered.

Other men spoke for and against. Then Robert rose. It was
just past sunset. Flares and torches were beginning to be lit here
and there at the edges of the crowd and by the platform.
Robert stood on the driving seat of a cart, waited until the older
Redmond acknowledged him, and then began to speak as
quietly as he could and still be heard.

He lifted up a copy of the poster which the graziers had
printed to advertise the meeting, and read from it. '*A Grand
Meeting of Citizens to Determine the Future Conduct and Government
of the Colony.*'

'Gentlemen,' he said, 'since that is what we are here for, I
will make two points about the form of government. While the
previous speaker was on his way to reminding us – but no more
than reminding us, as he made plain – of the fact that the
American colonies once seized their independence, he forgot I
think to mention that his father, who is in the chair of this
meeting, had already submitted to the Governor the draft of a
new constitution, which I have seen. It does not read at all like
the American Declaration of Independence. I do not think the
word independence anywhere appears in it. It provides for an
elective lower chamber, but proposes a property qualification
which would give the vote to perhaps one in five of those present
at this meeting. It also provides for an upper chamber, to be

composed of an hereditary peerage very much on the English model. "The Four-Legged Oak" may, as a song, have passed into tradition, but the idea of the great oak of aristocracy is still very much alive, certainly as a proposal.'

The crowd was silent now.

'But the speech we heard was really about transportation. That is what this meeting is about. Men may speak out for their own interest, and that is what has happened this evening. Mr John Redmond has spoken for the graziers' own interest. That is a perfectly proper thing for him to do. But it is also right for us to be very clear that this is what he was doing. Very well then, transportation. Mr John Redmond told us that in his opinion the life of a shepherd could humanize and restore a fallen human being. He did not say that these words are a quotation from a memorandum addressed by him and his fellow graziers to the Secretary of State in London at least a year ago, or that this memorandum was debated in Parliament and reported in the newspapers. He also did not say that this same memorandum contained these words, which I now quote. They are as follows: "No other country in the world could furnish such an effectual penitentiary as the sheep-walks of Australia." Mr John Redmond is offering to provide a penitentiary. Those of you who were transported here will remember the years before you became free again. And when you remember them, will you wish to inflict a punishment of the same severity on others, so that they can live again the lives you led?'

Most of the men in the crowd had stopped drinking, and were listening intently. There was hardly a sound.

'Mr John Redmond fairly stated his own interest. He stated openly that he was a grazier. I must state my interest. I have for many years worked as counsel for many men who had served their sentences but then found they were not really free. It is a man's right to do what he considers in his own best interests, as long as that does not hurt the legitimate interests of other men. I feel bound to say that Mr John Redmond has consistently opposed grants of land to emancipists, their right to sit on juries, and their right to hold all but the pettiest public office. His interests are those of perhaps one hundred other graziers. They are called the sheep-kings. What he proposes

would be in the interest of those one hundred men, but I believe
against the interest of almost all the other one hundred thousand
inhabitants of this colony. And I cannot believe that what he
proposes would be in the interest of the thousands of convicts
who would once again be transported here. Wool is the staple
of this colony, and the prosperity of everyone does depend on
it in some way. But flocks are not yet, I think, being melted
down into tallow. Wool is, perhaps, the Golden Fleece of this
colony. It has been called that. But we must not sell our souls
for the Golden Fleece, particularly when the profits from that
sale would go largely to others, and to so few others.'

He sat down. The points he made had gone home. The
graziers' cause was as good as lost. The crowd gave almost a
sigh. The men on the platform asked each other what to do.
Then Susannah stood up.

It would have been better if she had not, so much better,
but at that moment she stood. The light was now quite gone,
and her figure was picked out by the flickering flares. Everyone
there knew her as the Governor's daughter, though most likely
they did not know of which governor. They all knew she was
the older Redmond's estranged wife. She was cheered before
she said a word, and then she asked, 'Would the chairman say
whether he believes, as his son does, that men should once again
be transported to this colony?'

The crowd made Redmond answer. Yes, he said, he favoured
the return of transportation.

Susannah said, 'We were speaking just now of "exiles". That
is the new word. I have been here more than forty years, and I
have heard many words used. There have been fashions in
words. First men were felons, then convicts, then government
men, and now there may be others called exiles. Most have been
slaves. Some have been lucky. They were pardoned early
because they were useful, because they could be useful as
teachers, or architects. It has been a lottery. Some have been
lucky, but most have been slaves. I have had many friends who
were transported here. My dearest friend came here as a
convict. She married here as a convict, from the female factory.
And her husband, although he was an emancipist by then, was
later sent to Newcastle, where he died.'

Everyone in the crowd still remembered what Newcastle used

to mean. Susannah would have told them how Bryant died in chains, except that his daughter Elizabeth was sitting by her at the meeting. 'And now,' said Susannah, 'are we really standing here, so many of us, to ask for other wretches to be sent out to us?'

She addressed her husband again, this time directly. 'William, do you want it?'

He could not answer. Susannah would not have said what she then did say if the death of Jane Bryant had not been still so much in her mind. And if Redmond had managed to say almost anything to her, any words, he could have stopped her. But he said nothing.

She said, 'Very well,' and went on. 'If I talk of my father you will smile, and say it is many years ago. It is many years ago. But he always said that a man while he was a convict was no slave, and that after he served his sentence, and was freed, he was less than ever a slave. But my son John – whom you all know to be my son – wishes to retain a virtual slavery of his own emancipists, and now wishes to import more convicts, more exiles. As for the convicts themselves, some were no angels, but I think no less of a man who has been a convict. How could I, seeing that I married such a man?'

She paused. At first the crowd did not take it in.

Susannah said, 'William Redmond came to New South Wales as a convict. He was soon emancipated, because he was a surgeon. I married him when he was a surgeon.'

This was unknown. Few there knew Redmond had ever been a surgeon. None knew he had been a convict. At first there was silence, and then the murmur of 3000 voices grew, and became a shout.

'And now,' Susannah continued, 'he wishes to bring others? My son John, my son and William Redmond's, is himself the son of an emancipist, but will not associate in the least with the other sons of emancipists. And now he too wishes to bring out men to a kind of slavery.'

John was on his feet shouting, but could not be heard over the crowd which was yelling, 'Answer, answer.'

William Redmond closed his eyes and sat looking straight ahead. He had given up trying to control the meeting. But when the roaring of 3000 voices died away, he looked to his side and saw John about to launch into a furious refutation of Susannah, who still stood facing him. He reached over and took his son by the arm. Redmond was a big man, and he pulled John towards him and said, in a silence which made his words audible to those near the platform, 'Say nothing against your mother. *Nothing.*'

John shook him off, and turned again to Susannah, who was being urged by Robert to come away. She would not. But John was not finding it easy to speak. He was so angry, so evidently shaking with anger, that the gathering, which he had so easily swayed an hour before, now laughed aloud at him. The laughter of 3000 men is terrible to face. The scene was almost too much for Susannah. She could not stand and watch him derided in this way, and she would have left there and then, but she found she could not move out of the press of bodies round her. She looked round, and saw there was nowhere to go. Robert stood by her to prevent her from being carried away by the crowd, who were now swaying rhythmically from side to side as they picked up once again the old tune of 'The Four-Legged Oak.'

Then a huge man, who had once been dismissed by John, stood and shouted and waved the crowd into silence.

'Great Oak?' yelled the man, gesturing towards John. 'Him a Great Oak? Wool king? Wool king he may be. But as to a Great Oak, the cove's no oak. He's a scrubby cottonwood.'

This got a laugh, but it also made a pause in the bedlam, and John was at last able to speak.

'You have heard my father's wife speak. She lied to you. My father was always free. Everyone knows that. And now my father's wife, to make a political point, to make a fraudulent political point, declares he was a convict. I call her my father's wife, and not my mother, because she long ago abandoned the rights of a mother. She has been no mother to me.'

There was an angry howl at this. It was splendid entertainment to hear the greatest of the sheep-kings called a former convict. It was splendid entertainment to watch Mr John Redmond making a fool of himself. But when he attacked his mother he lost any tatters of sympathy which still remained for him in all that crowd. And it was sad. Because John believed what he said. He had never known his father was once a convict.

That had been kept from him as carefully as it was kept from the colony.

He believed that Susannah had lied. And he had also, for many years, believed bitterly that it was she who had abandoned him. When his father first took him away, he expected to return to his mother, and asked to see her. But then, about a year later, he was told that his mother and a man called Wyndham were lovers. The groom who saw Susannah come down so eagerly to meet Wyndham in the night described the scene in the lighted doorway not only to Redmond but later to John. He was hurt, and horrified. His mother had a lover. He did not even know what the words meant. But he carried that picture of the lighted doorway with him in his mind – his mother in her nightdress embracing the man who came to her in the night. The idea haunted him. His child's mind believed, and his man's mind persisted in the belief, that it was because of his mother's treachery that his father left her. After that John refused to see his mother, even when Redmond relented and offered it.

So when John called his mother a liar, he believed it. When he said she had abandoned the rights of a mother, he believed it.

Then he saw Robert standing by Susannah in the crowd, the pair of them now lit by the flares. As a boy, thinking himself abandoned, he had hated Robert, who was cherished. He knew the history of Robert's birth. It was no secret. It was accepted. Now John prepared himself for another onslaught. Once again Redmond caught him, and said to him, quietly and steadily, 'Say *no more* against your mother.' John, in spite of all his hardness, feared his father, but he was carried away with bitterness.

He spoke again to the crowd. 'My father's wife is no mother to me, and for years has been no mother to me.'

The older Redmond brought his fist down with a crash on the table, but there was no stopping John.

'If my mother has a son, it is a certain gentleman, standing by her now, whom you can all see. He is a gentleman half French, the son of a Frenchman. He is her only true son. And this true son, who stands so nobly by his mother now, is a man who has disgraced her. . . .'

Here the crowd growled, but John rushed on, now almost having to scream to be heard.

'A man who has disgraced her, and himself, and his new wife. For what did this true son do, a few years past? He is now a husband and father. His young wife sits near him at this moment. Yet it was he who took as mistress. . . .'

More howls from the crowd. Many men there knew and liked Robert. But it was a crowd in which John had hardly a friend left. Still he persisted. 'It was he who took as mistress the wife of the very man who saved his life.'

At this several men tried to drag John from the platform, but still he shouted on.

'That true son took as mistress the wife of the Yankee captain who rescued him. And that man, Robert King, is the only true son. For she is no mother of mine.'

John stopped. The cries of 3000 men died away. In a silence which was the silence of John's disgrace, they turned their backs on him to a man.

Robert put his arm round Susannah's shoulders. The roar gradually fell away. Robert looked down at Elizabeth, who rose and took his hand. Anna was no news to her. With one woman on each side, Robert began to make a way slowly through the throng. Men stood aside and made a wider passage for them. Robert then let his mother go first. She walked across the park, through the crowd that opened to let her pass, and as she walked she looked straight ahead.


And it was all for nothing. The Secretary of State in London, the other side of the world, had already signed the piece of paper placed before him, and exiles were on the high seas on their way to New South Wales.

But John Redmond had publicly repudiated his mother, and because of that he and his half-brother Robert King were ever after enemies.

# PART FOUR

# 31

# The Wildest Flower is Gold

Edward Hargraves sat whittling a stick with his knife, sharpening it with quick strokes to a point, then slicing away at the stem, not rapidly but pensively, thinking between slices. When only the stub was left, he tossed it on the floor. Then he drank a little whisky, the last in his glass. He never drank much, but he called, 'Boy,' and the Negro waiter glanced easily at him and came over, bringing another glass and a handful of whittling sticks. There were ten other men in the room. Six of them were whittling as they talked languidly to their companions. Most were American, but there was a German, a Frenchman and a Chilean as well. The San Francisco Hotel supplied whittling sticks by custom. One day a few weeks before, the hotel had run out of sticks, and the customers had whittled the table legs instead. The marks showed. Hargraves took up a new stick, shaved it smooth with sweeps of his sharp blade, and then cut accurate notches one by one along its length. Twenty-eight. He had been there twenty-eight days and it was time to move on to Sacramento and the Sierra Nevada.

Hargraves' Hotel in Sydney had done well at first, but soon other hotels had opened and taken away his monopoly, and then his restless nature became bored. He bought houses too, but in the slump of the 1840s rents fell until they were not worth keeping. Late in 1848, a President of the United States whose name Hargraves could never remember announced to Congress that gold was discovered in Upper California. He read the report in the Sydney newspapers and turned over in his mind the golden phrases of the leader writers. El Dorado existed – not in the minds of dead Spanish adventurers, not in Utopia, but in a place ships could sail to. He took aside the captain of a British brig that he knew had lain in Sydney three months looking for a cargo.

Hargraves said, 'What is this place called San Francisco?'

They went to the brig, and spread out the charts of the western coast of North America. The captain had never sailed those waters. He traced the coast northwards with his finger.

'Ciudad de los Angelos,' he said, 'S. Luis Obispo. Monterey. Yerba Buena.' There was no San Francisco.

But they found a range of mountains called the Sierra Nevada, and a River Sacramento, and these names also appeared in the newspapers Hargraves had brought with him.

The captain said, 'And the name California is on the Admiralty charts, but I daresay that's its closest relation to the civilized world, being on the map I mean. As for your Saint Francis. . . .'

The captain owed Hargraves for two months' board and lodging. Hargraves made him a proposition.

'But there may be no gold,' said the captain. 'There is *probably* no gold.'

'And if there is not?' said Hargraves.

The captain looked at him as if he were mad.

'If there isn't gold,' said Hargraves, 'there will still be ten thousand men who think there is. Men wanting shovels, trousers, tents, coffee, guns, hats, rum. How plentiful do you think those things will be in a town not on the map?'

The captain said, 'It is the other side of the world.'

'No, the other side of the Pacific.'

The captain shook his head.

'Man,' said Hargraves, 'how far is it to sail from New York to California round the Horn?'

'Sixteen thousand miles. Six months.'

'They'll be American ships. Let's say five months. Right. Five months. And how far from Sydney to California?'

The captain agreed it was half the distance, and in calmer seas. He had also begun to despair of a cargo of any sort, and he certainly could not pay his bill at Hargraves' Hotel. He accepted the proposition.

It remained for Hargraves to get a cargo. He sold his houses, but that did not raise nearly enough. He visited Robert King to ask how to mortgage the hotel.

'I could do that for you,' said Robert. 'The banks will lend on the security of the hotel. But times are very bad. What will you do if they call in the mortgage and your venture has failed?'

'It will not fail.'

'Why not?'

Hargraves had the gift of bold sight. It was then that he saved his venture, and raised the money he needed. He pointed out that it was easier to get to San Francisco from Sydney than from New York.

'You are telling me,' said Robert, 'that Sydney and San Francisco are two Pacific ports, and not to be afraid of distances on maps?'

'I am.'

Robert could hear Anna saying that. She would have thought in the same way. He told Hargraves to keep the hotel free of mortgage, and himself lent him the £3000 still needed.

In three weeks Hargraves assembled a cargo and 150 passengers, gold-diggers to a man. By agreement with the captain, Hargraves took a commission of 20 per cent of their fares. The brig was the first vessel to sail from Sydney to San Francisco, and the men were the first of 6000 who left the colony for America that year.

They were three months on passage. It was no wonder they could not find San Francisco on the Admiralty chart. Francis Drake never saw that bay, though it is a fine legend that he did. He sailed past. It was first seen by white men, a small party of Spaniards, only a year before Captain Cook saw New Holland. At the time gold was discovered, a few hundred people lived there. It was only the year before the gold strike that the United States sent a sloop to take possession of the place, and only then was the city given its name. But it was not a city. It was a collection of shacks when Sydney was a metropolis.

As they entered, Hargraves did not give a glance to the splendid bay. What he saw was a forest of masts, and he knew that his speculation had succeeded.

'Three hundred sail?' he asked the captain.

'Three hundred vessels,' said the captain. 'Perhaps four. But as for sail, not a sail among them.'

There was not. The masts and spars were bare, and the canvas was shrouded and reefed. The crews had deserted to the goldfields. As soon as the brig anchored, where she could, her crew also deserted. Hargraves and the captain bribed three passengers to remain and unload the merchandise at a dollar an hour. When he was later received in audience by Queen Victoria, Hargraves mentioned modestly that he had voluntarily stayed to help the captain unload when all his crew had fled, and the Queen commended him.

'Mr Hargraves,' she pronounced, 'that was a British act. We are always pleased to hear of such. For it is the sum of such small deeds, unsung though they be, that creates and maintains the good name of a great nation. And unsung such deeds, by their nature, must be. Or, we should rather say, by the nature of their authors. For it is not in the nature of the authors of such deeds – as, Mr Hargraves, it was not in your nature – to advertise such selfless acts.' Hargraves inclined his head in grave assent. He did not tell the Queen the goods were his, and were sold at a whacking, ten-fold profit, and that he smothered the town in handbills for his shovels, trousers, tents, coffee, guns, hats, and, above all, rum.

By the time he was whittling sticks in the San Francisco Hotel, so called because it was the only one there, Hargraves had sold the last of his 10,000 shovels at ten dollars apiece, keeping only a hundred or so which he would take inland to sell at thirty, and his thoughts were turning to gold. He tipped the black waiter with a tiny nugget of gold, at which the man scarcely nodded, but ran his finger nail through it to see that it was soft, and was gold. Hargraves was waiting for his companion to return in a few minutes' time from the cat-house, and then they would be off.

His companion would be more than a few minutes, and he was not in the cat-house, but he was with Yvette Rivière. She was a singer, and therefore naturally thought a whore. She was not. She was an opera singer, and had got to San Francisco by a chain of events possible only in an operatic libretto or in life. She was young. She had her chance early. She was hardly more than in the chorus of the Paris Opera when the director attempted a revival of Bellini's *Norma*. The *prima donna* of that season, wishing to assert that she was indeed *prima donna*, agreed

to sing the performances but not to rehearse them. 'Dear lady,'
said the director, 'I am desolated.' Then he threw her down the
stairs and offered the title part of Norma to Yvette, whom he
had noticed. This earned him the enmity of the entire company,
but he was old and honoured and did not care. The girl
Rivière did not have a large voice, but it was true, excellent for
the *bel canto* arias of Bellini, and she sang as if her heart was in
what she sang. She even sang as if she understood what she
sang. In a week she was beloved of all Paris, and in two weeks
the mistress of Ingres, who painted her. At Florence a year later
she created the role of Lady Macbeth in Verdi's new opera, but
Verdi, as usual, quarrelled with both his leading lady and the
impresario. The impresario, in a pique, cancelled engagements
in Milan and London, and took Yvette as his *prima donna* and
mistress to Mexico City, where *Macbeth* was ill-received by the
critics and lost a great deal of money. After shooting the most
outspoken critic, but missing, the impresario fled north to a
town where money was to be made from entertainment of any
sort. He took Yvette to San Francisco, rapidly made a lot of
money, but then was lured by gold into the interior. He deserted
Yvette, taking the money with him. There was nothing for it.
She continued to sing programmes made up of arias from this
and that. Hargraves and his companion heard her one night.
Next morning the companion went back to the make-shift,
shake-up theatre, sat unseen at the back, and heard her rehearse
again and again and again a couple of phrases she was unhappy
with. A San Francisco audience could not have told if she were
singing 'Three Blind Mice', but she wanted to get that line
right.

> *Qual cor tradisti, qual cor perdisti.*

She was recalling the role which made her famous in Paris, the
unfashionable Norma, and was going through her part in the
last duet. 'What a heart you have betrayed and lost.'

San Francisco was a cosmopolitan place, and after she sang
the line the fourth time she was not taken too much by surprise
to hear a voice answer her in Italian from the unseen back of
the theatre.

> *Ah, troppo tardi t'ho conosciuta,*
> *sublime donna.*

'And I have come to know you too late, lovely woman.'

Yvette was a self-possessed woman. She could look after herself in San Francisco.

She stood on stage with her hands on her hips and answered the voice. Her Italian was operatic. She could demand a chalice of poison in that language, but not ask for a cup of coffee. Her English was no better. She replied in her native French, telling the stranger to get the hell out and come back, if he must, that evening. 'And pay at the door,' she said. Her dealings with impresarios had a little coarsened her natural sweetness.

The man begged her pardon, thanked her for her invitation to return that evening, and said it had been a great pleasure to hear a voice that would grace the Paris Opera.

'Monsieur,' she said, 'it has. But my God, you speak French like Louis XVI.'

'I suppose it must be archaic,' he said. 'I will return this evening.'

As he stood up to go she saw him.

'Perhaps,' she said, 'a glass of wine first?'

That is how they came to know each other, and to spend many hours together, and that is why he was with her the afternoon Hargraves was whittling sticks.

She was singing for him and herself in the same shake-up theatre where they had met almost a month before. She ended with the same lines from *Norma*. Then she walked to a sofa, the only prop on stage, and arranged herself on it.

'Come, come,' she called out.

He came up from the auditorium.

She took her long chestnut hair in her hands, and swept it forward across her face.

'Tell me I am a filly, with the handsomest mane in the golden west.'

With both hands he parted the shining hair, just enough to see her eyes.

'I have said that, Yvette.'

He sat on the other end of the sofa, by her feet, stroked her ankles, and then smoothed her skirt and petticoats up to the waist. She *had* been painted by Ingres.

'*Et ainsi,*' he said, '*je retrouve le marbre.*' 'And so I come to the marble again.'

He was leaving next day, and she knew it, and did not too much mind. She would probably never see him again. She would have other men. She did not think coldly, but what use to kick against such things? They had the moment. They had the hour.

Hargraves had to wait rather more than an hour for his companion to return. He had whittled away all his sticks and was hacking at the chair leg when Robert returned.


It would be impossible to give a coherent account of why Robert left Sydney, because his reasons were not themselves coherent. It was those words of Hargraves' that did it, Hargraves' bold look at the world, and his bold way with distances. Robert had no need for gold. He did not want gold. He had no interest in trading shovels either, and was taking no profit from the transactions. He had lent Hargraves the money to buy the supplies, but had not bought a partnership. Robert loved his wife and his children. He would return to them. 'If I were a sea captain,' he said, 'it would be as if I were making one voyage.' He never intended to stay, but he wanted to see. That makes it sound too much like an adventure and no more, but it was more than that. It was his father's restlessness coming out in him. He wanted to see, and so he went.

Next day Hargraves, with Robert and four other men, moved inland, two days up the San Joaquin river, and then seventy miles further on to the goldfields in a waggon drawn by eight bullocks. The driver eyed the baggage. 'Mighty lot o' plunder.' Hargraves was suspicious. His profits, in gold nuggets and gold dust, were disposed about his person and in his various bags and trunks. He and Robert were dressed in blue shirts, mud-caked trousers, filthy boots, and wide-awake hats, like any diggers. To be thought prosperous in San Francisco was dangerous. Hargraves did not like to hear the word plunder, and was only reassured when it appeared that the man used it, as all the drivers did, to mean baggage of any kind. Hargraves then recalled his own days as a baggage-snatcher in Liverpool, took the word plunder as a good omen, and felt relieved and at home. He still kept his eyes open, but there were six of them in the party. All were armed. All but Robert were getting a small share of Hargraves' profit, the size of which he had concealed. A party of six strong men was safe.

In the high country, winter came on. They camped, having to wake several times each night to shake the heavy snow off the tents, to prevent the weight caving the canvas in on top of them. They did not know the country. No one they met knew the country. All were strangers. None knew when spring would come. Robert cut with his knife into the trunk of an oak tree to see how far the sap had risen.

Then, when at last the buds sprouted, and the birds sang, and the snow was gone, they moved on to Sacramento City, a city of tents without a single bed or bedstead in it. Hargraves wrote home, entrusting his letters to bullock-drivers or prospectors returning to San Francisco. Some of the letters arrived in Sydney. He wrote, 'Treasure smiles at the feet of the seekers, and woos them to clutch it. They pick it out of the ground just as a thousand hogs, let loose in a forest, would root out ground nuts.'

The six of them, in the first week, made two dollars.

Hargraves wrote, in another letter, 'Men open a vein of gold as casually as you would a potato hill.'

The six of them, in the second week, made twenty-two dollars.

Robert wrote back more circumspectly to Susannah, Elizabeth, and the children.

They worked throughout the year 1850. They did not make much. But Hargraves watched. He observed the landscape – quartz, slate, flat-topped iron mountains, gravel. He learned how gold was panned, and though he panned very little himself he put this knowledge to two good uses. First, he took a dozen frying pans which were unsaleable at his asking price of twenty dollars each, removed the handles, and sold them to pan gold, at thirty. Second, he noted and remembered how gold was panned: he stored it in his mind. Then he saw how gold was separated by sluicing, and by rocking paydirt in wooden cradles. Robert watched too. He saw all Hargraves saw, and he also watched the dealings of the diggers with the gold merchants and banks. The diggers were always cheated.

But Hargraves kept something to himself, telling not even Robert. His eye kept going back to the land. It was summer now. He walked through tall pines in the lower foothills of the

Sierra and idly picked wild flowers. He said to himself, 'Slate, quartz, granite, red soil, gravel, blue clay, brooks and creeks, and everything else that appears to constitute a goldfield.' He remembered New South Wales.

One day he and Robert agreed that the time had come to leave. Hargraves sold the dozen shovels he still had left, which by then fetched forty dollars apiece, shared the rest of his effects among the four men who were remaining, and then he and Robert, carrying only Hargraves' profits, wandered as if they were defeated miners back to San Francisco. Robert asked after Yvette, but she had moved on. No one knew where. Hargraves and Robert took the first ship that offered. On shipboard, Hargraves read his Bible a great deal. By January of 1851 they were back in Sydney.

Robert was reunited with his family. He embraced his mother. He lay with his wife, at peace. His son and daughter were disappointed that he had brought back only a few specks of gold, as souvenirs. He told them Hargraves had more, and would show them. Hargraves promised. On his third day back he went to Susannah's carrying in his arms a brilliant bouquet, and also a smaller posy of the same flowers. Susannah's grandchildren were her delight, and were with her that afternoon. Susannah-Jane was twelve. In every way she had Susannah's features. George-Nicolas, a year younger, was Baudin strengthened by the Dorset blood of the Bryants. Hargraves gave the bouquet to Susannah, and the posy to her grand-daughter.

'Now *you* tell us about gold,' said George-Nicolas.

Hargraves described San Francisco, Sacramento, the sap rising in the oaks, and the gold falling in the streams of foothills.

'The gold of Ophir,' he said, 'in the stones of the brooks.'

'What is Ophir?' George asked.

'The city,' said Hargraves, 'where King Solomon sent to find the gold to build his temple.'

'What is gold?' asked the little girl.

She was sure there must be more to it than her father made out.

'You have seen gold rings,' said Hargraves.

'Real gold,' said the girl, 'not made gold.'

Hargraves regarded the children and their grandmother, paused, and then broke into what was a soft incantation. Susannah, remembering how the blacks 'sang' an object to make it theirs, would have said Hargraves was singing gold.

'Precious,' he said, 'opaque, lustrous, dense, the densest of metals, ductile, the most workable of metals. Sometimes found as flakes, less often as nuggets, rarely as crystals. It does not tarnish. Some say that in the beginning it was carried up from great depths, when the world began; others, that it descended with a hot lava and was precipitated in crevices. I have seen it glisten in streams.'

He stood up, looked at them all again, and then opened one hand in front of him, to display a gold nugget of two ounces weight. He held it between his thumb and first finger.

Susannah saw that the eyes of the children were full of awe. She thought Hargraves had a great deal of the conjuror in him, a good juggler, a good entrepreneur – with a touch of the alchemist.

'I could beat this to a sheet so thin that it would cover the room, the floors, and the ceiling, and the walls, and then it would reflect greens among the gold.'

Silence from the children. Hargraves took a small pen-knife from his pocket and opened it.

'Or I could cut it with this knife.'

Susannah-Jane called out, 'No.' It was too lustrous to cut.

So he did not cut it, but offered it to her. She held out her hands cupped and he placed it in them. She took it between her fingers.

'Feel it,' said Hargraves. 'Press it with your finger nail. Your nail will go into it.'

She tried, and it happened. She offered it back.

'Keep it,' he said. He took two more nuggets from his pocket, gave one to George-Nicolas, and offered the other to Susannah, who shook her head.

'I will keep my flowers,' she said.

She picked up the bouquet from the table. 'I recognize the Banksias. What are the others?'

'All wild flowers,' he said. 'You know the Banksias. And there are the geebung, with pine leaves, and the wattle.' The flowers of all three were yellow, orange, or gold.

'And what will you do now you are back?' asked Susannah.

'Trade,' said Hargraves. 'I went to California as a trader. I'm not a miner. Those nuggets were paid to me, a nugget for a shovel. I am not a gold man. I walk a lot. California taught me how to walk. I have become a botanist, in a modest way. My first day back I took a long walk, and again this morning. I shall go further. I picked the flowers I brought you. I shall look for wild flowers.'

Susannah smiled, 'And, Mr Hargraves, the wildest flower is gold?'

He was right to say that he was not a digger. Susannah was right to think that he was nevertheless a gold-man, with something of the juggler in him. Practical men who dig for gold sell it for what it buys. The getting is a fever, but the possession, for its own sake, no joy. But for Hargraves, gold was an idea. He revealed himself by the incantation.

The next day Robert went back to his law practice. Hargraves went to the Governor. If he could find gold in New South Wales, what reward would the Government offer? The Governor sighed to himself, but told Hargraves that the Government would not be ungenerous. He could of course not be more precise than that. Mr Hargraves would appreciate that he could not commit the colony further than that? Of course. Good morning. And Edward Hargraves, a good man of business when it came to shovels, changed, when he was overcome by an idea, the idea of gold, into a man who gave his entire energy and resource in return for a promise that promised nothing.

The Governor mentioned the meeting to his secretary as they lunched together. 'Well,' said the Governor, 'if this is gold country, it will stop the emigration that is costing us so many men. Nobody will go to California from here any more.'

'And the Government back home will send us no more convicts.'

'Presumably not,' said the Governor. 'But if it is gold, it will come on us like a clap of thunder.'

That was all they said. Then they forgot the matter.

Hargraves began to ride out every day. Then he rode further,

over the Blue Mountains, always going where he had been
before, in previous years. In his time he had travelled over large
parts of New South Wales. Before he left for America he had
earned a living not only as a lodging-house keeper and landlord,
but also as a small dealer in sheepskins. He had acted as agent
for American shipping lines and had often ridden far into the
interior to procure cargoes of wool. Now, as he rode, he was
searching for the formation of landscape which had come so
clearly to his memory once he saw its like in California. He
could see it before his eyes, but he could not remember where.
Wherever he went he wore in his buttonhole one of the species
of yellow wild flower. Australian wild flowers are abundant. It
is part of the circle of life in a continent where nectar-eating
birds abound, and where small animals like possums feed on
nectar too. The wild flowers of Australia are by and large
yellow or red, or of the tinges between yellow and red. Golden.
Hargraves' wild flowers became a joke.

'Wilts soon in the sun, Hargraves,' said John Redmond,
meeting him one day. Wild flowers wilted in a few minutes
when they were picked for buttonholes. Hargraves waved back
at Redmond. After that he dismounted regularly to renew the
flower, sometimes ten times a day. He never spoke of gold in
public, but it was assumed that was what he was after. Any man
back from California must be after gold. There could be no
other explanation. It was obvious. Just as obviously, he was
assumed by everyone to be mad. No one bothered to ask him,
or follow him. He hired a black guide. He was several times
seen on horseback, standing in a circle of twenty blacks describing to them in pidgin English the landscape he was searching
for. They had nothing to tell him. Then he dismounted and
drew landscapes on red sandstone for them to see. They brought
him yellow and black dyes, and he carried white chalk with
him. He drew many landscapes.

As he rode he began to talk to his own black fellow, although
the man could not understand him. It was a monologue.

'I tell you,' he said, 'this is gold country. But mind, unless
you knew how to find it you could live a century here and never
know it.' A shepherd overheard him, and the monologue spread
by word of mouth to the taverns of the Rocks in Sydney, where
it became a familiar amusement to draw landscapes on pub

walls, complete with figures of Hargraves, his horse, his black
fellow, and his golden flower.

On 12 February 1851, Hargraves found his landscape. He
dismounted. He said to his black, 'The same class of rocks.
Slates, quartz, granite, red soil. A creek.'

'Where him?' asked the black.

In a gesture, Hargraves took from his pocket a nugget of
gold, the largest he had, four ounces. It came from Monterey.
That is a large nugget. It was the only sizeable one he ever found
himself. He held it above his head so that it took the sun's rays,
and said, 'I feel myself surrounded by gold.'

'Where him?'

'We are now in the goldfields. Here. Under our feet.'

The black uncomprehendingly agreed.

Hargraves took a small pick, and in the bed of the creek
scratched the gravel and dug a panful of earth. Then he took
the pan hanging from the saddle of the black's horse, and
washed the dirt with the elliptical motion he had learned in the
Sacramento Valley. The creek water slid round the pan, the
sludge moved to one side, and the heavier particles were
precipitated to the other rim. The particles were gold. At his
first panning he had found gold.

'I am a great man,' he said.

The black stood grinning at him, understanding nothing.
Then Hargraves said his ever-memorable words. He took the
black by the shoulders, and said, 'This is a famous day in
history.'

The black smiled widely. Then Hargraves spoke exultantly,
still to the black, as if to convince him, 'Man, I shall be a
baronet, you will be knighted, and my old horse will be stuffed,
put into a glass case, and sent to the British Museum.'

# 32

# Never So Many Craft in the Cove

There was a gentleman with a letter for Mr King. He was shown in. He was very young, only twenty-two, and very American, just off the ship that morning from New York. He introduced himself, 'Cobb's the name, sir.'

'Cobb?' said Robert.

'Freeman Cobb, sir.' It was the American 'sir', spoken without a shade of deference, between equals, simply a polite form of address. 'And I have this for you.'

Robert took the letter, asked his visitor to sit, and opened the envelope. He looked at the signature first. The writer signed herself in full, Anna Cobb. Robert had not heard of her or from her since the day they parted fifteen years before. It was a letter of introduction. The young man was a cousin from Massachusetts who intended to set up business in New South Wales. 'You will think him young,' she wrote, 'but he already has several years' experience in the express business, and manages his men, his horses, and himself, soberly and well. He has prospered in California. He has what I think we once agreed to call get-up-and-go.' She asked Robert, for the sake of their old friendship, to do what he could for her cousin. She said very little about herself. Her husband was dead. She had heard from American captains who called at Sydney that Robert had married and had two children. She sent him her love.

Robert folded the letter, and offered Cobb some wine. He declined.

'I knew your aunt well, Mr Cobb. I am sorry to hear of her husband's death.'

'Six years ago, sir.'

'What can I do for you? Your aunt says you are in the express business. I do not know what that is.'

Freeman Cobb explained. He ran a stage line. He figured the miners would need to get to the diggings, and he could take them. He figured they would need to ship their gold back from the diggings to the city, and he could do that. He had come out with four of his boys, all young men his age. He had brought two coaches to start with, and was aiming to ship out two others later.

'One of them's just being hoisted on to dry land, sir, if you'd care to look.'

Robert's house was 300 yards from the quay, and several of the wharves and docks could be seen from the windows. Cobb was sitting by a window and jerked his head. Robert crossed and saw a coach being lifted by two cranes on to a dock. It was swung up from the ship's deck, to which it had been lashed all through the passage, and was now poised in mid air. He had never seen such a contraption. It was as large as the biggest coaches he remembered from London and Paris, but much heavier. It was still covered with tarpaulin canvas, but the parts he could see were painted a brick red.

'Care to walk down and see?' asked Cobb, very much at his ease, sitting with his long-booted legs stuck out straight in front him, and his hands in his trouser pockets.

They went down to the dock together. Cobb's boys were superintending the lowering, watched by a hundred sight-seers.

'Bigger'n you have them in this country, Mr King?'

Robert said it was.

The coach was lowered gently, the canvas covering removed, and Cobb pointed out its features, not only to Robert but to the crowd in general. The wheels were heavier than a farm cart's, with iron tyres shrunk on. Inside the seats were plush, but the floor was bare. Six passengers rode inside, three on each of the facing benches; or eight at a pinch, four on each bench. Two more could ride up front beside the driver.

As the crowd pushed round it and against it, the coach swayed. There were no steel springs, just heavy leather straps, running longitudinally.

'See,' said Cobb, 'some of our roads back home are a mite rough. Steel springs won't take it.'

'Some of our roads,' said Robert, 'are not roads at all yet.'

Cobb nodded unconcernedly, as if he had expected this. Robert thought he was a cool young man. While the second coach was being lifted from the deck, they strolled back to the house. Freeman Cobb was already at home in Sydney. He was also very evidently the boss, although casual with it. While his boys got on with the unloading, he explained what he wanted. Who should he see to get the mail franchise? Robert supposed the Postmaster General, and he imagined the young man presenting himself to that high official, leaning back in a chair with his boots stuck in front of him and his hands in his pockets, and stating the terms on which Cobb and Co. would carry Her Majesty's mail. He smiled to himself. He liked the young man, and he knew the Postmaster General was a pompous ass. And where, asked Freeman Cobb, could he find a good man who knew the goldfields? Robert said that was easily answered. If Mr Cobb would wait, Edward Hargraves would be coming to dinner in half an hour's time. No one knew better than him. Robert said he had been to California, but never to an Australian goldfield.

'That so?' said Cobb. He was very pleased to wait. He had heard a lot about Hargraves. He declined another offer of wine, saying he never drank alcohol. Robert remembered Anna never had.

'How is your aunt?' asked Robert.

'Anna?' said Cobb. 'Well, sir, maybe this will tell you more than I rightly could,' and he fished from his pocket a crumpled pamphlet and handed it to Robert. It was a paperbound copy of a publication entitled *The Wealth and Biography of the Wealthy Citizens of New York*. It was much thumbed.

'Always carry it with me,' said Cobb, 'seeing as I mean to be in it one day soon.'

The booklet contained an alphabetical list of the citizens of New York whose personal fortune was 100,000 dollars or more. Robert flicked through the entries at random. *Collins, E. K.* ($100,000) ran packet ships across the Atlantic. *Slocum, Daniel* ($200,000) was the famous maker of solid-headed Yankee pins. *Pease, John* ($100,000) was the famous horehound candy man.

*Astor, John Jacob* ($25,000,000) came from Heidelberg and made his money in the fur trade. *Cavanna, Augusta* ($150,000) was the distinguished hairdresser. *James, John B.* ($200,000) had simply 'married Miss Johnson'. Robert looked up Anna last.

*Cobb, Anna*, formerly Mrs James Cobb III, had by her flair and diligence increased the Cobb line of packets from two vessels to sixteen, the finest fleet of its kind in the American mercantile marine. 'Would not appoint Noah himself to be master of a Cobb vessel until he had served five years as a mate, most of that under her personal superintendence.'

Robert looked at the figure against her name. The young man spoke it out for him. 'One million, five hundred thousand dollars; for real. Some of it is in those coaches. She owns half the equity in those.'

Hargraves arrived with Elizabeth, whom he had brought back from a drive round the bay to Vaucluse, which commands a view of the harbour from the headlands to the cove.

'We took your mother,' said Elizabeth to her husband. 'She said she had never seen so many craft in the cove.'

Hargraves remembered his Bible once again. 'And they came to Ophir and fetched gold from thence in a navy of ships.'

A few months before he had named the first of the Australian gold towns Ophir. He and the young American talked about gold and the roads to goldfields.

That night, after Hargraves and Cobb had gone, Robert and Elizabeth sat in their drawing room together. She read. He pretended to read, leafing through the tattered *Wealth and Biography* which Cobb had lent him, pressing it on him, saying it was always good to read about the people who had made it, and how. Robert was not reading the booklet, but thinking of the letter in his pocket. Anna had asked him to help her cousin for the sake of old friendship. They had not been friends, but lovers. It was a formal letter. She said so little about herself. And yet, under the signature Anna Cobb, she had written in Pahlavi script, as she had once before, the name Anahita.

Elizabeth looked at him. Earlier that evening she had entered just in time to hear Freeman Cobb pronounce the figure of his aunt's wealth, and she knew there had been a letter.

'Anna?' she said.

He nodded.

'Long years,' she said.

He opened the booklet and read aloud the sentence, 'Would not appoint Noah himself to be master of a Cobb vessel until he had served five years as a mate.'

'A good publisher's fanciful phrase,' she said.

'No, I can hear her voice saying it. She once told me, I remember it, that the first Armenian king was descended from Noah. She was Armenian.'

'She is American now. And in New York. And it is how many years?'

'She was from Boston when I knew her. I asked Cobb why she went to New York. He said she insisted they should move there soon after they returned from Sydney. She said the city was growing faster, and would be the capital of the world.' Robert did not say it, but he supposed that New York must have seemed to her a city where one could demand even more of the Cosmos than one could in Boston.

He had a feeling that New South Wales was about to demand more of the Cosmos. It was true, there never had been so many craft in the cove. Hargraves believed that what they were seeing was only a beginning, and Robert thought he was probably right.

Elizabeth came over, and stood by her husband. She was peace, peace, peace. She took him to bed.


John Redmond was also confident that it was only a beginning, and he wanted to be in at the beginning. So he left the management of the sheep kingdom to the old emperor his father, and went to Ophir. He did not propose to prospect for gold. The colony had started charging all diggers a licence fee, and he secured the post of licence commissioner. The salary meant nothing to him, but he reasoned that the power to licence or withhold licences would give him some control over a rabble of emancipists, new English immigrants, disappointed European revolutionaries, and Yankees. The Americans were the worst of the lot. The revolutions of 1848 in France, Sicily, Prussia, Hungary, and Poland had sometimes succeeded, sometimes failed, but whether the insurgents succeeded or failed, the most extreme of the extreme had been rejected and had emigrated to

America or Australia. John Redmond would have thrown them
back into Sydney harbour, along with the Chinese who were
coming in, but he comforted himself that they would in any
case murder each other on political principle. He was not too
worried about them. Americans were different. They worked.
And the damned insolence of them: the few he had already met
talked to him as if they were his equals. Ten thousand Americans
had come. He thought they were the first of many more. It
would be convenient to know who they were and where, and
that could be achieved if he had the discretion to grant licences.

That was not his only interest. Men of whatever nationality
drank rum and whisky. Redmond was a Justice of the Peace,
and could grant and revoke licences. He naturally favoured the
grog shops which sold rum from the distilleries in which he held
large shareholdings. And then he noticed that diggers, when
they once found gold, had one thing uppermost in their minds,
to sell it. They did not want to carry it round long enough to be
robbed. They had no way of getting it back to Sydney. Under
the cover of various nominees, Redmond set up companies to
pay cash or notes of hand for gold, on the goldfields. He
contented himself with a discount of 20 per cent, offering three
pounds sterling for an ounce, if it was pure. His powers as
commissioner also enabled him to assay gold. So he was buying,
at his own price, gold which had been assayed by his own agents.
There was not a shred of speculation in all this. He stood to lose
nothing because he risked nothing. Whoever profited from the
goldfields, Redmond would take one-fifth of that profit.

His first instinct was to run this racket honestly, but he was
frustrated in this desire by second thoughts which arose from
experience. It was impossible to find anyone to work honestly
on any terms. It was no good offering double or even treble
wages. A digger stood one chance in a hundred of becoming
rich, but that was a chance a man would take more eagerly
than treble pay.

Redmond cursed at this and called it greed. So it was. He was
incapable of seeing that it was also hope. To thrive on sheep, a
man needed capital to buy them. On the goldfields, five minutes'
luck could make a man a fortune for the price of a shovel. Gold
could make the poor rich, as well as the rich richer.

Convicts would have been ideal men for Redmond to hire,

but there were now so few. Only a couple of boatloads of
'exiles' had come to the colony in recent years in spite of the
sheep-kings' frequent requests for more. But there were still
a few convicts serving out long sentences as ticket-of-leave
men. It was these men who seduced Redmond into his second
thoughts.

He took six from his Tongala Section and put two at each of
his first three gold-purchasing branches. Each branch was
guarded by an armed policeman. The men first shook the gold-
dust round in a burnished copper pan, to spread it and see no
dirt remained in it, and then tipped it on to scales to be
weighed in front of the diggers. The policemen, who were well
bribed by Redmond's nominees, kept a close watch but saw
nothing. His picked villains were apparently honest.

Then a large Dane named Olofsen was brought before
Redmond in his capacity as magistrate. He was accused by his
mates – a German, a Swede, and a Frenchman – of stealing
gold dust they had jointly worked to get. After they worked for
three weeks, and the time came to sell their gold, he was trusted
to divide the amount. He had golden blond hair. It was only
by chance that it was noticed afterwards that his hair glinted
in the light of an oil lamp. It had not shown by day, but his hair
was dusted with gold. As he divided the dust, he had passed his
hands through his hair. Redmond jailed the man, and afterwards put on a shabby wide-awake hat and corduroy trousers
and watched his own men weighing gold dust. The transaction
was carried out in the shade of a tent, so the diggers, coming in
out of bright sun, were at a small disadvantage. Redmond
watched the men weighing the dust, and saw nothing. He
watched twenty times and noticed nothing. None of the weighers
had blond hair, or passed his hands through his hair. Redmond
was about to walk away satisfied, when an original thought
came to him. Instead of watching the men weighing the gold,
he watched the eyes of the diggers. They watched their dust
tipped into the pan. They watched closely as it was swished
round the pan. They watched as it was tipped on to the scales,
and watched closely as it was weighed. Then Redmond saw it
in a flash. Where were the eyes of the diggers? Always on the
gold, first in the pan, then on the scales. When it was on the
scales, they were so intent on the weighing that they did not give

second look at the pan, which was left on the table in plain
view. But Redmond looked at the pan and there, barely visible,
in one patch only, high up against the rim, was a fine coating of
dust.

Redmond reached across and picked up the pan. He passed
his finger under the brim, and it came away gilded.

The man at the table sat stock still.

Redmond felt the pan again. The dust had adhered to the
pot just beneath the brim, because that spot was lightly
greased. In the shade of the tent, and again the burnished
copper of the pan, the dust could not be seen unless you knew
it was there.

'Stand up,' said Redmond.

He felt in the man's hair. Nothing but lice. He ran his hands
over the wrinkles in the man's neck. Nothing but dirt.

'Hands,' he said.

The man held out his hands. There was nothing in the creases
of the palms, but something was wrong. Then Redmond knew
what it was. They were not the hands of a working man. The
nails were not long, but neither were they as short and cracked
as those of his shepherds. Under the finger nails was gold. This
was discovered near the end of the day. In his nails the man had
half an ounce of gold, worth two pounds sterling. Redmond did
not charge the man or have him flogged. He sent him and his
mate back to Tongala that night, to get them well out of the
way. Within a week all Redmond's buyers were growing their
nails, only the proceeds came, through his nominees, to
Redmond. To add to his discount of 20 per cent, he made
another 2 or 3 from long finger nails and greasy pans.

John Redmond never spoke up publicly for the gold interest as
he had for sheep. He kept in the background. Gold needed no
champion. Hundreds of diggers came by every ship. They were
frequently met by Hargraves who urged them to go inland to
his Ophir where, he said, there was more gold to be picked up
than Mr Cobb's coaches could carry away, with the coaches
running day and night and loaded so heavily they had to be
drawn by teams of six and eight horses. Hargraves was the great
golden man of New South Wales, but took no interest in the

realities of mining. He still mined nothing for himself. He accepted a reward of £10,000 from the colony for making his discovery known, and was spending the money fast. He planned to go to England to see the Queen. He assumed that the Queen would see him. He was famous, and fame was what he wanted.

At Ophir he addressed gatherings of diggers at night, after the day's work was over. In the midst of enormous real wealth he told them tales of the fabulous. He told the story of Croesus, King of Lydia, and the noble Athenian who helped him build a temple to the oracle at Delphi. To reward the nobleman, Croesus told him to enter the royal stores and take as much gold as he could carry on his person. The nobleman put on a cloak with large pockets, boots several times too large, and stuffed the cloak and the boots with gold dust so that he could hardly walk – and then, into his mouth, he crammed as much gold dust as he could carry there. And when Croesus saw this he laughed, and gave the man as much again, for his ingenuity. 'The goldmines of Ophir,' declared Hargraves, 'are your Croesus, and every digger among you is an Athenian nobleman. To every man that digs, twice as much shall be given.'

In Sydney, he also addressed other assemblies, not of diggers but of bankers, gold-changers, and bullion-shippers. He was in an especially elated mood one evening. That day he had received an indirect assurance that Her Majesty would receive him if he went to England. He intended to go there as soon as he had done what he could to help the citizens of Melbourne. This city, only six years old, was being swamped by the increasing prosperity of Sydney, and seeing all its men lured away to the goldmines. Melbourne offered a reward if he could find gold within 200 miles of the city. Melbourne wanted a gold rush of its own, and sent as an inducement a golden goblet filled with sovereigns. So Hargraves' confidence was at its height, and to the bullion men he proposed this toast, 'Gold – the mainspring of commerce; gold – the forerunner of civilization; gold – the handmaiden of Christianity.'

The toast was drunk in silver goblets. The next time, he assured them – raising the golden goblet sent to him that day – they would all of them drink from gold. Wild cheers.

John Redmond was not at the banquet. Fearing tumult and uproar if miners of so many different nationalities continued to pour into the goldfields, he got himself a major's commission in the cavalry militia. He was a believer in peace and order.

# 33

# The Absurdity of Conveying Offenders

In one morning two messengers came to Susannah. One was from Government House, and she sent back a reply that she would come that evening. The second was from her husband. He had written only twice, about the Comtesse d'Estaing's bequest, in all the years of their separation. Now he asked her to come and see him, and to bring her grandchildren if she was able. He very much hoped she would be able. The note ended, 'I would come to you, but do not get about so easily.'

'Is Mr Redmond ill?' she asked the messenger.

'No, ma'am.'

She glanced at the letter again.

'Are you sure he is not unwell?'

'Not that I have seen, ma'am, though I do not see much of him. He does not leave the house. But ill, no.'

The note said that any day would be convenient, and any time. Would she please come? She gave the messenger a note in reply: 'Yes. Soon.'

That evening she went to the Governor in his turreted, crenellated, Gothicized Tudor palace.

'My dear Susannah,' he said, welcoming her.

'Charles, what is it?'

There was something odd in his demeanour. She could not tell what.

'Good news,' he said.

Of all the governors since Brisbane, Sir Charles Fitzroy was the man Susannah had known most intimately. When he reminisced with her, as he often did, he was fond of describing his earlier career as that of 'obscure governor of obscure places'. He had spent four years at Prince Edward Island, quite the smallest province of Canada, and then another five in the Leeward Islands. 'In the Antilles,' he would explain. 'The Lesser Antilles.' In New South Wales he was hit hard by the death of his wife in a carriage accident for which he could not stop blaming himself. Afterwards, in his loneliness, he got to know Susannah well. And at the end of his career, a sad man, he had suddenly become no longer obscure. To become Governor of New South Wales was a great promotion after the Leeward Islands, but now, since Melbourne had grown and Victoria had become a separate colony, he was Governor-General of both New South Wales and Victoria, the first Governor-General of Australia.

'It is good news,' he said again. 'I have a despatch from London, and before I publish it I should like you to see it. It is a long document. I have folded back the page which says what matters.' He gave it to her.

She sat down to read it. The document said, 'It would appear an absurdity to convey offenders, at the public expense, with the intention of at no distant time setting them free, to the immediate vicinity of those very goldfields which thousands of honest labourers are striving in vain to reach.'

She looked up at him.

He nodded. 'Just like that,' he said. 'But read the next couple of sentences too.'

She did. They said, 'It is quite true that the offenders have to undergo a preliminary period of imprisonment and labour; but these are not likely to daunt reckless minds. It must be admitted by every impartial observer that transportation would be disarmed of its terrors, and that a very undesirable impression would be produced in the minds of the criminal class, if offenders should long continue to be sent to the immediate vicinity of the goldfields of Australia.'

Susannah put the papers down. She was almost angry. 'Rotten reasons,' she said.

'Rotten reasons,' said the Governor. 'But it is done at last,

that's an end to it all, an end to convicts, and I knew you would
be happy to know.'

'I am happy. But I see all those men and women in my mind;
the men and women of my whole life-time. I see Tyrone at
Newcastle.' She had told Fitzroy that story long ago. She also
saw herself cheered by a convict road gang as she walked up
from the jetty the day she took the children to Manly, just before
Redmond left her.

Fitzroy said, 'Well, it is done. I shall publish this tomorrow.
Now. . . .'

He stopped.

'Now,' she said, and took his arm, and they walked through
the open french windows on to the terrace. They would not
walk far. He was younger than her, but tired more easily. A man
never easily recovered from years in a Caribbean climate.

'Do you know,' he said, 'I was looking through my father's
journals the other day. Oh, papers of sixty years ago. And, it
was the strangest thing, I came across the time when he was
*aide de camp* to the old King. And he mentioned the visit of a
black called Bennelong and a Lieutenant King, about 1795 I
suppose. That must have been your father.'

'It was. He told me Bennelong would only make legs, and
couldn't be induced to say a word.'

'The journal said the King took to your father.'

'They talked about Virginia. The King had not liked to lose
America.'

'Sixty years ago,' said Fitzroy. 'Nearly sixty years. Your
father and mine, and now the two of us here. It is strange.'

'No. Things go in circles. Events go in circles.'

They went in again. Her mind went back to the convict gang
cheering her, and Redmond leaving her, and then jumped
years to the message she had received that morning. She said,
'My husband wants to see me, Charles. Does *that* strike you as
strange? He wants to see me and the children.'

'No,' said Fitzroy. 'It doesn't.' He had seen the older
Redmond more recently than she had. 'You will go?'

'Of course.'

'Susannah, when you do, ask him – I don't know how I can
put this – but somehow suggest that he might keep an eye on
his son.'

'Yes?'

'I can't put it more clearly,' he said. 'But, goldfields. I don't know very much. But there's something.'


Susannah went to Redmond's mansion the next morning, taking the two children. It was a drive of two hours. At the outer gate they were met by two armed men, who passed them on to a butler at the door, who passed them on to the man who was now Redmond's sole companion. It was Halloran, the man who for years had looked after the Abandon Hope shanty at Tongala, and had now come to look after Redmond. Halloran said, 'You will not mind if I say a word, ma'am? Mr Redmond will be very happy to see you. He has talked of nothing else for days. But, you see, he may not show it. He does not show much at all. He is an absent man.'

He took them along darkly panelled corridors lined with dark paintings and the spoils of great wealth – Meissen vases, Sèvres porcelain, Gobelin tapestries, brocaded sofas with cabriole legs, all acquired by agents in Europe, paid for, shipped out, and then forgotten. The only life in the house was in the huge kitchen which Susannah glimpsed across a wide courtyard. The food cooked there was no longer for banquets but for the battalion of servants.

'Mr Redmond is not ill?' she asked.

'Not ill, ma'am,' said Halloran, and then they were ushered into the great drawing room, which contained the most magnificent of the great house's spoils, and Redmond. Although it was summer, he was sitting in a screened armchair by a crackling fire. He tried to rise. Susannah saw it was difficult for him, and walked rapidly to him. He settled back in the chair.

'And you have brought the children,' he said. 'It is good of you to come to me.'

Susannah-Jane was presented. She dropped the lightest curtsy. George-Nicolas was presented to the old man, and they shook hands. Redmond looked at the boy's features and saw Baudin again, almost as much as in Robert. He looked at Susannah-Jane until she lowered her eyes.

The two children looked openly around.

'Yes,' said Redmond. 'I am a sheep-king – you will have

heard me called that – I am a sheep-king who has not seen a sheep for many months, and this is my palace.'

Susannah had not seen him since the night of the open-air meeting in Sydney seven years before. Then his red hair was turning grey. Now it was white. His face still looked as full as ever, his hands as strong, and his frame as large, but he had lost all energy.

'I never see my other grandchildren,' he said.

'Where is John?' asked Susannah. She knew he was often at the goldfields, but did not know he was constantly there.

'They prefer to live away, his wife and the children,' said Redmond. His mind was still on the children he never saw.

'And John?'

'Oh, the sheep station is mine again now, you know. I had made the running of it over to him, but now he has given it back to me. Not that I do much. My overseers manage it. And I think Halloran manages my overseers. Halloran is the man who brought you in.' And it was true. The keeper of the Abandon Hope shanty was now running the entire sheep kingdom of the Redmonds.

Redmond recollected Susannah's question. 'Ah, *where* is John? Gold. He is at the gold. Where are the goldfields?'

It was then that Susannah saw that there was no point in mentioning the Governor's fears about John. It was then she saw the extent to which her husband's mind had gone.

Halloran entered with champagne in a bucket.

Redmond said, 'You will take champagne with me? It is my own. It is my own make. Morning is the time for champagne. It gives a fizz to the day. The children?'

Halloran had opened the bottle and Redmond was offering the children champagne, as he had once given it to John.

'No,' said Susannah. Then she said, 'Mr Halloran, would you show the children the gardens?' He met her eye, and took the children away. Susannah had never entered this house before. She crossed to the long windows and opened the curtains wide so that the sun streamed in.

Redmond did not notice. He poured two glasses, and held out one to her by its long stem. His hand was steady enough.

She saw he had something to say, and knew he would have difficulty saying it. She remembered her own great pride as a young woman, and could understand how heavily the burden of pride rested on an old man.

He did manage to speak, starting with the smallest matter. 'When I took that legacy, from France. . . .'

'William, you did make two offers to me. I have not thought of legacies. Do not let that be on your mind.'

He said, 'I have provided equally for all four of my grand-children. But it was not that, or any thought of that, which made me want to see them now.'

'I know.'

'Yes, I think you do.'

He re-filled his own glass. She had not finished her first. He continued, 'And, that meeting in Sydney, what was said that night. I did not wish it, what John said.'

'I know that. I too said what I wish had not been said.'

'And when I took John. . . .' He could find no more words, but she knew he was trying to make some amends, by saying whatever he could say, for having taken John away when he was a boy, and left her.

Susannah watched the man who had once been her husband, and who still was. She knew that when he left, it had been for the best. She knew the marriage had been hopeless. She could not have continued to live with him. But she knew also that this did not matter any more. All that mattered now was that he should be able to say some words which would unburden his mind of the guilt of that long-ago desertion. She willed him to be able to say what would ease him. She waited. He could not say it, but she saw he terribly wanted to. She had to say it for him.

'William, I know what you are thinking. And it's all right.'

'I think you do know,' he said. The relief showed in his face, but now his hand shook as he raised his glass. This moment was the nearest they approached, in the whole of their marriage, to a community of feeling and understanding.

She let the moment stay, and then pass. Then she said, 'I shall call the children back.'

They came back, and Redmond said goodbye to them. Susannah said, 'Goodbye, William,' and he held her hand. The children went first, and Susannah was almost at the door when Redmond said, 'You. . . .'

She turned.

'You will not see it so clearly, but the girl will be you. She will be you as I first saw you.'

She nodded. 'I see it.'

Redmond said, 'Goodbye, Susannah.'

The last word he ever spoke to her was the first time he ever called her by her name.


By that evening the Governor had published the despatch, and there were fireworks in Sydney. It was a night for memories, but above all for rejoicing. It was a night that was itself remembered. The Chinese, who had been arriving in great numbers, somehow had fireworks. These were almost all bought up or stolen, and the end of transportation from England was celebrated with Canton crackers that blazed in the streets of Sydney in the form of snakes and dragons. The vessels in the cove lit flares. The American and French ships sent white and red rockets high into the Sydney sky. The English ships followed their example. To some it was a display. To others each rocket represented someone remembered. Susannah took her two grandchildren to watch from the flat outcrop of sandstone at Bennelong Point. They were joined by Elizabeth and Robert. A red flare, climbing and then extinguished, was for Jane. Another, for George Bryant. Another, for Tyrone's man, with his back flogged to the polished bone – for him, whoever he was, because Susannah never knew his name. The crackers and whirling fire-wheels were for a multitude of others. It was not just that transportation was gone, and that there would be no more felons, convicts, government men, exiles, or offenders, and no more chain-gangs of men in yellow slop clothes with the broad arrow. The fireworks also celebrated the confirmed freedom of those who watched. There would be no more shuffling convicts to remind the citizens of Sydney what they or their parents had once been. All that was past.

Susannah-Jane, standing with her brother and grandmother, wore the blue broadcloth cloak with fur collar and silk lining stolen by her grandfather from the town house of James, Lord Bishop of Peterborough. She had become attached to it. It had become hers. She knew its history well. She was fourteen.

George Bryant had been only two years older when he stole it. The night of the fireworks she wore it for him.

On the semi-circular quay, in front of old Government House, an English actor–manager, directly arrived by public demand, as he expressed it, from the California diggings, drummed up an audience and declaimed, in very actorly fashion, the well-remembered old lines in praise of the felonry of New South Wales:

> 'From distant climes, o'er wide-spread seas they came,
> Though not with much éclat or beat of drum:
> True patriots all, for, be it understood,
> They left their country for their country's good,
> And none will doubt but that their emigration
> Has proved most useful to the British nation.'

So ten years – a speck in time – before the United States abolished the slavery of black men, England abandoned the slavery of white men, because of the absurdity of conveying them to gold.

# 34

# Ballarat

Even a god could have been seduced. Even a god surveying the terrain of Eastern Australia at the turn of the year 1853 into 1854 – looking down from an infinite height on a sheep-run called Balla'arat, letting his gaze wander sixty miles to the south-east over a rain forest until it reached the city of Melbourne, and then letting it wander a few hundred miles north-east to Sydney – observing the events of those places, knowing the minds of the men beneath him, and then giving a quick dismissing glance across the Pacific to San Francisco, just to check – even a god could have been seduced into the opinion that the New World was no longer America.

In Melbourne business was at a standstill, the schools closed, and not a man left in the police force. The population was transient. No one stayed more than a week before going on through the rain forest to the goldfields. But that transient population was on any day five times the size of the resident population of a year before. The banks and hotels were still open. In the marble hall of the principal bank, a miner took off his encrusted boots, pared off the two-inch soles with the sharp end of a spade, and extracted from the space between the lowers and the uppers £1700 in banknotes, on which he had walked all the way from the goldfields. A man who until two weeks before had been an ostler waited behind him to bank £950 earned since then in tips from diggers for holding their horses outside an hotel. In the banking hall a man lit a cigar with a five-pound note. No one took any notice. It was no longer an original gesture.

From the port of Melbourne, Edward Hargraves had departed for England to see the Queen, still exhorting the crowd on the quay to go north to the goldfields. 'My friends, lumps of gold are to be picked up, any one big enough to make a diadem.' For the first time in his life he was understating the truth. The American clipper *Marco Polo* came in from England in seventy-four days. No one believed the captain until he showed them the dates on the Liverpool newspapers he brought with him. No vessel had ever made the passage that fast. Ships from San Francisco anchored every day. All this was because of gold found at Bendigo and, above all, at Balla'arat. Balla'arat is an aboriginal name meaning Place of Rest. In this Place of Rest there was alluvial gold to be picked up or panned from the beds of creeks. But there was more than that. There was also gold to be mined. These were the layers of soil the diggers had to penetrate one by one. First there was turf, then rich black alluvium, then grey clay, then red gravel, then red or yellow clay. In all these gravels and clays gold was found. Then there was a solid barrier of hard white pipe clay. Most diggers blunted their picks, turned their backs, and went off to another claim. But one man broke through this barrier and found a chocolate covered clay, rich and soapy. In this layer, nuggets – first one of 1117 ounces and then one of 2640 ounces – were found. Within months, the Place of Rest was occupied by the tents and claims of 132,000 men.

The god looking down, not wishing his opinion to be decided by the observation of a moment, and not wishing his judgement to be swayed by the ephemeral, could have allowed himself to glance ten years into the future. He would have seen Hargraves, returned from England, having seen the Queen but received no baronetcy, only words of praise, and so broke that he was unable to pay his hotel bill in Melbourne. But that was the fortune of one man. The god would also have seen that Balla'arat and its nearby fields had in those ten years produced, in that tiny part of one continent, four-tenths of all the gold mined in the whole world. Balla'arat was far and away the richest goldfield on earth.

Balla'arat was soon abbreviated to Ballarat. A road was constructed from Melbourne, through the rain forest of ferns and cabbage trees, Livingstone palms with sheer trunks and

dense foliage high up, giving everlasting shade and dampness
beneath. When it rained, Cobb's coaches struggled through
axle-deep mud. Then Cobb constructed corduroy roads made
from the branches of trees laid like railway sleepers, only close
together, touching each other, forming a continuous wooden
path.

On such a road, in a wildly bucking coach sawing back and
forth on its leather springs like a whale-boat in a gale, three
men and a woman made the voyage to Ballarat in early 1854.
They were Mr Dryden Hall-Kean, an impresario, the actor–
manager last seen at Sydney reciting the prologue from the old
convict play; an American who preferred not to give his name;
a travelling lady writer of Polish–Russian provenance whose
name no one could visualize or pronounce; and a handsome
young man in black suit and white top hat who, when asked for
his name, said the one word Cecil, which he pronounced Sissle.

'Mr Sizzle?' said the American, thoughtfully, steadying himself in the lurching coach by placing his booted feet on the plush
bench between the young Englishman and the foreign lady.
'Good name, sir. Tells nobody nothing, sir. Good name to give
yourself, that one. Now me, sir, I always says . . .', and at this
he said nothing but performed a cabalistic ritual with the right
hand. First with his index finger he touched an eye. Then he
touched his nose. Then with index finger and thumb he made
a circle, through which he peered in turn at each of his fellow
passengers, and then settled back mighty satisfied.

'See?' he asked.

'I do not see.' The reply came only from Mr Dryden Hall-
Kean.

The American sighed. 'I,' he said, pointing to his eye.
'Knows,' he said, pointing to his nose. Then, forming the circle
once again, he said, 'Nothing.'

Still no reply, at which the American sighed again and
repeated, as if he were attempting to make children understand,
'I Knows Nothing'.

'Very likely,' said the travelling lady.

The American spat out of the place where the windows would
have been if there had been any windows, settled his two pistols
into the holsters at his waist, tipped his hat over his eyes, and
went instantly to sleep. The gold rings in his ears swayed with

the movement of the coach. The impresario, sitting beside him, mimed the seizing of one ring and the leading of the American by it, as a man would lead a bull by the ring in his nose. The lady allowed herself a smile. The young man lifted the canvas flap and looked at the everlasting rain forest.

The impresario inspected the young man's clothes – the elegant shoes, the waistcoat with the last button correctly unbuttoned, the sit of the coat shoulders, the poise of the white hat. He addressed the young man.

'Are you in the profession, sir?'

The young man turned away from the open flap. 'The profession?'

'The profession, sir.'

'I do not know to what you allude.'

The impresario had concluded from the cut of the young man's clothes, and from his accent, that he had procured his clothes at a good theatrical tailor's, and his accent on the boards of the most fashionable London and provincial stages. The poise of the man also suggested that it assisted him to earn his living, that it was part of his stock in trade. 'Sizzle,' of course, was a strange name, but it must be, as the vile American surmised, a travelling name, no more.

'Are you of the theatrical profession, sir? Are we fellow actors?'

'We are not.'

The young man's tone was final and peremptory. Mr Dryden Hall-Kean was offended by this, but at the same time relieved that he would not have to face competition at Ballarat. More than 100,000 men was a large enough audience, but he would rather not share it. But the impresario still had his doubts, and, in order to learn more, kept the conversation going by offering information about himself.

'You will have wondered at my own name, sir?'

'No.'

'Kean, sir, speaks for itself. My father, sir.' So far as this suggested that his father was the great Edmund Kean, it was a lie. But it was true that his father had been a Kean, though a butcher by trade.

'And Dryden, sir, my given name, also speaks for itself.'

Still no reply.

'But *Hall*-Kean; now that Hall is the proudest part of all, sir.'
No reply.

'The great bard of Avon gave his eldest daughter in marriage
to one John Hall, a gentleman of Stratford. The Shakespeares
in the male line are extinct. The Halls remain.'

The young man said, 'I know that to be true.'

'Yes indeed, sir.'

'I have a butler of the name.'

The conversation died.

Once the coach slipped off the corduroy road, hurling the
passengers in a heap. The American untangled himself, drew
both pistols, swore vilely, and repeatedly said, 'Put a bullet
through his brain, put a bullet through his brain.' The travelling
lady smoothed her skirt. The actor–manager carefully picked
from his elegant grey trousers the bits of straw from the floor
which had been thrown round the coach. The American spat
in the straw. The young Englishman looked away in disgust.
In fifteen minutes they were back on the road again.

Near the end of the second day they came close to the
diggings. The bright red of the coach was coated with grey dust.
The bright yellow paint was abraded from the wheels. The
travelling lady felt sick from the motion of the coach, and
several times they had to stop to let her get down. The American
repeatedly spat in the straw until the young Englishman told
him to desist or he would give him in charge, at which the
American laughed and laughed, and spat on the floor with new
gusto. Then the coach stopped.

On the road in front of them they saw two miners on foot
and five uniformed men on horseback. The two men were
carrying a sack. An order was given. The men with the sack
made a protest, and looked round at the mounted and armed
men, and then back at the halted coach. One of the mounted
men nudged the man with his horse, knocking him over. He
scrambled to his feet. Another of the mounted men drew a
carbine and waved it at the sack. The two miners tipped its
contents on to the corduroy road. It looked like a heap of gravel.
One of the uniformed men dismounted, turned the sack inside
out, put it in his saddle-bag, and then kicked the heaped dirt
in all directions. The two miners watched it as it scattered into
the ferns. Neither said a word.

The travelling lady got down from the coach and walked up. She saw that four of the armed men were police constables. The fifth was a major of militia.

'What is this?' she asked.

'Paydirt,' said a policeman. 'Paydirt is what that *was*.'

The major said, 'Will you return to the coach, madam?'

'Why has this been done?' she asked.

'Christ, ma'am, because it's Sunday,' said one of the miners. 'Three weeks' bloody work gone because it's Sunday.'

The lady traveller was protesting, and the major was showing signs of impatience, when one of the Cobb drivers strolled lazily up to the group. Not exactly addressing the major, but rather speaking into the air beside the major's head, he said, 'Better take stock before you get your boys to throw her into the trees 'long of the paydirt, mister. Better take stock who we got inside.'

The Cobb and Co. drivers were a freelance élite on the gold-fields, not loved by the police or the militia, but given a lot of freedom. Freeman Cobb, expecting graft and extortion, made tactful and continuing monthly bribes in the right places and bought immunity for his coaches and men. He had come up the hard way. He had seen it all before.

The major rode his horse at a walk back to the coach. 'So who?' he asked the driver, who told him.

The major leaned down, glanced at the passengers through the open door of the coach, found his man, and saluted.

'Lord Robert?' he said.

'Good evening, Major . . .?'

'John Redmond, sir.'

'Good evening, Major Redmond.' The American in the coach went very quiet. The actor–manager congratulated himself on having spotted a gentleman. He had always known there was something distinguished about the fellow. A few words were exchanged. Lord Robert Cecil accepted the major's offer of hospitality at Ballarat. They would reach the camp in another two hours.

The two men on the corduroy road watched the Cobb coach and its escort of four mounted policemen and Redmond disappear towards Ballarat. Their sack had been taken. They searched in the forest for their paydirt, and recovered about a quarter of it, which they stuffed into their pockets and hats. It was not a fortune. It was not gold dust. It was quartz and gravel containing very little gold which they had not the means of extracting on the goldfields. They would have got ten pounds for the lot. Now they might get two or three. Because they had been detected working on a Sunday, their paydirt had been scattered. Their only protest had been that they were not working on a Sunday, but just carrying the results of their weekday labour. It had not helped them, and they had after-wards remained silent. Cecil mistook their silence for resignation to a just authority which properly insisted on the keeping of the Christian Sabbath.

He also found, as soon as he arrived at Ballarat, that he had been wrong to expect only shacks. First he took a bath at the United States Hotel, and, as he stood allowing one of the hotel servants to towel him dry, he saw from the back window a panorama of a slope and then a plain with a thousand tents lit from inside by candles and oil lamps. He had expected the tents but not the bath. Redmond gave him a glass of tolerable port, and suggested that this was a good time of day, with the sun gone, to take five minutes' walk along the main street. He showed his guest the Post Office, the gold office, the auctioneer's, the Chinese laundry, the apothecaries' hall, the free library and mechanics' institute, the blacksmith's. The dust of the day had settled, but the natural town smells of the time were still there – the pervading smells of horse stale and horse dung. He was given a guided tour, and shown what he should see, but what most convinced him that this was at least an infant civilization was not anything Redmond showed him but a grocer's shop he spotted for himself.

'The Sabbath,' John Redmond was telling him, 'is invariably honoured on the diggings, even by the French,' when Cecil stopped and gazed at a shop window.

'Dog soap,' he exclaimed. Cecil had many dogs and two packs of hounds, which were all washed by his kennelmen and hunt servants. Well-groomed dogs were strong evidence of probity.

Then his eye went to an advertisement in the window:

ICE!
ICE!
ICE!

Pure Canadian ice was to be bought, having been shipped in
sawdust in the holds of clippers all the way from the St
Lawrence, as ballast.

Displays of Westphalia and Cumberland hams, bottles of
Scottish marmalade, and tins of tea bearing the label 'Jackson's
of Piccadilly', convinced him of the civilization of Ballarat. He
ate a passable dinner, and retired to a passable bed. He was
given a choice between a camp bed of stretched cowhide and a
feather-bed. The mattress was a woolbag stuffed with bush-
feathers – dry and crumbled eucalypt leaves. It was fragrant,
but he reasoned that the cowhide would be freer from lice and
took that. He slept well, being disturbed only once, by the
sound of sporadic gunfire. It died away, no one came to rouse
him, and he drifted back to sleep.

'Dingoes?' he enquired at breakfast.

'Americans,' said Redmond.

'Ah,' said Cecil, between sips of Jackson's tea, 'they like to
discharge their firearms to convince themselves they have them?'

Redmond assured him that this was so. There was no disorder. The Queen's Peace was maintained.

Cecil was shown Poverty Point, a mine abandoned by the
first miners but which had since made a fortune for their
successors. Then he saw the shafts known as the Jewellers' Shops,
where lucky diggers made more in a week than they had
dreamed of earning in their whole lives.

'How are things going?' he asked, and not one man replied.
He came away convinced that this was a satisfactory response.
He had been told before that it would be most satisfactory. A
miner making money never talked. A man working a rich vein
wished to reveal nothing, and was too busy anyway. The only
talkative miner was an unsuccessful one.

He left next day on the same stage as the travelling lady,
whom he had not seen during their stay. She was a sharp
observer. She had seen what he had not. She had talked to
many miners.

'There is no lynching,' he said. 'No vigilante committees.'

'No.'

'It is a government not of the mob, but of the Queen.'

'By the police, if you wish; yes. But the miners are harried
for their licences, which some lack the means to buy.'

'I did not see that. The licence is only three pounds for two months.'

'Did you look at their hands?'

'What?'

She said, 'There is a sort of terracing, on the slope, extending for two or three miles. You did not walk over it?'

'I did not walk two miles.'

'It is like a colander. The earth is dug over and over. Some men have dug two and three shafts. There are more than a hundred thousand men now. I do not know how many have been there before and given up.'

'Yes?'

'Their hands suffer horribly. They dig with a pick, or with a spade, or with their fingers when they come to the blue clay. There is a pain in the fingers which starts under the nails. Then it goes up the arms to the shoulders, and from the shoulders to the backbone.'

'Did they tell you this?'

'Yes. And I tried for myself. I do not have the hands of a miner, or of a man, so I did not try to do much. But I dug for a quarter of an hour, in soft clay. That was yesterday. This morning I know what they mean.'

She took off her right glove. Her fingers were cracked and swollen.

No woman of Lord Robert's acquaintance had ever worked with her hands. He gazed in horror at those fingers and at the blistered palm.

'I wanted to find out,' she said. 'Also, they *are* harried over their licences. Sometimes they are required to produce them four times a day. I saw a man chained to a tree because he had not a licence.'

Lord Robert Cecil, direct descendant of the first minister of Elizabeth I, a man who would go into Parliament for one of his family's boroughs as soon as he returned to England, a man who would become three times Prime Minister of England, looked at the hand of the lady travelling writer and admitted to himself that she had seen much that he had not.

'I believe you about the licences,' he said.

She thanked him.

'And the shooting late at nights?' he said.

'Oh,' she said, 'Americans.'
At least he had not been misinformed about that.


Two hours after Lord Robert Cecil and the lady traveller left, John Redmond began his burnings of sly-grog shops, those not licensed by him. Prodded by policemen, the man and woman who owned one grog tent were forced to bring firewood, bits of timber which had shored up an abandoned shaft, and pile them on their forfeited tent, which first sagged and then collapsed under the weight. The woman pleaded for a small sewing-box which had come with her all the way from Ireland. The policemen took no notice. The man stood silently by, watching as the police lit and burned everything he had. The two kegs of contraband rum did not burn with the rest. They were taken into police custody. The policemen rode off with them. The man and woman watched as the last flames flickered and the smoke curled upwards.

From the window of Bentley's hotel, Frederick Vern watched the bonfire. He was from Hanover, a failed revolutionary, and now a failed miner. He had drunk a lot.

'Europe,' he said, 'is striking off its fetters.'

His two drinking companions, both Irishmen, said nothing.

'The divine right of princes is being scattered to the winds. But here we have a government more despotic than anywhere in the world.'

'Better overthrow it then, Fred,' said one of the Irishmen. 'And by the by, who's king these days in Hanover?'

Vern threw the contents of his glass at the man. There was indeed still a king in Hanover. The Irishman dodged and laughed.

Bentley, the inn-keeper, stood polishing glasses behind the bar, and listening.

# 35

# An Era of Their Own

'Mr Cobb,' said Susannah, 'you did promise to take me to Melbourne whenever I wished. You offered it. And now I ask, you will not.'

Freeman Cobb caught the eye of Lord Robert Cecil across the room, and then glanced at Robert King, and then at Elizabeth. The eyes of them all said to him, 'Nothing will stop her.' Cobb looked over at Susannah-Jane, who was sitting with her feet drawn up under her in a chair. He saw that she was already smiling directly at him. Her eyes said the same as the men's, and more. If Susannah went, Susannah-Jane would want to come too. He could see no way of stopping either. Cobb carefully put down his tea cup. He had come to tea and found himself surrounded.

'Now ma'am,' he said, 'won't you see reason? Sure I promised to take you to Melbourne. Sure it was my idea. But that was when Melbourne was something to see, when the gold country was in New South Wales and people were only just beginning to leave Melbourne. Now the gold's in Victoria. Melbourne's nothing but ships moored as close as they can get, with all their crews deserted, and buildings left half-finished because all the men have gone, and there's nothing there to see but what I would take no mother of mine to see. Drunken diggers and roving women. Apart from them, everyone is gone to Ballarat. I will take you anywhere else; but, for the moment, not Melbourne.'

'Ballarat then.'

'Ballarat? Ma'am, my boys were mostly in California before

they came out here, and they say there are more hangable
rogues in Ballarat than ever they saw in San Francisco or
Sacramento City.'

Susannah said, 'I am old enough not to be your mother, as
you suggested just now, but your grandmother. I lived in
Sydney when nine men out of ten were hangable rogues.'

Cobb looked at Cecil, who had come to say goodbye. He was
on his way back to England. He had already said the government of Ballarat was that of the Queen and not of the mob, and
he said no more.

'Mother,' said Robert, '*why* do you want to go to the goldfields?'

'Perhaps for the same reason that took you to San Francisco?
Wanting to see all that's happened. Once upon a time here, a
man pounded up two brass doorknobs and it took weeks to
discover they were not gold. It was said they were all the gold
that ever would be found in New Holland. And anyway,
according to Lord Robert, Ballarat is civilized.'

Cecil was bound to reply to this. 'Well, you can buy there,
apart from revolvers, pistols, and bandoliers, Jackson's tea and
ladies' side saddles. The peace is kept.' He thought it safer
than Melbourne. At Ballarat men were working, not spending.

'OK,' said Cobb, 'my boys will look after you, and I'll come
right along myself too.'

He saw Susannah-Jane flicking her hair from her eyes and
about to pounce on him with her request. He got there first.
'Miss King, are you still young enough for me to ask how old
you are?'

She considered. 'No, Mr Cobb, I am not.' She was fifteen.

'Then,' said Cobb, 'I guess you are old enough to come, and
I guess I have two of you to take now.'

She sprang up and kissed him on the cheek. Young American
women did not do that in Massachusetts. He was very pleased.

George-Nicolas would have wanted to go too, but he was at
sea. He showed some of his grandfather's vocation for the navy,
and was acting as temporary midshipman on a Royal Naval
sloop out of Sydney making a visit of inspection to Fiji, which
would keep him another two months. Before he embarked,
Robert gave him the sword presented to him by Bligh. It was
scarcely longer than a midshipman's dirk, having been made

for a boy of six, and the commander smiled at it and let the
boy wear it. Its having come from Bligh gave it cachet.

Cobb left with Susannah and Susannah-Jane.

Two days later Robert was offered a brief which would take
him to Ballarat as well. The messenger came late in the evening.
Robert knew he would have to sail for Melbourne at dawn the
next day. He knew he would have to tell Elizabeth.

He lay in their bed waiting. From the closed door which led
off to her dressing room he could hear her voice and her maid's,
but not catch a word of what they were saying. He knew the
girl was brushing out Elizabeth's hair. She came in, wearing a
cotton dressing-gown, walked over to the bed, and stood by
him. He reached out an arm, slipping it under the dressing-
gown and round her hips. He nestled his head into her, pulling
her towards him with both arms, encircling her hips and then
sliding his hands up to her waist.

'I have to go tomorrow early,' he said.

'Why?'

'Ballarat.'

'Don't go,' she said. She leaned over him and rubbed her
cheek against his hair. 'I will make you not go.'

He did not reply. She knew he was serious. She stood, then
shrugged the dressing-gown off her shoulders and let it fall to
the floor. They slept with nothing on. She came to bed, and he
encircled her and pulled her to him. She was warm. He cupped
her head in his hands, and then let his head rest on her breasts.
Then they lay quietly side by side.

'I *must* go,' he said.

'Yes, but why? When you went to California you said I should
think of it as if you were a sea captain and it was just a voyage.
I tried to. But it was a year. I hated being alone. I was afraid.'

'You knew I would come back.'

'I knew, but I was afraid. The sea, and danger. We had not
been apart before.'

'This is nothing like that. It is not a year's voyage. It is a
couple of weeks. I have often been away that long.'

'Why go? Robert, I do not want you to go. Susannah has
gone there. Susannah-Jane is there. Our son is at sea. I do not
want you to go too.'

Elizabeth and Robert shared everything. They never

quarrelled. She was steadier than he was. He loved her. But he was sometimes unreasonable, sometimes fierce or sudden. He could not altogether lack these qualities of his father and mother. When he was impatient or angry, and it was not often, Elizabeth left him alone until he came back to her. She had the sense to leave him to come to his own senses. He always did. He would come back in a couple of hours, sometimes saying nothing, sometimes making a gesture of apology with his open hands. They had been happy. She had never before asked him not to go away. He told her why he had no choice.

'It sounds like a riot,' he said.

She sat up, 'What?' She was afraid for her daughter, and for Susannah.

'Look,' he said, 'Cobb is going to hear this news too. It will be known tomorrow. He did not intend to stop in Melbourne, but they will tell him when he lands. He will not go on to Ballarat. He will bring them back.'

'But he may not hear.'

'No, he may not. I cannot think how he may not, but he may not. And that makes it all the more necessary for me to go. I do not want Susannah-Jane and my mother there, even with Cobb and his men to look after them. So I have to go for them. That settles it. But I think I should have to go anyway.'

He told her what he knew. A miner had been murdered by a police spy. The miners were outraged that the spy had been only cursorily arraigned and had every prospect of being released by the police magistrate. The military had placarded the streets of Ballarat with posters enjoining all true subjects of the Queen, and all strangers receiving hospitality and protection under her flag, to help preserve social order and the supremacy of the law, and to desist from riotous and violent action. In view of all this, the Australasian League had asked him to go and represent the interest of 10,000 miners.

'Elizabeth,' he said. 'It may be nothing, or it may be everything. It may have blown over by the time I get there. It may not. But it does look as though Cecil's wrong in his certainty that the Queen's Peace reigns at Ballarat. You see why I have to go, and I must go at dawn.'

'Yes I see that.' There were the beginnings of tears in her voice. He held her and rocked her.

Then they talked about their children. They were very much married in every way, but both knew their children were the strongest bond between them. He had never forgotten and neither had she – as how could they? – her bold first words to him, 'And I should love to give them to you.' The words that revealed her.

'George-Nicolas will be all right,' she said. 'But I wish he had not chosen the sea.'

'He will be more than all right. I am not sorry he has gone to sea. I think it will be his career. My father, after all. The patterns of our ancestors are very strong in all of us, you know. I do not know whether it is stronger than in other families, but I do see it clearly in all of us. I never saw my father. But my mother thinks George-Nicolas very like him. I am glad he has gone to sea. I was meant to, you know. The sword I gave him was mine. I do not know whether I still retain the rank Bligh gave me.'

'The oldest midshipman in the Royal Navy,' she said.

They lay still. Then she said, 'But it is Susannah-Jane.'

'She is a splendid girl.'

'She is a splendid girl, Robert; but she gets what she wants. Did you notice, with Cobb?'

'Oh, yes. There was no chance he would not take her.' Robert was amused. He had watched his daughter get what she wanted.

'But all the time?'

'Elizabeth, my dear wife, do not worry about your daughter. She will get what she wants. I think all her life she will get what she wants. It is a natural force of spirit. But hers is a generous spirit, too.'

'But it gives her such power.'

'*Oh yes.* That is true. But I think she will be one of those few people who enhance everything they touch.'

'That will be fortunate for those she loves, but they will still be in her power. Most of all they will be in her power.'

'Yes.'

Elizabeth and Robert dozed. They did not sleep.

They lay all the short night in the dark, talking sometimes, and then dawn began to break. She slid over her hand and entwined his fingers in hers. He kissed her. The kiss, of all embraces, is the first that goes, even when husband and wife are as close as Elizabeth and Robert. Both knew they had not kissed that way for . . . how long? They could not remember. With the happy ease in which they had always been so fortunate, she enclosed him in her slim arms, and he entered her sweetly. It was an embrace familiar over so many years, in a bed known to them all those years.

She clasped him closer. 'I do not want you to go, I do not want you to go, I do not want you to go, I do not want you to go.'


Cobb, had he heard the news, would certainly have turned back. But he wished to avoid Melbourne entirely, so he landed to the west of the city, at Geelong, and took the slower but safer road from that port to Ballarat. He heard nothing.

Robert, having landed at Melbourne, learned more details from his companions on the Ballarat stage.

'Poor Scobie was just drunk.'

Scobie was the murdered man. He was a Scot. He met another Scot. They drank until the Lord Byron closed at midnight, and then went to Bentley's, which usually stayed open all hours. But it was closed that night. Scobie smashed a window with an empty bottle, and Bentley chased him and killed him with a spade. The body was dumped in a shallow abandoned digging. Ballarat had enough abandoned shafts to provide a hundred thousand undetectable graves. Scobie was found only by chance.

'Murder,' said Robert's companion, 'is common enough, but this one smells.'

Robert was beginning to think less and less of Lord Robert Cecil's judgement, and to fear for his mother and daughter.

The man in the coach said Bentley was well-known to be a police informer. The magistrate at Ballarat had been unwilling to issue a warrant for his arrest. When a private warrant was taken out, the magistrate first allowed Bentley bail, which in a case of murder was extraordinary, and then, when he examined him, provided a chair and asked him to be so good as to sit while he answered a few questions. The diggers feared he would be discharged without even coming to trial. This,

added to the continuing grievances of the licence fee, and
increasing bitterness at the constant burnings-down of tents by
Major Redmond, had brought the diggings near riot.

'Major Redmond?' said Robert. 'John Redmond?'

'The sheep-king. Now the gold- and liquor-king. The
goldfield-king.'

Robert willed the horses to go faster. He arrived the same
evening as his mother and daughter arrived, from another
direction. He was looking for them when the diggers burned
down Bentley's Hotel.

It was as they had expected. The magistrate who offered
Bentley bail, a chair, and all consideration, finally discharged
him, finding he had no case to answer. He further announced
that Bentley was honourably discharged. This was too much.
The news spread at dusk, the end of the working day when there
were a thousand diggers drinking or lounging in the main
street. There were no apparent leaders. A column marched to
Bentley's. They hardly talked. They did not shout. There was
no shooting of pistols in the air. The sound was that of shuffling
feet on the dirt road. Those not at the front of the column were
choked and smothered in the rising dust of two thousand feet.
Their hair was grey. Their faces were grey. Grey dust lay in the
wrinkles of their faces and in the folds of their clothes. Above
the shuffling there rose a sound like a tapping on planks,
magnified an infinity of times. It was the blue trousers of the
men, caked hard with dried mud, knocking against the leather
tops of their boots as they walked. It was not at first a mob.
Outside Bentley's the men halted, waiting for others to come
up, and then a Scottish voice said,

'Shall we drink to Mr Bentley first?'

A roar of, 'No.'

'In his own liquor?'

They changed their minds and entered Bentley's in orderly
rows. Two bartenders waited petrified behind the bar. Bentley
himself was gone.

'Whisky,' said the Scottish voice. 'Scotch whisky.'

The bartenders poured ten glasses from a bottle, and waited.
The ten glasses stood on the counter.

'There are more of us,' said the Scotsman.

No one touched the whisky until the counter was covered with

200 glasses, all there were in the house, and then these were handed backwards, through the windows and doors, to the men waiting outside.

Then the men inside allowed themselves swigs from the remaining bottles, until all Bentley's whisky was gone. They did not touch the rum, gin, beer, or wine.

The Scotsman stepped forward, picked up a full barrel of Madeira, held it above his head, and threw it through the back window. It took window-frame, glass, and all with it and rolled down the slope behind. Then the men seized more barrels, hogsheads, kegs, bottles, lamps, tables, chairs, and anything that could be removed, and threw them through the same back window. They broke down all doors, broke all windows, smashed all plate-glass mirrors, and brought the chandelier crashing down. They stripped the panelling from the walls of the bar parlour. They smashed everything that could be smashed. Two barrels remained, too heavy to be lifted. They were staved, and the rum spurted out over the floor. Then the men left. All this was done with hardly a raised voice. The burning was by accident. A boy at the back tossed a blazing rag not into the pub but into a canvas bowling alley at the side.

The Scotsman, who remained inside until the last, saw the danger and beckoned to the bartenders. 'Better come out.'

They hesitated.

'It is not you we are after. Better go.' The flames burst in through a side wall. The timber of the wall caught with a dry crackle, and the two barmen had barely scrambled through the door when the spilled rum on the floor caught with a whoosh. The crowd watched silently, falling gradually back before the flames. One vat exploded, bringing the roof in. It had taken twenty minutes from start to finish.

The militia were two miles away in the diggings carrying out their own, legal burnings of sly-grog tents. By the time they arrived in force, Bentley's hotel was a smoking ruin, the street before it was empty, and Australian, English, Irish, Scottish, American, German, and French miners were drinking soberly at the bars of the eighteen other pubs in the main street. It was Cobb who found Robert, placing a hand on his shoulder.

'Where?' said Robert.

'Safe. At the hotel where my boys told me Cecil stayed. Good beds. Fair food.'

'Look, how could you bring them here into this?'

'Came from Geelong. Heard nothing. Saw the fire first, and then you. Come to that, how are you here?'

'Get them out tomorrow,' said Robert. He was angry.

Cobb looked at him. 'How close were you to that little bonfire? You're more shaken up than they are, I tell you.'

Robert's face was blackened. He had been close to the fire. He put his hand on Cobb's shoulder in apology. 'Please get them out tomorrow.'

Cobb nodded. 'Sun-up,' he said. I already told them. They don't want to go, but I told them, no way do they stay here.'

But when next morning came there was, on the contrary, no way at all they could leave. Reports said that 100, or 250, or 450 Irishmen, having found little gold and not having the money to pay for their next month's licences, had marched off in the night to plunder the bank vaults of Melbourne. No one knew the truth of this. Certainly many of the Irish tents were gone, and others left abandoned. And it was the sly-grog tents belonging to the Irish that the police had been burning the evening before, while Bentley's was destroyed. If they had been 450, and if they were armed, and if they could have reached Melbourne, they could have taken the city. There were no police left there. But it was doubtful if they were more than a hundred, they had only their picks and shovels and a few old pistols, sixty miles lay between them and Melbourne and twenty miles of that distance was rain forest. But Major Redmond had heard the news and he went in the middle of the night to the police magistrate and recited the facts. Besides, he said, two of the Cobb coaches had gone from the livery stables where they had been left the night before, and the Irish had taken them. They must be cut off. On his authority and the magistrate's, horse-police were sent riding cross-country to wreck the corduroy road to Melbourne, and, in case that should be used as a means of escape, the road to Geelong as well. The police found a few Irishmen straggling through the bush, but no coaches. They made a thorough job of wrecking the timbers of the corduroy roads. Then it rained. For two hours it rained, a drenching downpour which completed the ruin of the roads. The Irish had not taken the coaches. Cobb had moved them himself, late the night before, to open ground where he reckoned they were less likely to be burned than at the livery stables. He had coaches but no road. His own boys could repair the roads, but not until the track was dry. Then it would take days. So Susannah and Susannah-Jane had to stay.

Robert watched his mother and daughter as they sat surrounded by amiable diggers in the long room of the United States Hotel. Some of the diggings were flooded and there was no work to be done until the water seeped away. The diggers saw few women. Most of the men were Americans, gentle and full of courteous high-talk.

'And the next nugget I find, ma'am – the next sizable nugget, say more'n a thousand ounces – shall be named for you ma'am. And the one after that – say five hundred ounces? – shall be named for you, miss. That do you?'

Robert caught his daughter's eye. She smiled with pleasure and then, remembering that they should already have gone but for the Irishmen and the roads, looked suitably grave. He shook his head slowly at her, but he was reassured in his mind. She would come to no harm with those men.

He went across to his mother's side. 'We will stay inside,' she said. 'Today at any rate.'

He went to see the representatives of the Australasian League who were his clients. They told him the name was now the Reform League.

'I am sorry for the change, gentlemen. The old league did a great deal.'

'For convicts,' said Frederick Vern, the Hanoverian. 'We are not convicts, and what ended all that was not the league, but what we are getting from the ground here.'

The other three men were John Humfray, an Englishman; John Maguire, an American; and Peter Lalor, an Irishman. They wanted King to represent to the Lieutenant-Governor in Melbourne the iniquity of the licence fee and the brutality of the police and militia on the diggings. Could he do that? There was to be a meeting of 10,000 miners that evening, and a report of that would convey to the Governor the strength of their feelings.

Robert listened, and surveyed the men. He thought Vern a liability to any cause. Humfray was moderate. Lalor, when he spoke, was quiet and convincing, but he did not say much. The American said nothing at all, but sat knowing he was being sized up, and sizing up Robert in return.

'Well, Mr King?' said Humfray.

'Gentlemen, I am no use to you at all unless we are honest with each other. I shall play devil's advocate for a few minutes, and tell you how this looks from Melbourne; how it probably looks to the Governor; and how it looks to the military and the police here. Because if we don't take what they think into account, we shall get nowhere.'

'Why bother about the Governor?' said Vern. 'To hell with him.'

'Because he is the only man who can give you any part of what you want. He is a new man. I have never met him, but I know a little about him. He knows nothing whatever about gold, except that it has emptied Melbourne, and ruined the trade of the colony in anything but gold.'

The American asked slowly, 'And what do you know about gold, mister?'

'I was in California.'

'Right,' said the American. 'We're listening.'

'I can complain about the way the licence fees are collected. I think that would be put right. I know the militia officer in charge here, and I think the Governor would be heartily glad to get him off the fields. For that matter, if you do nothing, and wait a week, I think he will very likely be removed anyway.'

'So?'

'So, that can be done. But I am now going to put myself in the place of the Governor and tell you how I think he will see the rest of your grievances. You want the licence fees revoked. He would like to see them done away with himself.'

'Like Christ he would,' said Vern.

'He would like them done away with because they are too much bother to collect. The inability to collect them makes his police look fools. He would much prefer to drop the licences and levy a simple tax on gold exported from the colony. That is something he could easily collect from the bullion shippers. Naturally they do not like the idea, but he will do it, very likely he will do it; but he cannot do it overnight. So again, wait. Evade paying, but don't attack the principle, forcing him into defending something he wants to get rid of himself.'

'Subtle, Mr King,' said Lalor. 'But what do you say to the rest of our demands?'

'If I were the Governor, they would frighten me. First, make a simple concession in your use of words. Don't talk about "demands" to the Governor. Ask him. Make requests. Soften it. He has face to lose. He cannot be seen to lose face. But as to the rest of your points – well, look, manhood suffrage, State parliaments, miners represented in those parliaments, miners' members, and so on. Not new ideas, but add them to your refusal to pay your licences, and then add great open-air meetings, and a hotel burned down, and what does the Governor see?'

Humfray said, 'What does he see, Mr King?'

'In a word, then. He sees more than one hundred thousand miners here. He sees he has two hundred policemen here. He sees the miners are not only British but German, French, Irish, and American, and I tell you what he thinks. He thinks of revolts all over Europe; that is very recent. He thinks of English landlords burned out in Ireland: that is the usual state of affairs. He thinks of California and lynch-law: he has never been there but that is what he reads in the newspapers. So, gentlemen, I will do what I can to carry out your instructions. But the burning of the hotel last night will make bad reading in Melbourne. And I beg you not to hold the meeting this evening of which you spoke earlier. That would only make things worse.'

Vern lit a cigar. 'You put yourself very easily in the place of the Governor, Mr King.'

'I told you why.'

Lalor said, 'One thing you did not tell us, Mr King. You said you would tell us in one word what the Governor saw here. You did not put it in one word.'

'In one word then, what he will see is a revolution.'

Robert walked with Lalor and Humfray over to the United States Hotel. The mud in the street was drying out in the steaming heat. Flies were everywhere. 'Gentlemen,' said Robert, 'I am unhappy with Vern.'

'Yes,' said Humfray.

'And the American said very little.'

Lalor said, 'Maguire is a man with a head on his shoulders.'

They had lunch with Cobb, Susannah, and Susannah-Jane, the six of them together. Robert left them early to visit the three men arrested after the fire. Cobb had found a bakery just down the main street run by a man from New York, and was promising Susannah she should taste American bread. The real thing. Susannah-Jane was leaning back with her hands between her skirts while Lalor told her about the beauty of Dublin. Even as an Irishman he had to admit it, he said; in Ireland it might be, but really it was the most handsome of all English cities. Robert left the hotel, walked past the Theatre Royal next door where Mr Dryden Hall-Kean, ringing a handbell, was proclaiming the magnificence of the entertainment to be offered that very afternoon and evening, an unprecedented and never-before contemplated *mélange* – he relished the word *mélange* – of the spoken, terpsichorean, and lyrical drama, of Shakespeare's *King Lear* presented by himself, one of the lineal descendants of the great bard, and of dances and songs by Madame Ophir, as performed before King Solomon and the great Inca monarchs. But Robert had work to do. The police commissioner let him see the three men arrested the night before, who said they were miles away from the burning. The commissioner was reasonable. Robert was relieved he did not have to deal with Redmond. He asked after him.

'Bringing up reinforcements from Melbourne, Mr King, as far as his ruined road will allow him.'

'Yes.'

'Mr King, I hope this evening's meeting will be quiet. I should welcome a little peace for my men, and would rather not disturb either them or the diggers. Short of absolute riot, I shall do nothing. I should like those responsible for the meeting to know that. But it would be better still if there were no meeting.'

But it was hopeless. Five thousand men assembled, only half the number expected, but a vast crowd. The voice of moderation was Humfray's. They were all the loyal subjects of their Sovereign Lady the Queen, but she was misled by corrupt ministers. They would respect her authority and her person, but they would not respect her manservants, her oxes, or her asses. This was spoken with Redmond in mind, and received with irreverent laughter, into which Vern stepped to seize his opportunity.

'Are we not free men?' A crowd of five thousand has only one answer to this question. Five thousand men roared that they were free.

'Why not have a chronology, a date, of our own?' Vern sometimes played with this idea of starting time again, at least starting the calendar again with the Year One, as the French revolutionaries had done in 1792. This too was cheered. Anything he said would have been cheered.

'There has been talk of the Queen. God may save the Queen, but no one will save the Governor in Melbourne.' More cheers.

'But I will not talk of the Queen. The people are the only legitimate source of power. As to the associations of the Old World, let us leave them behind. Let us leave the Old World, because it is old. We are new. Why not, I say again, have a chronology, a date – an era – of our own?' Five thousand men were so inflamed that they burned their licences on a ceremonial pyre.

Major Redmond returned late and tired.

'What,' he asked, 'were they saying they wanted, besides not to pay their licences?'

The trooper helping him off with his mud-caked riding boots suppressed the reference to oxes and asses. He said, 'They have burned their licences. It's more than licences now, sir.'

'What?'

'At the end, sir, they said it was an era of their own they wanted. Which they voted for, raising their hands.'

# 36

# The Making of the Maiden Flag

When he got back to the hotel, after the meeting, Robert could not find Susannah-Jane. His mother was asleep. His daughter's room was empty. The bed was made and not disturbed. It was like looking into the room of a woman he knew intimately, but in some ways did not know at all. The United States Hotel was marvellously more comfortable than a tent, but its rooms were sparsely furnished. Any furniture had to be made there, or brought up from Melbourne or Geelong at great cost. There were no wardrobes. He could see his daughter's dresses, skirts, and petticoats arranged over chairs or hanging from hooks. If she had been a woman he had not known he would have thought, entering her bed room for the first time, that there was a lovely disorder about her. Then he did think that because of course she was a woman whose bedroom he was entering for the first time. When he last went into a bedroom of hers, at home, she was a little girl of eleven. Now she was fifteen, sixteen in a few months.

And where was she?

It was past midnight, but still hot. He went into the empty lobby. Two last drinkers were sleeping over an empty bottle of whisky. The porter was dozing. Robert woke him. He had not seen Miss King. Robert walked into the empty street. Not a soul. There was still some sound from the nearest tents, a fiddle playing a tune he could not catch, laughter, two voices raised and then dying away. He walked closer to the music. Tents have no windows, but it was the custom to sew panels of calico into the sides of tents, and then saturate the calico in linseed oil until t became translucent. This gave some light. In one tent, through such a panel, lit from behind by an oil lamp, he saw the embracing figures of a man and a woman.

He walked rapidly to the hotel, and took the stairs two at a time to Susannah-Jane's room. Still she was not there. He walked down the corridor and woke Cobb.

'Take another look,' said Cobb. 'If you can't find her then I'll get all my people and we'll go through this town. But take another look.'

Robert stood in the middle of the street. The last sounds from the tents had gone, and the last lights. He listened. A dingo howled. A night breeze rustled the leaves of a eucalypt. And, somewhere, horses were restless. He walked towards the livery stables and then stopped and listened again. Why were the horses restless? He half ran the 200 yards, turned in through the arch of the stable yard, and stopped. One of the stables was lit. Through the open double doors he saw Lalor and his daughter. Lalor was standing looking at Susannah-Jane. She was stooping, examining something at her feet with absolute attention. Then she knelt, and smoothed something in her hands. Lalor must have made some remark, because she turned her face to him and spoke. Robert walked across the yard and showed himself.

'Mr Lalor,' he said.

Lalor turned and met Robert's eyes but said nothing. Susannah-Jane rose from her knees, brushing off her skirt. She said, 'You have discovered us.'

Robert was possessed with anger against Lalor, fear for his daughter, and anger and bewilderment that she should take part in this mystery. He had recognized, so shortly before in her room, that his daughter was a woman he did not quite know, and now she was exactly that. Most of all he was afraid for her. He turned with anger on Lalor – and then the long, black moment ended because he saw two things. Behind Lalor, in shadow, were two other figures: one was the American Maguire and the other a woman. He hardly gave her a glance. And stretched clean across the stone floor of the stable was a flag. It was on a corner of this that his daughter was kneeling.

His relief was so great that he was not discovering Lalor and Susannah-Jane alone, his sense of gratitude so great that she was safe, that he said no word at all.

His daughter said, 'We have made a flag.'

It was twelve feet wide, and had been made on the scrubbed stable floor. The fabric of the background was a brilliant blue, except for one quarter where the texture was silkier and the tint darker. It was a flag with a blue ground, on which was superimposed a white cross and five eight-pointed stars, one at the end of each arm of the cross, and the fifth at the centre.

'No flag like that in Europe,' said the American. 'Well, we'll be going.' He and his woman left. Robert nodded to them. He had been standing outside the doors. Now he entered and went over to his daughter.

'No flag so chaste and natural,' said Lalor. 'A maiden flag, never yet flown.'

Robert looked hard at him.

'It is late,' said Lalor. 'I am sorry for that. But the flag *is* chaste and natural. It is your daughter's. She told us where to put the cross and the stars, and made most of it herself. She even found. . . .'

Susannah-Jane said, 'We just made it.'

'She called it the Southern Cross,' said Lalor. 'The five stars. We shall fly it tomorrow.'

He saw the two strands of Robert's disquiet. The first was his daughter. 'Mr King,' said Lalor, 'I did want to bring your daughter back earlier, but she would not go.'

Robert nodded. He could believe that.

The second strand of disquiet was the flag.

'Mr King, you are putting yourself once again in the position of Governor in Melbourne? You are thinking how he will see this?'

'He will see it as your tricolor.'

'It is,' said Lalor.

They left the stable, Lalor locking the doors, and parted.

Robert and Susannah-Jane walked slowly back together, both with their hands clasped behind their back. He put his arm briefly round the shoulders of his beloved daughter. She met his eyes, then looked down and then quickly up.

'All right,' he said.

Then he realized what she was wearing. Round her shoulders was the old cloak of George Bryant, the one she had insisted on wearing the night of the fireworks, the bishop's cloak.

'I used the lining for the flag,' she said. 'For part of it. There was not enough blue. I used the cloak.' She opened it to show him. The silk lining was gone.

They were facing each other. He took both her hands.

They were at the hotel, and she ran inside. He watched her fly up the stairs, and then saw a figure by the door. It was Cobb, who raised a hand in greeting. Robert returned the salutation. They went in together.

All his life, certainly since that afternoon in the Bois de Boulogne when he was seventeen, Robert had been aware of the power of women. But he had never felt it so strongly as he did then, when he saw it possessed by his daughter. It was not just the evident sexual force of the girl. She had made the flag, and called it the Southern Cross.

# 37

# An Oath, and the Arraying
of Armed Men

The next day was oppressively hot. Flies, the curse of the diggings, were everywhere – in men's hair, in their nostrils, in their ears, crawling at the corners of their mouths. Major Redmond drank scalding coffee from a tin mug which almost burned the lips, and addressed his servant.

'Good hunting weather.'

'Sir?' said the trooper.

'You said they burned their licences?'

'I saw it, sir.'

'Then this morning we shall require them to show the licences they have already destroyed. But first take a note for me to Mr King. You will find him at the United States Hotel.' The note ordered Robert to desist from further assisting the miners in their rebellion, on pain of instant arrest, and to leave Ballarat, taking his mother and daughter with him.

Then Redmond briefed the senior police officer. The man was in a difficult situation. John outranked him, but his major's commission was only in the militia, and the policeman thought his authority doubtful. If Redmond had not been heir to the largest of the sheep kingdoms, the man would have questioned his authority. As it was, he did as he was told, assembled a force of fifty mounted men, and reported back to Redmond, who had just received Robert's reply. It was brief:

I have always advised the miners to act within the law. My advice to you is the same. You have no conceivable authority over my mother and daughter. They would, however, have left long ago if you had not torn up the roads.

Major Redmond screwed up the paper in his hands. He swore at the heat, the flies, and his servant, and mounted his bay. Then he led the policemen at a canter across the diggings. He was proud of his horsemanship, but a canter was a reckless pace. The ground was honeycombed with old diggings. Old tunnels ran only a few feet below the surface. The miners watched the approaching cloud of dust hoping Redmond's distinctive bay would founder beneath him, and break its rider's neck. 'Jo, Jo,' went up the warning cry from the miners to their companions – always the cry when a digger-hunt was spotted – but there was no need this time for a warning. The horse-police were so many. Their dust was visible two miles away. They arrested twenty miners who could not produce their licences. The mass of the miners were so incensed that they retaliated by throwing stones, timber, and anything that they could lay their hands on at the police, whose horses shied and reared. The police fired a volley over the miners' heads, and then a magistrate read the preamble to the Riot Act, requiring all persons assembled together to the disturbance of the Peace to disperse within one hour or be adjudged felons and imprisoned for life.

Vern, Maguire, Humfray, and Lalor took their flag to a hill and hoisted it on a pole eighty-one feet high and straight as an arrow. Work stopped on all the diggings. From all over the goldfields groups of twelve or twenty men conferred together and then walked towards the hill. By early afternoon the workings and the town were deserted. Twelve to fifteen thousand men swarmed over the hill. Troops from 12th and 40th Regiments were withdrawn into their own camp. There were at most two hundred of them, and they knew they could be overrun.

Robert and Susannah-Jane watched from the foot of the hill.
'It is my flag,' she said.
'Then listen to what is said under your flag.'

Cobb joined them and stood with his hands on his belt. He had been inspecting the state of the roads, and had found them still impassable. He shook his head.

It was Lalor who spoke. Robert thought this a mercy. It could have been Vern. He could not see Humfray at all. Maguire was by Lalor's side. Robert reflected that Humfray could very likely not have commanded a hearing. Humfray himself had thought the same, and stayed away. Of them all, Lalor was likely to be the least violent, but this time it was Lalor carrying a pistol.

'I look around me,' he said; and as he began to speak the meeting quietened. 'I look round me and see brave and honest men, who have come thousands of miles to labour for their independence. The grievances under which we have all suffered, and the attack of this morning, are in my mind and in yours. And it is not only ourselves. I know there are hundreds, hundreds upon hundreds, now in great poverty, who could possess great wealth and happiness if they were allowed to cultivate this – wilderness – which surrounds us, and which without us would remain a wilderness. We will not be stuck up and robbed for what is called a licence. Twenty of us were arrested this morning. We shall demand the release of those twenty.'

The cheers were rousing. Lalor waited.

'Gentlemen. Gentlemen.' He could now be heard again. 'I feel bound to ask you to speak your mind. Should any one of us be dragged to the lock-up – for not having a licence, or for being unable to hear a proclamation telling us we are felons unless we disperse, or for being here on this hill now – will a thousand of you volunteer to liberate the man?'

'Yes. Yes.'

'Will two thousand of you come forward?'

'Yes. Yes. Yes.'

'Will four thousand of you volunteer to march to the camp and open the lock-up to liberate the man?'

'Yes. Yes.'

'Are you ready to die?'

'Yes. Yes.'

Lalor then asked men to come forward to enrol themselves in companies, and to take the oath by the flag. Any man who did not intend to take the oath should leave straight away. Any man who stayed to take it, and then failed to stand by it, was a coward at heart. He waited. No one left.

'Listen to me with attention then. Let all divisions under arms fall in around the flagstaff.'

Five hundred diggers carrying pistols gathered round the flag. Lalor knelt, pointing his right arm to the flag and began:

'We swear . . .'

'*We swear,*' the men echoed.

'By the Southern Cross . . .'

'*By the Southern Cross . . .*'

'To stand truly by each other . . .'

'*To stand truly by each other . . .*'

'And fight to defend our rights and liberties.'

'*And fight to defend our rights and liberties.*'

A universal Amen rose from the thousands on the hill.

Robert took his daughter's hand. 'That is enough,' he said. Together with Cobb, they walked back to town. Cobb's boys told him that his two coaches and both teams of horses had been commandeered by the military.

'Thought it best not to shoot it out with half a regiment,' said one of the drivers. 'They went off Melbourne way. They don't know the horses. The horses don't know them. Way they drive, reckon it would take them a month anyways. Way the roads are, reckon they won't get two miles.'

Susannah already knew about the oath from Cobb's boys.

'I have seen two rebellions,' she told Robert. 'One over rum; this one over gold. The first lot of rebels hardly had a good intention between them. These seem full of high principles. But it doesn't make much difference to the reality of things, does it?'

'Not a bit,' said Robert. 'Not a damn bit. Not in the least.'

The diggers marched from the hill, following the flag as it was carried to the Eureka diggings. There they put up the flag again, and erected a stockade round it. The enclosed area was about an acre. By evening it was an armed camp of 1500 men, though the arms were only pistols, pikes, and a few muskets.

Robert came down from his mother's room and found Cobb and Susannah-Jane returning from the New York Bakery with bread and English muffins. She offered him one. 'Now,' he said, 'this evening you must give me your word to stay in. Above all you must not go near the stockade. But you must not go out at all. I do not know what will happen tonight. Stay with Mr Cobb if he will have you, or with your grandmother. I shall not go far. You must stay here.'

She nodded.

'No, *tell* me you agree.'

'I agree.'

He did not go far, only to the Theatre Royal. There was nothing he could do. He was helpless. He wanted diversion, and so he went to be entertained by Mr Dryden Hall-Kean's *mélange*, along with 1200 diggers who, after the day's excitement, did not return to work. It was even more of a *mélange* than was promised. First there was a curtain-raiser called *The Stage-struck Digger*, composed by Mr Hall-Kean himself. After its performance, only a mad digger would have remained stage-struck. Then there were great rhodomontades delivered by Mr Hall-Kean from the works of his illustrious precursors Dryden and Shakespeare. Shakespeare, as he once again explained, was his ancestor through the Hall side of the family, the female line. Then came Madame Ophir, lavishly introduced by the impresario himself. In Ballarat, Ophir was a name of the past, though of the recent past. Gold rushes are rapid. But Ophir, thanks to Hargraves, still had both Biblical and golden connotations.

'We present,' declaimed Hall-Kean, 'the Queen of Dance bedecked in the gold of Ophir. She shall be led unto you, gentlemen, as she was led – I refer to the Book of Proverbs – unto King Solomon, in embroidered work, her clothing inlaid with gold, and her garments strewn with myrrh and cassia. And in ivory palaces, stringed instruments shall make her glad.'

At which the impresario bowed off the forestage and the curtain rose to reveal a girl dressed head to foot in gilded tinsel, with tinsel veil and tinsel ear-rings, and banging a tinsel tambourine. The solitary stringed instrument to gladden her was a fiddle played backstage by Mr Dryden Hall-Kean. The girl was handsome but could barely dance, and the diggers pelted her with tiny nuggets. It was half derisive, half good-natured, and she pleased them by dextrously catching a few nuggets, and at the end of her act making a sweeping curtsy which enabled her to pick a few more off the stage. The curtain fell, and the rest of the nuggets were rapidly gathered up by Mr Hall-Kean for his own benefit.

It was tat revue. The great man roared and yowled his way through the last scenes of *King Lear* – a revised version with a happy ending – and then ended the *mélange* in a way which showed that, roaring hack though he was, he knew the best act in his show, and how to display it to advantage by putting it last.

'To complete your pleasure, gentlemen, we once more present Madame Ophir [groans], this time not to delight you with her dancing but to seduce the soft air with her voice – the High Priestess of the Inca Gods invoking the golden plenty of the Sun.'

Madame Ophir it was again, similarly arrayed except for the veil. This time she held no tambourine. She sang unaccompanied. She did sing in the person of a High Priestess, though not of Mexico but of Gaul. And it was not a golden Sun-god she invoked but a goddess of silver, the Moon. Considering the place was Ballarat, Mr Hall-Kean's slight transpositions were fair enough, but what she sang was 'Chaste Goddess', from *Norma*, in Italian. Few of the audience could understand a word. While she sang not a man stirred, or coughed, or made any sound, and at the end there were many seconds' silence before the audience broke into a stampede of applause. That is as great a triumph as any singer can achieve, at Ballarat or La Scala. They showered her with nuggets, made her sing again, and showered her again.

Later, Robert went backstage to her.

She said, 'Further and further from Paris? That's what you're thinking?'

'Yes,' said Robert.

'You know how long it is since I was in Paris? Paris, Florence, then it was going to be Milan, Berlin. But I ended up in Mexico City – I told you that – and then San Francisco. Where can you go from San Francisco?'

'The way the ships are sailing.'

'Right. I came here. I last sang in Paris six years ago.'

'Go back.'

She shook her head.

Robert thought she lacked the fare and said, 'You know me well enough to let me give you a passage home.'

She smiled and opened a drawer. It was full of small nuggets. There was at least 500 dollars in gold. 'Look,' she said. 'The dance – I keep the nuggets I catch. The aria – I take half of everything that's thrown. I make ends meet. Robert, I make four times as much here as I ever did anywhere before.'

'But you should have heard yourself tonight.'

'I did. Paris? I'd do, I know; but for how much longer? Oh, if you have a big name you can keep going until you sound like a moorhen, and longer. But I was never much of a name. I would have been. Perhaps. What I was, was a new young voice. There'll be other new young voices now. How many since me? I'll stay.'

He nodded.

'Build me an opera house in Sydney.'

'One day.'

Outside the open door the impresario passed for the third time, obviously wondering who the visitor was.

'Him?' asked Robert.

'My God, no. There's an American. Dryden and I just happened to come from California. But not together. I never even saw him there. We met here.'

'Ah.'

'Robert, you have a memorable daughter.'

'What?'

'You know, you really were surprised to see me this evening.'

'Astonished. But what do you mean about my daughter?'

'You saw me last night, in the stables. Or rather, you were so engrossed you never even looked at me.'

'You were with Maguire?'

'My American,' she said.

'You helped make that flag?'

'I watched. Your daughter did it. When you came in, you were afraid for her, weren't you? You needn't have been. Lalor has great charm, but she has much more than that. She is utterly memorable. I'm glad she's your daughter. I remember you.'

'Yvette, you know where Maguire is tonight?'

'Yes. I pray for him.'


At the Eureka stockade, Lalor drilled his men by the light of flares. Sixty Americans calling themselves the Independent California Rangers rode by and asked, 'What's up?' They had Colt revolvers and knives. They listened to Maguire, and then bivouacked in the stockade. A hundred British infantrymen marched into Ballarat late, to reinforce the garrison. The California Rangers laughed at their uniforms. 'Greenhorns in red padding,' they said. Lalor let it be known that he had appointed a 'Minister for War'. The Major in charge of the new detachment roused the printer at the *Ballarat Times* near midnight and ordered him to print, immediately, 500 posters proscribing all those who had rebelliously and traitorously levied and arrayed armed men in the Eureka stockade, with a view of making armed war against their Sovereign Lady the Queen.

# 38

# The Eureka Stockade

The stockade at the Eureka was not a fort. It was made of
timber slabs whose normal use was to shore up the diggings,
boulders, upturned carts, and sharpened staves driven into the
ground. 'Great works!' exclaimed an Italian, Carboni Raffaello,
surveying the corral as if it were a feat of fortification and
engineering. He was constantly taunting Vern. 'Where are your
five hundred Hanoverian marksmen?' There were none. Vern
ignored him and went round encouraging the others by
promising to lead them to victory or death. He particularly
addressed the Americans, who in turn ignored him. They sat
silently oiling their Colts, spinning the chambers, cleaning the
barrels. A blacksmith from Mexico worked all through the
day forging pikes which he sold at ten dollars apiece. Raffaello
denounced the pikes as poor, rough things, but they were
bought by the Irish, who resolutely drilled with them.

'Shoulder pikes. Order pikes. Ground pikes.'

A broad Irishman, once a sergeant major in a British regiment, instructed his men in a combination of remembered
ceremonial drill sequences, and in a technique of defence
hardly used since Agincourt.

'Pre-*pare* to receive cavalry.' The men formed up two deep,
the first row kneeling, the second standing.

'Ad-*vance* pikes.' The men smartly raised their pikes, making
a wall of pointed metal rods on which jumping horses would
impale themselves.

'Poke your pike into the guts of the horse,' said the sergeant
major. 'Poke it in, and draw it out by the tail. Now, pre-*pare*

to receive cavalry.' He drilled them for two hours in the sweating sun.

'Good boys,' he said. They were all Irish. Only thirty had iron pikes. Twenty others went through the motions with wooden staves. There were no Hanoverian marksmen, but there was a Hanoverian band. Five men played the *Marseillaise* on trumpet and drums. The Americans observed everything. They watched the pike drill with a feeling that was part admiration and part amazement. Some of the Americans did not even recognize the *Marseillaise*. Raffaello told them. He was every-where, addressing revolutionary lectures to anyone, in Italian, English, French, and very bad German. Vern at length seized a half-wrought pike from the Mexican's forge, with the end still glowing red, and hurled it at the Italian. He missed. Lalor quelled Vern, and took Raffaello by the shoulder and walked with him, talking quietly. The Italian revered Lalor, and quietened down. A messenger rode in, reporting large bodies of redcoats coming up from Melbourne. The Americans talked about ambushing them. At six o'clock, a patrol of cavalry militia, a dozen strong, reined in 200 yards from the camp, on a slight hill where they could overlook the drilling. An officer dismounted, took a pair of field glasses, and swept them over the stockade and up at the flag.

'None other than Major Redmond,' said the Italian, 'with his gold lace cap, and red frock coat, and jingling sword, such a precise Puss-in-Boots.'

The long hours of Saturday afternoon and evening dragged themselves out. It was still very hot, a stinker of a day.

At the army camp the men of the 12th and 40th Regiments were confident for the first time in days that they were not about to be attacked and overwhelmed by armed diggers. They were much encouraged by the arrival the previous midnight of the reinforcements from Melbourne, and by the young Major Hannay, who commanded them. He had immediately posted double pickets but ordered the rest of the men to stand down and rest. He assembled his officers and asked who was the senior. They told him Major Redmond was asleep in his own quarters.

'Ask him to be so good as to attend on me now.'

He was told that Redmond, though only a major of militia, was heir to an empire of sheep.

'Good,' said the young man. 'I have some livestock of my own back in Shropshire. We shall have an interest in common.'

He was just the kind of commandant the colonial officers would ordinarily have suspected and disliked. He was English, he had been seconded to Victoria from a fashionable English light cavalry regiment in which he still held his commission and to which he would return, and he did not give a damn for Redmond. But as things stood, his officers were pleased to have him.

Redmond, summoned in the middle of the night by a much younger officer who did not even rise to greet him, was not pleased. He was told that the military command was no longer his. He would continue to command his own troop, but was relieved of the garrison.

'Now,' said Hannay, 'I do not know the terrain. I have been told that you are intimately connected with the goldfields, Major Redmond. Instruct me.'

He listened to what Redmond grudgingly told him, sent out his own patrols in the morning, and then in the afternoon told his officers, 'It looks like the Irish and the Americans.'

Redmond wanted to attack. He proposed a cavalry charge straight away.

Hannay said, 'I should not care to order a charge by tired horses, ridden by tired men, in the heat of the day. If it can be avoided, I shall not care to charge at all. I shall prefer to pray for rain. If it rains they will go away. That would be best for us all. I have no wish to risk my men, or to make martyrs out of diggers. If it does come to a fight I have no wish to command a massacre. I shall use the infantry, with cavalry in reserve. We will disperse the diggers if we can, or take them prisoner if we can. If they fire on us, we shall return fire. If they drop their arms and run, we shall let them run. There are no field-marshals' batons to be gained from such a little rout as this. We shall do it as quietly as we can. So, wait. And, gentlemen, pray for rain.'

It was Susannah in the end who convinced Robert that he
ought to go back to the stockade to make a last approach to
Lalor. Since the oath-taking there had been nothing he could
do. He had come away from a meeting of 15,000 men. If 15,000
diggers were intent on armed rebellion there was nothing to be
done. On the Saturday evening he sat talking late with his
mother and Cobb. The United States Hotel was bustling. So
were the Eagle, the Excelsior, the Byron, and the Liverpool.
The main street was packed with happily drunk diggers. The
next day was Sunday. Sunday was kept, according to the way
it was looked at, either as the Sabbath or as a holiday. There
was at any rate no work. But that Saturday men had been
working their claims as usual. And in the evening the street was
full. It was still full at midnight. The waiter said it was as full as
any Saturday night. Outside, beyond the town, there were still
lights in a thousand tents.

Susannah said, 'So how many men are still in the stockade?'

'This afternoon,' said Cobb, 'maybe fifteen hundred. Maybe
not.'

One of his boys said, 'Maybe not. A half hour ago, I was
down by the Free Trade bar, and Maguire and oh, maybe fifty
riders passed by. I saw Maguire and I called out to him, and
he said they were out to ambush some more redcoats coming
up from Melbourne. "At night?" I says. "They did last night,"
he says back, and then he says he surely hopes the stockade can
hold out till they get back. Now, you can say it was a joke the
way he said it; but maybe, maybe not. I wouldn't bet on any
fifteen hundred sitting there.'

Susannah said, 'There were fifteen thousand on the hill,
listening to speeches in the sun. Tonight, there may be only a
thousand in that stockade, and how many of those would come
away if they were given the occasion?'

'I shall go and see,' said Robert.

'Good,' she said.

'You'll need the password,' said Cobb's man. '*Vinegar Hill.*'

'*Vinegar Hill,*' said Robert. 'How did you come by that?'

'Just heard talk of it.'

It was a bright starlit night. A hundred yards from the stockade Robert was challenged.

'Vinegar Hill.'

At the compound he was challenged again. He went it. He
did not look for Lalor straight away. Another man had slipped
in with him at the same time. Robert said, 'Good night.'

'Good night, friend,' said the man exultantly. 'The excitement is of Satan.'

He disappeared towards one of the three fires still blazing.
Robert made for another fire, round which a dozen Irishmen,
three Scots, and an American were standing.

'Nobblers all round?' said a Scot. A tot of brandy was pushed
into Robert's hand. He knocked it back with the rest, and
looked around. The pikemen lay near the perimeter of the stockade, each one nursing his pike. Four hobbled horses scuffed
round a fragment of hay. The stockade itself was more insubstantial than he had thought. A horse could easily jump it,
or a man vault it. Behind the stockade, against the sky, rose the
mass of Mount Warrenheip. The army camp, which lay in the
other direction, was not visible, but the stockade and the men in
it could be seen by any spy who stood on the rising ground a
few hundred yards off. Robert was lost in a survey of the terrain
when he was startled by a clashing and hammering close by.
What he had taken to be a third bonfire was the Mexican's
forge, and he was still shaping pikes. Robert saw the metal glow
white and then red, saw the red sparks fly as the hammer beat
the iron against the anvil, and saw the steam rise in the light of
the flames as the man doused the sharpened point in a trough.
The sparks and clatter scared one of the hobbled horses, which
neighed. Its call was answered from somewhere in the dark,
outside the stockade.

Robert asked for Lalor. The man indicated the group round
the other fire. Lalor was not there, but a group of Irishmen were
lying back listening to a story intensely told by the man who
had come in with Robert. It was a tale the Irish liked, as
fantastic as a story of Brien Boru, ancient King of the Irish, as
exotic but more recent. The little man was talking in English
and translated bits of Italian about his defence of Rome a few
years before, with Garibaldi, against the might of the French.
And when the battle was won in Ballarat, he said, and in all

Australia, and the tyrants had all fallen, then he would be back
to his native country to overthrow the oppressors in all the states
of Italy.

'You have a fine command of the English,' said one of his
listeners, 'being an Italian as you are.'

The man said he had lived in London after being driven by
the French from Rome. But he and Garibaldi would enter
Rome again. They would conquer all Italy, starting from the
very toe, from Sicily, from Palermo. They would stop in
Palermo only long enough to construct in honour of freedom
an opera house grander than Paris, and then they would fight
their way up through all Italy. 'And I shall write a grand opera
of the Revolution for Palermo; and a pantomime; and historical
dramas; and comedies and ballets.' He saw in his mind the
opera house they would build at Palermo when he and Garibaldi entered. 'Great works!' he exclaimed. 'The greatest opera
house in Europe or the world.'

'That is a fine thing,' said an Irishman. 'And I wish you well.
We have a fine theatre at Waterford too; and your grand
comedies, if they were translated, could be performed there to
the applause of thousands, when the English are gone.'

Then the Italian overstepped himself. He began composing,
to the accompaniment of much hilarity, a satirical letter to Her
Most Excellent Majesty Queen Victoria, London, inviting her
to the diggers' celebration dinner six months hence in Melbourne, when the Diggers' Parliament was inaugurated. He
went too far when he proposed to extend the invitation also to
His Holiness Pius the Ninth, Pontifex Maximus, Rome. The
Catholic Irish diggers would not mock the Pope. The Italian
had already launched into a mock blessing of them all in
Latin – for had he not once spent a year in a seminary intending
to be a priest before he saw the light? – when he found that his
audience was now silent and offended.

Robert found Lalor alone at the edge of the stockade, gazing
at the sky above Mount Warrenheip. He came up on him
unawares.

'They will not attack from that direction,' said Robert.

'Mr King,' said Lalor, 'I did not expect you. But shall we be
attacked?'

'How many men have you here?'

'How did you get in, Mr King?'

'Your password is known in town.'

'And I daresay in the barracks as well?' asked Lalor.

'I daresay.'

Lalor said, 'As for men, see for yourself.'

There could not have been more than four hundred.

'The Americans were seen to go,' said Robert.

'Off star-lighting,' said Lalor, 'intercepting reinforcements from Melbourne. They call it star-lighting. Now tell me why you have come. With an offer from the commanding officer?'

Robert did not answer him.

'I beg your pardon, Mr King, that was foolish of me.'

'Where is Humfray?'

'He never came in here with us, and has been persuading others not to join us.'

'You and he, and Maguire, all seemed to have heads on your shoulders; when we first met.'

'Maguire would be here too. He is out with the Americans.'

'Mr Lalor, why did you speak as you did on the hill? Why the oath?'

Lalor stared at the sky, but did not answer.

'Mr Lalor. If Vern had said what you said, I could understand. I was glad when you spoke and not Vern. But you asked four thousand men if they were willing to die. I do not know why you selected that figure, but you said four thousand. And they took the oath. Well, Mr Lalor, there are not four hundred left here to die with.'

Lalor said, 'I would not say now what I said on the hill. That does not mean we shall not fight. We shall fight. I would not say it now, but I have an hereditary disability which is apt to show itself sometimes. My name in Irish is O'Labhaimir, which I am afraid means "descended from a man who is a great speaker".'

'Mr King,' Lalor continued after a pause, 'do you have a brother?'

'A half brother.'

'I had a brother. Mr King, I am from Queen's County, Ireland. My father was what the English call a gentleman farmer. He was in the Westminster Parliament as member for

the county. That was only ten years ago. He is dead. Now, I
went to Dublin – Trinity College. I was telling your daughter
about Dublin. A city not in England, but the loveliest English
city of them all. My elder brother would have been angry to
hear me say that. He was oppressed in spirit by the English,
and brooded over the English, and did not wish our father to
sit in the English Parliament. My brother brooded over plans
for Irish freedom. I could meet the English and drink with
them. He could not in any way. He said the land was for the
Irish. He wrote that Irish tenants should not pay rent to
English owners of Irish land. I could follow his grievance, but
did not feel it. He wrote again and again, for the newspapers.
Then a friend of his, who had done no more than write just
such articles, was transported. I think he will still be serving out
his days in Tasmania. The newspapers my brother wrote for
were suppressed. When the last was suppressed, he founded
another. It was called the *Irish Felon*. After five numbers, that
too was suppressed and he was arrested. He was imprisoned.
He was a persuasive man. A man of original and vigorous mind.
After nine months he was so broken by the jail that the English
released him, not wanting him to die in jail. He died afterwards,
out of jail. Now, I was the one who could always talk with the
English, and drink with the English, but when it came to it,
I said what I said two days ago on the hill. And now I suppose
I too am an Irish felon.'

While he listened, Robert had been looking up at the flag,
looking anywhere so as not to see Lalor's features as he spoke
about his brother. Against all usage, the flag had been left to
fly all night. A flag by day can be an inspiriting sight; at night,
when its colour and features cannot be seen, it can hang like a
damp sheet.

It was half past two in the early hours in the morning.

Robert kept silence for a long time. 'Well then,' he said. 'I
see. You have told me about your brother, and about Queen's
County, and Dublin – Ireland. Now, forgive me, I have also
heard Vern speak about Hanover – and what he hopes will be
one Germany. He speaks differently, violently, and senselessly,
but the point is that he is thinking of Hanover, and of what he
did not achieve in Hanover. An hour ago, here, before I found
you, I heard a man speaking in English and Italian, with Latin

thrown in as well, about a triumphal march through an Italy
of the future. Starting at Palermo.'

'He is Italian,' said Lalor. 'In Italy his name was Raffaello
Carboni. When he came here he said he would change it round
to Carboni Raffaello, to fit the southern hemisphere.'

'Lalor,' said Robert, 'this is not Ireland, or Hanover, or a
notional Italy which may exist one day. Men are here in this
stockade for far-flung, different reasons which have nothing to
do with Ballarat. And look around. Count. Tell me how many
are left now.'

The fires had died down. The groups of men were sparser.
While Robert and Lalor had been speaking, men had melted
into the night. Raffaello had gone, though only to his tent a few
hundred yards outside. The rest had considered, had second
thoughts, and left.

'How many?' said Robert.

'Two hundred?'

'Lalor, listen. You may be an Irish felon, but you are not an
Australian felon yet.'

'My dear King, what does that mean?'

'I want to speak to these men.'

'Do.'

'You must tell them who I am and why you asked me to come
here in the first place.'

It was done.

The men gathered round the last of the fires. Most of those
who remained were Irish.

'Gentlemen, there's precious little legal advice left for me to
give. I can give you a couple of pieces of information, and then
an opinion or two. The rest is up to you. Now, the new commander of the troops has stuck up posters proscribing those
who have traitorously and rebelliously levied and arrayed
armed men with a view to make armed war against the Queen.
That is you. That on the face of it is what you have done. He
will have got that proclamation out of his manual of military
law. It's a matter of form. But the form is more ancient than
the reality. Those words date back to the year dot. He can no
longer declare the lot of you outlaws and say there's an end to
it. I have been talking to Mr Lalor. He said a few minutes ago
that he supposed he was an Irish felon. I don't know whether

he is or not. But he certainly isn't an Australian felon until he's been tried and found guilty of felony in Australia. It can't be done by a magistrate. And the commander here has not declared martial law. Either he's forgotten, or he's had the good sense not to, or he hasn't got enough officers to make up a court-martial. So if there are trials, they will have to be trials by jury. That's all the *legal* advice I have. Now, opinions. If the new major were to send a patrol tomorrow and find nobody here, he'd write a report to Melbourne saying how successful he had been in preserving the Peace. I doubt if he would pursue anyone. But suppose some men *were* later found and charged, how easily do you think a jury could be empanelled in Ballarat, or Melbourne, to find anyone guilty of treason – which, since he's put up that poster, is about the only charge left open to him? My opinion, gentlemen, is that if you left, no jury would convict any digger of treason.'

And that was all he would have said, praying that it was enough, except that Vern said, 'So you are telling us to run? That is your coward's advice?'

'I am telling you what I think will happen if you leave. And I am advising you to leave. Yes, I am.'

'You talk of traitors,' said Vern, 'but you are the only traitor here. We' – here he indicated those around him with a sweep of his arm – 'we shall not be traitors to our own destiny. Our destiny is in our hands.'

Robert said, 'Lalor, tell them to go, for God's sake.'

Lalor hesitated. And then something of the same quality of change that came over Lalor on the hill came over Robert. His coolness left him.

'Destiny? Look at yourselves. How many are you? There were fifteen thousand on the hill taking the oath, but how many was that compared to the one hundred thousand on the diggings? There were once fifteen hundred in the stockade, but how many was that compared with the fifteen thousand on the hill? And how many are left now? Two hundred? I doubt two hundred. For God's sake, go. If you stay here you will sooner or later be attacked. Vern says you can decide your own destiny, and so you can. So you can. Stay here and you will decide your own destiny: you will decide your own deaths.'

And with that he would have left – and how many would

have gone with him? – but it was ten minutes past three in the morning, and at that moment the first digger sentinel fired the first shot as he saw in the light of the coming dawn the storming parties of the 12th and 40th of Foot with their bayonets, the dim forms of the mounted 40th standing back in parade order on the right, the foot police and horse-police with their carbines in the centre, and the cavalry militia with sabres drawn on the left. Hannay knew the Americans had gone to intercept reinforcements. He knew he could take the stockade easily in their absence. He decided to do so in the minutes before dawn. He did not expect to use cavalry. He had ordered the captain of the 40th to invite surrender, but the digger sentinel fired first.

In the stockade the Irish pikemen formed their two rows. They prepared to receive cavalry, the front row kneeling, the second row standing. They advanced pikes. There were fifty pikemen in all. They had stayed in the stockade to a man. The infantry came on at a march in drill formation. Two diggers had borrowed rifles from the Americans. They picked off the officers who marched in front of their men, presenting ceremonial targets, easily distinguished because their men had bayonets and the officers alone carried swords. The captain of the 40th fell, and the lieutenant leading the 12th. Their sergeants took command. One hundred and sixty infantrymen knelt, fired a volley into the stockade, and then advanced at the charge. At the first volley, Lalor was badly hit in the shoulder. Vern ran. The pikemen stood their ground, prepared to receive cavalry. Only it was not cavalry that overcame them, but the bayonets of the 12th. The pikemen suffered most. They stood firm and were cut to pieces – a few cuts, kicks, and pullings-down, and all was over with them.

It was really finished by the time the cavalry came, Redmond's militia from the left of the stockade. Major Hannay, holding his own cavalry back on the right, swore as he saw the militia let loose at full gallop and leap the stockade. Two riders were injured, but that was because they fell. It was not the work of the pikemen, who were all lying dead or injured. The diggers fought while they could fight, and then they ran. They were helpless now. The few with muskets had no powder or shot. The two riflemen were bayoneted. They had fought. Now, anyone able to run, ran. The cavalry militia pursued and ran

down an already defeated force of men. The sabre wounds
were nearly all across the back of the shoulders, neck, or head.
Robert dragged Lalor to a heap of timber slabs, and, with the
help of an American, hid him there. Lalor was bleeding badly
from the shoulder. The American screamed a warning, and
Robert turned to see him fall to a thrust from a militia officer,
who wheeled his horse and came back. Robert recognized the
bay, and then its rider. It was John. Robert crouched, struggling
to rise, but the bay ran him down. John wheeled again and
then, as if he were at field exercise, trotted up to Robert, leaned
to the left out of his saddle, and cut at him casually with a
backhand sweep of the sabre.

Robert fell. Major Hannay, who had just come up with his
sergeant, saw the slash at the wounded man and shouted with
anger at Redmond, whom he saw caracolling his bay, turning
her on her hind feet, to attack again.

Hannay drew his pistol. 'Damn you, man, for a butcher.
Damn you and your elegant horsemanship, and damn your
bloody men. Call them off or I will shoot them.' It took longer
to bring the militia to order than to defeat the defenders of the
stockade.

At ten past three there had been not 200 but rather fewer than
150 diggers in the Eureka. Ten minutes later 22 were dead and
three times that many wounded. The attackers numbered 274
in all, including the regular cavalry who never took part in the
action. Besides the two infantry officers picked off by the
snipers in the first minutes of the attack, three other soldiers died.

A police trooper hauled down the Southern Cross, and
Redmond's militiamen, having at length been rounded up and
brought back to the stockade, tossed it from sabre to sabre,
hacking at it, until Hannay's sergeant took it from them and
threw it over Robert and the American, who had fallen close
together. It was just full light. Hannay's charger cast a long
shadow as he stood still, watching his men collect the dead. He
found that he was still holding his pistol, and put it away.
Redmond walked his bay up to the bodies covered by the
tatters of the flag. As he looked down at the dead American,
and at Robert, he felt the contemptuous eyes of Hannay on
him. John had hated Robert, but had not wished to be seen to
kill a brother.

# 39

# In Which Susannah Awaits
# Her Lover

Susannah-Jane faced Cobb on the boardwalk outside the hotel. It was twenty minutes after the last shot had died away. Cobb had found a light cart, and one of his men was holding the horse's head.

'I will *not* go back,' she said.

'Where is your grandmother?'

At that moment he saw Susannah at the top of the hotel stairs and went in to help her, but she walked steadily down herself. None of them had slept since Robert left. They expected him back at one o'clock, then at two. At three they decided he would stay the night and not return till morning. Ten minutes later they heard the first shots. Cobb ran to find any cart. Susannah walked slowly to her room, stripped the sheets off her bed and Susannah-Jane's, for bandages, and came downstairs.

Cobb again told the girl, 'Go back,' and again she fiercely refused.

'Miss King,' he said, 'go back of your own accord, or one of my men will hold you back. I will not take you.'

She turned to Susannah. 'My father is out there.'

Susannah answered her gently. 'Yes. But go back.'

The girl defiantly obeyed her, so defiantly that Cobb asked Susannah, 'Do I need to leave a man with her?'

'No,' said Susannah.

They overtook hundreds of diggers on the way to the Eureka. It was hard going. The light wheels of the cart jarred against boulders. When they came in sight of the Eureka they found it was guarded by a double line of police with carbines. They had to get down and walk the last 300 yards. They met a file of prisoners being led away by soldiers of the 40th. They were the remains of the Irish, and the Italian. Those men who still had hats, took them off to Susannah. She looked at them, and no man met her eyes. She faltered. Cobb put his arm round her shoulders, and they went on. A police sergeant let them pass. Six military carts were heaped with dead. They lay with their faces upwards, looking like lead. Cobb and Susannah went from the first to the second carts. Neither had ever seen a battlefield. Some men lay apparently untouched, but lifeless. The sabre wounds were the most terrible. A sabre can remove half a man's face. On the third cart one man was still breathing. At every breath blood bubbled from a wound in the throat, and trickled on to the floor of the cart. Cobb called out to a sergeant of the 40th, who glanced at the man and called two orderlies. He also took the sheets from Susannah. There were three more carts of the dead to see, and then the wounded, propped against the slabs of the stockade, some lying still, some moaning and turning, one screaming without stop. Susannah looked over at the man and then at the sergeant, who understood her and said, 'There is only one surgeon we have. But believe me, ma'am, if a man screams he has life in him. I have seen it.'

Then he recognized her, and took Cobb aside. Susannah still looked towards the screaming man.

Cobb went back and stood before her.

'You have found him?' she said.

He took her arm and led her over to a heap of rags, which was the Southern Cross. The sergeant came with them. 'I am deeply sorry,' he said. He rolled back the flag from the two faces – the American, and Robert King.

Susannah gazed at the face of her son, disfigured with the dark slash of a sabre. Then she looked at the other face, lying so close that the hair of the two dead men mingled.

'Who was he?'

'An American,' said the sergeant. 'We showed him to the prisoners but no one knew his name.' He looked over at Cobb, who shook his head. He did not recognize the man either. The flag where the sergeant held it was very bloody. He shifted his grip to a part of the fabric that was not sodden and coagulated.

Susannah suddenly knelt, and the sergeant sprang to her and took her shoulders in both hands. 'No . . .,' he said. He almost cried the word. But Susannah knelt erect, only putting one hand to her son's forehead. The sergeant held her in a firm hold, as if she were his own mother. He wished to spare her what she could be spared of the ordeal. She rose without tears and looked up at the bare flagpole.

Cobb jerked his head to summon his men, who had stayed with the cart. 'We will take both,' he told the sergeant.

'Take the lady first,' said the sergeant. His eyes said, 'Do not ask me why.'

Cobb took Susannah back to the cart himself, leaving his two boys with the bodies and saying he would send the cart back. The sergeant had seen so much blood – not at Ballarat but in miserable African campaigns – that it had made him tender. Only a man already a brute is made more brutal by familiarity with the scenes of violent death. It gentles others. The sergeant had pulled the flag back carefully, and cried out, 'No,' when Susannah knelt, and then held her, because he would not let her see too much. She had to see her son's face. The sergeant could not disguise a sabre wound, which was terrible enough, but he did not uncover the face far enough to show that the chin was mostly gone, or that the chest was caved in by the trampling of the bay.

Susannah-Jane, watching them return, did not need to be told that her father was dead. Her grandmother sat in the lobby of the hotel, not caring who saw her. Her dress was bloody at the shoulders where the sergeant's hands had held her. She would not change the dress for two hours. Susannah-Jane half sat and half knelt by her, holding her hands and speaking quietly to her, asking her to go and rest, asking her to. . . .

'To do what?' said Susannah. 'What should I do?'

'Your shoulders.'

Susannah looked at her dress and saw the blood for the first time. 'It does not matter,' she said.

'It's all right, then. It's all right.'

But then Susannah did allow her grand-daughter to take her to her room.

Cobb had stood by them the whole time. When Susannah-Jane came down again, he said, 'You were brave.'

The girl would let no one see her tears. She asked to see her father. By then Cobb's men had brought the two bodies into town, laid them out as best they could in a stable, and covered them with a blanket. At the Eureka, the troopers had taken the remains of the flag. Cobb took her to the stable and did for Susannah-Jane what the sergeant had done for Susannah in the morning, carefully uncovering her father's face, concealing from her what he would by no means allow her to see. She too asked who the other man was. Cobb had discovered a letter in the man's pocket. It was a letter home, saying he had panned forty-four ounces of gold in three days, that he was in good health, and that he hoped the crops in Fayetteville County were good and fair. He had not finished the letter, so he had not signed it. There was no address, so not even his family name was known. Cobb said there was a Fayetteville in Virginia, and that it was likely to be very poor.

Susannah-Jane looked at the face of the young man from Fayetteville, and then she went back to her father, standing for a long minute at the foot of the trestle on which he lay. Cobb waited at the door. She bowed her head so that her hair hid her face, and Cobb could not see her features. Then she looked up and round. It was the stable where her father had come to fetch her at midnight only three days before, and had found her kneeling on the floor by the flag she had made.

It was December, nearly mid summer. The burials had to be rapidly done. The coffins were made of wooden slabs salvaged from the stockade. The coffin lids were of rough-hewn eucalypt. The dead Irishmen were supposed to be Catholic. Not all of them were, so the Roman Church took back a few souls that day from the Established Church of Ireland, which was Anglican and Protestant. Robert King, together with the American, a Canadian, and two Germans, was buried according to the English rites. Susannah heard the terrible and beautiful words, which had no comfort for her. She felt the sting of death, and plainly saw the victory of the clay grave. Her hope of the Resurrection was neither sure nor certain. And when it came to that part of the service which recites that the past is no more than faded grass, she denied this with all her instinct and soul and heart. In that triumphant denial she came away, supporting Susannah-Jane, whose courage had at last given way when

she heard for the first time the words spoken at the burial of the
dead, and the clods of earth striking the coffin.

No one told Susannah – they all thought to be kind so no
one told her – that her first son had been killed by her second,
or in what way, but she came to know, because it was common
talk and not be kept from her.

Then she cursed John. If she could have spoken a formal
commination it would have lessened her anguish, but she had
no easy anathema to pronounce. When she knew, she said, with
soft intensity, 'Oh may he live in Hell. Oh may he live in Hell.'
And that was all. But then she wept bitterly, and her spirit
broke.

Cobb would have killed the man. Many men in Ballarat
would have killed him, but he was gone. Susannah-Jane would
have killed him. Cobb held her hard by the wrists until her fury
exhausted itself and she sat with her head between her knees.
When she lifted her head again, he said, 'Go to your grandmother.' She did, mourning her father, but most of all com-
forting Susannah in both their griefs.


They took Susannah home to Sydney. The news had preceded
them. Governor Fitzroy had taken Elizabeth to the Residence,
not caring for her to stay alone in Robert's house, and it was to
Government House that he ordered Susannah to be brought
too. She was put in the old sandalwood bed in which she had not
slept since it was hers as a girl. She had slept there alone, and
with Baudin. When she married she left it with the Governor's
furniture: she had never shared it with her husband. Susannah
remembered nothing of the journey from Ballarat to Melbourne
or the passage from there to Sydney. Only as the ship entered
the harbour, and rolled in the swell between the north and
south heads, did she look up at the rocky outcrops on the right,
then at the wooded slopes of Vaucluse on the left, and then, as
they entered the cove, up at the Domain.

Already the legend of Ballarat had begun to grow. It was as
she had once told Wyndham when she was speaking about the
myths of her own life – legends are the spiritual side of events.
The spirit of Ballarat grew, as it had been destined to grow.

The charge of the militia cavalry into the Eureka stockade was five weeks almost to the day after the charge of the Light Brigade at Balaclava, and the first event became as memorable a legend as the second. The diggers had demanded a great deal of the Cosmos, and got it. The *New York Times*, reporting the skirmish, called it the Battle of the Southern Cross. The legend became no skirmish, but a revolution. Even the very young legend dominated events. Lalor, hidden by Robert King and the unknown American from Fayetteville County, escaped detection that night and recovered. When he was found, and became one of thirteen diggers to be tried for high treason, no jury would convict them. Licences were done away with and the diggers enfranchised. Cobb and his boys became the Wells Fargo of Australia. Carboni Raffaello, becoming again Raffaello Carboni, did march with Garibaldi, five years later, through the length of Italy, and they did land at Palermo, where they built a stupendous opera house. Carboni wrote his grand operas, ballets, dramas, and pantomimes, but they were never performed. In Australia, Lalor became Speaker of the State parliament. Yvette Rivière, once of the Paris Opera, lived to coach the young Nellie Melba.

But Susannah knew nothing of even the first beginnings of the legend. The two months after she learned that her second son had killed her first, Baudin's child, were a chaos of near-madness. When she saw Elizabeth, she recognized her and comforted her as she would have comforted anyone in distress for the loss of a husband. By instinct she comforted a bereaved woman, but her reason did not see that they shared the same loss. She did not identify Elizabeth's lost husband with her lost son. They were not in her mind the same man. A letter came from William Redmond. When she was told of this, she did not recognize her husband's name. Elizabeth opened and read the letter herself. It was written in the sharp, illegible scrawl of old age, and expressed sympathy, deep regret, and deeper shame. Elizabeth knew there was no point in reading it to Susannah. She replied to Redmond herself, explaining. Redmond had disowned and disinherited his son. John Redmond appeared once in Sydney and was received everywhere with contempt. No house or hotel was open to him. No one would give or sell him food or drink. No one would stable his horse. He left – it was said for California. No one knew. Old Redmond lived on in his palace. The Redmonds were long-lived.

Susannah was never left on her own. Elizabeth and Susannah-Jane took turns to be with her. She and Elizabeth had been close, but it was to Susannah-Jane that she talked now.

'Bring me my pictures,' she said.

The girl went to Susannah's house and fetched the sketch of Susannah by Wyndham and the framed engraving of Baudin. Susannah smiled at the sketch, looking into the eyes of the woman she had been, and gave the drawing to Susannah-Jane.

'This is for you.'

Susannah-Jane took it. It was familiar to her. She had known it since she was a child. For the first time she saw that it could be a sketch of herself.

A letter came one day from Bengal. Elizabeth recognized the handwriting of the address. As long as she could remember, Susannah had received letters addressed in that hand, once or twice a year, most from England but others from all parts of the world. Elizabeth had never known Wyndham and so did not know the handwriting was his. She saw by now that Susannah spoke to her young grand-daughter more freely than to her. She did not know why, or whether there was any knowing why. Perhaps it was because the girl had been with her at Ballarat. She asked her daughter to give the letter to Susannah.

Susannah did not open it. She said to Susannah-Jane, 'Bring me the two boxes.'

The girl brought her two rosewood boxes, inlaid with ivory, and the two tiny brass keys.

'You knew where to find the keys?' said Susannah.

The girl admitted it. She remembered from the time she was a very young child the drawer of the writing desk where the keys were kept.

Susannah opened one box and took from it more than thirty years of letters in Wyndham's hand. They were first the letters of a lover, and then the serene letters of an old friend. She replaced them, together with the new letter, which she did not open. She locked the box, put it to one side, and never once looked at it again. She put the second box by her bed.

Susannah-Jane knew what she was witnessing. She had known

for a week now what no one else knew – and she had told no one else, not even her mother. Susannah no longer remembered Robert's death. His death had broken her, but she had forgotten it. Ballarat, and all recent events, were forgotten. Susannah was living in herself. It was not that she had forgotten Robert. But she remembered him only as a boy, as a child. She had forgotten his death, but still remembered his birth. She talked about his birth. She told Susannah-Jane about the naming of Australia.

'He said, "I will call you Australia." And the next day, at dinner, I asked if it would not do very well for a name for the whole continent. And Sir Harry said he would willingly abduct a continent of that name.'

She often talked like this. Susannah-Jane sat and listened, and came to understand very well. The recent past no longer existed in her grandmother's mind. And now, by laying aside the letters, and by giving her the sketch done by Wyndham, she was also putting away any flickers of memory from her middle years and earlier. Now, only the events of Susannah's earliest womanhood were alive to her.

One day a high wind rose from the south. In the gardens, not fifty yards from Susannah's window, a clump of giant bamboo strained, creaked, clattered, and sang as bamboo does in a high wind, like the spars and rigging of a hard-driven ship. The wind fell as suddenly as it came. But it had stirred Susannah. From the second box her grand-daughter had fetched for her, she took Baudin's last, sea-stained journal in which, a week out from Batavia, he had written his last words to her.

She gave Susannah-Jane the box, the key, and the journal. 'That is for you to read and keep,' she said.

Susannah-Jane took the box to the edge of the Domain lawns and sat down, folding her skirts around her. She took out the journal and read:

Heavy seas all night, pitching, labouring, spraying all over. . . . Morning and the sea is fair. Susannah, you were the greatest gift that was ever made to me. . . . May you be cherished in your heart, and in your mind, and in your bed. . . . I believe we are at latitude 7 degrees 30 minutes S., and longitude 95 degrees 41 minutes E., but I do not know where I am.

Then she sat for a long time, surrounded by the scent of the frangipannis, with her head on her knees. Her grandmother had given her the Indian Ocean in the year 1803. Susannah had put from her mind the dying Baudin, and kept for herself only the living Nicolas, whose portrait still stood by her bed.

That night, when Susannah-Jane went to see her grand-mother, she found that she had left the sandalwood bed and was at the window.

'What is it? What is it? 'the girl asked.

Susannah was searching for the Southern Cross. 'My father had a gardener,' she said, 'who used to say it was the evening star and the seven stars all intermixed, as he never saw in his life in any part of the world before.'

'It is too early in the year,' said Susannah-Jane. 'It is February. It is in the south-east, too far round to see from the window.'

'I cannot see it.'

'Not in that part of the sky, not now.'

'No,' said Susannah. 'It was an October evening that he came.'

On the last night, Susannah-Jane found her again at the window, looking not at the sky but over the lawns and the acacias and the tall, grown cedars of the Domain, down into the cove at the lights of the ships riding easily. She said she was waiting for a ship.

'What ship?' asked Susannah-Jane, but as she asked she knew what ship.

'She will come in under topsails,' said Susannah. 'She will anchor first, and then she will come to her mooring. She will come to her mooring in an hour, and I will wait for him. When I am on board, there is something, there is a feeling, I could be in the gardens of the Domain. I asked. I told him. He says she is made of cedar, which is a fast wood for a ship, and that is what I sense. He says her timbers might be from the young timbers of the Domain – when they are a little grown. I will wait for him.'


*Peralta, Sydney, Ballarat, Papeete, Deptford*
*1977–8*

# A note, and acknowledgements

This is a novel, not a history, though I hope the characters who live through it are true to the spirit of Australia and of Sydney, that magical city. The principal historical events of the story, particularly the more terrible, are based on fact. They happened. Sydney was settled by the convicts of the First Fleet. A group of such convicts, a woman and two children among them, did escape in an open boat to Timor and around the world. The flag of the Southern Cross flew over the Eureka Stockade, and the battle between diggers and the military was fought round it. Some of the people of the novel are real. They lived, and I have used some of their words. Captain Bligh of the *Bounty* did become Governor of New South Wales, where he suffered a second mutiny. Philip Gidley King was third Governor of the colony, and I have portrayed that courageous man much as he was, though his acquisition in this novel of such a daughter as Susannah has necessarily changed the course of his life a little. The French explorer Nicolas Baudin, Susannah's lover, was sent by Napoléon to New South Wales, and sailed into Sydney Cove one day in 1802. Susannah herself is a creature of the imagination; and the hearts and souls of those around her are, also, created.

I owe a debt of gratitude to many people. To Peter Kay, Ian Dawes, and Peter Davison of the Australian Information Service in London and Sydney; to the staff of the Observatory, the Royal Botanic Gardens, and the Mitchell Library in

ydney; to Nina Valentine of Sovereign Hill, a marvellous
econstruction of the Ballarat gold diggings; and to the staff
f Old Sydney Town. I particularly wish to thank Harold
Iarris and Chris Chippindale of Hutchinson, London; Alan D.
Villiams and Georgette Felix of Viking, New York; and
Clizabeth Douglas of Hutchinson, Melbourne.

Now, a great debt. I first saw the Eureka flag on 2 December,
973, when its tattered and restored remains were unveiled at
he Ballarat Fine Art Gallery by the Prime Minister of Australia.
That was on the anniversary of the battle of the stockade. I
ever forgot Ballarat or Sydney. In 1977, when I returned to
London after a second visit, a history of early Australia was
roposed to me, but I doubted whether I should dare undertake
ny history of a continent that has been and is blessed with fine
istorians. It was then that Rosalie Swedlin, herself a publisher
f distinction, told me to write it as a novel.

And, last, I thank her whose generous heart gave me the
neans to write *Southern Cross*.

# ESTSELLERS FROM ARROW

All these books are available from your bookshop or newsagent or you can order them direct. Just tick the titles you want and complete the form below.

| | | |
|---|---|---|
| A CHOICE OF CATASTROPHIES | Isaac Asimov | £1.95 |
| BRUACH BLEND | Lillian Beckwith | 95p |
| THE HISTORY MAN | Malcolm Bradbury | £1.60 |
| A LITTLE ZIT ON THE SIDE | Jasper Carrott | £1.25 |
| EENY MEENY MINEY MOLE | Marcel A'Agneau | £1.50 |
| HERO | Leslie Deane | £1.75 |
| TRAVELS WITH FORTUNE | Christine Dodwell | £1.50 |
| 11th ARROW BOOK OF CROSSWORDS | Frank Henchard | 95p |
| THE LOW CALORIE MENU BOOK | Joyce Hughes | 90p |
| THE PALMISTRY OF LOVE | David Brandon-Jones | £1.50 |
| DEATH DREAMS | William Katz | £1.25 |
| PASSAGE TO MUTINY | Alexander Kent | £1.50 |
| HEARTSOUNDS | Marth Weinman Lear | £1.75 |
| LOOSELY ENGAGED | Christopher Matthew | £1.25 |
| HARLOT | Margaret Pemberton | £1.60 |
| TALES FROM A LONG ROOM | Peter Tinniswood | £1.50 |
| INCIDENT ON ATH | E. C. Tubb | £1.15 |
| THE SECOND LADY | Irving Wallace | £1.75 |
| STAND BY YOUR MAN | Tammy Wynette | £1.75 |
| DEATH ON ACCOUNT | Margaret Yorke | £1.00 |
| | Postage | |
| | Total | |

**ARROW BOOKS, BOOKSERVICE BY POST, PO BOX 29, DOUGLAS, ISLE OF MAN, BRITISH ISLES**

Please enclose a cheque or postal order made out to Arrow Books Limited for the amount due including 10p per book for postage and packing for orders within the UK and 12p for overseas orders.

*Please print clearly*

NAME ........................................................................................

ADDRESS................................................................................

................................................................................................

Whilst every effort is made to keep prices down and to keep popular books in print, Arrow Books cannot guarantee that prices will be the same as those advertised here or that the books will be available.